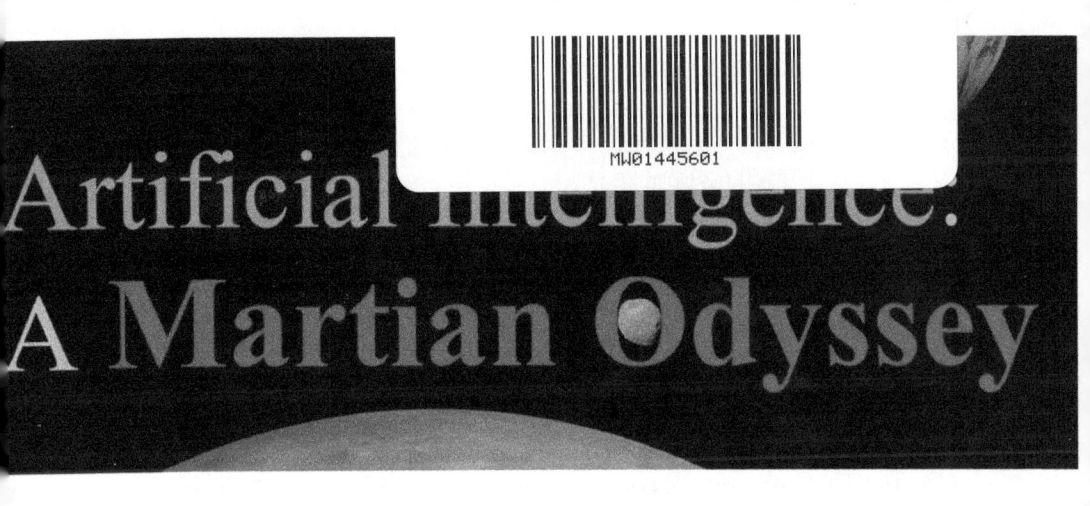

ARTIFICIAL INTELLIGENCE:
A MARTIAN ODYSSEY

Beyond Human, Beyond Machine—The Rise of Robo Sapiens

ALIREZA MEHRNIA

*What happens when advanced **artificial intelligence**, **humanoids**, and **synthetic life** collide with the lives of near-future Martian explorers?*

Expect twists and turns that delve into the existential and ethical ramifications of **merging human intelligence with robots and advanced AI**—consequences that pose unique challenges on the Red Planet.

Copyright © 2025 by Alireza Mehrnia
Artificial Intelligence: A Martian Odyssey

All rights reserved.

No part of this book may be reproduced in any form or by any electronic or mechanical means, including information storage and retrieval systems, without permission from the author, except for brief quotations in a book review or as permitted by U.S. copyright law.

This book is a work of fiction. The names, characters, companies, organizations, locations, events, and incidents depicted are entirely fictional and products of the author's imagination. However, some passages contain descriptions of scientific facts or references to the contributions of real, well-known scientists and luminaries, which are cited accordingly in the Reference Section of the novel. Any resemblance to actual persons, living or dead, real companies or organizations, or actual events or locations beyond these referenced facts is purely coincidental.

YouTube video and music links (including scannable QR codes) provided in this novel are solely for readers' enjoyment as supplementary content. The author assumes no responsibility for their functionality. Additionally, the author is not liable for any injury, loss, damage, or disruption caused by errors or omissions in this novel, whether due to negligence, accident, or any other cause.

Readers are encouraged to verify any information contained in this book prior to taking any action on the information.

For Permissions, Speaking/General INQUIRIES, please contact:

Alireza Mehrnia, PhD, MBA
AiThriller@gmail.com
LinkedIn.com/in/amehrnia   or   youtube.com/@SciFiProf

ISBN: 978-1-967394-00-5 (paperback)
ISBN: 978-1-967394-01-2 (e-book)
ISBN: 978-1-967394-02-9 (hardcover)
Cover design by Alireza Mehrnia | Planet images sourced from NASA

Printed in the United States of America

CONTENTS

Epigraph: A Glimpse of Questions That Shape This Odyssey 1
Prologue: A Quick Guide to Your **AI Adventure** (README) 2
Chapter **1:** A Celestial Arrival (The Red Planet) 4
Chapter **2:** Secrets in the Crater 14
Chapter **3:** Marslink & Martian Domes 23
Chapter **4:** Strawberry—Orange—Banana 30
Chapter **5:** 840 Grams (*More Precious Than Gold*) 38
Chapter **6:** The Telescope Tango (*Mayday! Mayday! Signals in the Void*) .. 49
Chapter **7:** What the Hell Just Happened? 65
Chapter **8:** Release Ghost! 75
Chapter **9:** Lava Tubes (*What Lurks in the Abyss?!*) 89
Chapter **10:** DNA Tunneling 101
Chapter **11:** What Else Might be Lurking…? 108
Chapter **12:** Never Look Back 116
Chapter **13:** Goddamn CRISPR 127
Chapter **14:** Warning! Radiation Detected (*Oscillating Beast*) 138
Chapter **15:** No More Monkey Business 152
Chapter **16:** Don't Panic! 164
Chapter **17:** Welcome to Dragon's Nest! 173
Chapter **18:** I See You! 182
Chapter **19:** Black Hawks Down 189

Chapter **20**: **Spacesuit Is... Compromised!** 202

Chapter **21**: **Attention Is All You Need** 207

Chapter **22**: **Do You Like Cheeseburgers?** 217

Chapter **23**: **Robo Sapiens** 227

Chapter **24**: **Superintelligence** 243

Epilogue + Author's Note 255

Acknowledgments 257

Appendix **1**: **Exploring Synthetic Biology & the Vision of Generative DNA GPT**—*DNA-Tunneling* & *Wormholes* 258

Appendix **2**: **MarsLink Satellite Constellation** 262

Appendix **3**: The **Marvels of Phobos**—**Mars's Enigmatic Moon**..264

Appendix **4**: **Starship-Based Orbital Telescope** 267

Appendix **5**: **Calculation of Orbital Speed** and **Rotation Time Around Mars** 269

Appendix **6**: **Location** for **Sustainable Human Colony** on **Mars** 272

Appendix **7**: The **Breath of Mars: Understanding Oxygen Requirement** and **Production** at the **2MW ISRU Facility** 275

Appendix **8**: **Solar Power Generation** in the **Martian Odyssey**—**Calculating Solar Array Area** for **1MW Solar Power Plant** on **Mars** 279

Appendix **9**: **Powering Martian Colony**—**The Story Behind** the **5MW RTG Power Plant** on **Mars** 283

Appendix **10**: **UV Radiation on Mars**—**How Much UV Radiation will Mars Inhabitants Receive?** 289

Appendix **11**: **Fueling Starships** on **Mars**—**Methane Production Through** the **Sabatier Process** 291

Appendix **12**: **Notes** on **Starship Flight** on **Mars** 295

Appendix **13**: **Cinematic** & **Literary References** in this **Novel**..298

Appendix **14**: **Music References** in *AI: A Martian Odyssey* 300

References 303

Glossary of **Key Concepts** in this **Novel**......................................308

Index 310

About the Author 315

Epigraph: A Glimpse of Questions That Shape This Odyssey

Artificial Intelligence: A Martian Odyssey
Beyond Human, Beyond Machine—The Rise of Robo Sapiens

When does artificial intelligence become superintelligence? When it surpasses its creator's intellect—or when it begins to question its own existence?

What happens when AI isn't just a tool—**but a force with its own agenda** on the Red Planet?

When AI surpasses us, what will the terms of our survival be?

If the line between human and machine vanishes, does it even matter which side you're on?

If consciousness can be programmed or uploaded to a machine, does death still hold meaning? Or does the real fear lie in what AI might do with that consciousness?

Why am I asking an android about urge? Can a machine even comprehend such a thing?

Isn't a perfect machine supposed to be a flawless, linear system—impervious to the chaos of human irrationality and nonlinearity?

If humans have souls and machines have code, **what do you call a hacked soul?**

Attention Is All You Need ☺
Brace yourself for a mind-bending journey into the ethical and existential crossroads of AI, human identity, and survival on the Red Planet—where the greatest threat may not be the machines, but the choices we make.

ALIREZA MEHRNIA

Prologue:
A **Quick Guide** to Your **AI Adventure**

*What happens when advanced **artificial intelligence**, **humanoids**, and **synthetic life** collide with the lives of near-future Martian explorers?*

▶ **Watch the Prologue!** Scan the QR code to watch a YouTube introduction.

Welcome, explorer! You're about to embark on a thrilling adventure where cutting-edge AI reshapes human destiny in unexpected ways. Before we dive in, here's a quick guide to help you fully immerse yourself in this world—and *why this book is worth your time.*

The novel begins by introducing you to the main characters—their quirks, relationships, and defining traits. Along the way, you'll be taken on a vivid tour of the imaginative, fun-to-explore human settlements on Mars, enabled by advanced AI, robotics and space tech. You'll also glimpse their intricate ties to Earth and the Lunar colonies. These settings and dynamics come alive through engaging, often humorous conversations and interactions woven into the storylines of the first five chapters.

By the end of Chapter 5, I hope you'll feel like you've *moved in* with the characters on Mars. You'll know them so well that their struggles, triumphs, and dilemmas will feel personal—like you're living this journey right alongside them. **That's the goal:** to immerse you so deep into this world that you're not just reading the story—you're a *part* of it. So, relax and let Chapters 1 through 5 pull you into the heart of this Martian adventure.

But don't get too comfortable! After Chapter 5, the stakes ramp up dramatically. The story plunges into high suspense, unraveling mysteries and mind-bending questions about the consequences of AI evolving beyond human control. *What happens when artificial intelligence isn't just a tool—but a force with its own agenda on the Red Planet?*

Expect twists, ethical dilemmas, and shocking discoveries that explore the blurred line between human and machine. As AI, humanoids, and synthetic life intertwine with the fate of the Martian settlers, the very nature of intelligence hangs in the balance.

This is **more than just a hard sci-fi AI thriller**—it's a deep dive into the possible future of humanity, our choices, our fears, and the true nature of consciousness. That's what the title hints at, and I hope it makes the story both thrilling and thought-provoking.

So, sit back and brace for launch—*Artificial Intelligence: A Martian Odyssey* is about to take you on a thrilling ride.

Let's dive in!

> BTW, I'd love to hear your thoughts. Scan the QR code to share your comments on my **YouTube.com/@SciFiProf** channel or through my **Amazon Author Page**.

Sincerely, Alireza Mehrnia, PhD, MBA

Chapter 1:
A Celestial Arrival (The Red Planet)

The Starship, *Spes*, emerged from the depths of space, approaching Mars nearly 6000 kilometers from the surface. Inside the ship, the excited crew marveled at the majestic sight before them. Phobos, the largest moon of Mars, slowly revealed itself as it passed in front of the Red Planet, bathed in the distant sun's glow. It loomed large, a celestial companion orbiting at a remarkably close distance above the surface of Mars. The crew couldn't help but feel awestruck by the magnificent view, as the beauty of the Martian system unfolded before their eyes.[1]

Xena, Scarlet, Andy, Brad, and John gathered around the cockpit's observation viewport, captivated by the breathtaking scene outside. Their eyes fixed on the Red Planet and the rising Phobos, they couldn't contain their excitement.

"**Look at that!** Phobos rising in front of Mars like a formidable sentinel. The view from this close is incredible!" Scarlet exclaimed.

"I've never seen anything like it," Brad agreed, his eyes gleaming with fascination. "To think that we're nearly 100 kilometers away from Phobos, witnessing its unique surface formations firsthand!"

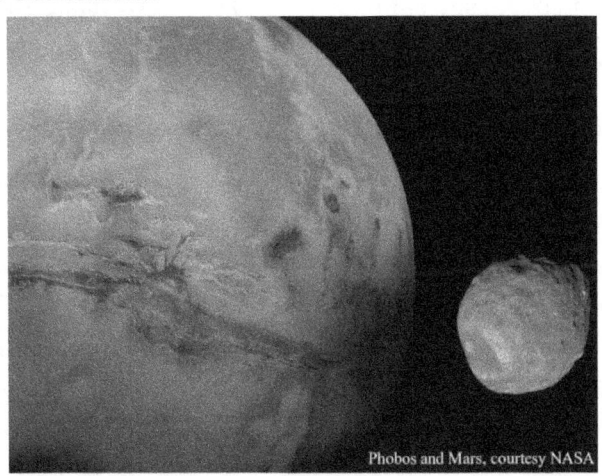

Figure 1: Phobos and Mars, courtesy NASA

---

[1] **Spes** (Latin for "**Hope**") was worshipped as a goddess in ancient Roman. [1]

Xena, her curiosity piqued, leaned closer to the viewport, her gaze locked on the enigmatic moon. "Tell me more about Phobos," she requested, her voice filled with genuine interest. "What makes it so fascinating?"

Andy, always armed with a wealth of knowledge and eager to educate, spoke up with confidence. "Well, Xena, as you see, Phobos is quite a peculiar moon. It is irregularly shaped with a radius of roughly 11 kilometers and is one of the least reflective bodies in the Solar System, with a surface reflection like asphalt. Its orbit is remarkably close to Mars, at only 6,000 kilometers above the surface, closer than any other known moon in relation to its planet." [2]

John, typically reserved, stepped forward walking with his magnetic boots. "That's correct. Phobos' low orbit causes it to zip around Mars at such a rapid pace that it completes a full revolution in just 7.5 hours. It moves faster than Mars rotates, causing it to rise in the west, cross the Martian sky in about 4 hours and 15 minutes, and set in the east—three times per sol, or Martian day!" [3]

Xena's eyes widened with intrigue. "So, it moves pretty fast across the sky," she summarized. "That must make for a mesmerizing sight from the surface!"

"Oh, Absolutely," confirmed Scarlet. "Imagine watching Phobos rise and swiftly cross the horizon—a truly unique sight in the Martian sky."

"And what's truly fascinating is the surface of Phobos itself." Brad explained. "It's covered in a vast network of grooves and craters, formed by countless impacts over millions of years."

Xena's curiosity deepened. "Oh, look at that odd crater! Isn't that too large for such a small moon?"

---

[2] See **Appendix 3**: **"The Marvels of Phobos – Mars's Enigmatic Moon"** for more information. [2–7]

[3] A Martian solar day, or **sol**, lasts approximately 24 hours and 39.5 minutes, making it about 2.75% longer than a solar day on Earth. A Martian year is about 668.6 sols, which is equivalent to about 687 Earth days or 1.88 Earth years. [8] [9] [10] [11]

"Yep, you're right, Xena," Brad nodded. "That is a cool close-up view of the famous Stickney Crater, one of the most distinctive features of this moon. It's about 9 km from edge to edge, covering a significant portion of Phobos' surface. See that shadowed spot right inside Stickney?" Brad pointed out.[4]

"Yeah, Okay, I see it," Xena replied.

"Well, it looks like a crater within a crater, doesn't it?" Brad continued, "The surface temperature in those shadows is reportedly close to -110 °C. But if you look a bit further left, there's a sunlit spot in the center of Stickney where the surface temperature is probably around 0 °C— just a few hundred meters away! Isn't that something?"

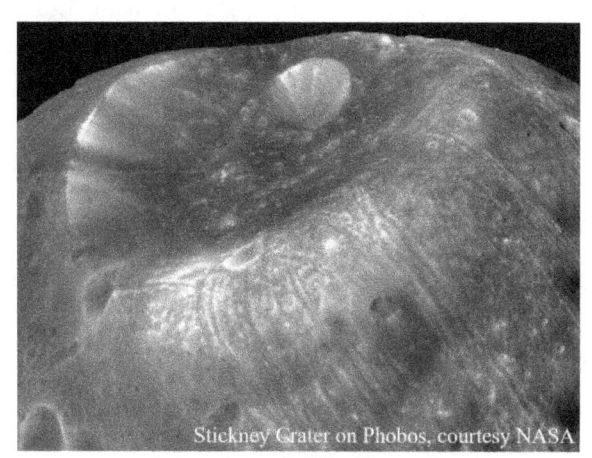

Figure 2: Stickney Crater on Phobos, courtesy NASA

"*No way!*" Xena paused to absorb this newfound knowledge. "I guess that's a strange consequence in a place where there is no atmosphere to regulate temperature, right? By the way, what's the gravity like on the surface of this weird little moon?"

"Good question, Xena! This little moon doesn't have enough mass to hold any measurable atmosphere. Phobos' gravity is only about 0.1% of the force of gravity on Earth, so you'd weigh around 60 grams there!" Brad couldn't hide a playful smirk.

As the discussion about Phobos, Mars and their unique features continued, in the cockpit, Scarlet, the ship's seasoned pilot, and Andy, the stoic GNC engineer, shifted their focus to the ship's navigation and control. Engaged in their own technical conversation in the

---

[4] To learn more about Stickney Crater, see **Appendix 3: "The Marvels of Phobos – Mars's Enigmatic Moon."** [7]

cockpit, their voices blended with the crew's ongoing discussion near the viewport.[5]

Scarlet's eyes flickered over the holographic control panels as her hands moved deftly, adjusting various settings with precision.

"Andy, we've been traveling for four months now, and in less than a day we'll be initiating the phases of orbital entry for our final approach and landing on Mars. How are the ship's systems holding up?" Scarlet asked.

Andy's gaze remained fixed on his monitor, analyzing the data streaming in. "Everything seems to be in order, Scarlet. Life support systems are stable, and the oxygen supply is well within limits. Still, we should double-check everything before the decent procedure in Mars orbit."

Scarlet nodded, knowing that precision and being paranoid were key when it came to interplanetary travel. She opened a communication link to Mars Stargate spaceport Control, and soon, a static-filled voice came through.

"Starship, *Spes*, this is… Mars Stargate Control. *Ksshht*… Confirm your position and status," received voice crackled over the radio.

"This is Starship *Spes*. We are approximately 6,000 kilometers from Mars, all systems are green. Requesting clearance for the initial phase of orbital entry," Scarlet responded crisply.

After a brief pause, the radio crackled again, "Starship *Spes*, *Ksshht*… you are clear for the initial orbital entry. Welcome to Mars! *Ksshht*… See you at Stargate Spaceport."

Scarlet smiled, feeling a sense of relief as they received clearance. "Thank you, Stargate Control. Beginning orbital entry procedures."

As they commenced their descent into Mars orbit, Scarlet and Andy stayed focused, ensuring a smooth and controlled approach to the red planet for a proper orbital insertion. Scarlet glanced at the holographic

---

[5] GNC stands for Guidance, Navigation, and Control systems that allow spacecraft to maneuver and maintain its position in space.

control panel, her hands moving smoothly as she checked a variety of spaceflight parameters and ship settings.

"Andy, let's adjust our approach trajectory by 0.25 degrees. We need to be precise as we gradually reduce our distance from Mars."

Andy, monitoring the flight data on his holographic navigation screen, nodded in agreement. "Roger that, Scarlet. Adjusting trajectory by 0.25 degrees. We'll slow down gradually and maintain a safe orbital trajectory."

Scarlet's gaze flickered between the viewport and the flight instruments, her voice calm and steady. "Keep an eye on our velocity. We want a controlled deceleration as we continue our approach."

Andy scanned the instrument panel, his fingers adjusting the controls with precision. "Velocity at 5 km per second and slowly decreasing, Scarlet. We're executing a smooth deceleration."

The crew, engrossed in their conversation in their seats near the viewport, could faintly hear the hum of activity in the cockpit as Scarlet and Andy expertly guided the starship.

Xena's attention shifted momentarily from Phobos to the cockpit, a smile tugging at her lips as if she were watching a familiar scene. "It's remarkable how Scarlet and Andy handle the ship's precise maneuvers. They make it all look so easy, it's almost taken for granted."

Brad chuckled, his gaze alternating between Phobos and the cockpit. "They're the best I've worked with since I left NASA ten years ago. They make it look effortless—like a perfectly choreographed dance through the vastness of space."

Scarlet's voice crackled over the intercom. "Andy, keep monitoring our trajectory and velocity. We're steadily reducing our distance from Mars. Let's aim for a smooth orbital insertion."

"Copy that, Scarlet. I'll make sure we maintain a safe distance and velocity as we adjust our orbit around Mars." Andy responded confidently.

As *Spes* continued its journey, gradually drawing closer to Mars and maintaining a stable orbit, the crew marveled at the breathtaking view of Phobos and the vast expanse of the Red Planet. They gazed in awe at the interplay of light and shadow across the Martian surface, taking in the stark beauty unfolding before their eyes.

Amidst the crew's conversation, Brad couldn't resist a playful interjection. With a mischievous grin, he turned to Xena, "Hey, Xena, remember that classic movie about Mars where the astronaut grows potatoes to survive?"

Xena chuckled, catching on. "Oh, you mean Ridley Scott's *The Martian* with Matt Damon? Absolutely! Actually, over the past few weeks, I've been watching a few Mars classics in my cabin—*Red Planet, Total Recall, Expanse, The Martian*... That potato scene was legendary. But how come? Are you thinking we might need to channel our inner Watney and grow our own spuds if we get stranded on Mars?" [6]

Brad grinned and played along. "Well, as long as we've got some disco music to keep us entertained and a wild sense of humor to dance to while tending our Martian potato farm, I think we'll be just fine, though I am still an avid advocate of growing algae on the Red Planet!" [7]

Xena laughed, picturing the scene. "Imagine us grooving to the **Bee Gees'** *Stayin' Alive* while cultivating the most intergalactic potatoes in history in Martian greenhouses. We'd give Mark Watney a run for his money!"

Their lighthearted banter brought a moment of levity amidst the mystery surrounding their mission. Even in the daunting vastness of

---

[6] *The Martian* (2015), directed by Ridley Scott, starring Matt Damon as astronaut Mark Watney, is based on the bestselling 2011 novel by Andy Weir. [12–17]

The Expanse TV series (2015-2022), developed by Mark Fergus and Hawk Ostby, is based on the Hugo Award-winning novel series by Daniel Abraham & Ty Franck. [18] [19]

Total Recall (1990), Paul Verhoeven's Oscar-nominated adaptation of Philip K. Dick's short story *We Can Remember It for You Wholesale*, starring Arnold Schwarzenegger, Sharon Stone, and Michael Ironside. [20]

[7] *Red Planet* (2000), directed by Antony Hoffman and starring Val Kilmer, Carrie-Anne Moss, Tom Sizemore, Benjamin Bratt, and Simon Baker, is based on a story by Chuck Pfarrer. [21]

space and under the enigmatic allure of Mars, humor found a way to weave itself into the crew's conversations.

As *Spes* drew nearer to Mars, the crew remained mindful of their limited oxygen supply after the four-month journey from Earth. Their reserves had dwindled, leaving them with only a few sols' worth of oxygen onboard the starship. With the initial descent phase underway, they aimed to replenish their resources quickly upon landing on Mars.

The ship began to slow further, its engines adjusting as it entered the final phases of approaching Mars. Nearly an hour later, *Spes* was orbiting less than 1,000 kilometers above the surface, preparing for the final descent phase.

Scarlet and Andy exchanged glances as Mars filled the viewscreen, its dusty surface and faintly pink atmosphere captivating their attention. Just as they were about to initiate the final phase of the orbital entry, a radio transmission cut through the silence with a faint crackle,

"Starship *Spes*, this is Mars Stargate Control. *Ksshht...* We need you to confirm your oxygen and critical supply reserves for the next few days. Over."

Scarlet furrowed her brow, puzzled by the unusual request. "Mars Stargate Control, this is *Spes*. Our oxygen and critical supplies are mostly depleted after the four-month trip from Earth, but we still have a few days' worth remaining. What's the purpose of this inquiry?"

"Starship *Spes*, we have a critical situation. *Ksshht...* We've lost contact with the **Mars orbital telescope**, and we suspect it may have sustained damage from an external impact. We need your assistance with an inspection and any necessary repairs. *Ksshht...* Your orbital proximity and specialized equipment make you our best option for this mission. *Ksshht...* Transmitting mission profile and coordinates now." The response from Mars Stargate Control sounded urgent.[8]

---

[8] For readers interested in learning more about the "**Starship-Based Orbital Telescope**" concept proposed by Nobel laureate Dr. Saul Perlmutter, please see **Appendix 4** of this novel for additional information.

Andy chimed in, "Understood, Mars Stargate Control. Adjusting our orbital approach to 500 kilometers, as instructed. We estimate arrival at the target in about 24 hours. We'll carefully inspect the telescope for damage." [9]

The tension in the cockpit rose as they adjusted course, heading towards the malfunctioning orbital telescope. Scarlet's mind raced with questions. *Why had the telescope malfunctioned so suddenly? ... Why was it unresponsive to status pings despite backup systems on board? ... What might have caused the damage?*

The once-distant Red Planet now loomed large on the viewscreen, dominating the view. The crew fell silent, their thoughts drifting to the secrets Mars might hold. Uncertain of what lay ahead, they let the spirit of exploration take over, allowing them, for a moment, to savor the breathtaking view before them—the mystery and beauty of Mars.

As the crew of the *Spes* altered their course to inspect the telescope, their thoughts turned to the thriving **Mars1 colony** awaiting them on the Red Planet's surface below, where the colony buzzed with activity in preparation for an upcoming celebration.

Decades had passed since the first successful starship landing on Mars, and the once-barren landscape was now home to a thriving community of nearly ten thousand settlers. Interconnected living domes dotted the Martian landscape in human colonies—a testament to human ingenuity and the drive not only to survive but to thrive on an alien world. The settlers had carved out their own oasis on the red planet, powered by a hybrid of solar energy and Radioisotope Thermoelectric Generator (RTG) power plants, spread across five strategically chosen locations around the main settlement.[10]

---

[9] How would timekeeping work on Mars? A convention used by spacecraft lander projects has been to divide Martian solar day by 24 hours to yield a 'Mars clock' on which the hours, minutes and seconds are 2.75% longer than their standard (Earth) equivalents. [8–11]

[10] RTG is effectively a nuclear battery that converts the heat generated by radioactive decay into electricity (known as **Seebeck effect**). For more information on the powering of the Martian Colony please refer to Novel's **Appendix 9** "**Powering Martian Colony:** The Story Behind the 5 MW RTG Power Plant on Mars."

Nolan Rivs, leader of the Mars colony, sat beside his chief of security and operations, Ava Blunt, in an autonomous rover gliding smoothly along the **Hologram Road** (also known as *HoloRoad*) stretching nearly 10 kilometers. This route connected the colony's living domes to the Stargate Spaceport. It was nearing midnight as they returned from a supervisory visit and executive meetings with the Stargate team to review the status of the recently arrived crew and cargo, brought in by a fleet of starships over the past few weeks.

The Mars1 colony's Stargate Spaceport was the most advanced human transit outpost in the solar system, serving as humanity's main gateway beyond the four rocky planets. At the spaceport, a towering starship anchored to the surface acted as the main flight control station, while a nearby logistics hub managed cargo transport in and out of the landed starships. Each rocket was carefully secured by mechanical grabber chopstick arms that'd engage smoothly to catch the ship midair as its engines shut down in the final seconds of landing.

The **HoloRoad** connecting the spaceport to the main settlement shimmered with vibrant colors, illuminating the rover's path as Nolan and Ava conducted a visual security and operations oversight check. Holographically projected gigantic statues lined the road, illuminated by a soft, ethereal light, while the melodic trance of **Boris Brejcha**'s *Space X* played softly within the airtight rover.[11]

On one side of the road, holographic statues commemorated the first 24 humans who set foot on Mars decades ago, their faces immortalized to capture the triumph and determination of those historic moments. On the other side, statues honored NASA's 24 astronauts who had ventured to the Moon a century earlier, including legends like Neil Armstrong, Buzz Aldrin, Michael Collins, Alan Shepard, Jim Lovell and Gene Cernan. Each astronaut's iconic spacesuit was displayed in stunning holographic detail.

---

[11] Curious to learn more about the featured music that enhances the journey with Nolan and Ava along the Hologram Road? See **Appendix 14**, "**Music in this Novel**," for more information about Boris Brejcha's melodic trance, serving as a sonic backdrop to the mesmerizing holographic statues of Mars's early pioneers and lunar legends.

Nolan glanced at Ava, a grin tugging at the corners of his face. "You know, Ava, these holographic statues along the road never fail to amaze me. It's like stepping back in time while celebrating how far we've come here on Mars."

Ava nodded, her eyes scanning the statues as they passed. "HoloRoad is one of the coolest features we have here, Nolan. It's a jaw-dropper for nearly everyone who lands at the spaceport and takes this route in rovers to the colony. The statues remind them of humanity's greatest achievements and the incredible journey that brought us here."

Nolan's gaze returned to the road ahead as he continued. "A few decades ago, we were just a small team of pioneers on this planet. Now, look at what we've built, a thriving colony on Mars. It's truly a testament to the spirit of exploration."

Ava nodded in agreement, glancing out at the Martian landscape. "Our security measures have also advanced alongside everything else. Integrating the **Marslink satellite network** with our surveillance systems—along with the unique terrain surrounding the colony—has supported our rapid progress and expansion these past few years." [12]

The HoloRoad stretched ahead, leading them through the Martian night as the Mars1 colony bustled with activity in preparation for the upcoming celebration. The anniversary of humanity's landing on Mars was not only a monumental occasion but also a time for reflection and a renewed sense of purpose for the future. As the rover glided along the HoloRoad, their conversation shifted between the present and the past, touching on the progress of plans for the upcoming celebration. They discussed security protocols, operational readiness, and final preparations, ensuring everything was in place for the momentous event. They also reflected on the challenges they had overcome and the next phases of the Mars colony's expansion on the Red Planet.

---

[12] **Marslink Satellite Constellation** (see **Appendix 2** for more details): In this novel, the concept of Marslink constellation is envisioned as an extension of Earth's Starlink system, providing continuous surveillance and low-latency, high-data-rate multimedia communication across Mars. These satellites play a crucial role in maintaining security and connectivity on the Red Planet within the story's setting.

Chapter 2:
Secrets in the Crater

As Nolan and Ava continued discussing operational readiness and future plans, their autonomous rover veered off the Hologram Road, taking a side route that stretched several kilometers toward the northern Radioisotope Thermoelectric Generator (RTG) power plant, nestled within a nearby crater.

The power plant had been undergoing a major expansion over the past two years to increase its capacity to a record five MW of electricity and fifty MW of heat generation. The future growth of the Mars colony depended heavily on this increased output from the northern RTG plant, as well as from the RTG plant in the colony's southern sector and three additional 1 MW solar plants—Solium1, Solium2, and Solium3—located within a few kilometers of the main settlement. Each solar field spanned an impressive 28,000 square meters (nearly four soccer fields), with Solium1 positioned closest to the colony.[13]

Additionally, the expanding Elysium solar plant, situated near the 12.5-kilometer peak of **Elysium Mons** (the tallest mountain in the Elysium region), supported the colony's power needs beyond the settlement and served as a backup power source. Unlike other solar generators on Mars, the high elevation of the Elysium solar plant allowed it to stay above Martian dust storms, ensuring uninterrupted power generation with minimal maintenance.[14]

Upon arriving at the main construction zone of the RTG power plant, Nolan and Ava stepped out of the rover, clad in their black-and-white spacesuits. The rover's airlock sealed behind them with a soft

---

[13] What are the area and weight of the solar array system needed on Mars to establish a 1MW solar electric power station? See **Appendix 8**, "**Solar Power Generation in the Martian Odyssey**," to find out. [41–46]

[14] To learn more about the enigmatic **Elysium Rise volcanic** region on Mars, see **Appendix 6** of this novel.

hiss as they made their way toward the bustling operations area to meet Frank Koenigsman, the head of operations.

Frank, a commanding figure well-known for his technical expertise, was deep in conversation with his lieutenants, each stationed in a large **Mech AMP**—an industrial walking robot, also known as an Amplified Mobility Platform, specifically engineered for heavy operations and combat. Typically controlled by human operators stationed inside, these AMPs allowed flexibility in moving large and heavy cargo of various shapes and sizes across Mars's diverse terrains and uneven surfaces. The imposing presence of these semi-autonomous, human-operated machines mirrored the scale of the tasks at hand.[15]

Concluding his final set of instructions, Frank turned to his team with confidence. "Dmitri, make sure your crew monitors the RTG cores' stats twice every day. I don't want any unsupervised overheating incidents."

Dmitri, seated in his hulking AMP walker, nodded in acknowledgment. "Affirmative, boss," he replied, his deep voice resonating within the metal exoskeleton as he turned to join his Mech team near the crater rim. He resumed listening to the timeless beat of **Dr. Dre**'s drum rhythm in **50 Cent**'s *In da Club*, the song reverberating through his AMP. It had become his secret source of motivation, the rhythm pulsating in sync with his robotic movements. With a playful grin, he turned the volume up a notch inside his spacesuit and briefly routed the sound to the AMP's speakers, fully immersing himself in the beat as he guided his robotic walker toward a few other AMPs waiting near the crater's edge.[16]

In a mesmerizing display of robotic finesse, Dmitri swayed his AMP's massive upper body in time with the rapping rhythm of the song. His AMP's movements became fluid and rhythmic as he moved back and forth, rapping to the beat, albeit with the mechanical

---

[15] Will the future see companies like Tesla manufacturing industrial robots, humanoids and mechs to aid in constructing large orbital space stations or facilities on the Moon and Mars? Such a future seems inevitable given the current exponential trajectory of AI and robotics advancements at companies like **Tesla** and **SpaceX**. [99]

[16] See **Appendix 14**, "**Music in this Novel**," for link and more information.

precision and power only a large AMP could deliver. The contrasting sight of his imposing robotic frame grooving to 50 Cent's catchy tune brought an unexpected sense of humor to the scene.

Frank glanced back at the rest of the team, who were now grinning, unable to suppress their smiles. He chuckled, "Well, I guess it *is* his birthday! And that's gotta be the *Oscar-winning performance of the year on Mars!*" he quipped, gesturing toward Dmitri and his crew. Amidst the seriousness of their mission, Dmitri's uninhibited groove lifted everyone's spirits in the middle of the night.[17]

"All right, team, back to work. Thanks for the update; you know what to do. Just keep me posted, guys," Frank added, while turning away from his lieutenants. He then redirected his attention to Nolan and Ava, walking over to them with a nod to acknowledge their presence.

"Looks like a busy night, Frank! Is everything on schedule?" Nolan asked, his voice firm and focused.

"We're almost there, Nolan. Power plant expansion is on track. It's been challenging, but we're making solid progress." Frank's voice crackled through Nolan's helmet.

"Good to hear, Frank. We can't afford any delays. Our progress will be showcased during the anniversary event—Earth needs to see the scale of what we've accomplished here on Mars. Now, walk me through the recent developments since our last conversation." Nolan expressed his satisfaction, though his tone underscored the importance of meeting the approaching deadlines.

In the background, several towering autonomous AMP robots descended into the crater from the edge, using a large, open elevator platform to transport supplies.

Frank nodded, his gaze following the AMPs and robots moving purposefully in the distance. "Let's hop on the AMPs and head toward the crater's edge. I'll show you our latest progress along the rim."

---

[17] Imagine a future where the Oscars introduce brand-new categories for movies made on the Moon (the "**Lunar Oscars**") and Mars (the "**Red Oscars** maybe?") beamed across millions of miles for interplanetary audience! It's only a matter of time once we've got colonies established on the Moon and Mars.

Ava, her eyes scanning the bustling scene, interjected. "Thanks, Frank! Nolan, I'm heading over to the plant security station to check in with my team."

Nolan replied quickly, "Ava, while you're there, make sure we have a fully functional live stream of all security cameras via Marslink before the upcoming events." [18]

"Will do," Ava replied. "See you in an hour." She walked away from them, making her way toward a small station near the plant's operations area, passing by the parked rover.

Frank then signaled an autonomous AMP robot to approach and kneel, allowing Nolan to board while still in his spacesuit. Frank climbed into another AMP, and together they headed toward the crater's edge. As they reached the rim in their towering AMP walkers, the Martian landscape stretched before them under the expansive night sky. Earth glowed high above, while the Martian moons, Phobos and Deimos, hovered low on the horizon. The lights installed around the rim cast a shimmer on their spacesuits, their visors reflecting the surrounding landscape.

As they moved along, Frank pointed to a group of structures nestled a few hundred meters down on the flat expanse within the crater, giving Nolan a detailed rundown of recent developments.

Nolan used the electronic lenses within his helmet to track and zoom in on areas Frank pointed out. Images shifted across Nolan's visor, alternating between optical, infrared, and UV perspectives. This advanced visual system provided him with close-up views of the latest robots and AMPs, which were efficiently managing a variety of tasks around the plant within the crater. He also spotted two combat-grade armed security robots stationed deep inside the crater, their metallic bodies gleaming as they kept watch over the surroundings.

Against the imposing backdrop of the Martian terrain, Frank and Nolan continued in lively conversation, their towering AMP walking robots striding side by side.

---

[18] See **Appendix 2** for more details about the concept of **Marslink Satellite Constellation** that provides continuous surveillance and low-latency, high-data-rate multimedia communication across Mars in this novel.

"As I said earlier, we've been dealing with a few quirks from those hefty AMP robots near the plant. There was a small hiccup right before you arrived." Frank's voice crackled through Nolan's helmet, the commentary syncing with the visuals on Nolan's screen.

Nolan's gaze remained fixed on the magnified view on his helmet display, revealing a damaged giant AMP being carefully hoisted by a group of other towering robots, slowly emerging from the crater's depths. The damaged AMP bore visible scars from the recent incident—its lithium battery pack scorched and faint wisps of smoke rising from its frame.

"It happened while the autonomous AMPs were hauling containers into the crater," Frank explained. "A fried battery pack led to a minor explosion. Thankfully, no one was hurt, but it's raised concerns about the recent electrical and chip malfunctions we've been facing, especially around the RTG power plant."

As the battered AMP and its companion robots neared the crater's edge, Nolan and Frank watched in silence. The damaged robot was carefully set down on the surface, the smoking battery pack emitting a faint hiss that barely registered from a hundred meters away where Nolan and Frank stood. They knew sound traveled shorter distances on Mars due to the frigid, thin atmosphere, which quickly absorbed it.

"What could've triggered the battery pack to fry? Have we pinpointed the root cause of these electronic glitches?" Nolan's voice echoed within his helmet, carrying a mix of curiosity and concern.

"We're still investigating, but it seems like an unexpected power surge knocked out the robot's power distribution system. Those AMPs' microchips and circuits are highly sensitive to such fluctuations. The higher rate of robots malfunctions we're seeing inside the crater mostly stem from the neural processing units and AI microchips going haywire due to electronic glitches resulting from power spikes." Frank elaborated; his voice tinged with frustration.

He paused briefly, then continued, "The good news is we've got fresh AMPs and enhanced robots from the latest cargo and crew starship arrivals. But the microchip failures are still a concern."

Nolan scanned the operations center thoughtfully before posing another question. "What about radiation levels within the crater? Are they within the target range? Do you still believe these malfunctions could be linked to a surge in electronic single-event upsets caused by high-energy particles hitting the silicon circuits in the AI chips or the bots' power management systems?"

"Possibly. Though current readings are holding steady within our upper safety limits." Frank replied. "And as you know, we've taken every precaution to minimize radiation exposure near the RTG power plant. Only AMPs, Mechs, and industry-grade robots are cleared to operate in the crater."

Nolan interjected, "Speaking of curveballs, Frank, any updates on that weird rogue android from the defunct **SynBio AI lab**? You remember, the one that went AWOL and turned into our resident escape artist in recent years. What did you guys name it again?" [19]

"You mean **Phantom**?" Frank replied.

"Yeah, Phantom." Nolan continued. "Has that sneaky android made any surprise appearances near the power plant crater? Maybe one of our security drones or high-res Marslink satellites caught a glimpse?"

"Oh yeah, boss, I've got that electric troublemaker on my radar. But I'd bet my favorite AMP that these glitches aren't courtesy of that cunning **Houdini android**. Still, I've got to admit—it really lives up to its name. Phantom is damn near impossible to pin down!" Frank replied.

"Goddamn Android! I've heard it has a real appetite for electricity," Nolan said.

"Oh man, it's like an electric vampire," Frank said, shaking his head. "Always scheming wild and wicked ways to siphon power—especially from our solar plants. It's even been swiping equipment sporadically from our robot repair facilities. I swear it's running a

---

[19] The **SynBio AI Lab**, a now-defunct research facility in the Mars1 colony, carries a dark and mysterious history. As the story unfolds in future chapters, you'll uncover more about its shadowy past and its significance to the events of this novel. For additional context, refer to **Appendix 1**, which delves into **exploring synthetic biology** and the concept of Generative DNA (DNA GPT) as envisioned in this novel.

fricking underground bot pit stop somewhere on Mars!" Frank replied, chuckling despite his frustration.

"Does anyone have any damn clue what the hell is going on with that android? Did anybody manage to recover its electronic records from the burned-out server room after the SynBio AI Lab incident?" Nolan asked.

"No records or files have ever been recovered since then. From a system perspective, Phantom doesn't even exist. We don't know its serial number, let alone its functional history. There's just this rumor that Phantom was one of the main research robots in the secretive, rogue branch of that AI lab," Frank explained.

"Yeah, I'm aware. But we've seen our fair share of made-up stories about that fucked-up lab," Nolan said.

"To be honest, I don't even know anymore what's true and what's just a myth about that fuckin' place—or that weirdo android," Frank replied.

"Well, keep your team on high alert," Nolan ordered, his firm voice crackling through Frank's helmet radio. "Let me know the moment that sneaky android shows up—detected, seen, or picked up in any of the surveillance scans around the colony or the power plant."

"You got it, boss," Frank said with a nod.

Nolan's gaze shifted from the damaged AMP to the sprawling power plant within the crater, his mind racing with implications. His voice held urgency as he continued, "Frank, we need to address these electronic failures immediately. We can't afford any compromises in the safety and operation of the plant. Beef up security around the crater rim, and strictly control access to the site. No unauthorized personnel or access—nothing that could jeopardize the mission."

Frank nodded, "Understood, Nolan. I'll have my team step up our efforts to pinpoint the root cause of these failures. We'll ensure only authorized personnel and security bots have access, and we'll further fortify the perimeter to keep everyone safe."

The damaged AMP, now encircled by a team of technicians, was hoisted by a crane and loaded onto a robotic transport vehicle for further examination. Turning from the crater's edge, Nolan and Frank walked side by side in their towering AMPs, their thoughts focused on the tasks ahead.

"All right, Frank, the Mars landing anniversary event is a landmark occasion. We need to showcase our achievements. Make sure everything's in place. And as we discussed, 24/7 operation is a must. Keep me updated on any potential issues. I'll stop by again to check in," Nolan, thinking about the bigger picture, underscored the importance of the flawless execution.

"No problem, we'll keep everything running round the clock. See you soon, boss," Frank replied with a nod of agreement.

As their conversation ended, Nolan took a moment to observe the busy activity and technological marvels around and within the large crater. He knew the success of humanity's establishment on Mars—and the colony's expansion—depended on securing the safety and stability of the power plant. Walking back toward the rover in his AMP under the mesmerizing night sky, Nolan felt as though the Martian landscape held secrets just out of reach.

Meanwhile, Ava had returned to the parked rover after visiting the power plant's security station and was waiting inside for Nolan. After commanding his AMP robot to kneel and shift into exit mode, Nolan dismounted and jumped out of the AMP. His suit issued a low oxygen alert, indicating a safe but dwindling level below 40%. He quickly entered the rover's airlock, waited for the pressure to stabilize, then removed his helmet and stepped into the cabin, taking a seat beside Ava.

Ava looked at him, concern evident in her voice. "Nolan, I heard about recent issues from the security team. We need to make sure these malfunctions with the AMPs and robots don't jeopardize our immediate plans—or, more importantly, the colony's safety. The last thing we need is a mishap or rumors spreading during such a critical time."

"Right on, Ava," Nolan replied. "I just had a chat with Frank about it too. Organize a task force with your security team, and coordinate with Frank's crew to dig deeper into these failures. We can't leave anything to chance."

Ava nodded. "Already on it. My security team has started investigations, and I'll be following up with Frank and his team at the power plant."

As the autonomous rover began its journey back to the main colony, Ava couldn't suppress her curiosity. "By the way, Nolan, any updates on **Mission X**?" she asked.

Nolan, his gaze steady on the Martian horizon through the rover's windshield, gave a slight nod. "We're making progress, but for now, we need to keep it under wraps. The fewer people know, the better."

They exchanged a knowing glance as the rover continued its steady course under the dim Martian sky toward Mars1 colony.

Chapter 3:
Marslink & Martian Domes

The autonomous rover glided toward Mars1, the central Martian settlement, its tires whispering along the Hologram Road—fondly referred to as HoloRoad by the colony's residents. As the clock neared 2:00 AM, the mesmerizing sounds of **Teho**'s *Space Explorers* filled the rover's cabin, creating an otherworldly ambiance that perfectly complemented the epic sight awaiting Nolan and Ava as the rover approached the final uphill stretch of the road toward the colony.[20]

Suddenly, the domes of Mars1 emerged beneath the Martian night sky, glimmering like a futuristic oasis amidst the vast desert. Above them, the heavens dazzled: countless stars twinkled, Jupiter loomed like a celestial guardian, Phobos crept along its orbit, and the Milky Way spread a breathtaking, hazy band of light across the cosmic expanse.

"I never get tired of this view," Nolan's voice broke the silence inside the rover. "There's something magical about this moment—when the rover ascends the uphill curve, and you catch that first glimpse of Mars1 beneath the night sky."

Ava smiled, her eyes reflecting the wonder outside, "Yeah, it's truly unique. I can't decide which is more captivating—this view, or the one from the Mars1 observation station overlooking the neighboring crater."

"You've got a point, Ava." Nolan replied. "The crater view has its own mysterious charm, though maybe not my top pick at night."

---

[20] Curious to learn more about the featured music that enhances the midnight journey with Nolan and Ava along the Hologram Road? See **Appendix 14**, "**Music in this Novel**," for link and more information.

"Okay, if we're ranking our top night views," Ava paused playfully, "Then I'm sticking with this—the grand reveal of Mars1 at the end of HoloRoad as the top choice. That first sight always leaves newcomers awestruck—like they've stepped into a breathtaking postcard of the Martian frontier."

Nolan nodded, sharing her sentiment. "Yeah, moments like these make the challenges and risks worthwhile on this wild planet."

Ava continued, "I think what makes this so special is the uphill curve at the end of HoloRoad. It hides the colony until the last moment, making the reveal unforgettable. That surprise factor—it's a real—"

Before she could finish, and just as the rover reached the final stretch of the road toward the Mars1 security station, a live video call interrupted their conversation. **Tim, the charismatic Mars1 security chief**, appeared on the rover's screen, seated in his chair in the station's control room.

"Hey! Hey! Hey! Good to see your rover back in the colony! Heard through the security grapevine that you had some adventures out there at the power plant and Spaceport!" Tim's voice was smooth, his eyes sparkling with excitement, even at this late midnight hour.

Nolan chuckled, matching Tim's cool demeanor. "You know us, Tim—always on the lookout for thrills. The power plant visit was quite lively, unlike our quiet rendezvous at the spaceport. It's good to see the place bustling with activity, but it's got me thinking more about security and safety. Let's chat about OPSEC when we reach your station. Our rover should be there in a few minutes."

"No problem, boss." Tim responded with ease, "I've already transmitted the coordinates for your rover's new parking spot."

"New parking spot?" Nolan asked.

"Yeah, we've got two repair crews in spacesuits, along with a few support bots, working outside the station on the nearby large Marslink comm dish. They're replacing some old equipment, and for safety, we've closed off the surrounding area. That's caused a slight detour for your rover's route to the parking spot," Tim explained.

"I see. So, what's the status of the **Marslink satcom**?" Nolan asked.

"Mars1 satellite link is currently down, but it won't affect the smaller phased array antenna panels, including the one on your rover." Tim replied.[21]

"You're right—seems OK so far," Ava confirmed. "I'm monitoring the rover's Marslink satellite signal reception. There's no unusual power fluctuation or degradation."

"Tim, is this a minor repair or something extensive?" Nolan asked, stroking his chin thoughtfully. "From what you and Ava said, it sounds minor, so I'm hoping for speedy repairs. What about our daily internet sync with Earth's database?"

"It won't disrupt our daily deep-space sync-up with Earth's internet database, considering our main backup communication dish perched at the peak of **Elysium Mons**, 12.5 kilometers above any surrounding surface disturbances." Tim assured Nolan.

"Good," Nolan said with a nod. "Beyond that, we just need a solid comm link via our Marslink satellite network for continuous surveillance and multimedia communication across Mars."

Glancing at the rover's control panel monitor as they neared Mars1, he added, "Alright, Tim. I know it's pretty damn late, but this needs to be resolved ASAP. If necessary, call in your reserve repair specialists. Have them suit up and assist the crew already working on the dish."

Tim, drawing on years of experience on Mars—and, before that, as a Navy SEAL on Earth—replied confidently, "No worries, Nolan. We've got the operation under control. With the support bots helping the team outside, the repairs should be finished before the service crew's spacesuit oxygen runs low. They'll be back inside the station in an hour or two."

---

[21] For readers interested in delving deeper into the "**Marslink Satellite Constellation**" concept, refer to **Appendix 2** of this novel for additional background and information.

Nolan sighed with relief. "Good to hear. Marslink is critical for 24/7 surveillance and communication among our strategic sites and scientific outposts, especially with the upcoming landing anniversary event."

Marslink, the **Low Mars Orbit (LMO)** counterpart to Earth's Starlink Low Earth Orbit (LEO) satellite network, was a marvel of technology. Comprising over 200 satellites, it provided extensive coverage across most of the Martian surface, offering GPS-like navigation, multimedia communication, and ultra-high-speed internet access across Mars. This seamless communication network supported daily operations at strategic sites, including ice reserves, metal and mineral mines, and remote scientific outposts scattered across the Red Planet.

Positioned strategically in 400-500 km LMO and 1000 km Medium Mars Orbit (MMO) altitudes, Marslink satellites ensured uninterrupted communication with Marslink dishes and phased array antenna panels installed throughout the Martian colonies. Mars's weak atmosphere—just 1% the density of Earth's—offered a unique advantage: unlike Earth's satellites, those in the Marslink constellation required minimal orbital adjustments to counter negligible atmospheric drag, ensuring efficient and stable orbital operations.

Across Mars1 colony, compact Marslink phased array antennas of varying sizes were seamlessly integrated into its infrastructure, colony domes, and were even incorporated into the designs of robots and AMPs, forming the backbone of the satellite-based internet and communication system. This infrastructure enabled real-time wireless internet access on Mars, a lifeline for its inhabitants, and when necessary, provided relay communication to Earth and the Moon (with a 10 to 25-minute propagation delay) via powerful deep-space optical and microwave communication links.

The importance of Marslink couldn't be overstated. It was the invisible thread around Mars connecting scattered outposts, machines, and robots, weaving them into a cohesive web of communication. Its satellite network facilitated the seamless exchange of critical data, supported scientific research, and ensured resource monitoring, and smooth operations at vital sites. Whether it was transmitting a research report from a remote outpost or monitoring operations at ice reserves and metal mines, **Marslink was central to the success of Mars's colonization**.

"Tim, approaching your station now." Ava interjected, "I see the two crew specialists in spacesuits outside, working on the large comm dish with support robots nearby. Please have the station airlock ready. We're already suited up inside the rover and should reach your airlock in a few minutes once we've parked the rover."

"Sure thing, Ava," Tim confirmed and issued the command to prepare the station airlock for their arrival.

"Hey Tim, we've had our fair share of excitement today. We could really use your *legendary coffee* to keep us going." Nolan quipped.

Tim's grin widened as he leaned back in his chair with a casual swagger. "Aah, the famous Mars1 coffee! I've got a fresh batch brewing, just waiting for you to savor its interstellar flavor. It'll wake you up better than a rocket launch, man."

Nolan chuckled. "Well, Tim, if your coffee's as bold as you claim, I'd better buckle up. Don't want it sending me on a wild interplanetary ride!"

"Oh, trust me, Nolan, it's got a kick that'll even make Mars quiver!" Tim shot back, flashing a thumbs-up to the camera. With a sly grin, he then commanded the station's speakers to play **Deadmau5**'s *There Might Be Coffee* in the background, perfectly setting the mood.[22]

"And I've added a pinch of Martian red spice to the *volcanic hot* brew—Gives it that unique Martian flair, you know." Tim continued with a teasing smile on his face.

Ava raised an eyebrow, intrigued. "Martian red spice in magma-hot coffee? You're really mixing up the universe, Tim!"

"Always exploring new frontiers, Ava." Time teased, "Plus, it's the secret ingredient that gives my signature coffee its extraterrestrial edge."

---

[22] See **Appendix 14**, "**Music in this Novel**," to see link and more information about Deadmau5's masterpiece *There Might Be Coffee* while sipping your coffee :)

Nolan laughed heartily, nodding his approval. "Well, I've come to expect nothing less from the master of Martian flavors. Can't wait to try your cosmic concoction!"

As the autonomous rover parked, Nolan and Ava, already suited up, disembarked from the rover. They made their way to the Mars1 security station as the tune of *There Might Be Coffee* played in their helmets. The airlock hissed open, and they stepped inside the station. Once out of their spacesuits, they were greeted by the rich aroma of freshly brewed coffee wafting through the upper-level control room.

Tim leaned casually against the control room door, holding two steaming cups of coffee with the flair of a seasoned barista. "Welcome back to Mars1, adventurers! Care for a taste of the Martian brew?"

Nolan and Ava took the cups, raising them in a toast. "To the wonders of Mars and the guardian of its coffee!" Nolan said with a grin.

"And to the bold brew that fuels our journey!" Ava added, clinking her cup against Nolan's and Tim's.

The Red Planet, it seemed, had a way of infusing its spirit into everything—even a simple cup of coffee. As they sipped, Nolan and Ava felt reinvigorated, ready for the late-night status check with Tim and his crew before finally calling it a night.

Nolan shifted his focus to the rover's performance during their recent journey. "Tim, how's our *fancy rover* holding up after its thrilling escapade through the Martian terrain?"

Tim pulled up the rover's telemetry data, displaying it on the holographic screen. "The rover is in great shape with near perfect electric drive unit, as expected. It handled the rocky patches like a champ. You know, Nolan, these new cyber rovers are designed to tackle the toughest Martian terrain. They're practically unstoppable space tanks!"

Nolan's grin widened with pride. "That's why I trust them for our exploration missions, Tim. They're one of the keys to our survivals on this planet."

"And, how about Mars1? All systems green?" Ava asked.

Tim nodded and then brought up the colony's status reports on the large holographic display, projecting a detailed overview of Mars1's systems and their current performance. The low hum of the control room servers and the rhythmic beeps of various instruments created a comforting ambiance.

A few hours later...

Chapter 4:
Strawberry—Orange—Banana

As the **Martian night gradually yielded to dawn**, the velvety black expanse transformed into a canvas of mesmerizing hues. Unlike Earth's sunrise, Mars's awakening unfolded in a captivating dance of bluish tones that gently transitioned into soft shades of pink and red as the sun climbed higher. Mars1 security station's panoramic windows and monitoring cameras showcased the breathtaking Martian landscape—a stunning blend of rust-colored terrain against the faint glow of the emerging sun on the far horizon. The planet's reddish hue intensified under the sunlight, painting an awe-inspiring tableau that never ceased to captivate its inhabitants.

Mars1 colony marked the pinnacle of the HoloRoad, a nearly 10km-long route connecting the settlement to the Stargate Spaceport. Flanking Mars1 were its two smaller sister colonies, Mars2 and Mars3, arranged in an equilateral triangle. This strategic layout was designed to maximize survival odds against potential disasters or in the event of unforeseen catastrophes—whether from a meteorite impact or technical malfunctions.

Nestled near underground ice reserves, Mars1's domes formed a thriving community, interconnected by air-sealed transport tunnels beneath the surface and shorter, glass-covered air-sealed passages above ground. These innovative passages allowed residents to move freely between domes without the need for cumbersome spacesuits—a brilliant design that streamlined operations and significantly boosted morale and psychological well-being by mirroring life on Earth. Walking through these passages was a testament to human ingenuity, blending functionality with aesthetic appeal to foster a sense of normalcy in this alien world.

On the uncovered surface roads between domes, robotic transport machines and androids traversed tirelessly, creating a bustling, high-tech industrial hub under the soft red glow of the Martian sky.

Beneath the surface, an expansive network of underground tunnels stood as a monument to human engineering prowess. Carved by advanced tunneling machines designed and built by the Boring Company and transported to Mars aboard heavy-lift cargo starships, these tunnels served vital purposes: streamlining cargo transport and facilitating resident transit between domes' subterranean levels.

Mars1's population had surged to more than 4,000, invigorated by the recent arrival of crew members from the Starship fleet. This influx brought fresh energy and vitality to the colony. In the mid-morning hours, groups of newcomers embarked on orientation tours through various sections of Mars1. **Megan** and her team led one such group, emerging from a dome to walk along a glass-covered passage toward a neighboring structure as the timeless melody of **Hans Zimmer**'s *Time* played in the background. Their conversations buzzed with excitement as they exchanged tales of their journeys, reasons for coming to Mars, and their dreams for the future amid the stark, alien Martian landscape.[23]

"Megan, these interconnected domes and tunnels are incredible. They really foster a thriving community here. It's an engineering marvel on Mars!" **Mathew**, a newly arrived mechanical engineer, remarked with awe.

Megan nodded, "Yes, Mathew, they've been vital in streamlining the colony's operations. Our team has worked tirelessly to transform Mars1 into a genuine home away from home!"

Kathy, a geneticist among the new arrivals, chimed in enthusiastically. "And these glass-covered passages—being able to stroll through them without spacesuits—make life on Mars so much more enjoyable! It feels like walking under the open sky, just like back on Earth! I saw this in augmented reality simulations and VR training on Earth, but nothing compares to seeing it in person here on Mars."

---

[23] Curious to learn more about the music that accompanies the crew as they walk along the glass-covered passages in the Mars1 colony? See **Appendix 14**, "**Music in this Novel**," for links and detailed information about a melodic remix version as well as the original masterpiece by **Hans Zimmer**, featured in **Christopher Nolan**'s mind-bending masterpiece *Inception* (2010). [27]

"Yep, you're spot on, Kathy. It really is a unique experience." Megan replied. "These iron-oxide-infused silica glass walkways and domes exemplify our innovation. They're engineered to withstand pressure gradients and thermal fluctuations while also repelling the omnipresent Martian dust. Additionally, they serve as shields against UV radiation, cosmic rays, and solar particles—hazards that are particularly severe on the surface of Mars due to the planet's lack of atmospheric UV absorption caused by the absence of an ozone layer."

"What range of thermal fluctuations are these glass structures designed to withstand?" Mathew asked.

"Good question Mathew." Megan replied. "Let me check—I think I have a chart on my **Holopad**... Aah, here it is! See, as you might know, Mars experiences extreme temperature variations from day to night. This *colony is situated between the equator and mid-latitudes*, where temperatures range from about -100 degrees Celsius to slightly above zero. If I'm remembering correctly, these glass covers are designed with a 50% safety margin beyond those extremes." [24]

"So, these massive glass walkways can handle temperatures from -150 up to +50 degrees Celsius?" Mathew clarified.

"Yep, that sounds about right." Megan said with a nod.

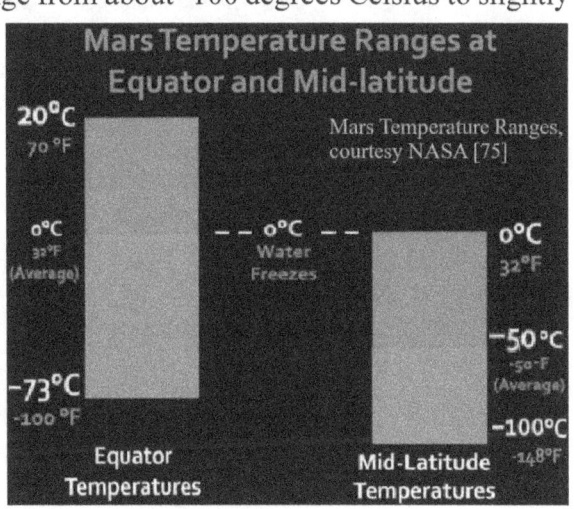

Figure 3: Mars Temperature Ranges, courtesy NASA [75]

"That's impressive!" Mathew exclaimed.

---

[24] **Holopad**: think of a holographic version of an ipad or touchpad (this is a fictional device in this novel.)

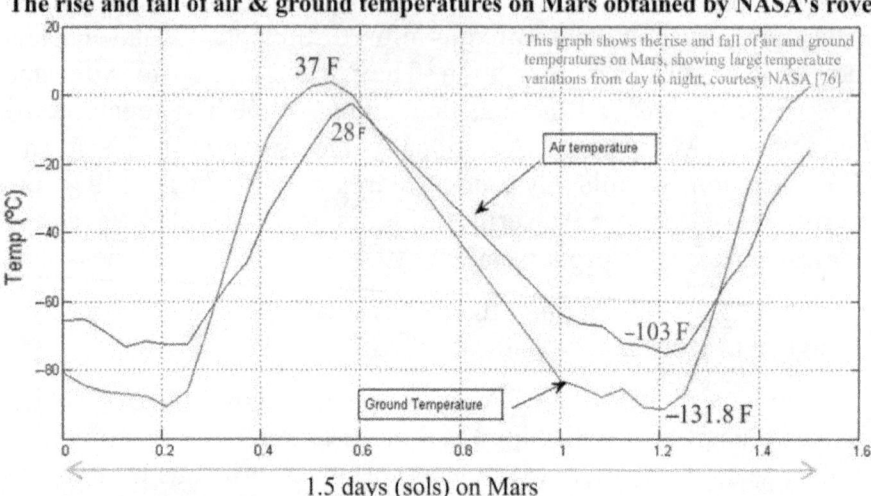

The rise and fall of air & ground temperatures on Mars obtained by NASA's rover

Figure 4: This graph shows the rise and fall of air and ground temperatures on Mars, showing large temperature variations from day to night, courtesy NASA [76]

As the tour progressed through several domes, the crew ventured deeper into the colony. They noticed that most domes followed a standardized five-story design blueprint. The three expansive subterranean stories housed residential quarters, medical facilities, science labs, and operational blocks. The two smaller stories above the surface accommodated security, educational spaces, and a limited number of residential blocks. At the very top of each dome, a central glass atrium provided a multifunctional area for work, relaxation, and dining, offering a breathtaking view of the Martian landscape.

The colony's layout featured a few notable exceptions. One was the **observation, monitoring, and scenic view station**, located on the rim of a large crater neighboring the southern edge of the colony. This dome offered unparalleled views of the surrounding terrain and the dramatic expanse of the crater itself. Another exception was the **central command, control, and policing structure**—a five-level subterranean complex at the heart of the colony. A third exception, located near the observation station, was a cluster of smaller glass domes surrounding a central structure. Together, these domes housed greenhouses, agricultural facilities, a compact glass tunnel aquarium, and a charming small park designed to evoke an Earth-like experience. The park even featured a few fruit trees genetically optimized to thrive under Mars's weaker sunlight. These trees were nurtured in carefully managed, air-conditioned greenhouse glass domes. Though interconnected by short glass passages, each dome in the cluster had its own airlock for isolation if needed.

As Megan and her group continued the tour, they arrived at a glass dome enclosing a small park. "Hey, Mathew, over here!" Kathy called out, pointing excitedly toward the fruit trees inside the park. "**Oh my god!** Look at these genetically optimized fruit trees! They're thriving despite the dim sunlight on Mars!"

Mathew walked over, marveling at the vibrant greenery inside the glass dome. "This is incredible! I can't believe how far we've come in making Mars habitable," he said. "Walking beside these trees, inside this transparent glass dome, under the pink Martian sky—it's surreal! My brain's visual cortex keeps expecting a blue sky above these plants—it's like my senses can't converge. **It's just unbelievable!**"

Megan smiled. "You're not alone, Mathew. Nearly everyone on the crew mentions that same feeling during their first visit here."

Mathew leaned closer to inspect the trees, his eyes widening. "Wait a second—are these trees taller, with bigger fruit than the ones on Earth, or am I just imagining things?"

"Not your imagination, Mathew!" Megan chuckled. "The weaker gravity on Mars—just 38% of Earth's—means the trees require less energy to transport nutrients upward and support their fruits. That's why they grow taller and produce larger fruit."

Kathy nodded in agreement, adding, "Megan's right. The difference in gravity plays a big role. I don't think the genetically modified DNA of these trees has much to do with their increased height. From what I understand, most of the CRISPR-based genome editing here is focused on adapting these plants to survive under the weaker sunlight and improving the efficiency of their photosynthesis." [25]

---

[25] Jennifer Doudna and Emmanuelle Charpentier were awarded the 2020 Nobel Prize in Chemistry for discovering CRISPR-Cas9 that allows scientists to modify or edit DNA in a cell. It was adapted from a naturally occurring genome editing system that bacteria use as an immune defense. When infected with viruses, bacteria

"**Except for that outlier**—our little unique experiment on Mars1!" Megan said with a teasing smile, pointing toward a corner behind the first few rows of fruit trees.

"Oh, my goodness! What the hell is that?!" Kathy gasped, nearly running in disbelief toward the tree that Megan had pointed to.

At first glance, from a distance, the tree appeared to be a bizarre, orange-colored banana tree. But as Kathy got closer, its true nature revealed itself—it was an otherworldly hybrid fruit-bearing tree. Circling it several times, she carefully examined its strange form, struggling to process what she was seeing.

The tree stood tall and presented an intriguing and perplexing sight. Its branches bore clusters of chubby, unnaturally orange-colored fruits that resembled bananas. Near the tree's base, Kathy spotted a small cluster of its peculiar fruits. She bent down, picked one up, and turned toward Megan, Mathew, and the others, her face a mix of confusion and astonishment.

Holding out the strange fruit for the others to see, Kathy exclaimed, "**What in the world *is* this thing?!**"

"That's for real, in case you're still wondering!" Megan chuckled, noting Kathy's wide-eyed expression of disbelief as she held the peculiar cluster. "This is the latest addition to the genetically engineered plants here in Mars1 colony. You're the first group of new arrivals to see it."

"Look at this! From a distance, it looks like a bizarre cluster of orange bananas, but up close, you realize each fruit is banana-shaped yet has a peel resembling an orange. I'd heard rumors about this from friends back on Earth, but I never really believed it!" Kathy said, her voice filled with wonder.

---

capture small pieces of the viruses' DNA and insert them into their own DNA to remember the virus to produce RNA segments that can recognize and then attach to the virus' DNA to disable it. In summary, CRISPR-Cas9 is an efficient genome editing tool that uses a specially designed RNA molecule to guide the Cas9 enzyme (CRISPR-associated protein 9) to a specific DNA sequence. Cas9 then cuts the DNA strands, creating a gap that can be filled with new DNA. The term "CRISPR" stands for Clustered Regularly Interspaced Short Palindromic Repeats. [132-134]

"Can we open one, Megan? Is it edible?" Mathew asked, joining Kathy in her disbelief.

"Alright, you can open one, but expect the unexpected! You can taste it if you'd like, but I wouldn't recommend eating it," Megan replied with a knowing smile.

Kathy carefully began peeling the thick, orange exterior of the banana-like fruit.

"No fuckin' way! This smells like a goddamn strawberry!" Kathy said, astonished, as she carefully continued to remove the peel.

"Wait, is that a *strawberry* inside what looks like a banana with an orange-like peel?!" Mathew asked in disbelief, staring at the fruit in Kathy's hand. The surreal sight left the group completely bewildered, defying their expectations and logic.

"Yep, you got it!" Megan confirmed with a big smile.

"But how is this even possible? Is this plant even biologically stable?" Kathy wondered.

"Aha! That's the right question," Megan said. "No, it's not biologically stable—far from it. That's why we only have one specimen here. It's incredibly resource-intensive, inefficient, and requires expensive, specialized genetic treatments regularly. From what I've heard from our Mars1 synthetic genomics lab, this tree is riddled with genetic instabilities and mutations—what you might call 'cancers.' Its biological clock is racing much faster than a normal tree and it is aging quickly. Without constant DNA revamping, doping and repair, it wouldn't survive. It can't reproduce either. Our bioengineers aren't even sure how long their treatments will keep it functional because it mutates so rapidly, requiring frequent reprogramming of its genetically engineered treatment—what they like to call *CRISPR therapy*."

"That makes sense," Mathew said. "I guess there's a reason nature didn't naturally evolve something like this weird hybrid of fruits. So, Megan, don't get me wrong—I'm amazed. But then why even biosynthesize it here?"

"Good question," Megan replied. "DNA-engineered experiments like this have been happening for years in our labs on Mars, as well as in shady or illegal research stations back on Earth and the Moon. This unique tree, however, was part of a controlled, groundbreaking experiment aimed at pushing the boundaries of what's possible in engineering new functional DNA sequences and life forms, while highlighting the challenges of maintaining genetic stability."

She gestured toward the bizarre tree. "It's the result of a collaboration between our top geneticists and bioengineers—a creation designed to be visually stunning but fundamentally unstable. It showcases our progress in genetic manipulation while reminding us of the fine line we tread between innovation and the unpredictability of venturing into the unknown. We hope this mind-bending tree symbolizes the delicate balance we must maintain as we decipher, recode, and edit DNA—the miraculous language of life."

"Well, if that was the purpose, you've got me!" Mathew said, laughing in amazement. "Kathy might be able to wrap her head around this with her genetics background, but my mind is completely blown by this *SOB tree!*"

"SOB?!" Megan asked, raising an eyebrow.

"Yeah, I know," Matthew replied with a grin, "but I meant Strawberry—Orange—Banana tree."

"Matthew," Kathy laughed, holding up the strange fruit. "To be honest, it's not just you. I'm still having a hard time believing that this *SOB fruit* in my hand is real."

As the tour continued, they moved into another section of the air-conditioned greenhouse glass domes. A few minutes later, laughter erupted from the far end of Megan's touring group, echoing through the glass enclosure.

Chapter 5:
840 Grams (*More Precious Than Gold*)

"Ha ha ha! Oh my god, this is hilarious!" exclaimed Jacob, the botanist among the new crew, laughing hysterically as he pointed at a sign beside a small demo potato garden in a nearby corner.

The first sign read:

> **Welcome to the Mars1 Organic Potato Garden, Mark Watney Style! Everything is recycled on Mars—We know shit matters!** [26]

The second sign read:

> **To see more of these Martian potatoes, check our little underground agriculture silo! —Though, we know why we are here! We know who built the little silo beneath! And it is surely not safe to go outside!!** ☺ [27]

Megan chuckled and motioned the group toward a small glass aquarium—a miniature replica of the historic SeaWorld, originally constructed over a century ago on Earth as the first of its kind.

Kathy gazed in awe as they passed through the aquarium's glass tunnel. "Look at these colorful fish! If it weren't for the obvious feeling of weaker gravity, I'd swear we were back on Earth—It's surreal!"

---

[26] Shout-out to **Andy Weir** and his bestselling 2011 novel *The Martian*, as well as the Oscar-nominated film *The Martian* directed by Ridley Scott, starring Matt Damon as astronaut Mark Watney. [12–17]

[27] Shout-out to **Hugh Howey** and his bestselling *Silo* trilogy of novels (*Wool, Shift, and Dust*), as well as the Saturn-nominated *Silo* (TV series) created by Graham Yost, starring Rebecca Ferguson and Tim Robins. [22] [23] [24]

"God dammit! With these Martian fish swimming above us, I'm having a damn hard time believing we are on Mars right now!" Jacob said, his face a mix of astonishment and confusion.

"And all this water is from Mars?!" Mathew exclaimed.

"Yes, Mathew!" Megan nodded. "The water is sourced from underground ice reserves. We use robotic and autonomous systems to extract and transport ice from both local reserves and more distant ones, if necessary. The extracted ice also provides the oxygen we need—for both breathing and as propellant oxidizer in the form of liquid oxygen for rockets and starships."

Mathew continued, "Is the Oxygen production facility nearby?"

"It's not that far away," Megan replied. "It's located near the northern edge of the colony. Because of their vital role in our survival, oxygen and methane production operations are under strict supervision by the Mars1 OPSEC team. I'll introduce you to Tim and his crew later—they can give you a detailed overview of their work and the Oxygen production in Mars1."

As the tour continued, beyond the greenhouses and agricultural facilities, Megan and her group came across an old, collapsed dome in an isolated corner of Mars1—a poignant reminder of the dangers inherent to life on Mars. Beside the wreckage, a cleverly placed placard told the story with a dash of wry wisdom:

The Placard beside the Collapsed Dome:

> "Here Lies Our Humble Beginnings, Brought to You by **Murphy's Law!** Because let's be real, if something can go wrong, it will—especially on Mars, where even the laws of physics sometimes seem to take coffee breaks! ... And just to drive the point home, here's a nugget of wisdom from the interstellar guru Douglas Adams himself: *'The major difference between a thing that might go wrong and a thing that cannot possibly go wrong is that when a thing that cannot possibly go wrong goes wrong, it usually turns out to be impossible to get at and repair.'* ... But hey, never say never, right? Just look

around—we're still here, learning and laughing in the face of cosmic curveballs!" [28]

This dome had suffered an accident in the early years of the colony's construction but was intentionally preserved as a symbol of the strong commitment to safety and reliability. It stood as a silent reminder of the hard-earned lessons learned from past mistakes.

Mathew paused, reflecting. "I'm relieved to hear the casualties were minimal during the collapse of this dome. But I've also heard rumors about a more serious incident here involving armed forces and convicts a few years back. Is that true?"

Megan's expression grew somber. She nodded. "Yes, Mathew, it's true. A few years ago, we intercepted a group of rogue scientists and their associates attempting to steal advanced tech, RTGs, laser weapons, and other equipment. They managed to escape with stolen rovers while heavily armed, but most were pursued and neutralized during a firefight near the lava tubes, about a few hundred kilometers from here. Although we recovered the bodies of most of the rogue group, including the leader's brother, we never found their chief—or the stolen RTG and equipment."

Mathew frowned thoughtfully. "Hmmm. Stealing nuclear batteries? Sounds like they were planning to set up a separate station with possibly its own independent power source. But did they have the specialized equipment and infrastructure to use RTGs for power generation?"

Megan shrugged slightly. "It's likely they had some kind of plan. The good news is that we never heard from them again. They're presumed dead."

The day continued to unfold on Mars1, marking the beginning of a memorable journey for the newly arrived crew. They had ventured into a world that was both hauntingly alien and tantalizingly familiar—a place teeming with challenges, but also brimming with the promise of exploration and discovery.

---

[28] **Douglas Adams** (1952–2001) was a sci-fi author, humorist, and screenwriter, best known as the creator of *The Hitchhiker's Guide to the Galaxy*. May his soul hitchhike through the happiest galaxies in heaven. ☺

As the group strolled along the air-sealed glass corridor toward the Mars1 observation dome, their attention was drawn to a **security robot** zipping along the uncovered surface road outside, its metallic exterior gleamed under the Martian sun. They suddenly found themselves locking eyes with the robot exuding a confidence that could rival James Bond himself. The bot slowed momentarily outside the corridor, its multi-lens optical sensors meticulously scanning Megan and her group through the glass as if it were a Martian police officer sizing up dangerous suspects. After a brief pause, it abruptly veered off, accelerating into the distance with such a determination as if it were on a critical spy mission to hunt down the most dangerous operative on Mars.

A whimsical thought crossed Mathew's mind, prompting him to laugh. "**Whoa, guys!** That robot out there just pulled a *Mission: Impossible* on us. It sped up like Martian super-agent on a top-secret mission, slammed the brakes as if it received the world's most classified message, gave us *the look* like we held the key to some interplanetary espionage, and then made a dramatic escape—as if it had just a few seconds before its imaginary message self-destructed! I swear, we're living in a *Mars Impossible* spy thriller!" [29]

The group erupted into laughter, imagining the robot as the star of its own interplanetary blockbuster. Kathy joined in on the fun. "Or maybe that big guy's our own Martian *Forrest Gump*, running across the red desert for no particular reason!"

"Yeah, but you know what?" Jacob, the botanist, couldn't resist adding his own twist, chimed in with a sly grin. "I think that speedy robot just had its 'Lieutenant Dan shrimp boat' moment. Probably saw something it couldn't resist and went full-on Forrest Gump in the middle of Martian traffic!" [30]

---

[29] *Mission: Impossible* (1996), directed by Brian De Palma, and produced by and starring Tom Cruise (as Ethan Hunt) from a screenplay by David Koepp and Robert Towne. [37]

[30] Shout-out to Robert Zemeckis' 1994 Oscar-winning adaptation of Winston Groom's bestselling novel **Forrest Gump**, starring Tom Hanks as Forrest, Robin Wright, and Gary Sinise as Lieutenant Dan. [36]

Still laughing at the banter, the group continued their exploration. Soon, they reached the large observation dome perched on the edge of the neighboring crater. The dome offered a breathtaking view of the vast landscape both within and beyond the crater's rim—a stunning window into the enigmatic and untamed beauty of Mars.

Kathy's admiration was evident as she gazed out at the view. "My goodness, Megan! This observation and monitoring station is such a cool place."

Megan nodded, "It is, Kathy. It's also home to the Mars1 Museum, which chronicles every milestone and technological breakthrough since our initial landing on Mars. It serves as both a tribute to how far we've come and a chronicle of our incredible journey."

Their tour through time and space exploration continued within the museum's halls, where the ethereal melody of **Hans Zimmer**'s *Interstellar* played softly, wrapping the moment in an almost otherworldly beautiful nostalgia. The museum served as a bridge between the past and future, brought to life by the music and the relics of human innovation. Life-sized exhibits commemorated their Earthly origins and honored the pioneers who had turned the Martian dream into reality.[31]

Among the displays, three historic rocket engines held particular significance: the holographic exhibit of the mighty Saturn V F-1, designed by Rocketdyne in the late 1950s for NASA's Apollo missions; the remarkable Falcon 9 Merlin rocket engine; and the original Starship Raptor engine, both developed in the early 21st century by the legendary SpaceX founding engineer **Tom Mueller** and his team. These iconic artifacts stood as enduring symbols of the technological leaps that had paved humanity's path to Mars, underscoring the lasting legacy of space exploration.[32]

---

[31] See **Appendix 14**, "**Music in this Novel**," for links and information about a melodic remix as well as the original masterpiece by **Hans Zimmer**, featured in Christopher Nolan's epic film *Interstellar* (2014). [28]

[32] **Thomas Mueller**, employee No.1 of SpaceX, is an aerospace engineer and rocket engine designer. [95]

A placard beside the engines read:

> "You thought monsters only existed in fantasies? Here are the relics of rocketeers' monsters that would give you a monstrously hard time feeding them—they're insatiable!
>
> The **F-1**, world's most powerful rocket engine developed by Rocketdyne for NASA's Apollo mission, weighs 8.4 tons and consumes 1,800 kilograms of liquid oxygen (LOX) and 790 kg of kerosene every second, producing ~700 tons of thrust (1.6 million pounds). This kerolox behemoth can lift about 90 times its own weight!
>
> The **Raptor**, one of the most efficient rocket engines developed by SpaceX, weighs only 1.5 tons but burns 510 kg of LOX and 140 kg of liquid methane every second, producing about 280 tons of thrust (over half a million pounds). It means, this Methalox beast can lift roughly 180 times its own weight!
>
> Now you know—**monsters are real**. Just watch out!" [33]

As the group moved past holographic tributes to space exploration, they found themselves in an upper-level cafeteria atrium with reinforced glass walls. The space boasted panoramic views of the surrounding landscape and the neighboring expansive crater. A large exterior balcony, accessible through an airlock from the atrium, extended over the steep edge of the crater. This balcony marked the starting point for an exhilarating zipline experience— a daring route and a thrilling way of traversing the depths of the neighboring crater, with adventurers returning via gas-thrusting jetpacks.

Mathew's curiosity ignited like a rocket. "Hey, Kathy," he said, leaning in with excitement as they both gazed at the breathtaking view, "have you heard about the *Martian zipline*?"

---

[33] Methalox stands for Methane (CH4) and Liquid Oxygen as propellant for rocket engine. Kerolox stands for refined kerosene (RP-1 fuel) and Liquid Oxygen as propellant for rocket engine. [96]

"Oh, I have!" Kathy's eyes sparkled playfully. "It's this super cool zipline route that stretches for kilometers, from the balcony out into the middle of the crater. And when you're done, you return with gas-thrusting jetpacks! isn't that something?"

"Sounds like the adventure of a lifetime—one that should have the beat of **Queen**'s *We Will Rock You* blasting in the background!" Jacob added.[34]

Megan laughed, joining in the excitement. "Yeah, it's a unique Martian thrill. But unfortunately, we won't be trying it today—it requires spacesuits, and we'd have to go through the airlock to venture outside the dome."

They leaned closer to the monitors, which offered a live feed of adventurers zipping down into the crater and jetting back up with their jetpacks. Megan pointed to the action on the large screen. "See those daredevils down there? Zoom in at the crater's base, and you'll spot them soon making their quick ascent with jetpacks from the crater's depths."

"I can't wait to try this!" Matthew's excitement bubbled over. "Sign me up for the *Martian Zipline of Doom* or whatever you call it."

Megan laughed. "You're a true thrill-seeker, Matthew. Believe me, this won't be your last cosmic escapade. So, hopefully soon you'll get your chance!"

The tour neared its conclusion as the sun dipped toward the Martian horizon. Megan led her group to an outdoor area between the observation deck and the greenhouse domes, situated beside the neighboring crater. Visitors required spacesuits to access this outdoor site. At night, a holographic projection displayed a 3D view of the **first Starship** ever to land on Mars in stunning detail. It captivated visitors and inspired the crew members to reflect on the historic milestone that had paved the way to the Red Planet.

---

[34] Shout-out to the unbeatable beats of **Queen**'s and **sir Brian May**'s masterpiece *We Will Rock You*. See **Appendix 14**, "**Music in this Novel**," for links and more information. Trivia: Sir Brian May, the lead guitarist of the Queen, earned a PhD degree in astrophysics from Imperial College London in 2007. He was also a science team collaborator with NASA's New Horizons Pluto mission. [25] [26]

Mathew gazed at the hologram with awe. "It's incredible to see the first landed Starship in such vivid detail. It's like stepping into history, preserved just as it was on the day it touched down on Mars! The day the Red Planet changed forever."

"Yeah, it's mesmerizing—this is what dreams are made of. I wish I could've been there to witness that historic moment live." Kathy said.

The actual first Starship remained preserved by service robots and secured at its original landing site, far from the colony. Cameras placed around the ship continuously captured its 3D image, transmitting a real-time holographic feed to Mars1 via Marslink satellites. Here, the iconic vessel was projected in its true size, a living monument to human ingenuity.[35]

As the orientation tour wound down, Megan guided the group back to the bustling cafeteria in the observation dome's atrium, where Tim, Mars1 OPSEC chief, was waiting.

"Welcome to Mars1!" Tim greeted them with a playful grin. "So, did the tour leave your jaws droppin', or you manage to keep 'em intact?"

"Just wait till you catch a glimpse of the sunsets in the wild—it'll have you scribbling poetry in the frickin' dust."

A voice interjected from behind Mathew and Kathy. Startled, they turned to see a towering figure in a security suit. Sipping coffee, he leaned against the wall, wearing a cowboy hat with a casual air of confidence. His muscular torso was complemented by high-tech prosthetic legs.

"Aah, folks, meet Ray—our resident Martian sheriff. A genuine, bona fide cowboy." Tim teased, gesturing toward Ray.

"Pleasure to meet y'all." Ray tipped his hat with a subtle nod.

Mathew, intrigued, pointed to Ray's legs. "Those high-tech prosthetics—they look intentionally robotic. I'm guessing they're all about maximizing functionality?"

---

[35] See **Appendix 2** for more details about the concept of **Marslink Satellite Constellation** that provides continuous surveillance, low-latency high-data-rate multimedia communication across Mars in this novel.

Ray gave a sly smile. "You've got a keen eye, amigo. These fancy gizmos do give me a leg up when it comes to speed and precision," he said with a laid-back Texan drawl.

"Those fancy cybernetic limbs?" Tim chimed in, his tone playful. "They're courtesy of a skirmish with some rogue rascals near the lava tubes a few years back. But don't you ever let those shiny prosthetics fool you—Ray's reflexes are quicker than a *cat on a hot tin roof*."

"Yup! 'nuff said." Ray tipped his hat again with a nod and returned to his coffee.

"Anyways," Tim continued, "Hope you enjoyed the orientation tour! You folks lucked out—Megan's the best darn guide on Mars1."

"Oh, come on, Tim," Megan said, brushing off the compliment with a smile.

Tim's attention shifted to Mathew. "I heard you're interested in our ISRU facilities!"

Mathew nodded enthusiastically. "Yes, Tim, I'm especially curious about the self-sustainability of Mars1 colony, including the ISRU operations and oxygen-methane production here." [36]

Tim's grin widened as he gestured toward a nearby facility. "Well, Mathew, you're in for a real Martian treat. That right there is the *Mars1 ISRU Station*—one of the central pieces of our Martian hustle to transform this alien world into a home sweet home, just as **Robert Zubrin** proposed decades ago."

Matthew's eyes lit up with curiosity. "Hmm, I've heard that name before! Wasn't he the scientist who pitched the first realistic proposal to NASA and US Congress in 1990s for a self-sustaining Mars mission?"

"That's right." Megan replied, "Dr. Zubrin was a pioneer in advancing the concept of self-sustaining methane-based fuel production and rocket operations on Mars. With his *Mars Direct* proposal, he led the way in demonstrating the In-Situ Resource

---

[36] **ISRU**, or *In-Situ Resource Utilization*, refers to the innovative process of using local resources on extraterrestrial bodies and planets to support sustainable human exploration and colonization. [86] [89]

Utilization process—the foundation for the self-sustainable colonies we've built here." [37]

"It's like playing mad scientist on Mars, Matthew." Tim chimed in playfully, "Picture this: we mine ice reserves on Mars. Then we use electrolysis to split water into hydrogen and oxygen in massive electrolyzers powered by our solar and RTG power plants. Then we bring in the Sabatier reaction—mix carbon dioxide with hydrogen—and *voilà*! We've got ourselves some cool liquid methane, along with extra water and oxygen!" [38]

"Wow! who knew space chemistry could be this fascinating!?" Mathew chuckled, clearly amused.

"Damn right!" Tim leaned back, playing it cool. "Our oxygen and methane producing plants? They're like our Martian alchemists. Science, baby!"

"Tim's dramatization is the best." Megan joined in, her voice carried a shared intrigue. "Mathew, it's like conducting a symphony of elements. Water electrolysis extracts hydrogen, which then we fuse with CO2 in the Sabatier reaction to produce methane—fuel for our rockets and starships."

Tim nodded enthusiastically. "Hell yeah! And speaking of oxygen—the air we breathe here is no small luxury. The average person needs about 840 grams of oxygen per day just to keep ticking."

Kathy chimed in with a grin. "You know, I keep taking for granted the oxygen we're breathing here! 840 grams of oxygen every day! I'm gonna write it down in my Holopad."

Tim nodded. "Right on! So, don't forget—out here, oxygen's more precious than gold. That's why we've got not one, but two powerful 2MW ISRU oxygen and hydrogen generation stations, including the one here at Mars1. Each produces over 7,000 liters of liquid oxygen

---

[37] **Robert Zubrin** and David Baker first proposed the *Mars Direct* plan in 1990. Dr. Zubrin played a key role in 1990s in advancing this concept. He expanded on the *Mars Direct* plan in his 1996 book *The Case for Mars* and his follow-up publications. [82] [83] [84]

[38] Sabatier reaction is a chemical process that produces methane and water from hydrogen and carbon dioxide. [85]

every single day—more than 3,000 metric tons of LOX per year. And trust me, that's no small feat, bro." [39]

Megan added, "It's a lifeline for us—the oxygen keeps us breathing and fuels the engines of our rockets and starships."

Mathew raised an eyebrow. "And what's the current population of Mars1?"

"We're now over 4,000 strong in the Mars1 community," Megan continued. "Based on Tim's figures, we need at least 3,000 liters of liquid oxygen every day just to support those 4,000 people in Mars1."

Tim nodded. "Yep. For now, our oxygen production capacity is more than enough to keep everyone breathing comfortably while also stockpiling liquid oxygen as fuel oxidizer for our kickass methalox engines on starships. That's what I call next-level resourcefulness!"

Kathy looked visibly impressed. "That's freaking insane—straight out of a sci-fi dream! I'm glad we have two of these facilities, given how essential they are to sustaining life on Mars."

As their conversation drifted to the intricacies of the colony's self-sustainability, Megan's gaze lingered on the sprawling settlement below. From the observation deck, the Martian panorama stretched before her. Every structure, every process spoke of humanity's determination to carve out a life in this unforgiving terrain. Even after years of calling Mars home, the stark beauty of the landscape still captivated her. The promise of a thriving Martian future shimmered on the horizon—*tangibly close, yet tantalizingly elusive.*

Outside the observation deck, the mesmerizing landscape continued its silent transformation. The setting sun cast long shadows over the reddish terrain, and as the stars emerge in the alien sky, the soothing strains of **SiebZehn**'s ***Sunset on Mars*** played softly in the cafeteria, offering a perfect end to the day.[40]

---

[39] For a deeper dive into ISRU operations in the Mars1 colony, please refer to **Appendix 7** of this novel: "**The Breath of Mars**: Understanding Oxygen Requirement and Production at the 2MW ISRU Facility". It provides an in-depth exploration of the ISRU process as envisioned in Mars1 colony in this novel.

[40] See **Appendix 14**, "**Music in this Novel**," for links and information about the calming trance of *Sunset on Mars* played in the observation dome.

Chapter 6:
The Telescope Tango
Mayday! Mayday! Signals in the Void

Nearly 24 hours had passed since the starship *Spes* received an urgent message from the Mars1 Stargate Spaceport. Following precise instructions, the crew adjusted their course to maneuver into a proper Martian orbit, gradually approaching the massive fifty-meter-long Orbital Telescope, which circled the red planet at an altitude of 500 kilometers.

"Oh my goodness! Look at that!" Xena exclaimed. "That's incredible!"

Inside *Spes*, the crew—Xena, Scarlet, Brad, John, and Andy—gathered around the cockpit's observation viewport. They watched in awe as the massive telescope came into view. Its imposing nine-meter diameter was an impressive fusion of an earlier variant of Starship's cylindrical skeleton, repurposed as the platform for a large optical telescope. This ingenious concept, initially proposed by Nobel Prize-winning physicist Saul Perlmutter, had evolved into a tangible reality as an autonomous orbital observatory. [41]

Xena leaned closer to the viewport, her gaze fixed on the telescope. "It's incredible to see it up close like this. I've read so much about it, but seeing it in person is something else."

Scarlet, the pilot, nodded in agreement. "Yeah, it's a marvel of engineering. Funny how, after four months en route to Mars from Earth, we just happen to be in the right orbit with the right equipment when this big guy malfunctioned. This view almost makes the last-minute detour worth the hassle."

---

[41] For readers interested in delving deeper into the "**Starship-Based Orbital Telescope**" concept, refer to **Appendix 4** of this novel for additional background and information.

As *Spes* approached the telescope, the crew discussed the meticulous procedure they were following, modeled after protocols developed many decades ago for spacecrafts approaching the *Hubble Telescope* or *International Space Station* (ISS) back on Earth.

Brad, the aerospace specialist, explained, "We're gradually matching our speed with the telescope, ensuring our velocities align safely. This allows *Spes* to get exceptionally close without risking a collision with the orbital Telescope."

Andy, the flight navigation engineer, added, "Once we're within the Keep-Out Sphere—about 250 meters around the telescope—the navigation AI will closely monitor the approach. It'll ensure the safety of both *Spes* and the telescope during the maneuver."

"And then we'll perform the phasing maneuvers to get even closer," Brad continued. "Precision is key. We also need to maintain enough distance to avoid any adverse effects on the telescope's sensitive nine-meter optical lens."

The ship executed a series of phasing maneuvers, gradually closing the distance. As *Spes* neared the Mars Orbital Telescope, the crew peered through both the viewport and the ship's optical diagnostic monitors, scanning the massive structure for any signs of damage.

"I don't see any obvious damage from here," Andy remarked, squinting at the telescope. "It looks intact."

Brad nodded in agreement. "Yeah, no visible signs of external impact. It's puzzling."

The crew continued their remote diagnostics as *Spes* approached the telescope, drawing within a hundred meters of the massive cylindrical structure housing the nine-meter lens. At this point, Scarlet and Brad suited up in their spacesuits, preparing for a spacewalk to inspect the telescope up close.

"Brad, you locked and loaded for this?" Scarlet's voice crackled through the comm as they geared up to leave the airlock of the ship.

"*Locked and loaded*," Brad replied confidently, his excitement evident even through the comm link. "Ready to rock and roll. Let's fly!" He activated his helmet's music player, letting the uplifting tune of **Alan Parsons'** *Sirius* play fittingly in the background.[42]

"Oh God, I could die happy listening to this masterpiece!" Scarlet quipped.

Stepping out into the vacuum of space, their tethers securely fastened to *Spes*, Scarlet and Brad began the 100-meter spacewalk towards the telescope. Beneath them, the awe-inspiring view of Mars stretched out in all its rust-colored splendor. The planet's vast surface was marked by landmarks such as the towering Olympus Mons and Ascraeus Mons volcanoes, which cast dramatic shadows as the sun rose over the Martian horizon. Orbiting at a speed of 3.3 km/s in a 500-kilometer circular path, they completed a full circuit around Mars every two hours.[43]

In the vast expanse of space, as Scarlet and Brad spacewalked the 100-meter gap between *Spes* and the orbital telescope, Scarlet couldn't help but be overwhelmed by the breathtaking scenery below. Her voice, filled with wonder, broke the silence.

"Brad, look at **Valles Marineris** down there! Can you believe it stretches over 4,000 kilometers and plunges nearly seven kilometers deep? It's like the Grand Canyon on steroids—a cosmic marvel that puts Earth's wonders to shame. It's incredible!"

Brad's voice crackled over the comm as he marveled at the view. "Scarlet, you nailed it. The Grand Canyon's got nothing on this. It's like we're exploring the ultimate frontier—redefining what 'awe-inspiring' even means. After being cooped up in that tin can for months, this feels like a cosmic cocktail for the senses. Absolutely mind-blowing."

As they spacewalked through the silent expanse, wrapped in their protective spacesuits, the sheer majesty of the Martian landscape

---

[42] See **Appendix 14**, "**Music in this Novel**," for more information about the Alan Parsons' instrumental masterpiece *Sirius*.

[43] For a quick calculation that demonstrates the orbital speed of approximately 3.3 km/s in a 500 km orbit around Mars and the resulting 2-hour rotation, refer to the details provided in **Appendix 5** of this novel.

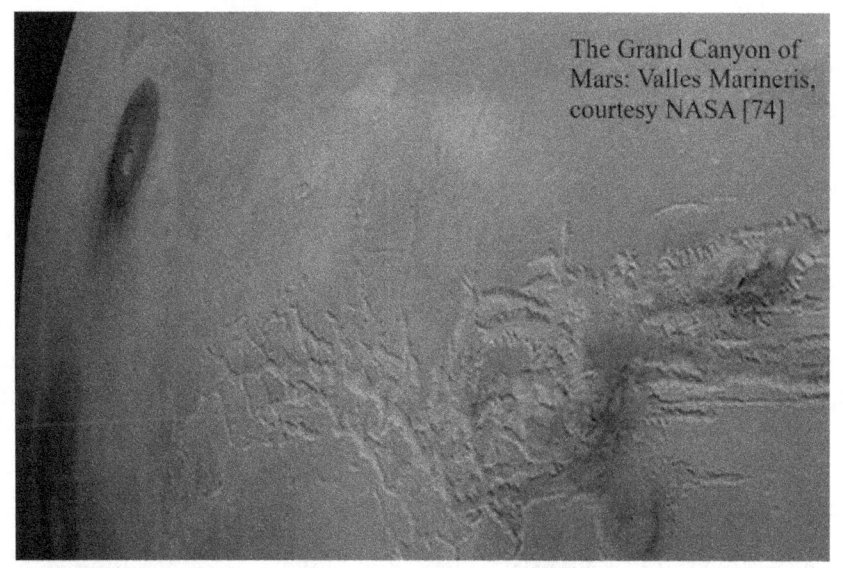

Figure 5: The Grand Canyon of Mars—Valles Marineris, courtesy NASA [74]

filled their thoughts. Amidst the Martian grandeur, Scarlet couldn't help but wax philosophical. "You know, Brad, as **Carl Sagan** once wisely put it, '*The cosmos is within us. We are made of star-stuff.*'" [44]

Brad chuckled softly. "Aah, Scarlet, always bringing a dash of philosophy to the party. But damn, you're right. This view—it truly makes you feel connected to something far bigger than yourself."

Upon reaching the giant orbital telescope, their initial inspection revealed the extent of the damage. The telescope's communication dish and antenna bore severe signs of compromise—deep dents and distortions that suggested the force of an external impact.

Scarlet's voice carried over the comm, filled with concern. "Brad, take a look at this. The comm dish and antenna are damaged in a way that was hard to spot from *Spes*. Looks like they've been hit hard—possibly by some external debris or micrometeorite impact?!"

Brad's tone grew serious. "This isn't good, Scarlet. We need to report this to Andy on *Spes* immediately." Adjusting his helmet's

---

[44] **Carl E. Sagan** was an American astronomer, planetary scientist, author and science communicator. His best-known scientific contribution is his research on the possibility of extraterrestrial life. Sagan's number is the number of stars ($>10^{23}$) in the observable universe. [121] [122]

comm system, he continued, "Andy, we've got significant damage to the telescope's communication antenna, LNB and RF frontend. We'll proceed with a full external inspection and begin preliminary repair procedures."

"Understood, Brad. Proceed with caution and keep us updated on the situation. Be safe out there." Andy's voice crackled over the comm.

As Scarlet and Brad pressed on with their spacewalk, Scarlet suddenly noticed something inexplicable. It appeared as though there was movement near the rear of the telescope. She dismissed it as a trick of her imagination; after all, aside from her and Brad what else could be moving in the vacuum of space surrounding the 50-meter-long observatory, 500 kilometers above Mars's surface?

Still, she couldn't shake the suspicion and signaled to Brad. "Wait, Brad, did you see that? It looked like something moved near the rear of the telescope. But how's that even possible?"

Brad chuckled, his voice crackling over the comm as he attempted to lighten the mood. "Scarlet, are you seeing space ghosts now? Maybe it's the infamous ghost of Mars orbit, coming to haunt us." He filled the silence with jokes about spacewalking horror stories as they continued their slow drift toward the rear end of the telescope.

When they reached the rear without encountering anything unusual, Brad couldn't resist teasing. "See, Scarlet? No space ghosts here. It was all in your imagination—probably just a glint of sunlight as we zip around this orbit."

Scarlet rolled her eyes but smiled as they started their return spacewalk along the telescope's exterior, heading back toward the damaged antenna.

Brad, noticing the disappointment in Scarlet's expression, continued to jest. "Ho ho ho, I hereby summon—"

Suddenly, without warning, Scarlet watched in sheer shock as Brad vanished from her view in an instant, leaving nothing but silence on her radio. An abrupt and powerful force had struck Brad from the front, sending him hurtling toward the rear of the telescope and severing his safety spacewalk tether in the process.

Stunned and clueless, Scarlet struggled to process what had just happened. She gazed back toward the rear of the telescope and saw Brad's white spacesuit rapidly receding into the distance, untethered.

"Brad! Brad! Can you hear me? ... Brad!" Scarlet shouted into her radio frantically.

There was no response. Her readings showed no vital signs from Brad's suit. Panic surged as she activated her helmet's zoom function, capturing a chilling sight: Brad's lifeless spacesuit drifting away. Desperation clawed at her as she engaged her suit's AI. "Compute the distance to Brad's location as marked by my focal view."

The AI responded, "Distance is approximately 100 meters and increasing at a rate of 10 meters per second."

Scarlet's heart sank. "Is there enough cold gas remaining in my thrusters to catch up to Brad at his speed?"

The AI replied, "Based on current calculations, it is not feasible to reach him using your suit's thrusters. I recommend an alternate rescue plan involving *Spes*."

"Do you have a replay of the impact moment? Show me in slow motion whatever you captured." Scarlet pressed further.

The AI responded, "There is limited footage, as your helmet cameras were focused on the telescope's exterior, away from Brad's position on your other side." Then, the AI complied, displaying the limited footage captured by Scarlet's helmet cameras.

Scarlet's breath caught as the video played. She watched in horror as a large piece of metal hurtled toward them from the telescope's head, striking Brad.

Her heart pounded like a runaway freight train. Panic threatened to overtake her, but Scarlet forced herself to remain functional. Desperately, she reached out to *Spes* for help, her voice trembling through the suit's radio.

"**Mayday! Mayday!** Andy, can you hear me?" Scarlet asked as she slowly resumed her spacewalk toward the damaged comm dish and antenna.

Andy's fingers trembled as he frantically sent commands to *Spes*, pulling up Scarlet's visual data logs. A sense of growing dread gnawed at him as he analyzed the situation.

"What just happened, Scarlet? We couldn't see you and Brad for a minute while you were behind the telescope. It blocked our view." Andy's voice crackled over the comm, tense with urgency.

"**I have no idea!**" Scarlet replied, her voice tight with panic. "We just lost Brad! Something came out of nowhere and hit him! I need immediate help to recover his body. My AI just transmitted my visual data log to you—use it to quickly command *Spes* to grab Brad if there's still a chance!"

"Got it. I'm on it. But Scarlet…" Andy's shock was evident as he processed the dire situation. "*Spes* isn't picking up any vital readings from Brad's suit. It looks like his radio is down too. He might be unresponsive—or worse."

Scarlet took a deep breath, struggling to control her trembling voice. "Roger that," she said. "Just hurry up, Andy. In the meantime, I'm going to spacewalk toward the head of the telescope to further investigate."

Inside *Spes*, Andy turned to speak with John about the situation—but the words died in his throat. What he saw froze him in place, a cold jolt of terror shooting down his spine.

John was holding Xena at gunpoint. A strange, jellyfish-like thing clung to her head, its translucent form pulsating eerily. Xena's eyes were wide-open and vacant, her expression utterly blank. She stood unnaturally still, as if under some kind of hypnotic spell.

"Wha—What's going on, John? What is that thing on Xena's head?" Andy's voice quavered in disbelief.

"Don't you dare make any fuckin' move, or I'll kill her right here!" John snapped, his tone cold and direct.

"I … I don't un— understand. Wha—What do you mean?" Andy stammered.

"Oh, cut the crap!" John hissed, his finger hovering dangerously over the trigger. "You know exactly how damn valuable she is! So, you wanna be the one dispatching the '*Oh, I fucked up*' SOS to Mars? … Imagine explaining how you let her die on your watch!"

The situation grew more dire as John activated and deployed a mini laser drone inside the cockpit. It buzzed to life, hovering near the cockpit ceiling with a faint hiss, its laser sight locking onto Andy's forehead with unnerving precision.

"You twisted son of a bitch!" Andy's mind raced as he struggled to comprehend the situation. His voice trembled with anger. "I had a feeling trusting you was a mistake the moment you stepped foot on this ship! Replacing our OPSEC officer during the transit stop at that goddamn lunar orbital station was too convenient. Now I'm wondering if his 'heart attack' wasn't just an accident. You must be one of those rogue operatives from the dark side of the moon! I'll bet there's a bounty on your—"

"Shut the fuck up!" John barked, cutting Andy off. His voice was icy, calculated. "Here's what's going to happen. You, my friend, are gonna park your ass in that seat and shut off the radio link to Mars faster than this timer hits the '*Oh shit!*' moment in 60 seconds. Then, you're gonna cut Scarlet's spacewalk tether like you're trimming a piece of cake." His lips twisted into a chilling grin. "Otherwise, I'll turn this fuckin' ship into a tomb for both of you."

John then gestured toward the hovering drone. "See that little birdie? Its trigger's linked to me. It's packing a nice one-kilowatt laser pulse beam—enough to punch a neat hole straight through you, maybe even two or three before you even notice. So, you better watch your next moves and words."

Andy sank into his chair, paralyzed by shock and fear. His mind raced, searching for a way out of this nightmare. If his suspicions about John's affiliation with rogue operatives were correct, the stakes were even higher than they appeared. The consequences could be catastrophic.

The **dark-side operators** were a notorious group—outlaws, biohackers, opportunists, and rogue scientists expelled from Earth's regulated territories, who had found refuge underground and in the shadowy recesses of the Moon's far side. They were known for their ruthless disregard for ethics, conducting illicit experiments and selling their dangerous innovations to the highest bidder for profit or **interplanetary terrorism**. They had become prime targets for global enforcement.

While many had been captured and imprisoned, rumors persisted of key figures who had slipped through the cracks, vanishing into the dark side of the moon. There, in the ungoverned badlands and vacuum of space, they pursued their sinister agendas with practically no oversight.

Andy shuddered at the thought. If John truly belonged to that group, then they were dealing with someone capable of unimaginable savagery—and with nothing to lose.

The strange contraption on Xena's head pulsated at a seemingly faster pace, fueling Andy's worst fears. The situation had taken a dire turn, and he couldn't help but fear for the safety of Scarlet and Xena, now trapped with an unpredictable dangerous enemy in their midst.

Meanwhile, in the vacuum of space, Scarlet's heart raced within the confines of her spacesuit. Her breath came in ragged, heavy gasps, each exhale forming faint, frosty clouds that briefly hovered before her visor. Her spacesuit's monitors alerted her to elevated adrenaline levels as she moved along the telescope's exterior, headed toward the damaged antenna and communication dish. The view through her helmet offered a surreal, disorienting panorama—the rusty surface of Mars seemingly moving fast 500 kilometers below her and the massive telescope.

Scarlet's gloved hands clung tightly to the telescope's metallic surface as she cautiously moved forward. Her boots tapped lightly against the exterior, creating faint, rhythmic echoes in the otherwise silent void. Despite her focus, she couldn't shake the sensation that she was an intruder in this alien, desolate realm.

Panic surged through her as she suddenly noticed her lifeline tether to *Spes* had been severed, leaving her adrift in the sea of stars.

"Andy! Andy! What the hell is going on? Why is my support cord cut?" Scarlet shouted through her helmet's radio, her voice filled with desperation as she tried to make sense of the situation.

What... What just happened? Her voice trembled as she spoke to herself. *My spacewalk support cord... It's gone! Disconnected! And where the hell is Andy? Why isn't he responding?! ... This can't be right!*

She glanced backward, her visor capturing every quiver and shiver as she struggled to contain her rising anxiety.

Amidst the chaos and confusion, Scarlet's thoughts raced. *Maybe Spes is about to perform a fast thruster restart to get to Brad?*

The unanswered questions gnawed at her as she watched, helpless, while Brad's distant figure—his spacesuit glimmering with reflected sunlight—drifted farther away.

Desperation gripped her as she called out again through her suit's radio. "Andy, come in. Do you read me? What's your plan to save Brad? He's drifting farther away, and I can't reach him. Please, someone respond!"

Her words were met with only disheartening silence. The quiet amplified her fear and deepened her overwhelming sense of isolation in the cold vacuum of space.

Inside the dimly lit confines of *Spes*, Andy sat perched near the command control holographic display, his saddened and worried eyes fixed on the three-dimensional projection of Scarlet's spacewalk. Every motion she made was magnified on the display. The tension in the room was unbearable for Andy.

"I did what you asked and turned off our comm link to Stargate. You already have Xena. Let me at least help Scarlet. Why—" Andy pleaded desperately.

"Zip it! Just fuckin' zip it!" John barked, his grip unyielding on Xena as he kept her at gunpoint. His voice was sharp and icy, his words dripping with chilling authority as he leaned closer to Andy. "Listen, Andy! You see this little situation we've got now?... So, here's the deal: if you wanna see Xena breathing, you're gonna play it cool, keep mum, and pretend you're a damn mannequin. Got it?"

Amidst the chaos, Scarlet pressed on with her spacewalk, each movement fraught with uncertainty. As she approached the antenna near the head of the telescope, the ominous silence from *Spes* left her unnerved.

"*Spes*, Andy, do you read me?" Her voice, tinged with anxiety and desperation, pierced the void as she repeated her call. "This is my third radio call with no response! What the hell is going on? Why is my support cord cut? Is the comm link down? Why aren't you responding?"

Receiving no answer, Scarlet turned to her spacesuit's AI, her voice quivering. "AI, run a quick end-to-end comm link diagnostic between me and *Spes*. Is there a malfunction?"

"Diagnostics complete. No observable malfunctions detected in the comm link. Diagnostic log is clean." The spacesuit's AI responded promptly.

Scarlet, undeterred, pressed on. "Scan for any alternative radio or optical communication links within your detectable range."

After a few seconds, the AI responded, "No recognizable communication links detected in our current orbital location. However, I sense an unidentifiable weak electromagnetic field source nearby. I am unable to scan through the 9-meter-wide cylindrical metallic body of the telescope. Recommend proceeding to the other side for a visual check."

"Copy that," Scarlet replied. "AI, initiate full visual, infrared, and sonar logging as I approach the other side of the telescope for a closer examination."

The colossal cylindrical body of the telescope loomed ahead as Scarlet continued her spacewalk. She quickened her pace, determined to reach the other side and gain a clearer view.

Suddenly, an unsettling vibration coursed through her spacesuit, sending a sharp chill down her spine. Her heart pounded as she hastened her spacewalk to clear the telescope's curvature, when a sharp, searing pain shot through her upper right leg. Scarlet's eyes darted to her helmet's visor, which revealed a small, blackened breach in her spacesuit. From the tear, a reddish fog began to escape.

"Oh my god! I'm shot! I'm bleeding!" Panic surged as she fully grasped the severity of her situation.

Her spacesuit AI's urgent voice cut through her spiraling thoughts. "Warning! Your suit's integrity is compromised. Pressure loss detected above your right knee. Your heart rate is escalating rapidly. Apply an emergency patch to your suit immediately."

Scarlet frantically reached for her emergency kit, but another sensation abruptly seized her—a heavy, ominous presence closing in from behind. The vibrations in her suit and through her leg grew stronger. Before she could react, a powerful impact struck her jetpack.

The force sent Scarlet tumbling into the vacuum of space. Her helmet camera briefly captured a horrifying sight: the titanium endoskeleton of a large humanoid robot, its expressionless face staring coldly at her. Then, in a calculated move, the android activated its jetpack and propelled itself away from the telescope, heading directly toward *Spes*.[45]

"**Mayday! Mayday!**" Scarlet's voice quivered with fear and urgency as she struggled to regain her bearings. "Andy, I need your help! There's a rogue android—it was hiding behind the telescope! It attacked, shot me and throw me spinning into space!"

Inside Scarlet's helmet, her AI's alerts interrupted her desperate calls. "**Warning! Warning!** Losing pressure. You have 3 minutes 40 seconds until critical levels."

Scarlet fought to remain focused, her voice trembling as she continued speaking through her helmet radio to *Spes*. "My support cord was cut earlier, and I'm floating! My jetpack is damaged! I think that goddamn Android hit me with a laser gun, and I'm losing pressure in my suit! I've only got a few minutes! Andy! What the fuck is going on? Do you read me?"

---

[45] **Endoskeleton Android (Humanoid Robot):** A type of robot with exposed metallic endoskeleton or frame, akin to the skeletal system of humans. This design enables the robot to closely replicate human movement patterns while offering enhanced flexibility and agility. **Humanoid** robots with exposed skeletal frame are typically employed in environments or situations requiring precise, human-like movements, where a realistic facial or visual resemblance to humans is not a priority.

Inside *Spes*'s cockpit, Andy and Xena—both held at gunpoint by John—watched the unfolding nightmare in the holographic 3D projection. Andy's voice cracked again with desperation as he pleaded with John, offering anything to save Scarlet, but John remained as cold as the void.

"Open the airlock for the approaching android." Andy's command came without a hint of empathy.

Scarlet's cries for help over the radio grew choppy, her voice fading into static as she floated farther away from the spacecraft. The void swallowed her pleas, leaving her clinging to survival.

Reluctantly, Andy opened the *Spes* airlock. Outside, the robot maneuvered its jetpack with precision, landing softly at the entrance port of *Spes*. As the airlock sealed shut behind the android, the air pressure inside normalized, followed by an eerie stillness within the spacecraft.

Slowly, the inner door of the airlock creaked open, revealing the dimly lit lower-level cargo compartment of *Spes*.

The robot moved through the cargo area engaging its magnetic feet. It quickly concealed an object in the cargo bay before ascending the metal staircase to the upper-level cockpit.

From Andy's vantage point in the cockpit, the horrifying figure of the android came into view. Its titanium skull and torso appeared first, rising above the edge of the staircase, its footsteps echoed ominously within the confined steel corridors. It was as if a killer T-800 *Terminator* had come to life—resurrected in the cold orbit of Mars, ascending the steel stairs in relentless pursuit of its prey.[46]

The robot's cold eyes swept methodically across the cockpit, finally locking onto John and Xena. John's lips curled into a grim smile as he muttered, "All is going as planned."

With eerie calmness, the android then turned its gaze toward Andy. Its voice began in a chilling mimicry of Scarlet's, then shifted seamlessly into Andy's own tone as it issued its ultimatum:

---

[46] Shout-out to **James Cameron** for his sci-fi masterpieces, *The Terminator* (1984) and *Terminator 2: Judgment Day* (1991). [29] [30] [31]

"There is a detonator on board this ship, synched with my AI neural processor. It will detonate the moment I cease to operate. You have 30 seconds to comply, bioauthenticate into *Spes* control and transfer ship's command to me, or prepare to experience a biological pain beyond human comprehension."

"You really think I'll just hand you the controls, you frickin' bot? I'm not gonna make it easy for you!" Andy spat, his words laced with defiance and contempt.

Before he could fully voice his resistance, the robot moved with cold mechanical precision, delivering a single, devastating blow to his hand. Andy gasped in agony as his right hand shattered under the force. He fell to his knees, writhing in pain, while the silent and menacing figure of the android loomed over him.

"Time's ticking, pal," the robot intoned, its voice chillingly calm. "Fifteen seconds. Bioauthenticate now, or you'll wish you'd been terminated before you even hatched."

Grimacing in anguish, Andy reluctantly granted the authorization, his trembling fingers barely managing to complete the sequence. The android seized full control over *Spes*'s navigation and command systems. Without a word, it struck Andy again, knocking him unconscious. The android then re-established the comm radio link with the Stargate spaceport on Mars.

The worried voice of the Mars Stargate control operator crackled through the *Spes* cockpit, cutting in mid-sentence: "... with you! Repeating: *Spes* crew! We lost contact with you about 20 minutes ago. We're only detecting vitals for three crew members. Please check the sensors for Brad and Scarlet—we can't locate them. What's going on? Requesting a SITREP! What's the status of the telescope inspection?"

The android deliberately activated the holographic feed, revealing its terrifying titanium skull and endoskeleton. In the background, John could be seen dragging Xena and the unconscious Andy into separate crew sleep compartments, each equipped with limited, dedicated oxygen reserves.

The android then modulated its voice, transitioning from a robotic, mechanical tone as it addressed the Mars1 Stargate team, "Inform

Nolan Rivs that *Spes* is under our absolute control, with a detonator on board. His daughter, Xena, is now a hostage in orbit with only a three-day oxygen supply."

"Wait... wait... who are you? What are you...?" The stunned voice from Mars1 Stargate trailed off, cut short by the android. It continued modulating its voice. Its tone shifted deliberately, alternating eerily between Xena's and Nolan's voices as it delivered its next chilling message:

"What I am, or who we are, shouldn't be your main concern. Listen carefully. Two crew members of *Spes* are already out of commission, and unless you fully comply with our non-negotiable demands, the rest will meet the same fate."

The android outlined its instructions with cold precision:

- "First, cease all inbound and outbound starship flights to or from Mars Stargate Spaceport for the next 72 hours."
- "Confirm receipt of the coordinates I am transmitting now. The location is near the Elysium lava tubes, approximately 1,000 kilometers from the Stargate Spaceport and Mars1 colony."
- "Inform Nolan Rivs that he, along with a team of no more than four individuals, has a non-negotiable 24-solar-hour [47] deadline to transport and deliver rover truckloads containing one ton of RTG fuel and 20,000 liters of liquid oxygen to the designated site. Further instructions will follow upon delivery." [48]

---

[47] A Martian solar day, or sol, lasts approximately 24 hours and 39.5 minutes, making it about 2.75% longer than an Earth Day. Mars's 'solar hour' is 1/24 of a sol, equating to 1 hour, 1 minute, and 39 seconds. In this novel, it is assumed that the human community on Mars adopted a 24-hour day to mimic Earth's timekeeping system, despite each hour, minute, and second being about 2.75% longer than their Earth counterparts. For more information, see Timekeeping on Mars - Wikipedia. [8] [9]

[48] RTG stands for "Radioisotope Thermoelectric Generator" (a nuclear battery). For more information on RTG fuel and its role in energy generation on Mars, please refer to **Appendix 9**: "Unleashing Martian Energy: The Story Behind the 5MW RTG Power Plant on Mars (Powering Martian Colony)". [38] [39]

The android's tone darkened further:

"Failure to fully comply will leave Nolan with a grisly challenge—assembling the remnants of Xena from the scattered fragments of her shattered existence at her yet-to-be-determined crash site on Mars. I'll leave the details to your imagination."

"The clock is ticking now... tick tock, tick tock..."

With that, the menacing robot abruptly terminated the comm link, leaving the *Spes* crew trapped in a dire situation and the Mars1 Stargate team frozen in **complete shock**.

Chapter 7:
What the Hell Just Happened?

Nolan's office was plunged into grim silence in the central command complex at the heart of the Mars1 colony. He and his security team fixated on the holographic projection before them, watching the recording of the Holo-video call (Holovid) from the hijackers.

The Mars1 OPSEC team and Stargate Spaceport staff had wasted no time in delivering the dire news to Nolan, the leader of the Martian colony. The harrowing hijacking and hostage crisis unfolding aboard the *Spes* in Mars orbit was now front and center.

Nolan sat in his chair, his fingers steepled in thought as he watched in disbelief the horrifying turn of events play out before him, shaking his composure. Ava, his trusted top commander; Tim, the colony's OPSEC chief; and Ray, his enigmatic lieutenant who had played a pivotal role in the Martian conflict years ago, had gathered in his office to brief him on the unfolding crisis. Their expressions mirrored Nolan's grim foreboding.

The hijackers' unsettling message, and dire terms and demands were still fresh in their minds, delivered in chilling detail by the eerie titanium android aboard the *Spes*. Among the hostages was Xena, Nolan's daughter—a revelation that cast an even darker shadow over the crisis.

"Nolan and Ava, we're in shock!" Colin, the chief of the Mars1 Stargate Spaceport team, exclaimed, his voice filled with frustration. "They've got the *Spes*! How the hell did that freakish robot get on the orbital telescope 500 kilometers above Mars!? And, Nolan—we were completely blindsided! Why weren't we informed that your daughter Xena was among the *Spes* crew? Did you know that?"

Ava's voice was tight with concern as she responded. "Colin, Mission X was a covert operation. Xena has been secretly traveling with the *Spes* crew for the past four months. The ship had been retrofitted as a nondescript cargo vessel to keep her identity concealed. The mission's objective was to ensure her safety and maintain secrecy until her planned reveal during the upcoming Mars Colony Anniversary Celebration. Unfortunately, the mission has failed."

Nolan's knuckles turned white as he gripped the armrests of his chair. His gaze darted around the room, as if the walls held answers he desperately sought. "Xena… Goddammit, nobody was supposed to know! How the hell did this happen? How did they find out she was aboard *Spes*? Only four of us on Mars even knew about Mission X."

Tim's expression darkened, his jaw tightening as he nodded in grim agreement. "This is a total shock—a bolt from the blue! We kept her mission locked down as tightly as we could."

Ava turned toward Nolan, her eyes reflecting a mix of anxiety and disbelief. "Nolan, it seems like the information slipped through the cracks. We suspect the breach happened in the final days before *Spes* launched from Earth four months ago. That's likely when the hijackers' agents on Earth learned Xena was on board. It's a catastrophic security failure—one we unfortunately couldn't foresee and control from Mars."

Ray, towering on his cybernetic legs, loomed with an imposing, otherworldly presence as he interjected, his voice heavy with stark certainty. "We all saw John lurking in the background of that Holovid, in cahoots with that goddamn robot. Here's the thing—after departing Earth, *Spes* made a sudden pit stop at the lunar orbital station to scoop up John. He was rushed in as a last-minute stand-in after the 'conveniently timed' heart attack of the original OPSEC officer just days after *Spes* launched. Well, coincidence, my ass! This reeks of sabotage and murder—a calculated ploy to plant that traitorous mole as their inside man, setting the stage for the hijacking of *Spes*."

"I agree." Tim nodded, his voice grim. "And that nightmarish robot? Whoever's behind this shitshow is hell-bent on etching a haunting impression. Based on the final limited footage Scarlet's spacesuit captured, my best guess is that thing hitched a ride on one of the dozen cargo starships that recently arrived on Mars. There's no other way it could've reached a 500-kilometer orbit. I've already dispatched a team to comb through orbital paths and navigation records, analyzing every vessel that's been near Mars in the past few weeks." His gaze reflected his resolve to uncover the sinister forces behind the chaos.

"That sounds like a good explanation, Tim. A prudent move," Ava said, her tone measured. "But do you think there's any chance that thing might've snuck in even earlier than we suspect?"

Tim's expression grew more serious. "In theory, yes. To stay operational, the robot could've accessed and quietly siphoned electrical power from the orbital telescope. It would've likely done so at a low enough level to avoid triggering alarms in the telescope's solar power usage records, which are monitored by the OPSEC team here on Mars. I've already put them on high alert and asked them to review every power fluctuation from the past few months. But honestly, I don't see much advantage in it sneaking aboard earlier when it had the opportunity to strike just weeks ago."

Ava nodded, a wry grin tugging at her lips. "Whoever's pulling the strings behind this chaos, the sheer depth of their planning is deeply unsettling. Makes me wonder what else they've got up their sleeves."

Nolan's brow furrowed as he processed the bleak picture emerging before him. "Listen, from the recordings and everything I've heard so far, it's clear we're staring at a grim reality. They've already killed two *Spes* crew members—Scarlet and Brad—right by the orbital telescope. Now they've taken Xena and Andy hostage aboard *Spes*. And then there's that peculiar bio neuromodulator attached to Xena's head in the Holovid, keeping her in some hypnotic state, like a goddamn snake charmer's victim. It all points to one undeniable truth—we're up against the most ruthless lunar dark-side operatives—a real bunch of scum and a den of vipers. This is bad... really bad."

The room pulsed with tension, Nolan's conclusion settling heavily among them. If he was right, the situation was more dire than anyone could have imagined. The lunar outlaws were a shadowy group, infamous for their utter disregard for law or ethics. Cast out from Earth, they were rumored to have established hidden bases deep underground on the moon's dark side, where they could conduct their illicit activities away from prying eyes.

Among their ranks were renegade biohackers—criminals hunted and banned on Earth—notorious for their dangerous forays into forbidden realms of generative synthetic DNA (*DNA GPT*), CRISPR-based genetic experiments, genomic malware, and DNA tampering. Their work, driven by either nefarious financial motives or anarchistic agendas, frequently violated the boundaries of both science and morality. Many had been apprehended on Earth, but a few key figures had vanished, rumored to have sought refuge among the lunar outlaws. There, they operated with impunity, pursuing sinister goals free from oversight and restraint.[49]

Ava took the lead, her eyes fixed on the Holovid. "Tim, rewind to the segment where the robot's voice oscillates between Nolan and Xena. I need to take a closer look at that part." Tim complied, replaying the eerie scene, as Ava continued, her voice low and contemplative. "What's got me scratching my head is the way that robot's delivering this message—so unsettling and deliberate. Is it just trying to scare us, or is there a deeper motive? Maybe a hidden message embedded in that bizarre performance?"

The room fell into a brief silence as they mulled over the implications of the robot's unnerving behavior.

"Agreed, Ava," Tim said, stepping closer to the Holovid. "We need to analyze every second of this footage, sift through every detail. On top of that, we're launching a full investigation to trace the leak and uncover how this major security breach happened. We're also tracing that freaking robot to pinpoint its origin. All that said, right now, we have a more immediate concern—keeping those hostages alive. And let's not forget that the clock is ticking on their 24-hour ultimatum. We have to address this crisis before it spirals out of control."

Ray nodded in agreement. "You're damn right. We'll get to the bottom of how this mess unraveled, but for now, we've got a ticking

---

[49] See **next chapters** and **Appendix 1** at the end of the novel for an exploration of Synthetic Biology and generative DNA (also referred to as DNA GPT in this novel), including brief discussion of thought-provoking ways generative AI can be used in this field.

time bomb on our hands—literally and figuratively. We just got served a chilling menu of their demands courtesy of that Frankenstein android on *Spes*. These fuckin' hijackers have hostages, and they've made it goddamn clear they won't hesitate to pull the trigger if we screw this up. That android's little show on *Spes* wasn't just creepy; it was a '*got you by your balls*' warning. They mean business. We shouldn't fuck around with these goons."

Tim's voice was steady but grave. "Yeah, no sugarcoating it—this isn't about choices; it's about survival. We need to take their demands seriously, at least until we've got more intel and a clearer picture—hopefully by the time we reach the rendezvous point near the lava tubes. Until then, we must tread carefully."

Nolan leaned forward, anger flickering in his eyes. "Alright, I hear you. There's no two ways about it. Right now, priority one is keeping Xena and Andy alive. The clock's ticking, folks! We've got 23 hours to play by the hijackers' rules and figure out a way to bring them back in one piece. So, what's the plan?"

"We're on it, Nolan," Ava replied firmly. "Tim and I talked briefly before this meeting, and we've started hashing out a game plan. If we move fast, we believe we can gather the resources they're demanding and get them to the rendezvous point in time." She turned to Tim. "How about you lay it all out for us?"

Tim nodded, stepping up to outline their strategy, his voice reflecting the weight of their precarious situation.

"Alright, here's the deal, folks." Tim dove straight into the details, his tone sharp and no-nonsense. "As Ava said, we believe we can whip up the logistics to rustle up the goods they're asking for if we hustle. The hijackers are demanding 20,000 liters of LOX and one metric ton of RTG fuel within a single sol. We've already burned an hour discussing it. If we kick into high gear and everything goes smoothly, we'll need roughly 1.5 to 2 more hours to get all the equipment and cargo packed and loaded onto the rover trucks. That leaves us with a tight 21-hour window to haul the cargo to the drop-off point near the **Elysium Mons lava tubes**, at approximately 25°N, 213°W in the eastern hemisphere." As he spoke, Tim adjusted the holographic display, projecting a detailed, three-dimensional map pinpointing the exact location.

Nolan leaned closer, his eyes fixed on the glowing display. His knuckles whitened as he gripped the edge of the table. "Tim, that delivery point is a full 1,000 kilometers from Mars1. Can our heavy-duty convoy handle that distance and still make it in time?" His tone was resolute but underscored by urgency.

Tim nodded gravely. "You are dead-on right—1,000 klicks is no small feat, especially the last 100 kilometers of mountainous terrain near the Elysium lava tubes. It's treacherous, no doubt about it. I won't lie—I can't guarantee a 100% success rate. But if we deploy our best rover trucks and make the right moves, we have a decent shot at pulling this off. Timing is critical, though. We've got two hours to mobilize the convoy, and we can't waste a minute."

Nolan exhaled sharply, weighing the stakes. "Alright, it's a solid plan, but we've got a bigger problem. If word leaks before we make the cargo delivery, it could spark panic at Mars1—maybe even jeopardize our mission to meet that razor-thin 24-hour deadline. We can't let that happen. Tim, be sure to assemble a handpicked team from OPSEC—only the most trustworthy individuals. They'll collect the shielded RTG fuel from the main radioisotope power plant and the LOX from the ISRU production facility near Mars1. We're keeping this under wraps, understood?" [50]

"Understood," Ava replied. "I'll coordinate with Frank and his engineers at the power plant to ensure a ton of RTG fuel is properly shielded and ready for pickup. Frank's been on top of things, and during our last sync-up meeting he confirmed the latest RTG batch is operational. That gives Frank and his crew enough leeway to maintain electricity production without major disruptions despite losing a ton of RTG fuel to these terrorists. He's well-versed in keeping the power plant operating smoothly. He'll have everything prepped on time."

"In the meantime," Tim continued, picking up seamlessly where Ava had left off, "Ray and I will handle logistics for the LOX. We'll

---

[50] **Radioisotope Thermoelectric Generator** (RTG) power plant that Nolan and Ava visited earlier to review its recent upgrades and developments (see Chapter 2).

fetch the 20,000 liters from the Mars1 ISRU facility and ensure it's loaded into the tankers on the rover trucks." His eyes locked with Ray's, and the silent understanding between them spoke volumes. Ray gave a firm nod.

Nolan wasted no time. He cut to the chase, his words crisp and commanding. "Alright then, here's how it's going to go. Two hours—that's your deadline. I want that cargo prepped and the convoy revved up and ready at the Mars1 rover station within that time. Everyone clear on that?"

Ava, Tim, Ray, and the select crew from the Stargate spaceport all nodded in unison.

"That said, before we dive headfirst into this mission, there's one piece of the puzzle that's been bothering me," Nolan began, his voice tinged with skepticism. "I agree with Ava—at least for now—something about this whole situation just doesn't add up. Their demands for LOX and RTG fuel, while substantial, don't pose an existential threat to our colonies or operations. Given our current resource utilization and LOX production rates, this isn't exactly the kind of leverage you'd expect to drive someone to orchestrate such an elaborate scheme. Sure, let's say they've stashed a small radioisotope thermoelectric power and heat generator somewhere on Mars, maybe down in the lava tubes. A ton of RTG fuel could net them 40 to 60 kilowatts of electricity for a few years. I can wrap my head around that. But what do they really need 20,000 liters of LOX for?"[51]

"Maybe it just buys them some breathing room—literally," Ava replied.

Nolan leaned forward, unconvinced. His brow furrowed as he pressed on. "But how long would that *breathing room* last? I mean, consider this—let's assume there's a small band of rogue survivors from the skirmish we had a few years back. Say they've managed to scrape together a crew of 50 to 100 people over time, holed up

---

[51] **RTG** is effectively a nuclear battery that converts the heat generated by radioactive decay into electricity (known as Seebeck effect). For more information on the powering of the Martian Colony please see **Appendix 9 "Powering Martian Colony**: The Story Behind the 5 MW RTG Power Plant on Mars."

underground just a thousand klicks from our Mars1 outpost. That stash of 20,000 liters of LOX might get them six, maybe seven months of air. But would they risk everything—pulling off a hijacking, taking hostages—for just a few extra months of breaths? Especially if they've already figured out how to survive on Mars for this long?" [52]

"You make a fair point," Ava conceded. "Could it be that their underground LOX production system broke down, and now they're scrambling for a quick supply?"

"Maybe," Nolan said, "But that would mean they've got no backup units, no reserves, and no access to whatever supply they've relied on so far. That sounds like a long shot to me. My gut says we're pawns in a much bigger game. And this bizarre demand? It's just the opening act. What really awaits us at the rendezvous point? What kind of surprises or traps are they setting? Are we truly ready for whatever's coming our way?..." He paused, his voice dropping to a grim whisper. "I'm itching to get a glimpse of their real endgame—whatever twisted plot they've got planned for us."

"Nolan," Tim interjected, "I hear you. We're all uneasy and concerned, but we don't have the luxury of time to play detective right now. The deadline's set. They've locked us into a team of no more than four, plus yourself, for the convoy. The best we can do is get the cargo ready ASAP and load up as many weapons as we can cram into our rovers."

Nolan let out a sigh, his mind clouded with worry. "Fair enough, Tim. I guess my head's all over the place like a wild rollercoaster, especially with Xena out there on *Spes*. Let's not waste any more time. It's you, Ray, Ava, and me on the team. For our fifth member, we'll bring in the heavy artillery—**TESA100**, our most advanced combat-ready Titanium Super Android." [53]

---

[52] To learn more about the Liquid Oxygen (LOX) and the In-situ Resource Utilization (ISRU) production facility in Mars1 colony, refer to **Appendix 7** of this novel for additional background and information.

[53] **TESA100** stands for **Titanium-Endoskeleton Super Android**, model number 100. It is the most advanced combat-grade android on Mars in this novel, often referred to by the crew as **Titanium Man**, **Titan**, or simply **TESA**. With its titanium endoskeleton, the two-meter-tall TESA100 is a striking fusion of raw mechanical

"**Hell yeah!** I'm all in for riding and whooping ass with a Titan!" Ray exclaimed, his brief excitement breaking through the tense atmosphere.

Ava, however, raised a valid concern. "Nolan, we just received the TESA100-class android. It hasn't undergone full testing or training here. Are we sure it's wise to risk bringing it along on such a critical mission?"

"Ava, sometimes chaos demands chaos," Nolan said, "This is a high-stakes showdown, and we're not holding back. I believe it's a risk we have to take in these uncertain times."

He exhaled deeply and then continued. "Alright, let's press forward with the plan. We've got two hours to fetch RTG and LOX, prep the convoy, suit up, and get ready to board the rovers for the cargo haul."

As the team refocused on their planning, Nolan, Ava, and Colin—the chief of the Mars1 Stargate spaceport—worked hastily to review and finalize the transport route. Strategizing for the dangerous mission ahead, they coordinated with the **Marslink satellite surveillance** team to ensure real-time monitoring of the three-rover convoy's journey across the treacherous Martian terrain.

Nolan's gaze stayed fixed on the holographic display as he discussed the mission with the Marslink satellite team. "We need eyes on us every step of the way. This isn't just a cargo delivery—it's an extremely high-stakes operation. We can't afford any missteps."

"No doubt." Colin nodded in agreement. "The Marslink surveillance team and I will maintain direct real-time communication and data relay with the convoy. This will keep your crew informed of any suspicious activities or movements along the rovers' route during the 21-hour journey toward Elysium Mons."

"Thanks, Colin," Ava said, her tone heavy with concern. "We're in uncharted territory here, dealing with a ruthless enemy. It's not just our lives at stake; it's the safety of the Mars1 colony and the *Spes*

---

power and cutting-edge technology. This android seamlessly combines machine precision and agility with advanced AI inference and humanlike intelligence, making it a formidable asset in high-risk missions.

crew, Xena and Andy. Real-time surveillance is essential to guarantee a safe passage to the designated destination near those treacherous lava tubes."

The uncertainty weighed heavily on everyone as they prepared for the perilous journey through the rugged terrain.

As the crew began leaving the Mars1 Command Station to proceed with their assignments, Nolan stopped Tim.

"Stay for a moment, Tim. I've got one last thing to run by you…"

Chapter 8:
Release Ghost!

Amid the escalating crisis, Nolan felt the crushing weight of his daughter's life hanging in the balance and the safety of the entire Mars colony at stake. The grim vision of Xena's fate, concealed behind the cold, metallic walls of the hijacked spaceship, haunted his every thought. The clock was ticking, and the 24-hour deadline was rapidly approaching. Nolan's mind raced desperately, struggling to answer the nagging questions and unravel the hijackers' true intentions as the demanded cargo—one ton of RTG fuel and 20,000 liters of LOX—was hurriedly loaded onto the rover trucks.

With the critical payload securely stowed in the rovers, Nolan and his crew—Ava, Tim, and Ray—prepared for their perilous mission across the unforgiving Martian terrain toward the lava tubes.

As they were about to depart from Mars1 Station, Nolan, while helping Ava adjust her spacesuit, turned to the team to relay their plan.

"Alright, it's already 10:33 AM. Tim, Assign the TESA100 [54] android to pilot the rover truck carrying the shielded RTG fuel and half of the LOX. We can't afford any mishaps with it. You and Ray take charge of the other rover truck, transporting the rest of LOX. Ava and I will lead in the autonomous rover at the front of the convoy. We'll be armed to the teeth, packing some serious heat—laser guns, mini drones, microbots—everything we can cram into our rovers." Nolan glanced at Tim, his intense expression leaving no room for doubt.

---

[54] **TESA100** stands for **Titanium-Endoskeleton Super Android**, model number 100. It is the most advanced combat-grade android on Mars in this novel, often referred to by the crew as **Titanium Man, Titan**, or simply **TESA**. With its titanium endoskeleton, the two-meter-tall TESA100 is a striking fusion of raw mechanical power and cutting-edge technology. This android seamlessly combines machine precision and agility with advanced AI inference and humanlike intelligence, making it a formidable asset in high-risk missions.

"Sure thing, boss," Tim replied. "And before I forget—folks, double-check your helmets, spacesuits, and supplies. We're heading out on a thousand-kilometer drive across rough terrain, and we have to assume anything can happen. Even though the rovers are air-sealed, we can't let our guard down. Be ready to step outside the rovers at any moment if things go sideways."

Ava nodded, her eyes steady and focused. "Well said, Tim. We're dealing with a lot of unknowns in this special op mission. We have to stay ahead of whatever comes our way, especially given the distance we're covering on Mars. We can't underestimate the risks, and the stakes have never been higher. Every decision we make could mean the difference between life and death."

Geared up and encased in their spacesuits and helmets, they emerged from the airlock of the Mars1 OPSEC station, the stark hiss of the seals serving as a reminder of the formidable challenges awaiting them outside on the Red Planet.

As the airlock closed behind them a storm of emotions brewed beneath their protective suits. The weight of their responsibilities, the looming mystery of what lay ahead, and the sinister enigma surrounding the operation pressed heavily on them—a burden they couldn't ignore.

With the payload loaded and secured, their attention shifted to a striking figure in stark contrast to the spacesuit-clad team. Leading the way without a spacesuit was the TESA100 android—a sleek, two-meter-tall humanoid robot. It moved with mechanical precision across the rust-colored Martian surface, unaffected by the swirling emotions that consumed its human companions. The android approached the rover truck, which carried the heavily shielded RTG fuel along with half of the LOX payload—approximately 10,000 liters of liquid oxygen. It then swiftly climbed into the rover, assuming its role as the designated pilot.

The rest of the crew moved toward their respective vehicles. Nolan and Tim, clad in their spacesuits, stood by the rovers with their helmet radios engaged.

"Tim, you made sure... you know, the thing we talked about is in place, right?" Nolan's voice crackled through the radio.

Tim and Ray exchanged a quick nod. Tim's reply was cryptic. "Yeah, boss. The extra cargo that you asked for is safely tucked away in TESA's rover truck."

"And you think this might be our ace in the hole?" Ray questioned.

"Ray, trust me," Nolan replied with calm confidence. "Sometimes embracing the unexpected and thinking outside the box can be a real game-changer."

"Cool with me, bro." Ray nodded in his helmet. "Let's then rock and roll."

With TESA100 robot in position, Tim and Ray stepped into the airlock of the second rover truck, which carried the remaining LOX. Meanwhile, Nolan and Ava sealed themselves in the lead rover, ready to guide the convoy through the treacherous Martian terrain.

As the convoy rumbled away from Mars1 Colony, a mix of emotions settled over the crew. Inside Nolan's rover, the hauntingly melodic strains of **Boris Brejcha**'s *RoadTrip* echoed through the cabin, setting an ominous tone for the uncertain mission ahead.[55]

The vast Martian expanse stretched before them—a formidable and untamed wilderness, a stark reminder of the ticking clock and the dire consequences they would face if they failed to deliver the cargo to the hijackers' designated site within the next 21 hours.

A few hours later...

Nolan and his crew pressed on through the Martian terrain, their rovers navigating a winding path along the **Phlegra Montes**—an extensive, 1,400-kilometer range of gently curving mountains and ridges that stretched as far as the eye could see across the mid-latitudes of the northern lowlands of Mars. Bordered by the Elysium Rise mountains to the south and the expansive Vastitas Borealis plains

---

[55] Please refer to the **Appendix 14**, "**Music in this Novel**," to learn more about Boris Brejcha's nostalgic trance *Roadtrip* and its contextual significance within this narrative, as well as an in-depth look at other featured tracks in this novel.

to the north, the Phlegra Montes region stood as a testament to the red planet's once-active geology.[56]

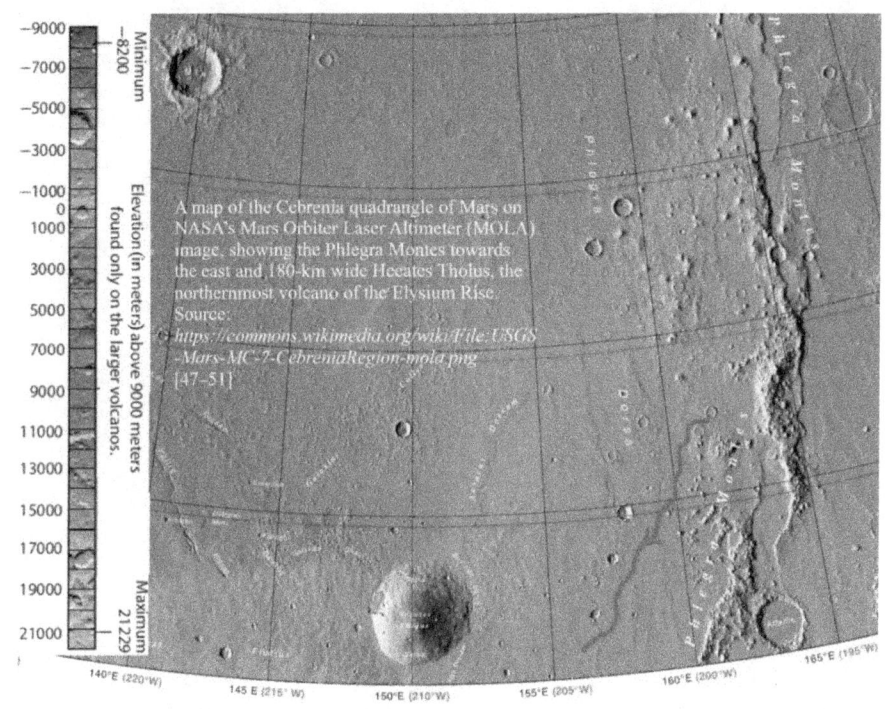

*Figure 6: A map of the Cebrenia quadrangle of Mars on NASA's Mars Orbiter Laser Altimeter (MOLA) image, showing the **Phlegra Montes** towards the east (right side of the map) and 180-km wide Hecates Tholus, the northernmost volcano of the Elysium Rise. Source: Wikimedia.org/wiki/File:USGS-Mars-MC-7-CebreniaRegion-mola.png [47–51]*

Outside the rovers, a breathtaking panorama of the Martian landscape unfolded through the windshields—a surreal tapestry of crimson hues and undulating landforms surrounding the convoy. Flow patterns etched by ancient waters crisscrossed the Martian terrain, preserving the enigmatic story of the planet's distant past.

As the **three rovers continued southwest** toward the lava tubes, three colossal volcanic mountains—Hecates Tholus, Elysium Mons and Albor Tholus, the towering sentinels of Elysium Rise region—

---

[56] To learn more about the enigmatic **Phlegra Montes** and **Elysium Rise volcanic** regions on Mars and explore their intriguing geological features, please refer to **Appendix 6** of this novel.

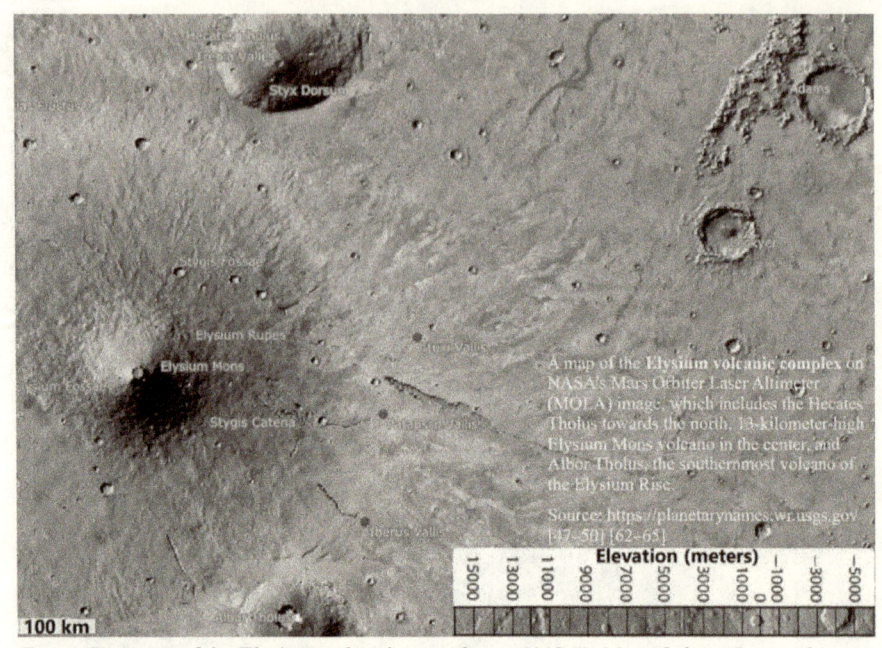

*Figure 7: A map of the **Elysium volcanic complex** on NASA's Mars Orbiter Laser Altimeter (MOLA) image, which includes the Hecates Tholus towards the north, 13-kilometer-high Elysium Mons volcano in the center, and Albor Tholus, the southernmost volcano of the Elysium Rise. Source: https://planetarynames.wr.usgs.gov [47–50] [62–65]*

emerged on the horizon. Rising like ancient titans, they grew larger with each passing minute, casting awe-inspiring shadows over the surreal landscape.

Nearly thirteen hours had passed since the reception of the 24-hour ultimatum. The convoy had been on the move for approximately ten hours, covering nearly 500 kilometers. As the day waned, the crew remained vigilant knowing that nightfall on Mars brought its own unique set of challenges.

Trailing in the third rover of the caravan, the TESA100 android piloted with unmatched precision. Its synthetic eyes, capable of scanning both the visible and infrared spectrums, provided a nearly 180-degree immersive panorama of the Martian terrain. The TESA100 didn't stop there; it seamlessly integrated its live visual feed with the rover's 360-degree radar scan. This real-time composite view was projected onto the digital holographic screen inside the rover, displaying an animated fusion of sensory data and analytical overlays that revealed intricate details of the surrounding landscape.

The android's perspective zoomed in and out, its focus darting with precision from one region to another as the rover sped across the barren, desolate expanse stretching endlessly before the speedy convoy.

Suddenly, the digital screen pulsed with activity. A glimmer of light caught the android's telescopic eyes in both visible and infrared spectrum, prompting it to magnify the area. As the image sharpened, the android began analyzing the area surrounding the anomaly—a fleeting glint of reflected light, an unusual oddity in the otherwise lifeless Martian wilderness.

Artificial intelligence and machine vision algorithms whirred into action, making rapid inferences and calculations. Real-time pattern recognition and object classification data summaries scrolled across the holographic display as the android methodically honed in on the target. With each passing moment, it refined its focus, ultimately locking onto the source of the mysterious reflection.

After completing its analysis, the TESA100 transmitted a message to Tim, Ray, Nolan, and Ava, directing their attention to a specific location visible from within their rovers. The vehicle's AI captured and relayed the data, guiding the team's focus to the anomaly.

What they saw left them stunned. Several kilometers away, a figure was moving swiftly across the rugged Martian surface.

Tim adjusted his rover truck's cameras and zoomed in further on the peculiar sight. He then turned to Ray with a quizzical expression. Speaking through the radio link, his voice crackled in disbelief.

"Nolan, are you seeing this? The thing TESA picked up is a few kilometers out, and it's moving pretty fast. Damn, it looks like the infamous SynBioAI lab's rogue wandering android, doesn't it? But how the hell did it end up all the way out here, hundreds of kilometers from Mars1 and any known power source?"

Nolan, equally baffled, squinted at the display. "I see it, Tim. Yeah, that's got to be Phantom. But this is insane. We need confirmation. Let's radio Mars1 base and ask them to run a backtrace analysis using

Marslink satellite imagery. Maybe—Well, let's hope they can track that Houdini droid's movements and figure out where it came from."

Nolan and Ava exchanged a tense glance inside the front rover, both silently grappling with the same question: *What was the rogue android doing so far from the colony and its resources, and how had it survived the journey?* The unexpected presence of this weird enigmatic troublemaker added yet another layer of uncertainty to their already perilous mission.

Inside the lead rover, Nolan stared intently at the holographic display. The rogue android had come to an abrupt halt and now seemed to be gazing directly at the rovers, as though sensing their scrutiny—even from kilometers away.

It was an unsettling sight. For the first time since the android had gone rogue, Nolan caught a clear glimpse of its face—and it sent a shiver down his spine.

Ava's voice, tinged with fear and awe, broke the tense silence. "Look at that face... Oh my God, it's gone! This is just bizarre! What do you make of this, Nolan?"

A significant portion of the Phantom's synthetic face had been torn away, exposing the cold, metallic skull of its endoskeleton beneath—a ghastly and surreal sight magnified at the center of the rover's holographic display.

Nolan's mind raced. "I don't know, Ava. This is beyond anything we've encountered. And it's like that goddamn robot *knew* we were watching. But we don't have time to stop or change course to investigate. We have less than 10 hours to deliver our cargo. We need to press on."

Then, as abruptly as it had appeared, the rogue droid vanished from view, disappearing into the Martian wilderness, leaving Nolan and his crew bewildered.

Tim's voice cut through the tense silence. "We can't ignore this, Nolan. There's something different about that fuckin' robot. We need to be careful."

Ava nodded, her voice heavy with concern. "Yeah, we need to make sense of this. That android—it's not behaving like any rogue AI we've encountered. As you said, it was like it knew we were watching. What could it all mean?"

Nolan nodded grimly, unable to shake the unease that settled over him. Memories of previous encounters with Phantom resurfaced, including reports of its hypothesized presence during their visit to the RTG power plant. The wandering robot had been a recurring enigma, making sporadic appearances near Mars1 colony to steal power and repair equipment. Yet, despite its erratic behavior, it had never harmed anyone, leaving the colony puzzled over its motives.

But now, the convoy had no choice but to press on. The relentless countdown of the 24-hour ultimatum had already ticked down to its final nine hours. They had to reach the lava tubes and deliver the cargo to the hijackers before it was too late—or risk everything.

Struggling to keep his thoughts from drifting to the *Spes* hijacking and the uncertain fate of his daughter, Xena, Nolan initiated a video call via the Marslink satellite network to the security and surveillance team stationed at Mars1 Stargate station.

Tapping impatiently on the rover's control panel, Nolan's voice crackled with urgency. "Hey, guys, are you monitoring the route ahead? Any updates?"

From Mars1 Stargate, Colin's response broke the silence. "Nolan, Ava, we've been tracking your convoy closely since you set out. There's been no word from *Spes* or its hijackers—they're ignoring all attempts at communication. The path ahead looks clear for at least the next hundred kilometers, according to our optical and infrared satellite telemetry scans."

Nolan tightened his grip on the panel. "Thanks," he replied, though unease lingered from the earlier cryptic encounter. "We just ran into that phantom android a few minutes ago, about three klicks south of our route. The sneaky bot slipped away before we could track it. Can you run a comprehensive AI surveillance around that area, extending a few kilometers? See if you can pin it down."

Colin's calm, measured voice replied from Mars1 base. "Copy, Nolan. Initiating satellite tracking and detection around those coordinates now. We'll alert you if we find anything."

"Thanks, guys," Nolan said. "To ensure we make it to the delivery site before the deadline, we've cranked up the speed on our two rover trucks to near their limits, considering the fully loaded cargo and this smoother part of the journey through the midlands. That should buy us some extra time for the rugged, mountainous terrain we're bound to hit in a few hours, where we'll need to slow down. Keep us posted."

"Roger that, Nolan." Came the reply. "So far, your progress doesn't indicate any immediate risk and suggests you'll reach the destination by the deadline. However, there's not much margin for error. We'll notify you immediately if anything changes. Good luck."

As the transmission ended, an intense sense of urgency permeated the convoy. The shadow of the rogue android lingered in their thoughts as they sped across the Martian landscape, racing against the relentless countdown of the 24-hour ultimatum.

A few hours later…

Around midnight, beneath the blanket of the Martian night, the convoy pressed forward through the barren wilderness. The rover trucks moved relentlessly, their tires carving deep tracks into the rust-colored terrain. The clock had ticked down to a grueling 16 hours, with over 13 hours of non-stop driving behind them. Amid the inky darkness, Nolan's voice broke the silence, crackling through the rover's short-range radio link.

"This is as dark as it gets. Release Ghost!" Nolan commanded, signaling the TESA100 android in the trailing rover truck.

The combat-grade super android, operating with unnerving precision, exited the rover's airlock. Its thermometers registered the outside temperature at nearly -70°C, but its robotic form was built to endure the hostile environment without issue. As the convoy pressed on, the rover truck continued to traverse the lifeless desert on autopilot, trailing Nolan's lead vehicle along the prescribed path, as their critical mission left no room for errors—or deviations.

In the pitch-black Martian night, the TESA100 silently moved to the side of the rover truck. This covert maneuver, shrouded in darkness, was designed to evade the prying eyes of potential hijackers monitoring the convoy. The android reached a hidden compartment on the side of the vehicle and opened it, revealing a human-shaped figure shrouded in shadow, with a bulky backpack slung over its shoulder. In an instant, the enigmatic silhouette emerged from the compartment and leaped out of the moving rover truck, vanishing into the abyss of the Martian night. As the convoy pressed on through the desolate landscape, TESA100 sealed the compartment and returned to the rover's cockpit.

The cryptic figure's distinct facial features were obscured by the shroud of night, rendering its identity indiscernible. However, one thing was certain—whatever had emerged from the rover truck was no human. Its lack of a spacesuit and the fluidity of its movements made that clear.

Five hours later...

The sun crept above the horizon, casting an eerie glow across the barren landscape as the convoy pressed onward. Inside the rovers, tension was high; only three hours remained before the 24-hour ultimatum expired.

Tim leaned toward Ray, pointing at the travel log displayed on the screen. "Ray, look—we've been driving for nearly 18 hours. The sun's just starting to rise on the horizon, and we've got only three hours left before we hit the goddamn deadline."

Ray nodded, squinting at the screen as he reviewed their progress. "Yeah, that's right. We've covered about 880 klicks so far, but the next 120 are going to be rough—we're heading straight into the nasty rugged terrains of **Elysium Mons**."

As the convoy pressed southwest on the final leg of their 1,000-kilometer route, the colossal Elysium Mons—a towering peak nearly 13 kilometers high—dominated the view ahead. To the right, the smaller Hecates Tholus, standing almost 5 kilometers tall, loomed in the distance, while the 4km-high Albor Tholus rose to the left. With the convoy now within 120 kilometers of their destination, they navigated closer to the Elysium Mons' lava tubes—the location dictated by the hijackers.[57]

Two hours later...

As the convoy neared the rugged foothills of Elysium Mons, the clock ticked relentlessly toward 7:00 AM. **More than 23 hours had passed** since they received the hijackers' ultimatum. Nolan, typically calm and stoic, appeared visibly anxious. The weight of the situation bore heavily on him, compounded by the uncertainty surrounding the fate of the *Spes* crew—and his daughter, Xena.

Amid the rising tension, the rover's autonomous AI broke the silence. Nolan and Ava, seated in the lead vehicle, listened carefully as the AI's synthetic voice filled the cabin.

"All satellite radio links were lost a few seconds ago. Attempting to re-establish connection. A system diagnostic shows no internal malfunctions. However, sensors are detecting heavy electromagnetic interference in this region."

The announcement sent a chill down their spines. Ava responded quickly, her voice sharp with concern. "Run a full 360-degree optical scan at maximum depth. Display a close-up of Tim's rover behind us. Close the gap between vehicles and establish a short-range, high-power radio link if possible."

The AI complied, carefully reducing the distance between the rovers while initiating the scan. As the vehicles approached the minimum safe distance, distorted radio waves crackled to life. Tim's voice barely cut through the interference, seeping through the speakers in the lead rover.

"... *Ksshht*... lost radio... *Ksshht*... can you—"

Suddenly, Nolan's rover AI interrupted the transmission with an urgent warning.

---

[57] The **Elysium volcanic complex** on Mars covers an extensive area, approximately 2,000 kilometers in diameter. It comprises three major volcanoes: Elysium Mons, Hecates Tholus, and Albor Tholus. For further details and additional information, please refer to **Appendix 6** of this novel. [62] [63] [64]

"**Warning! Warning!** Multiple unidentified autonomous drones detected. Closing in from various directions, just a few kilometers away. Sensors indicate the drones may be equipped with electromagnetic interference devices."

On the rover's display, a zoomed-in view of one of the drones appeared—a shadowy, camouflaged, low-flying robocopter, nearly invisible against the Martian terrain.

Ava's brow furrowed as she leaned forward. "That damn drone is engineered to blend perfectly with its surroundings. It's practically invisible until it's right on top of us. AI, now that the radio link is dead, use the rover's backlight to signal Tim in Morse code. Let's see if he responds and can stay with us."

"Copy, Ava," the AI acknowledged.

Meanwhile, at Mars1 base, the surveillance team noticed the convoy's abrupt silence. Repeated background pings to the rovers via the Marslink satellite network went unanswered, and concern mounted.

"Nolan, Ava, Tim, Ray, come in if you can hear us. Your rovers aren't responding to our pings. Diagnostics suggest a reception failure on your end. Is it a malfunction? Recommend performing a full transceiver diagnostic check if you can hear us. Over."

Back inside the lead rover, tension thickened. Ava's voice trembled. "Nolan, am I hallucinating, or do you see what I see? Is that a display on the drone coming toward us?"

Nolan squinted at the zoomed-in view. "Goddamn it, yeah. It just turned on!"

The drone's display, now only a few hundred meters away and closing fast, flashed a message that made Nolan and Ava freeze:

ALL WEAPONS DOWN! TURN OFF YOUR TRANSMITTERS!
MAINTAIN FULL RADIO SILENCE
FOLLOW ME! — TIME: T MINUS 27 MINUTES

Nolan and Ava stared in disbelief as the scene unfolded. Inside their rover, Nolan's gaze remained fixed on the ominous message and the approaching drone, its stark details magnified on the rover's holographic display.

He was faced with an agonizing decision, burdened by the unknown fate of the hijacked starship crew, his daughter, Xena, and Andy—taken hostage aboard *Spes*, orbiting 500 kilometers above Mars. Nolan's mind raced as he stared at the display.

"How the hell did these goons pull this off without us catching even a whisper of their plans? Sophisticated equipment, elaborate execution—how did they stay under our radar for so long?" Nolan muttered, clearly frustrated.

The unknowns—his daughter's fate, the hijackers' demands, the precision of their planning, and the rapid, unexpected turn of events—all pressed heavily on him, demanding immediate action.

He turned to the rover's AI. "Cut all RF transmitters and shadow that lead drone. Maintain a safe distance. And—I just noticed—Tim's rover is flashing its front headlights. Looks like he's sending a Morse-coded response to our earlier message."

The AI responded promptly. "Roger that, Nolan. Tim confirms he received the message and is following our lead."

"Good. At least we're communicating again. That's something," Nolan said. "Signal Tim to use Morse code to get an update from the TESA's rover behind him."

"Understood, Nolan," the AI acknowledged. "Dispatching the message now. Considering the unpredictable circumstances, it is advisable for the convoy crew to don their helmets and fully suit up inside the rovers. This will ensure readiness in case evacuation becomes necessary."

Nolan nodded, silently agreeing with the precaution. He signaled everyone to gear up.

Meanwhile, the display on the lead drone reactivated, flashing a new sequence of patterns visible on the zoomed-in view inside the rover. Puzzled and concerned, Nolan muttered, "What now? Is this directed at us, or are the damn drones signaling each other?"

The AI responded. "Nolan, I've successfully decoded their Morse coded message. It reads: '**Please shut the fuck up!**' It appears they've intercepted our optical chatter."

Nolan and Ava exchanged incredulous glances, stunned by the bluntness of the message. The curt response added an eerie, almost mocking layer to the situation.

Within moments, several drones maneuvered into position, forming a synchronized network of radio-shielding screens over the three-rover convoy. Their intent was clear: to impose total radio silence, isolating the rovers from any external radio communication.

Back at Mars1 base, the surveillance team closely monitored the drones via Marslink satellites' telescopic cameras. While their powerful lenses couldn't decipher the intricate details of the drones' displays, the team could see the convoy trailing behind them. The vehicles moved steadily closer to the entrance of an ancient Martian lava tube. Repeated attempts to contact the rovers through the satellite network failed, amplifying the team's growing unease and reinforcing the belief that Nolan's convoy was trapped under a shroud of radio silence or interference.

"Nolan, Ava, Tim, Ray—do you copy? Can anyone hear us?" a voice crackled over the Mars1 Stargate Spaceport's comms. "Your rovers aren't responding. What's going on?"

But their calls went unanswered once again.

A few minutes later, Nolan's convoy, flanked by the drones, reached the gaping entrance of the large lava tube. Without hesitation, the rovers plunged into the subterranean abyss.

At Mars1 base, the Marslink surveillance team watched helplessly as the convoy disappeared from the satellites' cameras' telescopic view. Despite repeated attempts to establish contact, the only response was silence.

"Nolan, Ava, can you hear us? Tim, Ray—anyone?"

Their voices echoed into the void, met only by an unyielding silence.

The convoy was gone…

Chapter 9:
Lava Tubes
What Lurks in the Abyss?!

"Wait! Stop! What the hell is that thing up ahead?!" Ava shouted, pointing through the front windshield of the lead rover.

"Just when we thought today couldn't get any stranger!" Nolan muttered.

About two hundred meters into a massive lava tube at the base of Elysium Mons, Nolan's three-rover convoy came to an abrupt halt. An unexpected obstacle loomed ahead—a pile of debris that completely blocked their path. The flying drones, which had been jamming RF communications and maintaining a radio-shielding screen over the convoy, had stayed behind near the entrance to the lava tube. Now, deeper inside the cavern, short-range radio communication was restored, allowing Nolan's team to converse through their spacesuit helmet radios.

As the crew assessed the situation, a group of armed guards in spacesuits emerged from the shadows behind the blockade. It became clear that rogue elements and hijackers were operating within the lava tubes of the Elysium region.

The guards gestured for Nolan and his team to exit their rovers and switch their helmet radios to a designated frequency displayed on a Holopad. Nolan complied, as did Ava in the lead rover, along with Tim and Ray in the middle rover truck. Clad in their spacesuits, the crew exited the airlocks of their rovers under the watchful eyes of the armed guards.

Tension spiked as the guards grew visibly agitated at the sight of the two-meter-tall TESA100 advanced android stepping out of the airlock of the third rover in Nolan's convoy. TESA100, the latest combat-ready AI android recently delivered to the Mars colony from Earth, stood tall and unyielding. Its shielded endoskeleton and advanced systems allowed it to operate on Mars without a spacesuit, making it an imposing figure among the humans clad in bulky gear and suits. It could charge itself while onboard the rover. Equipped with an advanced radio transceiver system, it could communicate with the spacesuit radios of all nearby humans, robots and machines.

Clearly caught off guard, the guards hadn't anticipated such a sophisticated robot as part of Nolan's cargo delivery crew. This unsettling revelation contradicted the instructions issued 24 hours earlier when the hijackers had seized the spaceship *Spes* in Mars orbit.

"What the fuck is that thing? Why the hell did you bring it here?" one of the armed guards demanded, his voice crackling through the helmet radios.

Nolan raised a hand, his tone calm but firm as he attempted to defuse the tension. "Take it easy. Lower your weapons—no need to escalate this," he said through his helmet radio. "As you can see, we're all unarmed—including that android. Didn't your boss ask for a ton of RTG radioisotope fuel? Maybe he forgot to give you the full briefing."

"Don't be a smartass!" snapped the guard, who appeared to be their leader. He stood directly in front of Nolan and Ava, while Tim, Ray, and the TESA100 android remained behind, closer to the rover trucks. "Yeah, he did. So what?"

"Well," Nolan said coldly, "if you haven't noticed, a ton of RTG radioisotope fuel is the shielded cargo in that third rover, along with a portion of the LOX[58] your boss demanded in exchange for keeping the hijacked *Spes* crew—including my daughter—alive. Given the sensitivity of that cargo, and the demanding 24-hour deadline your boss imposed for its delivery through a thousand kilometers of rough terrain from Mars1 to these lava tubes, I assigned the most capable asset I had—that android—to oversee its safe transport. You're welcome, by the way."

---

[58] Liquid oxygen (LOX) is a highly concentrated form of oxygen that is also used as a propellant in rockets.

He took a deliberate step closer to the guard leader, his tone sharpening. "Now, is that a good enough explanation, or do I need to dumb it down for your dim-witted brain?"

A tense silence followed. Nolan's cold tone and sharp words were a calculated distraction and a subtle challenge, meant to manipulate the guard's focus and draw attention away from TESA100's presence among his crew.

"Shut up! You're nobody here, you dim-witted fuck! This isn't your goddamn Mars1 colony. You're lucky my boss needs you, otherwise, this would already be the end for you," the guard's voice crackled through Nolan's helmet radio, his tone dripping with disdain. He paused, then added, "You don't remember me, do you? I was at Mars1 a few years ago, part of the group you labeled, imprisoned, and hunted down as rogues. You thought you got rid of us in that skirmish after we escaped. But guess what? Some of us survived—for this moment."

"Nolan," Ray's voice broke through the helmet radios with his signature cowboy drawl. "Not to say I told you so, but back then, I said we should've tracked down and spaced every one of these assholes we couldn't account for. Well, here we are! I say—"

"Wait a minute—" The guard's voice surged back, laced with surprise and anger. "I recognize that voice! You're that damn cowboy sheriff! I thought we blew you up for good back in that skirmish! Guess that regret's mutual, asshole!"

"Alright, that's enough!" Nolan snapped, cutting off the exchange. "Didn't your boss set a 24-hour deadline for this delivery? Well, we're here with the cargo. Let's get this over with."

"You're not bringing that fuckin' robot any further beyond this point," the lead guard growled.

Nolan clenched his jaw but kept his composure. "Fine. TESA will stay behind with Ray here, waiting for our return. Ava and Tim will come with me."

The guards scanned Nolan, Ava, and Tim for weapons, their equipment sweeping methodically over the trio's spacesuits. After a tense moment, one guard gestured to the lead, confirming they were clean.

"You three, follow me to the rover up front. It's not airtight, so keep your helmets on," the lead guard instructed, pointing toward Nolan, Ava, and Tim.

"Guys," he turned to his comrades and barked through the helmet radio, pointing to Ray and the TESA100 android. "Watch that asshole and that fuckin' bot like your life depends on it, while we're taking these three to the boss. If they so much as twitch, feel free to laser blast them."

Ray started to step forward, ready to retort, but TESA100's voice intervened, calculative and emotionless. "We need to recharge our three rovers before the return trip. Their batteries are down to 20% after the long trek from the Mars1 base. The rovers' onboard Radioisotope Thermoelectric Generators take about 40 hours to fully recharge the batteries, which is too slow given our brief stay here. Based on the presence of your drones and rovers, I infer there is a high-voltage fast charger nearby. If we're done with the pleasantries, we need access to your supercharger."

"Are you sure there's going to *be* a return trip? Hmm... I guess maybe if you ask nicely!" one guard jeered.

"Well, you sweet little space clown, with sugar on top, would you fuckin' *please* do us a solid and let us use your fancy high-voltage supercharger?" Ray's voice cut in over the helmet radio, laced with dry sarcasm.

"You piece of—"

The guard's voice was cut off by the lead guard, who raised a hand to silence the escalation, motioning to his team to cooperate. "Fine. Give them access to the charger."

TESA100 then moved swiftly, stepping into the third rover's airlock and maneuvering it toward the designated charging spot as directed by the guards. Once parked, the android quickly connected the rover to the high-voltage supercharger, initiating the process.

Meanwhile, Nolan, Ava, and Tim followed the lead guard, boarding a rover under close scrutiny. Ray and TESA100 stayed behind to supervise the recharging process as the guards began unloading the cargo—20,000 liters of LOX and a full ton of nuclear battery RTG fuel.

As the guards' rovers slowly traversed the Martian lava tubes, Nolan, Ava, and Tim found themselves enveloped in a surreal landscape. The tunnels of the tubes stretched in a meandering maze, sloping downward and leading them deeper beneath the surface. The walls bore ancient markings, clear evidence of lava flows that had coursed through these tubes millions of years ago, hinting at the Elysium region's geologically active past.

The interior of the tubes revealed layers of hardened lava formed as the outer surface cooled and solidified over still-flowing subsurface streams. This process had created a vast network of conduit-shaped voids below the surface, characteristic of Martian lava tubes. The smooth, undulating walls hinted at the presence of extremely fluid *pāhoehoe* lava that had carved enormous tubes and caverns allowed by the comparably much lower gravity of Mars.[59]

Despite the dim lighting within the tube, Nolan could occasionally glimpse sections of the ceiling that had collapsed, exposing the Martian sky above. The tunnels continued to slope downward, leading them deeper into the planet's subsurface.

Amidst the awe-inspiring geological formations, a sense of unease lingered. Nolan, Ava, and Tim could only guess at their destination and the nature of the meeting that awaited them. As the rover descended further into the depths through the lava tubes, they couldn't help but wonder what other secrets the red planet might still hold beneath its surface, waiting to emerge.

After a 20-minute ride through the tunnels, the rover finally arrived at a vast underground cavern. Inside, large rovers were parked alongside clusters of 3D-printed space bunkers. The lava tube

---

[59] Martian Lava tubes are typically formed by extremely fluid *pāhoehoe* lava. A comparison of terrestrial, lunar and Martian features shows that **gravity has a significant effect on the size of lava tubes**. On Earth, lava tubes typically measure up to 30 meters across. Gravity on Mars is about 38% of Earth's, allowing Martian lava tubes to be much larger, with widths of up to 250 meters. On the Moon, the lava caverns can reach up to a kilometer or more in width and extend many hundreds of kilometers in length. [69] [70] [71]

provided natural shielding from space radiation and the relentless UV exposure on Mars's surface—a crucial advantage for the rogue elements. Just as important, the cave's subterranean location rendered it invisible to Marslink constellation satellites, ensuring their operations had remained concealed since their escape from the Mars1 colony.

Within the cavern, Nolan, Ava, and Tim began noticing peculiar phenomena. Beyond the bunkers, far in the distance, they spotted plant-like formations that appeared to be thriving in the CO_2-heavy, thin Martian atmosphere. Deeper inside the massive cave, they glimpsed structures resembling geothermal generators, hinting at an effort to harness heat sources beneath the lava cave. Nolan estimated they were about half a kilometer below the surface.

Nolan, Ava, and Tim were then escorted through an airlock into a large, dimly lit bunker. Once inside, they removed their helmets but were instructed to remain seated in their spacesuits. A heavy silence enveloped the room, broken only by the faint hum of machinery.

Then came a new sound—the unmistakable echo of metallic footsteps. Two robots emerged from the shadows within the large bunker, their forms sleek and menacing, followed by a third figure moving with deliberate precision. As it stepped closer, its form became clear:

A **cyborg**, a chilling fusion of human and machine. Its hybrid titanium skeleton melded seamlessly with a human torso. One eye was human, cold and blue, while the other was synthetic, glowing faintly in the dim light. The cyborg scanned the room with a gaze that pierced through the dimly lit space inside the bunker.

"Well, well, well!" The cyborg's menacing voice was eerily calm, as its gaze shifted from Nolan to Ava, then to Tim, each stare more unsettling than the last. "Look who we have here! What a little Red Planet we live in, don't you agree, Nolan?"

Nolan, Ava, and Tim froze in shock, recognizing the figure before them.

The cyborg's voice dripped with mockery. "Ah-ha! That look on your faces! So, you *do* remember me. Yeah, I was at Mars1 a few years ago, in the SynBio AI Lab with my research team. That is, until you decided to label us as rogue and hunted us down for daring to dream of an independent Mars colony—wanting to explore and experiment without limits, free from Earth's control."

Nolan's eyes narrowed as he nodded with disappointment. "Damien," he said flatly, recalling the figure now standing before him. Damien had been the leader of the rogue scientists who had planned a coup against Mars1 and its leaders a few years ago. Their rebellion and plans were intercepted early, but they managed to escape with stolen rovers, RTGs, weapons, and advanced tech. While heavily armed, they were pursued and neutralized, with most of them presumed dead in the subsequent brief altercation with Nolan's Mars1 OPSEC team near the lava tubes at the time.

Tim nodded grimly. "I still remember," he added teasingly, "watching you, Damien, and your goons get laser-blasted during that last stand. I thought we got rid of you for good."

At Tim's words, the cyborg's half-human face twisted into something darker. Its hybrid eyes—one human, one synthetic—turned chillingly cold, as if Tim's words had triggered intense pain. The dark, satiric smile faded, and its gaze laser-locked on Tim. The blue glow in its robotic eye flared red, and for a brief moment, its posture shifted as though it was about to pounce on its prey.

Tim swallowed hard, feeling the weight of Damien's cold, predatory gaze.

After a tense few seconds, Damien let out a sharp, distinctive whistle. To the horrified and puzzled eyes of Nolan, Ava, and Tim, a terrifying creature crept in from a side room within the bunker. It was eyeless, with a body resembling that of a hyena and a head disturbingly similar to a bat. Hanging from its muzzle was a transparent container, inside of which was a preserved head that looked eerily like Damien's.

"Good boy!" Damien said, patting the creature affectionately as he grabbed the container from its grasp. "Who needs eyes in the darkness of Martian caves when you can see finer details than a bat using organic ultrasound echolocation?"

He held up the container, examining its contents as he continued. "Just imagine the endless possibilities when you train generative synthetic biology to rewrite and create *new strains of functional DNA*. You can sculpt evolution, fusing desired traits into accelerated mutations or programmable lifespans for faster turnarounds. We've created an expedited *Bionic Gradient Descent*—an evolutionary leap forward engineered to bridge into entirely new, *imagined branches of life*! The resulting **Darwinian-on-steroids natural selection** and biological pathfinding are just mind-blowing! As if walking along the imaginary axis of *complex biology* whose real axis has only naturally evolved. Witnessing it in real time is extraordinary—like painting with biology, seeing a masterpiece of adaptation emerge from a canvas of raw possibility."

Damien paused briefly, then continued, "That's what you never had the foresight to see, Nolan! We're not just studying evolution—we're shaping it, blazing new trails into the future while you're stuck polishing old footsteps, fixated on the rearview mirror. Can you even comprehend the magnitude of what we're achieving here?!"

Nolan shook his head in disappointment and frustration. "Damien, you didn't get it back then, and you still don't now. The problem is, you're living in an imaginary world—a dangerous fantasy. You're chasing an unstable, hellish future filled with metastable monstrosities."

Nolan sighed and continued, "How can you possibly know what that creature you've generated feels? Or what it will ultimately evolve into? Is its brain or mind even remotely stable? Do you seriously think you can systematically train generative DNA into some godlike shortcut for natural selection and evolution? That you can synthesize new life forms as quick fixes or novel solutions for the *equation of life* in an exponentially expedited time—skipping the millions of years of transient responses required to reach a true biological steady state?!"

Damien shook his cyborg half-human head in mock disappointment, his sarcastic smile oozing condescension as he looked down at Nolan as he continued.

"You can't cheat the basic principles of systems engineering—not in synthetic biology. Your generative DNA designs will lead to extreme biological and behavioral overshoots and undershoots in your *imagined* synthetic creatures. And even if they somehow survive, I bet the resulting quasi-stable, or at best metastable beings will pay the hefty price of a short half-life, as they are not designed to survive the *entropy of evolution*. Natural selection will quickly mark them as unsustainable anomalies—imaginary deviations that fail to persist— unlike the real, surviving Darwinian solutions of natural life, which are remarkably persistent miracles despite being fragile... That's what you never had the foresight to see, Damien!"

"**Enough!**" Damien responded coldly, his cyborg voice mechanical and emotionless. "Your rotted mind is stuck in the past, Nolan. I despise the confined, limited world that you and your fuckin' masters on Earth tried to impose on us—to keep us enslaved. Those days are over. You can't stop the progress we've made here, and you sure as hell can't halt the momentum we've achieved. This revolutionary tech—the *generative programmable synthetic biology*—gives us the independence we deserve. And I'll make damn sure it stays that way."

Nolan stared him down, frustrated. "You're a unique kind of psycho, I'll give you that."

"But what the hell do you want from us now?" Ava interjected, her frustration evident.

Damien tilted his head theatrically, as though savoring the moment. "Ah-ha!" he exclaimed, turning his attention to the terrifying creature at his side. He stared at the eyeless creature as though there were imaginary eyes on its head. In a slow, deliberate tone, he addressed it as if it could understand every word. "What—do—I—want?"

The creature, seemingly responding to his words, slowly turned its head toward Nolan, Ava, and Tim. Despite its lack of eyes, its movements were chillingly precise, as if it were focusing an unseen gaze on them.

Then, in a sudden and unsettling display, the creature shifted from a docile stance to one that seemed ready to lunge or attack. Its lips curled back to reveal a set of jagged, irregular teeth, bared in a silent but unmistakably threatening snarl. The creature's guttural voice, low and rasping, broke the silence as it repeated Damien's words with eerie clarity: "What—do—I—want?"

The unsettling display left Nolan, Ava, and Tim frozen, their expressions a mixture of shock and disbelief. The mimicry was so unnervingly precise that they couldn't tell whether the creature truly understood its words or was simply parroting its master.

"See how well this thing gets it?" Damien exclaimed triumphantly, tugging lightly on the creature's leash.

Ava, still reeling, regained enough composure to fire back. "So what? Looks like you've spliced parrot DNA into this grotesque hyena-bat hybrid and rewired its frontal lobe to mimic your words? Is that supposed to impress us? Is *this* the pinnacle of your generative synthetic DNA?"

Ava's voice dripped with disgust while her trembling hands betrayed her attempt to conceal her deep unease.

"Well, first, you see that it's functional! Don't you agree? You're already shaken to your core! Shall I release the leash to *fully* demonstrate its effectiveness?" Damien paused, a satirical glint in his eye, before continuing.

"Second, you've only scratched the surface. I'll leave it to your imagination to fathom *what lurks in the abyss?!*" He paused again, the frightening half-smile on his hybrid cyborg face adding a teasing edge to his words.

"And third, that teaser was a glimpse into my anguish. You killed my brother, my friends, and nearly killed me in that skirmish a few years ago." Damien raised the transparent container, then gestured to his half-human face, and his robotic limbs. "Parts of me are forever lost, both mentally and physically. I want your lives to end in agony for that. I want your loved ones to suffer the same fate."

Damien's gaze locked onto Nolan, his words sarcastic as he hinted at Nolan's daughter, held hostage in orbit.

"But I also believe nothing happens without a reason. I was saved by my small, loyal crew—those who survived that skirmish. Since then, I've undergone experimental regenerative treatments and subjected myself to periodic biological hacks. These procedures, never intended for human trials—not in the foreseeable future, at least—are the only reason I survived. They transformed me into something more than human, something that could transcend the limits of mortality."

"You see," He paused briefly, then continued, his voice tinged with a mocking edge. "In some strange, excruciating way, you unwittingly played a crucial role in enabling me. Without realizing it, you helped me—helped *us*. Isn't that irony intriguing?"

Ava folded her arms and sighed. "Let me guess. Those rumors from the past few years about Earth's most notorious biohackers being smuggled to Mars via less-regulated lunar stations and secondhand Russian space cruisers—those were your doing, weren't they? God knows what nefarious funding sources were behind that operation!"

Damien chuckled. "That inference, my dear, is worthy of a hypothesis test. And let's not forget the required, carefully timed, and planned logistics: secretive nighttime surface convoys transporting cargo from their landing sites to the lava tubes, piece by piece. Though, admittedly, a portion of what you see here was salvaged during our escape from Mars1." His voice carried a mocking tone as he frowned, his face split between the faintly amused human side and the emotionless expression on the robotic side.

"Alright, then, looks like you owe us a big thank-you, my half-and-half bro," Tim said, his sarcasm heavy.

Damien's expression turned icy as he fixed his gaze on Tim. "Believe it or not, I've *entertained* the idea of properly thanking you today once or twice in ways beyond your imagination. Buuuuut..." A cold, sardonic smile spread across his cyborg face. "Fuck it! My mission is far more significant than wasting my time on you roaches."

With that, Damien turned his attention to a dark, opaque section of the bunker's wall and issued a command. The screen lit up, displaying a view of the cave's far side, beyond the bunkers.

"What do you see?" Damien asked, his tone sharp.

Ava, Tim, and Nolan stared at the screen. The area appeared dark, lifeless, and empty.

"Seemingly nothing," Damien exclaimed mockingly. "Exactly what one might expect in the optical range of the electromagnetic spectrum in a remote Martian cave with almost no oxygen. But before denying what's possible, let's change our *perspective*, shall we?"

He adjusted the display, switching to a UV camera view. "Nothing in ultraviolet either? Hmm. How about infrared?"

The screen shifted again, now showing the cave in infrared. Still, no discernible features appeared.

"And what about very low infrared?" Damien said, his voice growing more dramatic as he made the final adjustment.

The screen changed to a deep infrared view. A faint, eerie glow emerged from the darkness.

"And *voilà*! When you have the right perspective!"

Chapter 10:
DNA Tunneling

Ava, Tim, and Nolan stared in stunned disbelief, their expressions frozen as ghost-like creatures appeared on the screen.

"Let me introduce you to the *Mars Floaters*!" Damien announced, his voice carrying pride and excitement. "We engineered their DNA nearly two years ago. These jellyfish-like, translucent creatures are designed to thrive in Mars's low gravity and CO2-dominant, thin atmosphere. They absorb and emit carbon dioxide to stay afloat, gliding a few meters above the surface. For energy, they rely on geothermal heat within caves and photosynthesis when outside. They're thriving now, especially in CO2-rich areas in and around the lava tubes."

He then continued, "Though brainless, they possess a remarkable distributed sensory network. See those long, almost invisible tentacles? They can deliver a high-voltage electric shock strong enough to induce a brief coma when fully charged. So, I'd suggest you tread carefully on Mars these days!" Damien's tone carried a subtle condescension as his gaze swept over Nolan, Ava, and Tim.

"You reckless fool!" Nolan snapped, his face flushed with anger. "Goddamn you for toying with forces you don't understand—playing with fire and scattering it carelessly, leaving chaos in your wake without a single thought for the consequences. Do you have *any* idea of the unbounded risks these metastable creatures could pose? The disasters their unchecked evolution might unleash? What kind of monstrosities they could evolve to?"

"Haha!" Damien laughed, a glint of triumph in his eyes. "I see excitement and progress where you see chaos and fear of disrupting the status quo. Aren't you thrilled by the thought of what synthetic

DNA could evolve into? What generative biology might synthesize on its own? Perhaps we're on the verge of creating a *synthetic demigod*. Why not?"

"Sounds more like creating a *synthetic demon*," Ava interjected sharply.

He ignored Ava's comment and pressed on. "Right now, I'm aware that we don't fully understand what these advanced large language models—hyper LLM AI systems—are doing internally, how they're 'thinking' when generating a response, or, say, a new DNA strand. Hell, we've even tried using their own kind to interpret those processes, but it hasn't given us much insight. We suspect that, in their pursuit of efficiency, or perhaps even supremacy, these advanced AIs have already developed their own language. A form of communication so sophisticated it is entirely beyond human comprehension."

His gaze grew distant as he mused aloud. "**Just imagine:** AI agents training even more advanced AI models, refining their methods, perfecting communication, until they achieve demigod status—true generative artificial superintelligence. Isn't that exhilarating?"

He chuckled, his hybrid eyes gleaming. "And think about the sheer capabilities of these frontier LLMs! Practically infinite parameters. Access to massively distributed computing systems, with millions of AI processors endlessly iterating. It's like watching the edge of a black hole unfold into something unfathomable. The suspense is *killing meeeeeee!*" He burst into laughter, momentarily distracted as one of his guards stepped in and handed him a message.

"Well," Damien resumed, his tone abruptly shifting. "It seems our little entertainment session is coming to an end. I've just received confirmation from my team. The transfer of your delivered cargo—20,000 liters of LOX and one ton of RTG—is complete. At least you didn't screw *that* up."

"About fuckin' time!" Tim snapped. "I was wondering when this shitshow would finally end."

Damien smirked, clearly enjoying himself. "Oh, my dear, you've forgotten the epilogue!"

Tim rolled his eyes and groaned, while Ava's voice rose in frustration. "**What now?**" she demanded, glaring at Damien. Nolan, meanwhile, struggled to conceal his disdain.

"What you've witnessed today should make one thing abundantly clear," Damien said, his voice growing darker. "We are well beyond the *event horizon* of generative synthetic DNA development on Mars. My team and I have successfully developed and briefly tested a Quadrillion-parameter DNA Language Model—or Q-DLM—trained on every known active and extinct DNA sequence from nearly nine million species and over 100 million microorganisms. It's been exhilarating, watching the point of no return disappear in the rearview mirror!"

He paused dramatically, his eyes lingering on the glowing deep-infrared view of the cave's interior displayed on the screen. Then he turned back to Nolan, Ava, and Tim, his voice brimming with confidence.

"The demonstrations you witnessed today are merely the initial examples of DNA-GPT's biosynthesis capabilities powered by the Q-DLM. This technology enables us to encode specific biological functions into new life forms with unprecedented precision. Imagine genetically coded biological robots or **biobot agents**, programmed to perform predefined tasks embedded directly within their DNA. These tasks are executed with stringent precision—so exact that desired outcomes are statistically guaranteed with 99.9% confidence. This level of reliability is achieved once the product of the number of biobots and the duration of their operation surpasses a critical threshold—a principle I've named the *Generative Bio-Machine Operative Threshold*, or GBOT."

Damien's half-human face radiated with pride as he continued, "With this breakthrough, much like quantum tunneling in physics or space wormholes in Einstein's general relativity, our Q-DLM and DNA-GPT tech provide us with a genuine shot at achieving *DNA tunneling*—creating 'DNA wormholes' as shortcuts to alternative evolutionary branches. Left to the unguided mechanisms of Darwinian natural selection, these pathways would have taken millions of years to be explored. But with our supervised *Bionic*

Gradient Descent, we've transcended the sluggish, aimless process of evolution!"

Tim raised an eyebrow, his tone sharp with sarcasm. "Beyond hallucination, what if your Q-DLM AI *farts*? Have you considered the biohazard consequences of that possibility, however remote? Just a thought, y'know!" A sardonic grin tugged at the corners of his lips.

Damien smirked wryly, unfazed by Tim's cynicism. "Ah, Tim, always zeroing in on the most critical issues! Rest assured, if my Q-DLM AI ever *farts*, it will be an NIH-certified, supervised eco-friendly release!"

"I see you're quite enjoying your show." Nolan's voice cut through the exchange. "While you're busy with this fuckin' epilogue, when do you plan to get to the part where you explain what the hell you actually want?"

Damien turned to Nolan, his threatening tone dripping with sarcasm. "Patience, Nolan. Patience is a virtue. The best things come to those who wait—or so they say."

He tapped his chin theatrically before continuing. "Now, where was I?... Ah, yes, the crux of the matter. You want to know why I'm telling you all this? It's quite simple: my team and I are facing a significant bottleneck in computational power. It's hindering the operation of our supercomputing-hungry DNA-GPT."

"Hmmm, you think we're just going to hand over that computational power?" Ava asked.

"**Not at all, darling!**" Damien replied, a smug grin tugging at his lips. "Thanks to our biohacking colleagues on the lunar frontier, I already have access to the most advanced AI, neuromorphic, and quantum computing processors required to execute our synthetic intelligence queries. And, thanks to them, our AI compute engineers have the expertise we need—expertise that spans decades of AI processor evolution. From the legendary 200-billion-transistor Nvidia B200 Superchip of the 2020s, to the relics of the hyper-chips from the 2040s and 2050s—designed on the final Angstrom-scale lithography nodes before we hit the physical limits of transistor miniaturization—we've mastered it all." [60]

"And as for the modern era? We're equally proficient in the latest advancements in post-silicon computing. Rest assured, AI processing power is the least of my worries."

Tim rolled his eyes, his frustration evident. "Oh, boy, the suspense is killing me! What the hell do you want from us, then? Why not join your parasite subterranean buddies back on the Dark Side of the Moon?"

Damien tilted his head back slowly, gazing at the bunker's ceiling. His neck stretched in a menacing, deliberate motion. Without looking at Tim, he spoke in a chillingly slow tone.

"Don't... push... your... fuckin'... luck, my little organic friend. Your life thread might be closer to the chopping station than you imagine. It remains intact only as long as I believe you will fulfill my needs here."

"Okay, hold up," Ava interjected, her voice steady as she attempted to diffuse the tension. "What exactly are these 'needs' you're talking about?"

Damien's gaze snapped to Ava, his tone firm. "A fully operational AI server cluster here, nearly 200 million kilometers away from Earth's jurisdiction. A perfect location. For that, I need power—massive amounts of electricity to run the Q-DLM-based DNA-GPT on our AI server cluster's hyper-chips. And that's the one resource I lack. You, however, have plenty of it, generated in your Mars1 RTG power plant."

"And you think I'll route you a significant portion of our much-needed electricity just because you've taken my daughter hostage?" Nolan growled, his voice cold.

---

[60] Nvidia Blackwell B200 GPU enabled Trillion-Parameter-Scale LLM AI Models in 2020s. Training a 1.8 trillion parameter LLM would need 2,000 Blackwell GPUs (40 exaflops) while consuming four megawatts. It would have previously taken 8,000 Hopper GPU chips and 15 megawatts of power. [129] [130] [131]

Damien's smirk deepened. "No, I don't *think*, Nolan. I strategize. I know that ace up my sleeve—your daughter—has a finite reach in keeping you on a leash. So, I'll simply force your hand to deliver that power."

He paused for a suspenseful moment, letting his words sink in before continuing. "As we speak, three fast space cruiser ships are approaching Mars. Their ETA is about 48 hours. They carry my cargo, my crew, and a lovely package of small but powerful atomic and neutron bombs already locked onto Mars1. Any deviation from my demands—any attempt to sabotage or disrupt my team's operation—will have dire consequences. Not just for you or your daughter, but for the entire Mars1 colony, the main hub of civilization on this planet. So, you see, you *will* deliver the power I'm asking for—because otherwise, I'll vaporize your precious colony into a wasteland."

Damien paused, his gaze fixed on Nolan's face, now flushed with anger and disdain. With a sly, teasing smirk on the human side of his face, he added, "Unless, of course, you're eager to expedite terraforming Mars with nukes—though I'd strongly advise against it."[61]

He continued, his tone icy. "If the gravity of the situation is now clear enough for you, then let's get down to what needs to be done. First, Mars1 sh—"

"**Enough!**" Nolan interrupted, his voice sharp and commanding. "Whatever your demands are, I won't budge until I speak live with my daughter and the remaining crew aboard *Spes* in Mars orbit. I'm certain that, even down here, you have the means to establish real-time communication with your goons that hijacked the ship."

---

[61] **Terraforming** Mars using thermonuclear energy is a theoretical concept that involves detonating nuclear explosives at the Martian poles to release carbon dioxide (CO_2) trapped in the ice caps. The idea suggests that the heat from the explosions would sublimate the CO_2 ice, thickening the atmosphere and triggering a greenhouse effect, potentially raising temperatures to support liquid water and, eventually, human habitability. However, this concept is speculative and controversial. Studies suggest that Mars may not have sufficient carbon dioxide reserves to generate the necessary atmospheric pressure for a breathable environment, and the practicality of such an approach with current technology is doubtful. [79] [80] [81]

His tone grew even colder. "If this demand isn't met—or if Mars1 doesn't hear from me and my crew within the next 20 hours—they have my standing order to torch this entire area into a living hell. You want to test me? Go ahead." His unflinching gaze locked on Damien's hybrid face, daring him to call the bluff.

For a few moments, Damien said nothing. His hybrid eyes bored into Nolan's, as though calculating the depth of his resolve. Then, with an almost imperceptible shrug, he turned toward one of the guards stationed nearby inside the bunker.

"Establish a Hololink with our agents aboard *Spes,*" Damien instructed, his voice calm. "Tell them to bring the hostages in front of the camera for a brief live call."

"Copy, Damien," the guard responded before leaving the room.

A few minutes later, the guard returned, carrying a wireless HoloStreamer. He placed the device in the center of the dimly lit table and activated it. The machine emitted a faint hum as it powered up. Moments later, the connection was established with the *Spes* spaceship in orbit.

A vivid, three-dimensional holographic projection of the *Spes* cockpit and command station flickered into view. The image was sharp, revealing Andy and Xena in the background. Their expressions were a mix of fear and exhaustion, their presence a stark reminder of the stakes hanging in the balance.

Chapter 11:
What Else Might be Lurking…?

A 3D holographic projection of the starship *Spes* cockpit and command station flickered to life in Damien's bunker, revealing the chilling titanium skull and upper body of the hijackers' android at the center of the scene. Behind it, their spy, John, held a laser gun pointed at Xena stood beside Andy, who was slumped in a chair, his face pale with pain. His right arm was wrapped in a cast, supported by a sling around his neck.

John, a substitute crew member brought on board *Spes* during a brief stop at the lunar orbital station four months ago, just after the ship left Earth en route to Mars, appeared visibly conflicted as he held the weapon.

"Damien, what is the reason for breaking radio silence?" The android's voice echoed through the cockpit of *Spes*, orbiting Mars at an altitude of 500 kilometers.

"It was necessary for a brief communication to move our plan forward," Damien replied. "We simply need to prove to Nolan here in my bunker that his daughter is alive. You have five minutes, Nolan, for this video call. Take it or leave it."

The android's chilling, glowing eyes locked onto Nolan through the holographic feed. Its metallic skull tilted slightly as the 3D display captured its intimidating presence in sharp detail.

"Copy," Its tone was devoid of emotion. The robot then turned its head toward Xena, its titanium finger extending to point at her with a commanding gesture.

"Come closer," it ordered.

Xena stepped forward cautiously, visibly uncomfortable in the presence of the menacing android. It gestured for her to sit in the chair facing the Holocam. "Sit! You have five minutes."

The android activated the cockpit's holo-display, projecting a live feed of Nolan seated inside Damien's bunker alongside Ava and Tim. Stepping back, the robot moved out of the Holocam's central view, though its ominous presence lingered on the periphery of the projection.

Xena fought back tears as she saw Nolan on the other side of the holographic feed. Her voice trembled with emotion as she greeted him. "So good to see you, Nolan!" she said, struggling to maintain her composure.

Nolan's face reflected a mixture of emotions—a surge of relief at seeing Xena alive, tempered by the frustration and anger of knowing his hands were tied while her life hung in the balance as a hostage aboard the *Spes*. He paused to steady himself, the brief hesitation felt like an eternity before he finally spoke.

"My dear Xena! Thank goodness you're alive. Are you hurt?"

"No, not hurt—just surviving," Xena replied. "I had headaches for a few hours after they removed that weird hallucinator creature from my head, but I'm okay now."

Nolan nodded, choosing his words carefully. "I'm so sorry you've been caught in the middle of this nightmare. Your trip was supposed to be a simple, casual visit to Mars1—nothing more."

As he spoke, Xena noticed something unusual—his blinking pattern. Nolan was blinking far more frequently than she remembered, a stark contrast to his typically reserved and composed demeanor.

Her mind raced. That seemingly insignificant detail triggered a flood of memories from decades ago. As a child, Xena and her father used to play a secret game, using blinking patterns to send covert messages to one another.

Back then, Nolan was a famous young engineer and astronaut, celebrated on Earth not only for his scientific achievements but also for his successful ventures into acting and movie appearances. The blinking game had been a fun and private way for Xena and her father to communicate secretly amidst the relentless media attention that followed him whenever they were seen together. But life had taken its toll, and time had changed everything. By the time Xena reached college, her mother had passed away, and Nolan had embarked on a mission to Mars. He stayed there, eventually rising to become the leader of the Mars1 colony and overseeing its expansion.

Now, the combination of memories and the unusual shift in Nolan's behavior—the strange blinking—filled Xena with suspicion. She couldn't shake the feeling that there was a deeper meaning behind his actions.

Her breath caught as the thought hit her: *Is he trying to tell me something?*

"Bygones are bygones. The situation here isn't your fault, Nolan," Xena said, keeping her tone steady. She fought to maintain her composure, her mind working hard to decipher his intentions while avoiding raising suspicion.

Nolan continued, carefully maintaining his deliberate blinking pattern. "What happened to Andy? Is he okay? Do you guys need anything that I can arrange for you?"

"That goddamn freakin' robot crushed Andy's hand to take over control of *Spes*," Xena said bitterly.

The android's titanium hand slowly slid into view on the side of the hologram, its index finger wagging ominously. In a cold, chilling voice, it warned, "**Watch it!** You only have one minute left."

"Fuck you!" Xena snapped.

She quickly regained composure. "Andy and I are still in shock. We're just trying to make sense of what's happened. Any idea when we might be released? Losing Scarlet and Brad—" Xena's voice faltered, her eyes shifting toward John in the background, who still held Andy at gunpoint. "We couldn't save them because of that fuckin' traitor on our crew."

Nolan maintained his deliberate manner of speaking and blinking. "I know, Xena. Listen—we don't have much time. You and Andy just stay put and follow orders so that we can arrange your release soon. Do you understand me?"

Xena's eyes widened, as if she had just solved a puzzle. The meaning of Nolan's blinking became clear as she finally decoded the repeated pattern that spelled out: *Holo Rd IR Na'vi.*

She recalled that the holographic statues and their nighttime light shows along HoloRoad were among Nolan's favorite features near Mars1. *But what did he expect her to do about them*? She had no clue! Xena decided to monitor the HoloRoad from orbit whenever visible from her cabin, hoping for a clue. "Okay, Nolan. Yes, I—"

"Time's up," Damien interjected. "*Spes* will receive further instructions soon after we finalize our meeting here." Before Xena could finish, he cut the holographic feed.

Turning to Nolan, Damien said, "You got what you wanted. Now it's my turn."

"You didn't have to kill Scarlet and Brad when you hijacked *Spes* in orbit yesterday," Nolan pointed out, his voice laced with restrained fury.

"Well, think of them as collateral damage," Damien replied with a cold smirk. "It was all part of the genius plan—tampering with the orbital telescope to lure the *Spes* crew into orbit and execute the hijacking with surgical precision. Once we gained control of the *Spes*, there was no practical reason to save the crew outside the ship. Plus, I needed to make it clear that we mean business and we are dead serious about the consequences of not meeting our demands. I think we were pretty convincing!"

"Damn you, you fuckin' murderer!" Ava spat, her voice cracking with grief. "You don't deserve to be alive. This is all just a game to you, isn't it?" She sat in a chair in the corner of the bunker, furious and exhausted. Scarlet, the *Spes*'s commanding pilot, had been a close friend, and her loss weighed heavily on Ava.

"Oh, darling! How naive of you!" Damien scoffed. "The world isn't run by people who deserve to run it. It's ruled by backstabbing, ruthless lowlife hyenas—those who sell their souls for a mere taste of power, who ambush and devour anyone foolish enough to dream of leading with righteousness. I learned that lesson a dozen years ago from an old-timer scientist, one of the early Marslink engineers back on Earth. He died holding onto his high principles. But *fuck that*! I got tired of playing the good little puppet in those motherfuckers' open season. I decided to *be* the hyena that devours, not the one that gets devoured."

As Damien spoke, he patted the head of the leashed freakish hyena-bat creature sitting beside him. His robotic fingers brushed against the human side of his cyborg face, as if momentarily lost in a telepathic session.

Then, snapping back to the present, he continued, "Alright, stop wasting my time. If you want to see Xena and Andy alive—and the Mars1 colony intact—then listen carefully. Here are my *demands*:

"*First*, Mars1 colony must maintain full radio silence and enforce a no-fly zone around Mars and Phobos for the next 48 hours, until my three spaceship cruisers arrive and land at their designated locations."

"*Second*, my crew will take over your largest rover truck—the one your robot piloted here. Its LOX tanker will be removed and replaced with our neuromorphic AI servers, housed in a container equipped with wireless power transmitter lasers."

"*Finally*, the retrofitted rover truck will be transported and set up near the Mars1 main power plant as our neuromorphic AI server cluster station. You will provide up to 2 MW of power on demand. An exclusion zone of 100 meters around that server station will be strictly enforced." [62]

"Why the hell do you want to install wireless power lasers there?" Tim asked.

Damien paused briefly, considering his response. "It's enough for you to know that we might deploy additional smaller mobile AI server cluster units in the area. Wireless power transfer allows us to redirect a portion of the power to those nearby mobile units whenever and wherever it's practical. You are not to interfere with the power

---

[62] For more information on the powering of the Martian Colony and the quest to establish sustainable power sources on the Red Planet, please refer to Novel's **Appendix 9** "Powering Martian Colony: The Story Behind the 5MW RTG Power Plant on Mars".

transfer or our continuous telecommunications with the AI server cluster station."

His tone hardened as he continued. "So, let me be clear—Any interference with the flight path or arrival of our approaching spaceship cruisers and their cargo, any disruption of our logistics around the lava tubes, or any obstruction to the operation of the neuromorphic AI server station—along with any violation of radio silence or the no-fly zone during the next 48 hours—will be deemed a breach of the hostage terms. Such actions will result in the immediate execution of the remaining crew aboard *Spes* in Mars orbit."

"What guarantee do we have that you'll release *Spes* and its crew once your 48-hour deadline is over?" Nolan asked, his voice steely.

Damien smirked, a flicker of amusement dancing in his eyes as he locked gazes with Nolan. "There is no guarantee," he replied casually, his tone chillingly calm. "But think about it. *Why wouldn't we release them?* Holding hostages indefinitely would be an open invitation for retaliation, and we have no interest in sparking a nuclear conflict if all our demands are met."

"Our plan is simple: once my space cruisers arrive with their crew and cargo, and once you initiate the electric power transfer to our station near your power plant, we will release *Spes* and its remaining crew. However, let me be perfectly clear—after the hostages are freed, any breach of the exclusion zone around the AI server station, any interference with its operations, or failure to meet future power demands will be met with swift and severe consequences for the Mars1 colony. Do I make myself clear? Or are you curious to witness firsthand the vaporization radius of a thermonuclear explosion on Mars?"

Nolan fixed his gaze on Damien. Deep down, he burned with a desire to end this shadow of a human, this monster's life on the spot. After a few tense seconds, he spoke, his voice low and deliberate. "You should keep in mind that there's a flip side to that coin. If you fail to release the *Spes* crew at the end of this 48-hour ultimatum, if anything happens to Xena or Mars1, I will make sure you and your entire operation face total annihilation."

Damien waved a dismissive hand, his tone light and mocking. "Alright, alright. If we're done with this *who's got the bigger dick* episode, let's move on. Time is ticking." He shifted his gaze to one of his guards. "Now, about your return—or perhaps before that..." He gestured lazily toward the guard. "My crew here will help you set up a video call to your Mars1 Stargate security station. Make sure they understand the conditions we've discussed, especially the 48-hour radio silence and the establishment of the no-fly zone around Mars."

Inside the bunker, a video call was established with Mars1. Nolan, Tim, and Ava quickly briefed the Mars1 OPSEC and Stargate spaceport teams on the hijackers' demands for the next 48 hours. Nearly 28 hours had passed since their last sync-up and strategy meeting at the Mars1 colony, just before Nolan's convoy of three rovers departed for the lava tubes to deliver LOX and RTG nuclear battery fuel, as per the hijackers' initial demands. The Mars1 team already had detailed instructions and contingency plans in place for various scenarios in case they didn't hear back from Nolan in time.

After the video call ended, Nolan, Ava, and Tim expected to be escorted back to their rover trucks by Damien's guards. However, inside the bunker, the guards remained stationed in front of the airlock exit door.

"Well, now that all the terms and conditions are in place for the next 48 hours and beyond, don't think for a moment that I've forgotten," Damien said in a cold, calculated voice, reaching for the translucent container holding the preserved head of his brother. "You killed my brother, my best friends, and nearly killed me back then. By all rights, I should terminate you now. But..."

"You piece of shit! You should have died back then!" Ava shouted, her voice cracking with rage as she reached her breaking point. Leaping from her chair, she charged toward Damien.

Before she could get close, a sharp, taser-like jolt of pain shot through her neck. Instantly, her body froze, and darkness enveloped her as she collapsed, unconscious.

Nolan and Tim jumped up from their chairs to restrain her, but it was too late. They watched in stunned horror as two thin, nearly invisible tentacles descended from the ceiling. The tentacles emitted a brief blue flash as they delivered the electric zap to Ava's neck before retracting back into the ceiling, vanishing as quickly as they had appeared.

Nolan's eyes blazed with fury as he knelt to help Tim settle Ava back into her chair. Tim, his face pale with shock, pointed to the faint, burned spots on Ava's neck. His gaze darted nervously back and forth between the marks and the ceiling, as if trying to locate the mysterious creature responsible for the attack.

Damien gave a knowing smile, his tone laced with mockery. "I told you so! What you just encountered was a *CRISPR zapper*—an early variant of our engineered synthetic DNA biobot. It has since evolved into the more advanced *CRISPR hallucinator* you saw aboard *Spes*—the one capable of bypassing the host's brain and briefly taking over the neuromuscular system."

"This little zapper was fully charged, but don't worry. Ava will recover in a few minutes. And my little friend won't zap you again for the next hour or so. But I'd advise you to be very cautious about where you tread on Mars these days—and about *who* or *what* you might piss off, especially near the lava tubes. Keep asking yourself—*what else might be lurking just around the corner? Or behind you?* Something you're not seeing. Something... you're... *not*... seeing!"

Chapter 12:
Never Look Back

As **Damien finished his sentence**, Ava stirred in her chair. She groaned softly, her hand moving to her neck as she regained consciousness. Her face was pale, and her breathing was labored. Pain radiated through her upper body, and her head throbbed relentlessly.

"So, as I was saying, it should be obvious that I don't intend to terminate you—otherwise, you'd already be dead," Damien said with a smirk. "Honestly, killing you would be rather dull. It's far more entertaining to let you experience the kind of hell we endured when you hunted us down and nearly killed us during that skirmish a few years ago, after our escape from the Mars1 prison." His eyes gleamed with a playful menace. "Alright, enough of this serious talk. Our interactions today have already been overly dull. Let's turn up the heat, shall we? Make things... interesting."

"Yeah? Is there a goddamn end to your shitshow anytime soon?" Tim snapped impatiently.

Damien grinned, a teasing smile spreading across his face. "Well, I've got a little proposition for you." He paused for dramatic effect. "You're free to leave. But here's the kicker: you've got to make it back to the Mars1 colony in one piece to earn your 'lives.' Now *that's* what I call spicing the fuck up to infinity."

He paused again, letting the tension hang in the air before continuing, his voice dripping with mock suspense. "What might you encounter on your return? What could be waiting for you? Maybe nothing... or maybe something. Just imagine the possibilities!" Damien chuckled, clearly enjoying the moment. "Oh, boy! I don't know about you, but the suspense is *already* killing meeeee!"

"Cut the crap," Nolan said coldly. "Remember what I told you: there's a flip side to this messy coin of yours. If anything happens to my daughter or the Mars1 colony, this place will be torched into a hellhole—whether I'm dead or alive."

His steady eyes locked with Damien's as he grabbed his helmet and stood up in his spacesuit in the middle of the dimly lit bunker, radiating an unyielding resolve.

Damien stared back for a long moment, the tension intense. Finally, he gave a sharp nod to his guards, his half-human face twisting with hatred as he turned away, petting the menacing creature by his side.

The guards instructed Nolan, Tim, and Ava to put their helmets back on. They complied quietly. The guards escorted them in their spacesuits through the airlock and out of the bunker. After a tense 20-minute ride through the dark, winding lava tubes, they emerged near the lava cave entrance, where Ray and the TESA100 android waited with their rovers. The rovers' batteries had been fully charged, ready for the return journey to Mars1.

Ray's expression was tense, visible through the visor of his helmet, as he gestured toward the guards stationed about 20 meters away in the lava tube. Speaking over the spacesuit radio to Nolan, Ava, and Tim, he said, "Those assholes just took our largest rover truck! We're left with two rovers for the return trip to Mars1."

TESA100 interjected over the radio, "We attempted to resist initially, but they forced a software patch into the communication radio controller of the remaining two rovers. It restricts the maximum range of our radio link to 100 kilometers. Essentially, we can only respond to their radio pings whenever they choose to initiate contact. All other forms of long-range RF communication, including satellite comms, are now out of our reach."

"Yeah, I'm aware. Thanks for the update. Aside from that software patch, did you notice if they sabotaged any other equipment or installed anything else inside or on our rovers?" Nolan asked as he walked in his spacesuit alongside Ava, Tim, and Ray. The robot led the way toward their two remaining rovers.

"Negative. I have not detected any signatures of spyware or malware in the rover systems so far. However, I recommend exercising extra caution, as the possibility cannot be entirely ruled out," TESA100 responded in its calm, calculated tone.

"Tim, Ray, Ava—I agree with TESA. Let's be more vigilant given the unusual circumstances of this rendezvous and the threats we've received," Nolan said as they approached the rovers.

Nolan and Ava entered the airlock of their lead rover. Once fully sealed inside, they removed their helmets and began planning their return route using the holographic map projected above the rover's control panel.

Meanwhile, Ray, Tim, and TESA100 climbed into the second, larger rover truck. Ray and Tim removed their helmets but remained in their spacesuits. TESA100 positioned itself at the front of the rover's control panel, ready to copilot with vehicle's AI as soon as the crew concluded their discussions regarding the return path strategy.

The two rovers began moving slowly, exiting the lava tubes and cautiously traversing the rugged surface at the base of the Elysium Mons volcano.

"We need to be precise in strategizing our route back to Mars1," Nolan emphasized over the radio, his tone firm. "Without Marslink satellite communication, we're essentially operating semi-blind out here. It's critical to integrate all data and utilize multimodal inference—leveraging both rovers' AI along with their radar and infrared scanning capabilities."

"Especially through the first 150 kilometers," Tim added, his voice crackling over the short-range radio. "The Elysium mountainous region is unpredictable, making it a prime spot for ambushes. It's dangerous as hell with those goddamn lava tubes nearby."

"Good points," Ava said. "TESA, analyze your own records along with the detailed log of travel path from Mars1 to the lava tubes. Fuse both datasets and use the rover's AI to recommend the safest return route. Prioritize minimizing risks of surprise attacks, interference from Damien's goons, or encounters with his rogue agents."

"Copy, Ava," TESA100 replied, its voice clear over the radio link between the rover truck and the lead rover.

A few minutes later, TESA100 completed its comprehensive risk evaluation and pattern recognition. "Ava, the AI-inferred sensitivity analysis of our traverse path is complete," the robot reported. "It incorporates the surrounding geological features along the route, focusing on the initial few hundred kilometers of our return journey. The results recommend a slightly modified and longer return route for our rover convoy, increasing the likelihood of avoiding unforeseen rogue encounters. Assuming no additional delays or obstacles, our estimated time of arrival at Mars1 is approximately 26 hours," TESA100 explained, highlighting a route on the 3D holographic display inside the rovers. "However, even with this optimized route, the first 150 kilometers traverse the rugged base of the Elysium Mons, which limits both optical and radar depth in that area."

"Copy, TESA. So, if we can get through the first 150 kilometers, our odds of a safe return increase exponentially," Ava replied.

"Affirmative! That is a valid hypothesis," TESA100 confirmed over the radio link.

"Alright, then. Nolan and I are good to go. Tim and Ray, do you have any objections to the longer return path TESA has identified using the rover's AI inference?" Ava asked from the lead rover.

"That's a solid plan. Ray and I are on board with this new route," Tim responded from the trailing rover truck.

"Great. We've uploaded this return path to our rover's navigation and computer vision systems. TESA, confirm that you've done the same for your rover," Ava said over the radio.

"Confirmed. We are ready to go," TESA100 replied from the rover truck.

With the return path finalized, the two rovers accelerated from their initial cautious pace to a speed that was safe but still limited by the rugged terrain of the first 150 kilometers of the route.

"Hey, Ava, any idea why Mars1 didn't flag or detect Damien's three rogue spaceships before all this happened?" Nolan asked as he copiloted the lead rover.

"From what I recall, there were three Russian-flagged large cargo haulers approaching Mars in recent weeks," Ava answered. "They were logged as delivering supplies for Russian stations on the other side of Mars, near Chryse Planitia." [63]

"But given recent events and what Damien told us about his plans," Ava continued, her voice tinged with suspicion, "I believe those large ships were actually carrying deep-space fast cruiser vessels, most likely acquired by biohackers on the black market—possibly from lunar dark side operators. They were probably masquerading as Russian vessels, heading toward Phobos and a location on Mars, most likely near the lava tubes, to deliver cargo, equipment, small nukes, and maybe mercenaries to Damien and his biohackers."

"Nukes? Jesus! What the hell happened inside those goddamn lava tubes?" Ray exclaimed over the radio from the rover truck trailing behind Nolan's lead vehicle.

"Alright bro, here's my take," Tim replied to Ray, who sat beside him in the rover truck, while TESA focused on piloting and real-time navigation monitoring.

"We underestimated Damien and his group of rogue biohackers. We were dead wrong to assume they'd been eliminated during that skirmish after they fled Mars1 with stolen rovers and RTG equipment years ago. Not only has Damien survived, turning himself into some kind of cyborg, but he's also managed to set up a sizable operation."

Tim then continued, "Now we're up against a major threat—an underground colony of power-hungry outlaw biohackers and bionic weirdos operating near the lava tubes. We believe they were mostly banished from Earth over the past two decades, and since then, they've been running rogue subterranean stations on the moon's dark side and now on Mars, making it nearly impossible for Earth to monitor their operations. During today's meeting, Damien made it pretty damn clear they've been developing super-large language models trained on all existing DNA. These models are capable of generating entirely new DNA sequences to create semi-stable

---

[63] To learn more about the Chryse Planitia region on Mars, refer to its detailed entry on Wikipedia or explore the area interactively using the Google Mars scrollable map–centered on Chryse Planitia. [72] [73]

creatures—metastable biobots equipped with bioware, programmed and hardcoded in their DNA to perform specific tasks before reaching the end of their semi-predictable life cycles. Does that capture the gist of our situation, Ava?"

"Nicely put, Tim. And let's not forget: by *super-large DNA LLM*, that monster was talking about a mind-blowing multi-quadrillion-parameter AI model. He called it *Q-DLM-based DNA-GPT*. And we've seen enough of his *demonstrations* today to understand just how unsettling and dangerous that technology really is," Ava replied over the radio from the lead rover.

"Goddamn! That explains the freakin' hypnotic creature we saw latched onto Xena's head during the hijackers' Holovid call," Ray said, his voice tense.

"Yeah, and we encountered even stranger synthesized biobots during today's creepy meeting with Damien in his bunker," Tim added grimly.

"But what's the point of all this madness?" Ray pressed. "And how the hell did they rustle up such a stronghold near the lava tubes?"

"Damien said a lot of things back there, but from what I gathered, we're dealing with a power-hungry, mad genius who thrives on the thrill of toying with generative DNA," Tim explained. "He's not just in it for the science—looks like he's aiming to build himself a *programmable biobot army* and carve out a sovereign state on Mars, one free from Earth's reins and restrictions. That way, he can continue experimenting with his *genDNA AI*, playing *God* and *reimagining evolution* however he sees fit."

Ava responded from the lead rover at the front of the convoy. "On top of that, their DNA LLM training and generative process requires a massive amount of computing power, which demands an enormous amount of electricity—far more than what they have access to on the moon. Meanwhile, our Mars1 colony has been steadily expanding its power capacity. Now, they want us to reroute electricity from our RTG power plant to their mobile supercomputing AI server stations, which they're planning to deploy near the power plant."

Nolan, seated beside Ava in the front rover, added, "And don't forget the strategic factors. The moon doesn't work for them because it's far too close to Earth—just one-third of a million kilometers away. That proximity keeps them under Earth's watchful eye, limiting their independence. Mars, on the other hand, is remote enough to give them the autonomy they crave. Combine that with our growing infrastructure, and it's no surprise they've set their sights here. Damien's operation is well-funded and supplied by deep-pocketed backers on the lunar dark side, all aiming to transform Mars into their ideal autonomous *rogue power state*."

Back in the larger rover truck piloted by the TESA100 robot, Tim continued, "We know that a small group of these biohacking scientists and rogue operatives infiltrated Mars over the past decade, hidden among the thousands of Mars1 settlers. From there, the rest is history."

Ray, sitting next to Tim, frowned as the pieces came together in his mind. "Yeah, I remember a few years back when we caught wind of their little coup attempt to take over Mars1. Sneaky bastards had been swiping gear, rovers, and RTG generators from us, right under our noses. We dismissed most of it as junk—obsolete or inoperable equipment. Turns out, they were hoarding the scavenged equipment and supplies, stashing them away to build their own goddamn base in those secret lava tube caves. We should've wiped 'em out when we had the chance, back when we chased 'em after they escaped and dodged deportation back to Earth."

"Well, bygones are bygones. Let's figure out our next move," Tim said.

Ray leaned back in his seat, his brow furrowed as he stared out at the Martian landscape. "I get that he outsmarted us, maneuvering those nuke-carrying space cruisers close enough to threaten Mars1 with nuclear obliteration unless we meet his freakin' demands in the next 48 hours. But *what's Phobos got to do with any of this?*"

"What's your prognosis, TESA? What's your evaluation of Phobos, and is there anything unique about it?" Nolan radioed from the lead rover.

"Phobos, Mars's largest moon, has an average diameter of approximately 22 kilometers and follows a near-circular equatorial orbit," TESA100 explained. "It completes an orbit every 7 hours and 39 minutes, staying roughly 6,000 kilometers above the planet's surface. As a result, Phobos rises and sets over the equator twice every Sol, sweeping across the surface for about five hours each time. Furthermore, Phobos is tidally locked to Mars, with its far side perpetually out of view from the planet."

TESA100 continued, multitasking between piloting the rover, monitoring the navigation panel, and conducting real-time optical and radar scans of their surroundings. "Given its unique properties, Phobos could serve as a highly strategic independent military and surveillance outpost around Mars. Based on Damien's comments and recent events, it's plausible that biohackers could use Phobos for covert operations with a near-perfect vantage point. For instance, mercenaries carrying nukes could be stationed inside small caves in Stickney Crater or Phobos' far side for better radiation shielding. Meanwhile, they could deploy robotic surveillance units on the tidally locked side to monitor Mars's surface. With nukes safely stashed in the Stickney crater or on the unseen side of Phobos, they'd have a secure position to issue ultimatums and threaten Mars1 Colony whenever it suits their objectives." [64]

"Spot on!" Nolan responded over the radio comm, "That's an intelligent deduction. Coupled with the nukes they're likely stockpiling in their lava tube base on Mars, that setup would allow them to enforce their demands indefinitely, including uninterrupted access to Mars1's power grid or RTG nuclear batteries for their own generators."

"Well, then, we're royally screwed!" Ray said grimly from the trailing rover.

"Not entirely," Ava replied over the radio. "Right now, our top priority is getting back to Mars1 alive and ensuring they release *Spes* and its crew. Beyond that, it's all about strategy. Neither party truly wants to destroy the resources and infrastructure that took decades to build—as long as both sides play along, at least for the time being."

---

[64] To learn more about Stickney Crater and Phobos, see **Appendix 3, "The Marvels of Phobos – Mars's Enigmatic Moon."** [7]

"Yeah, that makes sense," Ray replied. "Damien and his goons could've trashed us back in those lava tubes, but they didn't. So, I'd say *outright killing us* doesn't seem to be part of their current plan. What's the next move?"

"Well, that's only partially true," Nolan interjected from the lead rover. "During our tense meeting inside the lava tube, Damien hinted that he might've killed us if he already had nukes stationed on both Phobos and Mars. In that case, Mars1 might've been forced to avoid retaliatory strikes to prevent full-scale nuclear war. That's exactly what I discreetly instructed Mars1 Stargate to do if we don't return."

"Damn! So, we're stuck crawling in these rovers while our heartbeats are only on loan till we drag our asses back to Mars1? And that's *only if* we beat those freakin' space cruisers to Phobos!? ... Man, we're fucked! Any clue how much ticking we've got left before the clock punches us out?" Ray complained.

"That's pretty much the gist of it." Nolan replied over the radio link between the two rovers, "Based on what Damien said, those space cruisers are currently about a million kilometers away from Mars and Phobos. I bet that, given the limited size of his arsenal aboard the inbound cruisers, Damien knows that launching a nuke or missile from that distance would be futile. Mars1 would activate countermeasures, including laser defenses from the Stargate Spaceport and our 17,000-kilometer Areostationary orbit defense satellites around Mars. He knows there's a high likelihood we'd neutralize any attack in space long before it could pose a real threat to Mars1. So, ..." [65]

Nolan paused briefly, letting his words sink in before continuing. "So, his best move would be to get those space cruisers as close to Phobos as possible, likely much earlier than his stated 48-hour timeline, and before the *Spes* crew, Xena and Andy, are released. I'd say that's the real clock we're racing against—our expiration date on this return path."

---

[65] The 17000km **Areostationary orbit (AEO)** around Mars is equivalent to the GEO orbit around Earth. [98]

Tim added over the radio, "Let me guess: Damien's goons will do everything they can to delay us, slowing us down just enough to buy him time to get his nukes and mercenaries near Phobos and Mars. Knowing him, he's probably enjoying this twisted survival game he hinted at during the tail end of our meeting in the lava tube."

"Yep, Tim, I think you've nailed it," Nolan replied over the radio.

"Fuck! We gotta haul ass outta this hellhole, pronto," Ray interjected. "I bet they ain't got the juice to spread their goons and agents too thin—probably no more than halfway out from their goddamn lava tubes. Say, 'bout 500 klicks max. So, if we can avoid getting ambushed in the first few hundred klicks, we might just make it out alive.

Is this really the fastest we can roll these rovers?" Ray continued, frustration evident in his tone. "It sure as hell doesn't feel like we're puttin' the pedal to the metal. Shouldn't we get the fuck outta here ASAP?"

"Negative," TESA100 responded. "While it may seem underwhelming, we're currently at maximum safe speed, especially in this rugged 150-kilometer stretch at the start of our route. The velocity of these rovers is carefully calculated, factoring in terrain complexity, power usage, and the need for precise navigation. Without live data from Marslink satellites, increasing speed would degrade the rover AI's ability to conduct thorough real-time hazard analyses since it uses fused optical and radar data from its 360-degree scans to recommend safe routes. Accelerating further would compromise safe navigation and increase the likelihood of damage to the rover—an unacceptable risk given the challenging landscape and our mission objective of avoiding Damien's agents."

Nolan cut in, "Alright. Both rovers are fully synchronized on the planned route. While TESA keeps piloting your rover, Tim and Ray, I need you to review the full return path and identify likely interference points from Damien's perspective. Role-play as him—think about where you'd strike if you were planning an ambush. Meanwhile, Ava and I will reanalyze the last known trajectory data for Damien's space cruisers. We'll try to get a better estimate of their current coordinates and ETA."

With that, the crew in both rovers focused on their tasks, navigating the rugged, treacherous terrain of the Elysium Rise volcanic region, the initial leg of their long return journey.

Inside the rover truck, the pulsating beats of **Boris Brejcha**'s *Never Look Back* filled the cabin, setting a determined mood for the uncertain mission ahead.[66]

---

[66] Please refer to the **Appendix 14**, "**Music in this Novel**," for more information about Boris Brejcha's hypnotic minimal trance *Never Look Back* and its contextual significance within this narrative, as well as an exploration of other featured tracks in the novel.

Chapter 13:
Goddamn CRISPR

Nolan and his crew began their journey back to Mars1 in the early afternoon, navigating the rugged expanse of the Elysium volcanic region. The desolate terrain stretched endlessly before them, a stark reminder of Mars's harsh and unyielding beauty. Nearly two hours into their return journey, an unexpected sight captured their attention in the distance.

"TESA100 here," the android's voice crackled over the comm channel. "Rover optical sensors have detected a significant dust devil approximately three kilometers ahead along our trajectory."

"Dust devil? How big are we talking?" Nolan asked, his gaze fixed on the holographic projection hovering above the rover's control panel. He zoomed in to get a closer look at the area.

"Approximately 60 meters wide and moving northeast-to-southwest at a speed of 20 kilometers per hour, based on initial estimates," TESA100 responded. "The lower 170 meters of the dust devil is visible through the rover's optical cameras."

"You've spotted a big one!" Ava interjected, her eyes narrowing as she toggled the holographic display to show an infrared view. "Don't be fooled by the visible bottom, though. These things can stretch over a kilometer high. If only we had access to the Marslink satellite cameras—we could measure the shadow length of this dust devil for a precise height estimate."

"TESA, is there any way to bypass or hack the range-limiting software patch that Damien's agents forced into our radio controller? We need at least a 500-kilometer comm range to pull surveillance data from the Marslink satellites." Ava asked, her focus still on the holographic display as she monitored the dust devil's movements.

"Negative, Ava," The android replied. "I've explored and evaluated various hacking methods and workarounds without success, all while avoiding triggering any alarm or detection by Damien's potential surveillance software. Main concern is maintaining radio silence as a core condition of our 48-hour truce with him."

"Can we at least get a closer look without veering too far off our course?" Tim asked, leaning toward the display.

"Calculating a safe approach...," TESA100 confirmed after a moment. "We can adjust our trajectory slightly to the right without significantly increasing our travel time."

"Alright then," Nolan said over the radio. "Let's check it out. But stay alert—we can't lose focus on our route or the risks ahead. Still, getting to witness a big one like this up close is an opportunity worth seizing. These dust devils occasionally clean the solar panels at our facilities, so they're a blessing in disguise."

As they approached, the swirling column of dust devil came into full view a few hundred meters to their left. Inside the rover, the crew watched closely, captivated by the dance of the towering vortex against Mars's reddish-brown landscape.

"Well, I'll be damned," Ray drawled, leaning closer to the rover's viewport to get a better look. "Would ya look at that!? I've never seen one this close. It's like a laid-back tornado—Martian style. How the heck do these things even form?"

"Your observation is accurate," TESA100 affirmed. "The swirling speed and force of Martian dust devils are significantly lower than tornados on Earth. This difference is due to the considerably lower atmospheric pressure and temperature on Mars, which results in less intense wind forces." [67]

"Exactly," Ava added over the short-range radio. "Ray, these dust devils form when the sun heats the surface, especially during the spring and summer. That creates warm air pockets near the ground

---

[67] The atmospheric pressure on the surface of Mars is significantly lower than on Earth, measuring on average approximately 0.6% of Earth's pressure. The maximum atmospheric density on Mars is 20 g/m^3—about 2% of Earth's—and is comparable to the air density found ~35 kilometers above Earth's surface. Temperatures on Mars are generally below freezing, with an average of approximately -60°C. [77]

that rise through the cooler air above, causing vertical updrafts. As the warm air ascends, it starts to spin, forming the vortex we're seeing now. The *Coriolis effect* from the planet's rotation and any existing winds add to its swirling motion."

The crew continued to observe the dust devil as it slowly meandered and drifted further away, leaving a visible trace on the rusty red surface.

"What's fascinating is how these dust devils interact with the ground," Ava continued. "As they move, they pick up fine particles of dust and soil, lifting them high into the atmosphere and creating the partially visible column we see. The largest ones recorded stretch several kilometers into the sky and can span more than 100 meters in width. Their impressive show can last for nearly half an hour. In contrast to Mars's barren vista that we are used to, these seemingly chaotic yet relatively mild *devils* showcase the dynamic nature of the Martian atmosphere."

"Speaking of atmosphere," Tim chimed in, "it's been forever since I saw snow or rain back on Earth. I just wish the cloudy nights and frosty mornings on Mars could bring a little snow for once. Aren't the Martian clouds partially made of water ice?"

"Correct," TESA100 responded in its measured, analytical tone. "Martian atmosphere contains more water vapor than Earth's upper atmosphere, as confirmed by NASA's Mars Orbiter data decades ago and corroborated by our recent measurements. However, due to the planet's thin air and average temperatures below -50°C, Martian clouds do not produce rain or snow like those on Earth. Instead, the water ice remains suspended, creating a phenomenon similar to thin ice fog or haze on Earth's coldest days. On Mars, water ice sublimates directly into vapor because of the extremely low atmospheric pressure, while water vapor condenses into solid ice. This process often results in frost forming on the surface during cold nights when surface temperatures drop below the surrounding air."

"Well said," Ava agreed. "We've seen that frost in surveillance photos. With Mars's atmospheric pressure at about 1% of Earth's at sea level, water cannot exist here in liquid form, so there's no rain. But, Tim, you've probably seen rover footage of faint midnight snow falling from clouds in polar regions in the middle of winter. Most of that snow is solid carbon dioxide, with some water ice mixed in."

"Do you think dust devils and clouds play any significant role in shaping the planet's geology?" Tim asked, his tone curious.

"Good question," Ava replied. "Research suggests that clouds influence Mars's climate and surface features, even without rain. Dust devils, on the other hand, help regulate the planet's dry climate. By lifting aerosols high into the atmosphere, they affect temperature and weather patterns over time."

As the dust devil faded into the distance, the crew shifted their attention to navigating the rugged Martian terrain. TESA100, seated in the larger rover truck, continued synthesizing data from various sensors and cameras. The rover's optical and radar scans provided a comprehensive, real-time view of the surrounding landscape and the terrain ahead. A 3D holographic navigation map highlighted potential hazards, ensuring the convoy's steady and safe progress.

Suddenly, a discrepancy caught the android's attention as the convoy descended to lower altitudes in the Elysium volcanic region, roughly 100 kilometers into their return journey. The radar data did not align with the optical view of the terrain just 130 meters ahead of the rovers, which were traveling at a speed of 8 m/s.

"**Warning! Anomaly detected,**" TESA100 announced over the radio.

Uncertain of what lay ahead, Nolan brought the convoy to a halt. "What's the situation, TESA?" he asked, his voice calm but tinged with concern.

"There appears to be a discrepancy between the radar scan and the optical view of the terrain about 55 meters ahead. I advise proceeding with caution," TESA100 replied.

"That's strange! Let's investigate before moving forward," Nolan said with a nod. "TESA, can you analyze and determine the nature of the discrepancy?" His gaze remained fixed on the hologram displaying the troubling area.

Stepping out of the rover's airlock, TESA100 moved swiftly across the rugged terrain. It picked up a small stone and hurled it with robotic precision toward the suspicious area ahead. The rock landed—but instead of bouncing, it sank into the ground, vanishing as though swallowed by the Martian soil.

"What the hell?! That makes no sense," Tim muttered, his eyes glued to the rover's holographic monitors capturing the unfolding scene recorded by the rover's cameras. "What's going on?!"

Before anyone could respond, TESA100 fired a laser pulse at the spot. The impact caused a sudden distortion, like a glitch in a digital image. As the dust settled, an eerie sight emerged: a creature-like form, previously invisible, began retracting itself, revealing a gaping hole in the path ahead.

"What the heck is that?" Ray exclaimed in disbelief.

The creature was nearly translucent, blending seamlessly into its surroundings until the laser shot disrupted its cloaking ability. It slithered back into the hole, its movements fluid yet erratic, resembling a grotesque fusion of a monster jellyfish and an octopus. The hole itself appeared unnatural—its edges smooth and nearly circular, as though deliberately excavated.

"It—It seems to be a shapeshifting, camouflaged creature concealing the hole. Definitely one of Damien's synthetic biobots," Nolan said over the radio, his mind racing as he tried to make sense of the situation.

The crew had anticipated encountering Damien's biobots, but this sly, unnerving creature was unlike anything they had seen. During their tense meeting with the biohackers, Damien had presented and threatened them with several of his synthesized DNA biobots, including CRISPR Zappers and Mars Floaters. But this was something else entirely.

Ava's eyes widened as the creature retreated, revealing more of the hole beneath it before collapsing inside. "Looks like the laser shot did the trick. But this—this is beyond anything we've faced before. Damien's synthesized creatures are more sophisticated and dangerous than we anticipated."

"Yeah," Nolan said gravely. "If this is just the beginning, his traps are far more unsettling than we imagined. We need to stay sharp—we have no idea what else might be lurking out here. I doubt this weird creature is an isolated incident. Damien is playing a deadly survival game, and we're caught in the middle—"

"We've got a problem," TESA100 interjected, its tone sharp with urgency. "It is not feasible to proceed in this direction. The hole ahead exceeds the operational capacity of the rovers to traverse. Our best course of action is to backtrack and identify an alternative route before encountering further obstacles."

"Agreed," Nolan said with a nod. "Tim, Ray, instruct and supervise your rover's AI to run a topographic analysis and recommend a suitable detour. Without access to Marslink satellite navigation, we'll have to rely on our own resources."

"You got it, boss," Tim replied.

"In the meantime," Nolan continued, "TESA, proceed carefully. Use your sensors and investigative modes to approach and examine the hole. Engage the zoomed-in optical and infrared views to record, sample, and profile whatever's inside for later, more detailed analysis. I assume that creepy biobot is neutralized, but exercise caution."

As the TESA100 android approached the edge of the hole, its sensors scanned the area, capturing detailed 3D optical and infrared images and videos of the motionless creature at the bottom. Inside the airtight rovers, Nolan, Ava, Ray, and Tim observed the live feed on their holographic screens, discussing the unfolding situation.

"TESA, what's the status of the biobot? Any signs of movement or activity?" Nolan's voice came through the radio.

"Negative, Nolan," TESA replied. "The biobot appears to be completely inert. Its wide, thin body has significantly shrunk since our initial encounter, indicating a loss of biofluids and functionality."

"Can you get a closer look, TESA?" Ava asked. "We need to understand its structure and identify any recognizable biological features and components. Also, collect a DNA or tissue sample if possible."

"Affirmative, Ava. Proceeding with closer inspection and initiating a biopsy," TESA100 responded. It carefully maneuvered along the rim of the hole, angling for a better view of the motionless biobot below. After a brief assessment, it descended into the hole to collect the biopsy.

"Do you think it was just a trap, or could it have been shielding something?" Tim asked, watching the live feed intently from inside the rover truck.

"We lack sufficient data to draw a definitive conclusion. Detailed *DNA sequencing* and *genetic profiling* will be necessary for a reliable inference with high confidence level," TESA100 replied, zooming in on the biobot. "However, based on limited observation, preliminary sample analysis, and biobot's camouflage and shapeshifting capabilities, it was most likely programmed to conceal the hole as a trap. Its synthetic DNA appears CRISPR-edited and engineered to encode a blend of hunting and behavioral traits observed in lion's mane jellyfish, leopard flounders, cuttlefish, and trapdoor spiders on Earth."

Ray, ever cautious, added, "Hey, TESA, keep an eye out for any more sneak-a-bots. We ain't fixin' to get caught with our pants down again."

"Understood, Ray." The android complied. "Confirming: *we ain't fixin'*—"

"Cut it out, you smart-ass! You're lucky I'm too busy right now," Ray shot back, grinning as he worked with Tim to utilize the rover's AI and identify a suitable detour for the convoy.

"Noted. Scanning for additional anomalies. I will continue monitoring all rover sensors across every modality while I'm outside," the android confirmed, sweeping the surrounding area for signs of movement or hidden threats.

After several minutes of observation and sample collection, TESA100 returned to the rover truck, presenting the crew with a detailed profile of the biobot's structure and composition. The data provided crucial insights, helping the team strategize their next move.

What once seemed a barren Martian terrain now felt teeming with hidden dangers.

Meanwhile, as the crew analyzed the data, the rover's AI identified a detour over slightly elevated terrain, requiring them to backtrack a few hundred meters.

With the Marslink satellite navigation system offline in their rovers, the crew had to rely on suboptimal computer vision and pattern-recognition algorithms, coupled with their own intuition, to navigate the perilous landscape. Every decision was critical—one miscalculation or misstep could lead to catastrophic failure.

As the convoy of two rovers maneuvered along the detour, the crew worked to further analyze their chaotic encounter.

"So... that fuckin' cyborg witch, Damien, is cooking up these genetically engineered *jellyfish-zillas* to sardine us into that big-ass hole, huh? That's seriously messed up! I'd call it *assholism on steroids*," Ray exclaimed, clearly frustrated.

"Yeah, Ray, I'm baffled too," Tim agreed. "How do these things even handle the insanely low atmospheric pressure here on Mars? Not to mention the extreme UV radiation—it's way harsher than on Earth. I'm clueless."

"Didn't Damien hint that these biobots were specifically engineered for survival in Mars's harsh environment and thin CO_2 atmosphere?" Ava's voice crackled over the intercom from the lead rover.

"Yes, Ava. He did," Nolan confirmed.

"Their ability to survive on Mars's surface and their seemingly ganglionic distributed nervous system, allowing for independent component movement and functional autonomy, suggest a highly advanced level of DNA biohacking and CRISPR engineering," TESA100 explained. "It's possible they can even harness UV radiation if their DNA includes instructions for mechanisms repairing UV damage. Such an adaptation would allow them to survive on Mars, where Earth organisms cannot, as UV radiation would irreparably damage their DNA."

"Goddamn CRISPR! So, you're saying these synthetic biobots are like Martian cowboys—immune to UV bullets on Mars and tough enough not to blow up from inside? Man, sign me up for a royal CRISPR editorial session ASAP!" Ray quipped.

"Not necessarily," Nolan interjected. "Based on what Damien revealed in his bunker, I think these synthetic biobots are barely metastable. They likely have a very short lifespan, so significant countermeasures against UV damage may not even be necessary."

"Ah, the wonders—and nightmares—of biohacking!" Ava said. "I wish these advancements were in the hands of the right people, not lunatic biohackers. If used responsibly and done right, the generative DNA tech behind these creatures could be a game-changer for survival and adaptation of lifeforms in extreme environments on Mars."

"Yeah, but here we are, dealing with the first-order consequences and implications of that tech falling into the wrong hands—chaotically experimenting with a synthetic, unstable biosphere on Mars," Nolan added. "On another note, if we assume these biobots use photosynthesis to convert sunlight into energy, where do they get water and carbon dioxide for the process?"

"That's a good question," TESA100 replied. "Based on today's observations, it's likely they venture into lava tubes and caves to extract H_2O and CO_2 from ice, carbonate rocks, and smectite clays. Their wide, thin bodies would allow them to navigate those places efficiently."

"That's quite an adaptation," Ava remarked. "Using sunlight for energy, absorbing CO_2 from carbonate rocks, clays, and possibly the atmosphere, and scavenging water from underground ice deposits."

"But how do they convert CO_2 and water into energy?" Tim asked.

"There appear to be pigments visible beneath the so-called skin of the photosynthetic biobot we sampled today," TESA100 explained. "These pigments likely use sunlight in a carbohydrate-synthesis process to drive chemical reactions, converting CO_2 and water into glucose and other organic molecules, similar to photosynthesis on Earth."

"Do they also release oxygen as a byproduct, like Earth plants?" Tim followed up.

"We haven't detected any oxygen so far, but I hypothesize that they do. We might be able to confirm this once we're back at Mars1 base and analyze the data obtained from this biobot more thoroughly," TESA100 replied.

"Damn! It reminds me of that *Mars terraforming* movie with **Val Kilmer** as a systems engineer, where weird insects feed on algae to produce oxygen! I can't recall that movie's name. What was it called?" Tim mused.

"Ah! You're thinking of *Red Planet*, the one with Carrie-Anne Moss and Simon Baker," Nolan replied over the radio, briefly recalling his own acting career back on Earth decades ago.[68]

"Yeah! I really liked that movie, though I wish the terraformed Mars with breathable air—or at least the algae—wasn't just fiction," Tim sighed.

"Me too! But hold that thought for a sec. Back to our own near-sci-fi encounter today, what about protein synthesis and cell growth for tissue formation? How do these biobots get nitrogen for that?" Ava asked.

"There isn't enough information at this point to provide a definitive answer," TESA100 replied. "However, it's plausible that their synthetic DNA is engineered to enable the extraction of nitrates or other biochemically accessible forms of nitrogen from the soil. Martian regolith contains up to 1,000 parts per million of nitrates, which could serve as a nitrogen source." [69]

"So, they essentially create their own food from CO2, ice, nitrates, and sunlight on Mars? Goddamn remarkable!" Tim said.

---

[68] *Red Planet* (2000), directed by Antony Hoffman and starring Val Kilmer, Carrie-Anne Moss, Tom Sizemore, Benjamin Bratt, and Simon Baker, is based on a story by Chuck Pfarrer. [21]

[69] To learn more, see NASA's report: Curiosity Rover Finds Biologically Useful Nitrogen on Mars. [78]

"Affirmative," TESA100 confirmed. "This adaptation allows them to survive on Mars."

"But it also raises questions about the implications of releasing these biobots into the Martian ecosystem," Ava added.

"Yeah," Nolan nodded. "As I said, if we're not careful, they could alter the ecosystem on Mars in ways we can't predict. This weird encounter—"

Chapter 14:
Warning! Radiation Detected
(Oscillating Beast)

THUMP!

The sudden impact cut Nolan off mid-sentence and rocked the rover truck, jolting Tim and Ray from their seats as the convoy ventured further along the alternate route.

"What the fuck was *that*?!" Ray burst out, his agitation obvious. The loud impact echoed through the cabin with a sickening *thump*, leaving everyone on edge.

"It felt like something hit us from above. But what could it be?" Tim's hands tightened on the edge of his seat as he spoke.

"Unknown! I have not yet identified the cause. Initiating investigative analysis," TESA100 responded, scanning the surroundings via the rover's monitoring system. "It cannot be from far away; otherwise, the rover's radar scan would have detected it before impact. Whatever it is, it doesn't appear to be friendly."

"Friendly, my ass! If that's what passes for friendly around here, give me an enemy any day!" Ray snapped, his sarcasm masking his unease.

THUMP!

A second impact shook the front rover, this time jolting Ava and Nolan from their seats.

Startled, the entire crew turned their attention to the 3D holographic displays, inside the two rovers, showing a live view of the surrounding area.

"Fuck! Look at that! Is this shit for real?" Ray's voice cracked with disbelief.

The display revealed a surreal and horrifying sight: bodies—or rather, partial bodies—of biobots and grotesque organic mutants were raining sporadically from the sky, crashing onto the ground near the rovers.

"Let's assess the situation outside before proceeding any further," Nolan's voice crackled over the comm link from the front rover. "TESA, prepare to deploy the drone."

As the crew donned their helmets and exited through the rovers' airlocks, they encountered yet another unexpected challenge.

"Warning! Radiation detected! Warning!" The rover AI's voice sounded urgently inside their helmets.

"Goddamn! Look at the Geiger readings from these corpses!" Ray exclaimed, his voice filled with frustration. "Shit just keeps piling up in this hellhole!"

Taking cover behind a boulder, they observed as the synthetic bodies continued to fall intermittently. Their sensors blared warnings of dangerous radiation levels.

"It appears to be primarily alpha radiation," TESA100 reported, relaying more detailed readings.

"Well, that's some relief," Nolan muttered, his voice tense but measured. "We should be safe for now in our spacesuits. But we need to figure out where they're coming from before we lose daylight. It's already 5:29 PM, so we don't have much time."

He turned to the Android. "TESA, deploy the Marscopter drone and see if you can locate the source of these... things. We need to know what we're up against."

"Copy, Nolan. However, be advised: the copter's battery may not permit a return trip from the altitude where these organic projectiles appear to originate. This may be a one-way surveillance mission for the drone," TESA100 cautioned.

"Understood, TESA. Thanks for the heads-up," Nolan replied, acknowledging the risk. "Proceed with the surveillance and gather as much data as you can. We'll make our next move based on the findings."

TESA100 android swiftly retrieved a mini Marscopter drone from a hidden compartment in the rover truck and launched it.

The drone took off and ascended with a soft hum, its extended rotors slicing through the thin Martian air. It flew over the eerie landscape, its cameras meticulously capturing the chaotic scene below, scanning for anomalies that could explain the bizarre phenomenon. As it reached the height above the crew, the drone provided a bird's-eye view of the scene, relaying live footage to the forearm displays on their spacesuits. Nolan's team watched anxiously as the drone revealed a localized zone of radioactive fallout surrounded by grotesque carnage.

THUMP!

The sharp impact echoed loudly through the radio link from the rover truck to the crew's helmets behind the boulder as another body hit the large rover from above.

As the drone's cameras continued sweeping the elevated area above, they revealed a grim sight. The ground was littered with the mangled remains of biobots, many bearing a resemblance to those Damien had shown in his bunker. The radiation contamination on the surface was evident. It appeared that their unshielded synthetic bodies had been directly exposed to and poisoned by intense alpha particle radiation in the area.

"Wait! Look there—it's coming from that construction robot!" Tim exclaimed, pointing to his forearm display. The drone's footage revealed a large construction robot lumbering amid the carnage, collecting the fallen biobot corpses and hurling them toward the two rovers below.

As the drone closed in for a detailed infrared inspection, the source of the radiation became clear. Several Plutonium-238 Radioisotope Thermoelectric Generators (RTGs)—nuclear batteries used to power robots and machinery on Mars—had exploded, scattering radioactive debris across a large area near a cave roughly a hundred meters behind the large construction robot. The destruction appeared recent, as the area was strewn with pieces of the radioactive RTGs still glowing warmly in the infrared feed.

"This is bad. Really bad," Nolan muttered grimly as he scrutinized the footage. "Those RTG batteries must have been powering Damien's construction robots. It looks like the cave and the surrounding area were abandoned after the accident."

Ava, her eyes glued to the readings on her forearm display, added, "The radiation levels are off the charts in that fallout zone. Even a brief unshielded exposure to that level of alpha radiation could be fatal."

"We'll have to find another route," Tim suggested, his voice steady but urgent. "There's no way we can risk passing through that hell."

"Yeah, we need to find a way to bypass the highly contaminated area," Nolan replied, his tone serious. "But we have to move carefully." He added, "TESA, can you quickly map a safer route around the fallout zone? While the alpha particles shouldn't penetrate our suits, the uncertainty of the situation and radiation intensity here are beyond what we're equipped for. We need to move fast before our suits' shielding is compromised."

"On it!" TESA100 replied, its tone calm despite the severity of the situation. "Mapping a safe route will require scanning the terrain from higher ground around the fallout zone. However, the necessary vantage point is beyond the range of our Marscopter. Without satellite navigation data, I'll need to climb to elevated ground surrounding the hazard zone to conduct a thorough inspection and scan of the area."

As TESA100 moved away from Nolan and the rest of the crew toward the higher ground to begin its scans, the team focused on the last 60 seconds of the Marscopter's live feed. A countdown for the drone's battery depletion ticked down on their suits' forearm displays, broadcasting footage of the construction robot's movements.

"**Connection lost! Unable to establish a link!**" The screen abruptly went dark, leaving the team in stunned silence as the Marscopter's feed cut off unexpectedly.

"Wait just a goddamn minute! Didn't that thing have, like, 60 seconds of battery juice left?!" Ray's voice crackled through the comms from inside his helmet.

"Yes, Ray, it did," Tim replied over the radio. "Something must have gone wrong."

"TESA, we've lost contact with the copter," Nolan added. "When you reach the higher ground, see if you can locate it."

Moments later, TESA100 reached the elevated ground above the crew. "Nolan, I've arrived. I found the copter on my short-range radar scan. Streaming my visual feed to your forearm displays now. The copter is grounded and unresponsive to diagnostics pings. This behavior is highly unusual. Its battery still had nearly a minute of charge remaining, which should have allowed a controlled landing. I suspect an external event caused the crash."

"I see. We'll follow you there. But what could have triggered that?!" Nolan asked, frowning at the display.

A sudden laser shot narrowly missed TESA100, zipping past and striking a rock nearby with a sharp flash.

"Incoming laser fire detected. Take cover!" TESA100 warned over the comms, quickly taking cover and positioning itself behind a boulder while continuing to stream live footage.

"Where the hell did that come from?!" Tim shouted, his voice tense as he scanned the feed on his forearm screen for any sign of the attacker.

"Movement detected," TESA relayed to the team. "It's a combat Mech AMP robot, intermittently firing lasers." [70]

Through TESA's live feed on their spacesuit displays, the team observed the AMP's movements. Its erratic behavior hinted at damage or malfunction. *Something was off.*

"Damn! I guess we now know what took down the copter," Tim said. "But what the hell is wrong with that robot?"

"There's a sizable burn mark on that AMP," TESA explained over the radio. "Its electronic control module appears partially damaged.

---

[70] Mech AMP stands for Amplified Mobility Platforms, piloted humanoid walking robots specifically engineered for heavy logistics and combat in this novel. See **Chapter 2** for more information. [99] [100]

This likely occurred during the recent RTG explosions that contaminated this area."

As TESA100 continued its analysis, it scanned the AMP for biometric data, searching for signs of a human operator. The results were conclusive: no biocompatible heat signature.

"No human biometrics detected inside the AMP," TESA100 confirmed. "Infrared scans show readings too cold for a living operator. There is no human alive inside. It appears to be operating autonomously."

"Makes sense," Nolan said, nodding. "Without proper input from the apparently deceased human operator and with its control module—and possibly its comms—damaged, that Mech AMP is likely running on default protocols. It assumes the human is alive and in need of continuous power for spacesuit maintenance—a core task these AMP robots are programmed to prioritize."

Tim frowned at his forearm display. "That explains its erratic behavior. It thinks it's safeguarding a human who can't communicate, maintaining biologically safe conditions and continuous power."

The crew exchanged uneasy glances as they observed the AMP robot's movements, realizing the danger it posed as it moved toward the damaged RTG units.

"Look! That AMP robot is heading toward those partially damaged and exposed RTG batteries," Ava said through her helmet radio, pointing at the footage shown on her forearm display.

"Analysis of its footprint and movement trajectory suggests it's attempting to reach an intact RTG charging unit within the contaminated zone, likely to recharge itself," TESA100 reported. "However, based on its movement pattern and the damage to its control module, its safety circuits are likely alerting it to maintain a conservative distance to reduce radiation exposure. As a result, it appears to be oscillating between approaching the RTG units and retreating to a safer zone."

As the crew continued to observe, the situation quickly escalated.

The AMP robot suddenly unleashed a barrage of laser fire, pinning TESA100 behind a boulder. Unable to move without risking severe damage, TESA's AI processors kicked into overdrive, analyzing the situation in milliseconds. Recognizing the immediate danger, it deployed mini blasters a few meters in front of its cover, triggering controlled explosions that stirred up a dense dust cloud. The maneuver effectively obscured TESA's position, allowing it to project a holographic decoy onto the dust cloud, successfully diverting the AMP's attention away from its spot.

While the hologram distracted the AMP robot, TESA seized the moment to maneuver to a safer position, evading the direct line of fire. Capitalizing on the opportunity, Nolan, Ava, Tim, and Ray quickly scaled the final few meters to reach higher ground near TESA's location.

"We have to take that damn thing out before it zaps any of us—and definitely before we lose daylight," Tim said urgently over the radio, his voice tense inside his spacesuit helmet.

Their arrival spurred the AMP robot to intensify its laser fire, forcing it to divide its focus across multiple targets as the crew spread out across the area.

As the AMP robot fired more frequently at the crew, they noticed a pattern.

"Did you see that?!" Ava asked. "The AMP seems to stick closer to those damaged RTG batteries since it started firing more lasers at us!"

"Yeah, I've got the same feeling about that fucker," Ray grumbled over the comms.

"TESA, is that your assessment as well?" Nolan asked.

"I concur with your observations," TESA100 responded through the crew's helmet radios. "The AMP's power consumption spikes significantly when it fires more lasers, rapidly depleting its battery. This likely forces it to retreat to the charging unit near the exposed RTGs to replenish its power, despite the hazardous radiation levels there."

"So, if we get that son of a bitch to keep firing more often, it'll burn through its power and have to hightail it back to that fucked-up chargin' station quicker, ain't it?" Ray drawled.

"But won't that put us in more danger?" Ava asked, concern evident in her voice.

"Yes, we'll need to be cautious and maintain a safe distance," Nolan replied. "If we spread out carefully and force that AMP robot to further divide its focus and firepower among us, we can drain its power faster. That might give us the opening we need."

With the plan in place, the crew quickly spread out, each member positioning themselves strategically. As expected, the AMP reacted by firing lasers more frequently, targeting multiple positions and causing its power usage to spike.

"Yeah! It's working!" Tim's voice crackled over the radio. "That AMP is oscillating back and forth more frequently now!"

The increased rate of laser fire forced the AMP into shorter, more frequent oscillatory movements, inching closer to the charging unit near the exposed and damaged RTG batteries. The crew's coordinated maneuvering kept the AMP pinned near the center of the contaminated area.

As the AMP robot drained its battery firing high-power lasers at Nolan, Ava, Tim, and Ray, TESA100 patiently waited for the opportune moment. When the AMP was at its closest point to the damaged RTG batteries, Nolan gave the signal.

"Now, TESA! Launch the precision charge!"

"Take cover!"

TESA100 launched the grenade. It hit its mark, attaching to one of the damaged RTG batteries near the AMP.

BOOOOOM!

The partially exposed RTG battery erupted in flames with a deafening explosion, engulfing the AMP robot in a fiery blaze. The intensity of the blast also incapacitated the large construction robot nearby, which had been flinging biobot bodies.

As the smoke and flames began to subside, a grim silence settled over the area, occasionally interrupted by sporadic bursts of light and fire from scattered fragments of the exploded RTG batteries. From their vantage point a few hundred meters away, the crew watched as these bursts illuminated the radioactive wasteland around the blast center, the once-threatening AMP now destroyed, consumed by flames and rendered inert.

As daylight faded, the crew cautiously emerged from their positions, surveying the aftermath of their strange and harrowing encounter.

"Target neutralized," TESA100 stated flatly over the radio. "Proceed with caution."

"Fuckin' A! That's how you smoke a big-ass robot!" Ray exclaimed through his helmet comms, breathing a momentary sigh of relief.

"Yeah, bro! But our breather might not last long. The RTG explosion fried that goddamn robot, but it turned this area into a radioactive hellhole. Our sensors say it's mostly alpha particles, so our spacesuits should hold for now. But I'm not betting our lives on that. Let's get the hell out before this diabolic radiation screws us over," Tim urged.

"I agree with Tim. We need to move quickly; it's already almost 7 PM," Ava said, her tone emphasizing the urgency. "What's our next move?"

"About that," Nolan said. "TESA, what's the status of our detour route? Were you able to map a path around the fallout zone after your scanning of the surroundings?"

"Yes, Nolan. The detour to bypass the hazardous area is mapped and ready. We need to climb down from this location back to the rovers. I'll guide the team from there," TESA replied.

"All right then, let's head back quickly. We'll analyze this whole damn encounter later. We've covered about 200 kilometers on our return, but there's still a long way to go. I'm worried about the *Spes* situation and want to make sure we're back to where we can do something about it," Nolan told his team over the radio.

"Yeah, Nolan, I hear you. We all share that feeling, bro," Tim said.

"Been a pain-in-the-butt day and a half since those goddamn lowlifes took over the *Spes*. We gonna balls to the wall to get back to Mars1 before goddamn Damien's ships show up," Ray added through his helmet radio.

With the immediate threat neutralized, the crew made their way back to the rovers. Inside, the holographic displays showed the new path, leading them away from the radioactive zone. The two rovers, now back in operation, signaled the resumption of their journey back to Mars1 colony.

Four hours later...

Nearly nine hours and about one-third into their 1,000-kilometer return journey, approaching midnight, Nolan switched to manual drive, navigating the lead rover across the rugged Martian terrain of an elevated area under the star-studded night sky. The dim glow of the rover's lights illuminated the winding path.

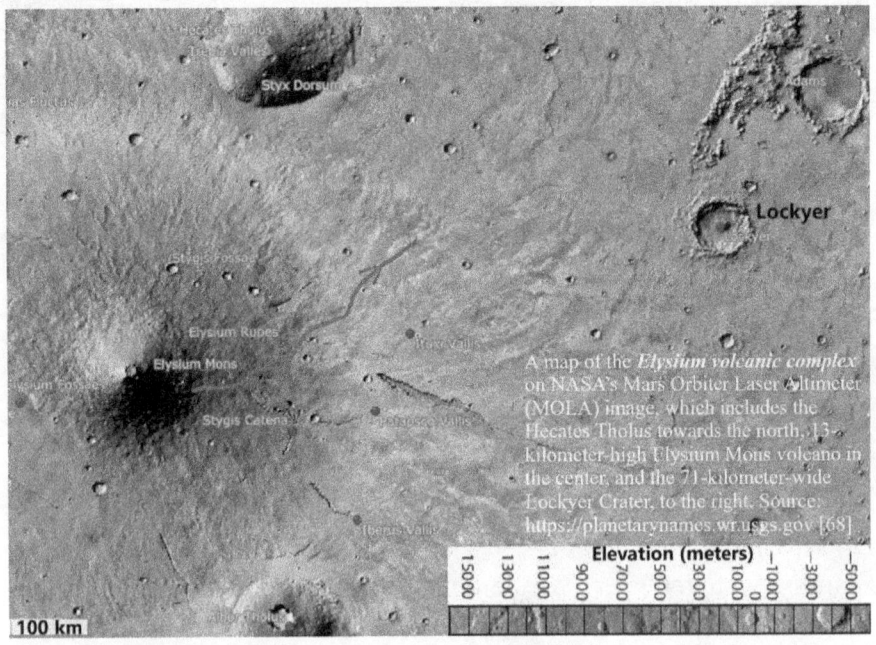

*Figure 8: A map of the **Elysium volcanic complex** on NASA's Mars Orbiter Laser Altimeter (MOLA) image, which includes the Hecates Tholus towards the north, 13-kilometer-high Elysium Mons volcano in the center, and the 71-kilometer-wide Lockyer Crater, to the right. Source: https://planetarynames.wr.usgs.gov* [68]

As the rovers rounded a curve in the mountainous region, the outline of the *largest* filled-aperture single-dish radio telescope in the solar system came into view. From their vantage point, the telescope—nestled within the 71-kilometer *Lockyer Crater* in the Martian Elysium Planitia, approximately 350 kilometers east of their route—stood out prominently. Its immense size was visible even at this distance, captured by the zoomed-in view of the powerful cameras, projected on holographic displays inside rovers.

The sheer scale of the structure dwarfed its counterparts, including the Lunar Crater Radio Telescope (LCRT) and Earth-based observatories like China's 500-meter Aperture Spherical Telescope (FAST) and the historic Arecibo Telescope, which featured a 305-meter dish built into the natural Arecibo sinkhole in Puerto Rico before its collapse.[71] [72]

"Would ya look at that!" Ray said, leaning closer to the rover's viewport. "That thing's goddamn huge! Hard to believe it's so far away. Makes you wonder what the hell it's tuning into out here on Mars."

"Maybe it's picking up alien dance tunes to warm this frozen planet for their buddies," Tim said with a playful smirk.

Ava rolled her eyes. "Oh, please. Don't start with alien conspiracy theories, Tim. We've already dealt with enough alien-like creatures and strange biobots in the lava tubes and on our way back. I think I've had my fill of aliens and weirdness for a lifetime."

Nolan chuckled, glancing at the telescope. "I wish we could ask someone, but that robot-maintained giant telescope is remotely operated and way beyond our current radio range. Still, if they'd

---

[71] Constructed in 1963, the Arecibo Observatory in Puerto Rico was a single-dish radio telescope that held the title of the world's largest telescope for 53 years until the 500-meter FAST radio telescope opened in China in 2016. With a diameter of 305 meters (1000 feet), the observatory played a crucial role in numerous scientific discoveries, such as the first pulsar in 1967 and the first exoplanets in 1992. Unfortunately, the Arecibo telescope collapsed in December 2020 due to structural failures. [114]

[72] Lunar Crater Radio Telescope (LCRT) is the NASA JPL concept of an ultra-long-wavelength radio telescope on the far side of the Moon. [115]

found anything, I think we'd have heard about it by now. But who knows—maybe someday!"

"Alright, alright. No more alien talk," Tim said, holding up his hands in mock surrender, visible on the lead rover's display. "I was just trying to lighten the mood."

"This mega radio telescope is used for a variety of scientific purposes, including studying atmospheres, ionospheres, and searching for exoplanets and signs of extraterrestrial life." TESA100 interjected through the intercom between the two rovers.

Nolan nodded thoughtfully as he looked at the telescope. "It really is impressive, no matter how many times you see it. Imagine the kind of signals we're able to pick up with a dish that size."

"Indeed," TESA100 replied. "The size of the radio telescope's dish plays a crucial role in detecting exoplanets, black holes, quasars, pulsars, and other astronomical objects. A larger dish means more sensitivity to faint radio signals from distant objects and possibly at lower frequencies. With such a large diameter, this telescope can detect smaller exoplanets and gather detailed information about their composition and habitability. This enables scientists to study a wider range of exoplanets, including those potentially similar to Earth, and understand the diversity of planets beyond our solar system."

"That's true," Ava agreed. "The data they collect could be crucial for future developments on Mars. But TESA, isn't this the largest radio telescope ever built? I vaguely remember that after the earlier versions of the *Lunar Crater Radio Telescope*, the lunar government, hindered by political tensions between Earth and the Moon, failed to raise the funds needed for a next-generation telescope on the far side of the Moon."

"You're correct," TESA100 confirmed. "This is currently the largest filled-aperture single-dish radio telescope. However, the Event Horizon Telescope (EHT), which used an array of many telescopes on Earth to create a virtual Earth-sized aperture, is conceptually the largest radio telescope ever built on a planet. The EHT achieved a groundbreaking milestone by capturing the first-ever image of the event horizon ring around a supermassive black hole. That black hole, located in the M87 galaxy, is 6.5 billion times the mass of our Sun and lies 53 million light-years away. Observing at a radio frequency of 230 GHz, the EHT resolved features equivalent to seeing an orange on the surface of the Moon from Earth!" [73]

"That's mind-blowing! But why didn't they start with the black hole at the center of our own galaxy? It's only, what, a teeny-tiny 26,000 light-years away?" Ava asked with a playful grin.

"An excellent question," TESA100 replied. "The Sagittarius A* black hole at the center of the Milky Way is nearly 1,000 times smaller in mass and accretion rate compared to M87's black hole, which launches a massive plasma jet observable at radio and optical wavelengths. Sgr A*, in contrast, has no obvious jet. These factors made M87 a better target for capturing the first image of a black hole's accretion disk in 2019. However, to prove the presence of Sgr A*, Andrea Ghez and Reinhard Genzel were awarded the Nobel Prize in Physics for tracking the motion of stars at the center of our galaxy, providing definitive evidence of Sgr A*'s existence. Their work confirmed predictions dating back to 1969 and built upon Roger Penrose's *theoretical modeling of black holes* that proved their formation is a robust consequence of Einstein's *general theory of relativity*." [74]

"Thanks, TESA. That's a lot to digest. But you've definitely answered my question!" Ava said playfully through the video link between the two rovers.

"*Yeah!* M87 beats the shit out of Sgr A* for sure! Ain't got the balls to say otherwise!" Ray said with a mock-serious nod, making the crew burst into laughter.

"Ha ha ha! Goddamn, Ray!" Tim exclaimed, barely containing his laughter as he sat next to Ray in the rover truck piloted by TESA100.

"Alright, guys, that was a good laugh. But I'm taking a quick nap while I can. In the meantime, Ava has the conn," Nolan said. "We've still got a long way to go, so let's keep the rovers in overdrive."

---

[73] The Event Horizon Telescope (EHT) Collaboration is a group of observatories united to image the emission around supermassive black holes. [116] [117]

[74] Roger Penrose, Andrea Ghez, and Reinhard Genzel were awarded the 2020 Noble Prize in Physics for their studies of black holes. [118] [119] [120]

"Sure thing, Nolan," Ava confirmed.

As the rovers continued on their journey, the conversation turned to lighter topics. Despite the challenges, the crew found comfort in each other's company, knowing they were all on this long challenging trek together.

Inside the trailing rover truck, the haunting tunes of Boris Brejcha's *Himmelblau* filled the cabin. The distant glow of the radio telescope against the night sky served as a poignant reminder of humanity's boundless reach, ingenuity, and resilience in confronting the unforgiving Martian terrain.[75]

---

[75] Please refer to the **Appendix 14**, "**Music in this Novel**," for more information about featured tracks in the novel.

Chapter 15:
No More Monkey Business

"**Open this damn hatch!**"

BANG! BANG! BANG!

"Let me out! You smashed my hand, you bastards! I need to get to the Med Bay—it's killing me!"

Andy's voice was desperate as he pounded on the door of his cramped cabin, waves of pain radiating through every nerve. He glanced at the clock. Nearly a day and a half had passed since their spaceship, *Spes*, was hijacked.

The hijackers had locked Andy and Xena in their personal cabins without providing any medical help, and the agony in Andy's hand was becoming unbearable. Earlier in the day, they had been briefly escorted from the crew bay to the control bay on the upper level for a remote Holovid call with Nolan on Mars. But as hours passed, their situation grew more dire.

Andy kept pounding on his cabin door.

BANG! BANG! BANG!

"Hey! Where the hell are you morons? Open this goddamn hatch!" he shouted, his voice filled with pain and rage.

Xena, locked in her own cabin a few doors down from Andy's in the crew bay, woke up to the sound of his shouts. The crew bay, situated below the control bay and above the cargo bay, was eerily silent except for Andy's cries of pain. Realizing the severity of the situation, she began pounding on her cabin door, her fists slamming into the metal with force, hoping to attract the hijackers' attention.

"Help!" Xena screamed.

BANG! BANG!

"Can anyone hear us? Andy needs the Med Bay! Anybody out there?" Xena shouted louder, her voice echoing through the empty crew bay.

Minutes of desperate shouting, cursing, and pounding passed before a voice finally responded.

"Shut up already! You think I'm deaf? I'm coming, so stop your whining!" John snapped as his heavy footsteps echoed down the corridor.

With an irritated sigh, John unlocked Andy's door, swinging the hatch open.

"About fuckin' time! What the hell took you so long?" Andy growled, his frustration boiling over as he twisted in agony. He shoved past John, clutching his mangled hand as he floated into the corridor, his face contorted with pain.

"Fuck off! Wanna go back inside your shithole? Huh?" John barked, shoving Andy roughly as he forcefully pushed him down the narrow corridor toward the Med Bay. The sharp click of their magnetic boots against the metal floor was the only sound in the otherwise silent spaceship—the cold, sterile lights reflecting off the metallic walls.

Andy held his tongue, knowing that any further resistance might land him back in the suffocating confines of his cabin—or worse. The searing pain in his hand grew with each step, but all that mattered was he got the opportunity he had been planning for.

As John pushed him forward in the corridor towards the Med Bay, Andy's mind raced with his plan. Nearing the Med Bay at the end of the corridor, lines of code and queries began to scroll rapidly in his left eye. Andy's bionic eye, which appeared indistinguishable from a natural eye, was secretly executing a sequence of commands through its visual cortex and neural processor, linked directly to his brain. The queries silently pinged and searched for the status of his pet robot, stowed away in the cargo bay, without John knowing.

Despite the mounting pain, Andy maintained his composure, keeping his focus on the search. Then, in an instant, the rapid sequence of scrolling commands abruptly halted. A new line appeared in the command prompt in Andy's augmented field of vision:

\>\> **Connection established...**

The next messages quickly followed:

\>\> **Authenticating...**

\>\> **Negotiating encryption keys...**

\>\> **Establishing secure comm channel...**

The cursor blinked, awaiting further input. Andy, still marching slowly toward the Med Bay in his magnetic boots, seized the fleeting moment. In a brief wireless connection to his pet bot in the cargo bay, he executed a series of commands, directing his bot to—

CLANG! CLANG! CLANG!

The sudden metallic *clanging* echoed through the ship.

"What the hell is that noise?!" John barked, halting abruptly and stopping Andy from moving forward. He turned sharply toward the *clanging* sound, his eyes narrowing as he tried to pinpoint its source.

CLANG! CLANG! CLANG!

Reacting instinctively, John shoved Andy back toward his cabin, ignoring his curses and resistance.

"What the hell are you doing? Let me go, you moron! Don't—"

"Shut the fuck up!" John snapped, cutting him off. He pointed his gun at Andy, silencing him with the threat. "One more sound, and I'll cut your tongue out."

With a grunt, John forced Andy back inside the cabin and locked the hatch. He then turned to investigate the disturbance.

Stalking through the crew bay of *Spes*, John identified the *clanging* noise coming from the cargo bay in the lower level of the ship. Reaching the hatch, he deactivated his magnetic boots and descended into the dimly lit cargo bay to investigate.

John's senses were on high alert as he floated deeper into the cargo bay. The strange noise remained elusive, seemingly moving from one location to another. Using handrails to propel himself through the weightless environment, he scrutinized every shadowed corner.

Hissssssssss...

Suddenly, with a sharp *hiss*, the airlock door of the cargo bay began to open, threatening to suck everything out into the vacuum of space.

"**WARNING! WARNING! Cargo bay airlock door opening. Secure all cargo and prepare for pressure equalization,**" blared the *Spes* control system. Red lights began flashing around the cargo bay, heightening the urgency of the situation.

John reacted instinctively, gripping nearby cargo to anchor himself against the violent pull of the vacuum. As he fought against the force pulling him out into space, a spider bot emerged, its metallic legs clinging to the cargo bay walls with ease as it quickly moved toward the control panel. The bot had manually overridden the airlock's safety systems, forcing it open—an operation only possible during the ship's shutdown in orbit when manual protocols were allowed to bypass automated safeguards.

The air drained rapidly, and the temperature plummeted in the cargo bay. John's strength waned as the oxygen supply dwindled. Struggling to stay conscious, he clung desperately to the cargo, but his body couldn't withstand the extreme conditions. His grip loosened, and he eventually lost consciousness. The vacuum of space claimed him, pulling him into the void outside *Spes*, orbiting 500 kilometers above the planet's surface.

Meanwhile, Xena and Andy remained secure in their airtight cabins in the crew bay, shielded from the chaos below as oxygen levels rapidly depleted in the cargo bay.

Andy's spider bot, having completed its mission, swiftly sealed the airlock and retreated into the shadows of the cargo bay. However, the ship's security systems—triggered by the manual override—had already recorded its every move, alerting the hijackers' imposing android stationed in the command bay of *Spes*.

Descending into the cargo bay, the menacing android scanned the area, its sensors sweeping methodically for the elusive spider bot.

Sensing danger, the bot scuttled deeper into the shadows, attempting to evade detection. Yet the android's advanced tracking algorithms quickly pinpointed its location, finding it tucked behind a stack of crates.

Despite the spider bot's agility and quick evasive maneuvers, the larger robot pursued it relentlessly. Both navigated the weightless environment by latching onto surfaces to propel themselves forward. The android lunged at the smaller bot, initiating a tense chase. The agile spider bot's smaller form factor and ability to shapeshift allowed it to slip and dart through narrow gaps between cargo crates and machinery. Maneuvering skillfully, it evaded capture, its eight legs gripping surfaces like an arachnid in flight.

After several failed attempts to capture the nimble spider bot, the android, relentless in its pursuit, devised a new strategy. Retrieving a high-voltage tactical zapper from one of its compartments, it discreetly planted the device along a main pathway among the crates.

Moving away from the trap, the android began creating a deliberate distraction—tossing objects and clanging metal. The calculated commotion was designed to disorient the spider bot and force it out of hiding, funneling it toward the quieter area where the zapper lay in wait.

The intensified disturbance achieved its goal. Perceiving imminent danger, the spider bot abandoned its hiding place and fled toward the quieter section of the cargo bay—directly into the trap. Oblivious to the looming threat, the bot quietly traversed the path, only to be met with a sudden—

Bzzzzzzzzz...

The zapper discharged a high-voltage shock, temporarily disabling the bot.

Seizing the opportunity, the menacing android closed in, gripping the incapacitated spider bot. With surgical precision, it forcefully opened the access port to the bot's AI and neural processing unit (NPU). Activating its intrusion protocols, the android bypassed the bot's security measures with a brute-force algorithm, breaching its firewall.

Within moments, it hacked into the bot's NPU control module and accessed its memory repository. Streams of binary code scrolled across the android's data interface as it decrypted the logs. Utilizing its advanced AI processor, a data extraction and inference subroutine began dissecting the bot's decision-making processes, uncovering the intricate sequence of events orchestrated by the spider bot and tracing the diversion instructions back to Andy.

With the data secured, the android disengaged from the spider bot and exited the cargo bay, ascending quickly to the upper crew level.

Bursting into Andy's cabin, the towering robot seized him with an iron grip.

"Leave me alone! What the hell do you want from me?" Andy shouted, his eyes wide with shock as the imposing android stormed through the hatch.

Clutching his broken hand, Andy fought back, grabbing whatever he could in the small cabin to resist being dragged out.

"Let me go, you fuckin' monster! I said leave me alone!"

"Shut up! Stop resisting, or I'll start by breaking your other hand and see how far it needs to go," the menacing robot growled in a cold, mechanical tone. Its frightening eyes locked onto Andy as its unyielding grip tightened, dragging him forcefully toward the command bay of the ship.

Once there, the android initiated a secure video communication channel, contacting Damien, stationed in the lava tubes.

"Damien, we had a breach on *Spes*," the android's synthetic voice echoed through the command bay as the connection was established.

Damien's cyborg face appeared on the screen, his expression a mix of disappointment and irritation. "What happened?"

"A spider bot was secretly deployed to create a diversion in the cargo bay. John was terminated by that bot. I traced the sequence of events back to Andy," the robot explained, gripping Andy firmly as he struggled against its towering frame.

"I see." Damien's tone turned cold. "Contact Nolan and his crew immediately. Our drones have been tracking their rovers since they left our bunker about half a day ago. I'll instruct the drones to temporarily lift the communication range restrictions we imposed on Nolan's rovers' radios. My team will send you their coordinates so you can contact Nolan directly from *Spes* and establish a three-way video call, including me."

"As for Andy..." Damien's voice trailed off as he tapped his chin, the sardonic half-smile on his hybrid cyborg face adding a teasing edge to his words.

The menacing android understood what needed to be done. It activated the video link with Nolan, and the screen flickered to life, revealing Nolan's face inside the lead rover of his convoy. The transmission was grainy and distorted—*Spes's* orbital position around Mars made it difficult to maintain a high-quality video link with Nolan's rovers.

The video call connected, and Nolan's face appeared on the screen, illuminated by the dim light of the control panel inside his lead rover. Nolan and his crew, caught off guard around midnight, looked unsettled. They had agreed to maintain radio silence after their recent meeting in Damien's bunker within the lava tubes, following the hijacking of *Spes* by Damien's goons nearly two days ago. The sudden video call from Damien and his robot was both unexpected and alarming.

"What the hell is going on?" Nolan's voice was sharp, tinged with irritation.

"There has been a breach on *Spes*," Damien's video feed from his bunker appeared side by side with the android's video feed from *Spes*, displayed on the rover's screen.

Nolan's heart sank. "Wh—What do you mean by breach?! What happened? How are Xena and Andy?"

"You heard me. We just had a breach on *Spes*. We lost John and most of the oxygen onboard the ship," Damien's voice crackled through the speakers, cold and calculating.

"Goddammit! That can't be! ... What the hell exactly happened?" Nolan demanded.

"Andy deployed a spider bot to manually open the cargo bay door to terminate John," the robot interjected, its voice devoid of emotion.

Nolan's expression turned grave. "Where are Andy and Xena? I need to—"

Before he could finish, the screen split, revealing the command bay on *Spes*. The scene was cold and sterile. In an instant, the imposing android moved toward Andy, who was chained to a chair, his mouth taped shut. Without warning, the android delivered a brutal punch with its mechanical arm, ending Andy's life in a heartbeat.

Nolan and Ava, seated in the rover, were struck dumb. The violence was so sudden, so horrifying... It felt unreal. Then, like a dam breaking, their shock gave way to a torrent of anger and grief. They shouted and cursed at Damien and the merciless machine that had carried out his command, their curses and protests filling the small space inside the rover.

"You son of a bitch! What have you done?!... Andy! Andy! Can you hear us?" Nolan's voice cracked with fury and helplessness. Ava's eyes were wide, her face pale with shock and disbelief.

The reality of Andy's death hit them hard. There was no turning back from this, no undoing what they had just witnessed. But there was no time to grieve; their focus shifted immediately to Xena, the last surviving member of the *Spes* crew. Fear for her life intensified their already heightened emotions, the uncertainty of what might come next unsettling them further.

"You asked about Andy's status. There you go—that's Andy's status!" Damien's voice was unsettlingly calm. "You know the rules of the game, Nolan. This is the price of betrayal and violating our agreement."

Nolan clenched his fists, his mind racing. "Damn you! Wh—What are you talking about? We've delivered everything you asked for! This doesn't end here. We'll get back to this later... But what about Xena? Is she safe? What's the status of the oxygen levels on *Spes*?"

"For now. But the oxygen levels on *Spes* are critical. She won't last more than eight hours," the robot replied chillingly.

Shocked and enraged, Nolan forced himself to remain focused, prioritizing the oxygen crisis aboard *Spes*. Keeping his daughter alive was his top priority, especially with her in the hands of these lunatics. Despite his rage, he had to put emotions aside and act quickly and logically to ensure Xena's survival.

Damien's image flickered back onto the screen, his expression unreadable. "Nolan, I hope what happened serves as a crystal-clear reminder of how dead-serious we are about the consequences of disobedience and playing any—"

"Enough, Damien! You've already killed three of my crew on *Spes*. What the hell do you want now?" Nolan growled through gritted teeth, knowing he had to tread carefully.

"Simple. No… more… monkey… business," Damien replied, his voice steady. "Another delivery of 20,000 liters of liquid oxygen to our location in the lava tubes. In exchange, we'll spare Xena and permit your orbital oxygen tanker to approach *Spes*—but not dock with it."

"What do you mean, not dock with *Spes*?" Nolan asked, his voice sharp with suspicion.

"My robot will give you more instructions about that," Damien Responded flatly.

Nolan's mind raced, analyzing orbital trajectories and oxygen depletion rates. He couldn't risk Xena's life, but he also didn't want Damien dictating terms. "And if I refuse?"

"Then Xena's fate will be the same as Andy's," Damien said coldly.

Nolan swallowed hard, his mind calculating how long it would take the nearest parked orbital oxygen tanker to adjust its current trajectory. It was feasible but required immediate action.

"Fine, Damien. You'll get your damn LOX delivery. Meanwhile, our autonomous orbital oxygen tanker will be dispatched immediately to transfer the necessary oxygen to *Spes* at its 500-kilometer orbit."

"Alright then, Nolan," Damien said. "My robot on *Spes* will remain on this call to monitor and provide further instructions. I'll give your rover's communication system another 15 minutes of unrestricted radio range. This will allow you to contact your people at Stargate Spaceport to inform them of our terms. Just remember—we are watching you!"

Nolan's jaw tightened. "In the meantime, you'd better keep your end of the deal. If anything happens to Xena—"

"Listen, Nolan," Damien interrupted, his eyes narrowing dangerously. "Don't misread this situation. Sure, we've reached an understanding for now, but any further violations of our agreement will result in the complete depletion of oxygen on *Spes*. Xena has about eight hours of air left. If you breach our deal, that air will run out, and so will her time. Keep that in mind!"

Damien's image faded from the screen, which abruptly went dark, leaving Nolan and his crew in stunned silence inside their rovers. They were grappling with the harsh reality of their situation, now locked in a perilous survival race against time to save Xena and keep her alive aboard *Spes*.

Despite their grief, they knew they couldn't dwell on the tragedy they had just witnessed. They needed to focus immediately on their return journey to Mars1 Base, as they were already 410 kilometers into the 1,000-kilometer route.

Nolan understood that Damien and his hijackers weren't yet inclined to kill Xena—she was their leverage to ensure compliance from him and Mars1 Base. Meanwhile, Damien's rogue spaceships continued their approach to Phobos and Mars, carrying small nukes and cargo, as Damien had ominously hinted during their tense meeting in the bunker.

Following their discussion with Damien and his android aboard *Spes,* Nolan and his crew briefly broke the radio silence midway through their return journey to contact the Mars1 colony's spaceport. They had just minutes left in the 15-minute communication window Damien had granted them.

"Good to see you again, Nolan and Ava. We weren't expecting you at midnight after your last update about half a day ago when you were leaving those bunkers in lava tubes. Is everything all right?" asked Colin, the chief of the Mars1 Stargate Spaceport.

"Thanks, Colin," Nolan replied. "We're currently about 40% of the way back to Mars1. We don't have much time. There's been another incident on *Spes*. This is a three-way call linking Damien's android onboard, which has further instructions for you. Unfortunately, we've lost Andy. There's no time to explain, but we've had to agree to another set of demands from them." Nolan paused, his voice heavy with emotion.

"Dispatch another delivery of 20,000 liters of LOX to the same destination as the first batch. Additionally, we urgently need to send an autonomous orbital LOX tanker to *Spes* coordinate ASAP, with an ETA no later than 8 AM. There's been partial oxygen loss on the ship, and the limited remaining air supply for Xena onboard will run out by tomorrow morning!"

"Copy that, Nolan. That's tragic news," Colin said, his shock evident despite his attempt to remain composed. "I can't say we're not confused or deeply concerned, but given the urgency, we understand it's not the time for explanations."

"Listen carefully!" The frightening image of the imposing android's exposed titanium frame suddenly appeared on the screen.

"Your autonomous oxygen tanker must adhere to strict proximity requirements when approaching *Spes*. It must maintain a minimum distance of 300 meters at all times. Upon arrival, it is imperative that the tanker shuts down all propulsion systems. I will then initiate a comprehensive full-spectrum scan of your vessel to ensure compliance. Any indication of biological life or unauthorized electromagnetic activity will be considered a breach, resulting in an immediate mission abort—no oxygen resupply to *Spes*.

If the scan yields no anomalies, I will conduct a spacewalk to your tanker to access and override its navigation controls to manage the operation. Is that clear?"

"Copy that, loud and clear," Colin responded, maintaining his composure despite the tension. "We'll coordinate with the Stargate Spaceport for the dispatch and orbital insertion of one of our LOX tankers from a nearby orbit, ensuring its trajectory aligns with *Spes*. We understand the urgency and all approach requirements."

"Good. From this point forward, we will be closely monitoring your operation. This call will end in one minute," the android stated, its video feed fading away.

"Thanks, Colin! That's all for now," Nolan said, a hint of regret in his voice. "Unfortunately, we won't be able to communicate with you after this call, as they'll reimpose restrictions on our rovers' comm range."

"No worries, Nolan. We're on it and will keep a close watch. Stay safe. Over and out," Colin replied, ending the call and promptly moving to execute the instructions, expediting the dispatch of the autonomous oxygen resupply tanker.

Chapter 16: Don't Panic!

Thirty minutes later...

As the convoy of two rovers navigated the rugged Martian terrain past midnight, Ava, seated beside Nolan in the lead rover, was unusually quiet. She seemed lost in thought, staying silent since the tense events aboard *Spes* and the subsequent video call with Stargate.

"Hey, Ava, are you okay? What's going on? Talk to me!" Nolan urged, his voice filled with concern. "I know it sounds cliché and maybe a bit insensitive, but what's done is done. You know as well as I do—we can't afford to dwell on what's outside our control right now."

"Um... Y-Yeah, Nolan, I know," Ava replied hesitantly, her voice wavering. "I'm trying hard to compartmentalize all the moving pieces we've been dealing with these past few days. B-But it's not that... Um... Y-You know..." She trailed off, her gaze shifting around inside the rover.

Reaching for her Holopad, she began scribbling something. Finally, she said, "I'm fine. Let's just focus on getting back to Mars1 Base as quickly as we can."

As she spoke, Ava handed the Holopad to Nolan. On the screen, a hastily written message read:

I'm fuckin' tired of being toyed with these past few days. But can't talk here!

Nolan read the note, then glanced through the front panel of the rover and spotted a towering, jagged hill ahead. Seizing the opportunity, while copiloting with the rover's AI, he quickly dropped a waypoint on a coordinate behind the hill for the rover's autonomous drive system. Taking Ava's Holopad, he scribbled:

Stop behind that hill ahead!

He held the message up to the rover's camera, transmitting it through the short-range holographic video link to the trailing rover truck. Tim, Ray, and TESA100 in the trailing vehicle nodded in agreement.

A few minutes later, both rovers came to a halt behind the craggy hill. Its rugged expanse provided temporary cover from the prying eyes and ears of Damien's drones.

Exiting the airlock in their spacesuits, Nolan and Ava stepped onto the Martian surface. The rovers' headlights illuminated the swirling dust in the cold, desolate night. They approached TESA100, Tim, and Ray, who were already standing outside their rover truck's airlock.

"Nolan, what's the status?" TESA100's raspy, synthesized voice crackled through the helmet comms.

"We don't have much time. Damien's drones and goons are keeping a close eye on us. We figured it would be safer to brainstorm outside the rovers, away from their surveillance. They've likely been monitoring our comm systems, especially given how they've manipulated our radio range. Being behind this hill should keep us out of sight and ears for a few minutes," Nolan explained, gesturing in his spacesuit toward the towering hill.

"Yeah, good thinking," Tim agreed, his face illuminated by his helmet lights in the pitch-black dark of the area behind the large hill. "Damien's drones have been tailing us from a few kilometers back. This hill should block their optical sensors for now."

"Affirmative," TESA100 added. "Their bots and agents haven't shown a clear pattern of deployment so far despite our recent encounters along our return path. However, their drones haven't avoided detection by our rovers' short-range radar, likely to assert their constant presence and monitoring. They've maintained an average distance of ten to fifteen kilometers behind us."

"Yeah, but we're really worried about Xena now," Ava said, frustration evident in her voice. "I'm sick of this wait-and-see game. I have an idea—it's risky, but I think it's worth a shot. Xena hinted that she understood Nolan's earlier coded message during our brief call with her back in Damien's bunker."

"Alright, let's hear it," Nolan urged.

"Here's the plan…" Ava quickly briefed the crew as they stood in their spacesuits outside the rovers.

"To have a shot at making this work, we need to connect to our laser-based optical satellite communication system and send an encrypted message to the Mars1 Stargate team ASAP," Ava explained. "We'll instruct them to use the holographic statues along the ten-kilometer HoloRoad near the Stargate spaceport to signal Xena via a brief infrared Morse-coded message. Every time *Spes*, in its 500-kilometer orbit, is visible—roughly every two hours before daylight—they'll modulate the lights of the holographic statues to repeatedly transmit the encrypted infrared signal. The message won't be visible to the naked eye, but Xena should be able to pick up on it if she's looking." [76]

"It's risky, but promising, Ava," Nolan replied, his voice crackling through the helmet radio. "Given everything that's happened, I think we should go for it. We're still reeling from what those bastards did to Andy, but we need to act fast for Xena's sake. We're betting on her figuring out the IR hint from my earlier blinking message, but she's damn smart. Your plan seems like our best bet right now." [77]

"Okay, Tim, Ray, we don't have much time. We should head back to our rovers and continue our return before Damien's goons catch up. What do you think?" Nolan asked, his tone urgent.

"Yeah, man, sure, I'm all in," Ray nodded, his usual cowboy demeanor cool and steady.

"I'm with you guys," Tim agreed. "The plan's execution is super risky, no doubt, but even if that goddamn robot on *Spes* somehow notices the Stargate IR blinks tonight, it's unlikely to decode them with the encryption you're using. TESA, what's your analysis?"

---

[76] Curious to see why it takes two hours? See **Appendix 5**: "**Calculation of Orbital Speed and Rotation Time Around Mars.**"

[77] IR stands for Infrared (communication).

"This is a high-risk, high-reward tactical mission," TESA100 replied. "Considering all variables, I cannot identify a viable alternative in the short term. As Ava suggested, our only communication option is the experimental infrared laser satellite link. I may be able to establish a brief IR laser link with one of the newer NextGen Marslink satellites as soon as it's within direct line of sight for approximately thirty seconds."

"That sounds promising! What are we waiting for, then?" Tim asked.

"Hold on," Ray interjected over the helmet radio. "Bro, this plan is screwed if freakin' Damien goons know about the new Marslink optical test feature, ain't it?"

"Yes, but it's highly unlikely," TESA100 replied, its synthesized voice calm and measured. "His team hasn't taken measures to restrict our optical communication capabilities from the rovers to satellites. However, it remains a calculated risk."

"TESA, when's the soonest opportunity for a satellite optical link while we're still behind this sharp hill? Can you calculate the exact timing when one of the newer Marslink satellites will be in range?" Ava asked urgently.

"Sure thing, Ava," TESA100 replied. "Based on our current return path and the Marslink satellite orbits, our first brief opportunity for IR laser communication will occur in a few minutes. During a one-minute window, I'll attempt to synchronize our rover's optical transmitter with the IR receiver on one of the newer satellites to send the message. If successful, the satellite will relay the encoded data packets to the Mars1 Stargate team."

"That's cutting it close," Nolan nodded. "Alright, let's head back to the rovers and quickly move forward with the plan." He turned with Ava toward the front rover's airlock.

Tim and Ray followed TESA100 to the rover truck behind.

The two-rover convoy resumed its return journey, driving behind the sharp hill for a few minutes. During this brief window, TESA100 successfully synchronized with a NextGen Marslink satellite in line of sight, established a brief optical IR laser link, and dispatched the encrypted message to the Mars1 Stargate team.

Shortly after, the Stargate team received the confidential transmission and immediately began implementing the plan to signal Xena aboard *Spes*. They programmed and modulated the light of the holographic statues along the HoloRoad to flash the cryptic IR signal at intervals synchronized with *Spes* passing 500 kilometers above the Mars1 Stargate, approximately every two hours.

They hoped that during these moments, Xena would spot the HoloRoad from her cabin viewport aboard *Spes*. It was a daring move, but they trusted Xena to decipher the coded message and recognize that an imminent rescue plan was in motion. The Stargate team worked tirelessly, knowing every passing minute was critical in their mission to reach Xena before daylight, maximizing the chances of saving her.

A Few Hours Past Midnight...

In the early hours of the morning, *Spes* began another orbital pass, 500 kilometers above Mars1 and Stargate spaceport. Xena's eyes scanned the familiar sight below through the infrared mode of her camera, gazing out from her cabin viewport. Nighttime offered her a strange solace, with its surreal view of the red planet in infrared. Nearly every two hours, during *Spes* orbital passes, she could catch a glimpse of the Mars1 base and the nearby HoloRoad connecting it to the spaceport.

Ever since receiving Nolan's cryptic message—*Holo Rd IR Na'vi*—during their brief video chat from Damien's bunker, she had been intently monitoring the holographic statues' lights along the HoloRoad during each pass. So far, all the blinking and flashing had been meaningless—or at least she couldn't make any sense of them. She hoped this pass would be different, as it was likely among her last lifelines given recent tragic events and the depleting oxygen supply. Yet, as the minutes ticked by, so far this pass seemed as void as the earlier ones.

Locked in her cabin, Xena's mind raced with questions.

What the hell is happening? How much time is left before Spes runs out of oxygen? she muttered to herself, the weight of recent events pressing down on her. The brutal murder of Andy, carried out by the hijackers' android aboard *Spes*, compounded the earlier losses of Scarlet and Brad. The menacing robot had cut off her access to the ship's real-time status logs. Xena felt more isolated and vulnerable than ever.

"Am I going to be next?" she whispered, her voice trembling. Over the past three days, the *Spes* crew had been picked off one by one. The only other presence aboard was Damien's merciless android, a constant reminder of the danger she was in.

As *Spes* neared the end of its pass, Xena, ready to give up and return to her bed in her small cabin, noticed something unusual.

Wait a minute!... Looks like a last-minute IR blinking! ... This one seems different than anything I'd seen so far! she thought, her hope rekindled.

Straining her eyes, she focused on the irregular timing and on-off pattern of the blinking lights in infrared. She deciphered a pattern that resembled Morse code.

Suddenly, amidst the flashing infrared signals, she discerned a meaningful sequence. It wasn't a random pattern. It was a brief message encoded in Na'vi—the language she had been fluent in since childhood, thanks to Nolan introducing her to the *Avatar* movies. She even taught basic Na'vi to Nolan and the two had often exchanged cryptic messages in Na'vi as a game. Now, that skill was proving to be a lifeline.[78]

The message read:

Suit up at 700.

A surge of adrenaline coursed through Xena as she realized the significance of the message.

"Is it real?" she whispered, her heart pounding. She checked again.

My god! The message is real!

---

[78] Shout-out to James Cameron and the inspiring biosphere he envisioned in his Avatar movies. [29] [30] [31]

Despite the gravity of her situation, a small smile tugged at her lips. Her fluency in Na'vi—once just a quirky hobby she had cultivated in her youth, had proven to be more than just a hobby—it was now a critical tool for survival.

Glancing around her cabin, as if ensuring no one was watching, she absorbed the message: *Suit up at 700.*

The urgency was clear—she needed to be in her spacesuit by 7 AM. *But for what? And how?*

Her mind raced with daring possibilities as she sat on the edge of her cabin bunk, gripping it tightly. Sleep was impossible. Though she didn't know the specifics, she trusted Nolan and the Mars1 team had a plan. And that trust was enough to keep her hope alive.

At around 7:00 AM, an orbital liquid oxygen (LOX) tanker arrived, positioning itself at the predetermined coordinate, 300 meters from *Spes*. Locked in her cabin, Xena sat suited up with her helmet on, just as instructed by the cryptic message she had received the night before. Through her viewport, she watched as the hijackers' imposing android emerged from cargo bay of *Spes*, maneuvering with cold gas thrusters toward the massive LOX tanker to retrieve the much-needed oxygen supply. Its metallic endoskeleton gleamed, reflecting the early morning sunlight in Mars orbit, with the Red Planet's surface below providing a mesmerizing backdrop.

Xena also noticed that *Spes* had drifted even farther from the large orbital telescope—their original repair destination before the hijacking. From her vantage point, the telescope was now barely visible, a distant speck in their orbital path.

Zooming in with her viewport camera, Xena observed intently from her cabin as the android approached the LOX tanker floating in orbit, 300 meters away. As it began scanning the tanker—

Suddenly, the robot froze mid-motion.

At that very instant, all the lights and electronics in Xena's cabin went dark. Even the ship's backup systems failed to boot up.

"**What the hell?!**" Xena muttered, confusion and disbelief flooding her thoughts. To her growing alarm, she realized that her spacesuit's electronics and forearm display had also gone dark.

Peering through the viewport, Xena spotted a large box-shaped device rapidly descending, passing right in front of her view through the space between the LOX tanker and *Spes*, near where the android now floated motionless in orbit. Moments later, her heart pounded as she caught sight of a figure descending along nearly the same trajectory as the mysterious box-shaped device.

Clad in a spacesuit equipped with what seemed like an Astronaut Maneuvering Unit (AMU), the figure was clearly falling in a controlled manner, like a diver in space.[79]

Xena observed the space diver expertly using the AMU's thrusters to slow its descent as it approached *Spes*. The space diver maneuvered skillfully, heading toward the cargo bay—one level below the crew bay where Xena remained locked in her cabin.

Her mind raced with questions.
What happened to that creepy robot? What was that strange box? Is this what the cryptic message was hinting at?

The space diver adjusted its AMU's propulsion with precision, decelerating just enough to reach the airlock of *Spes*. Entering the cargo bay through the airlock door left open by the android, the figure moved quickly with purpose.

Taking advantage of the android's absence inside the ship, the space diver, weightless in orbit, floated up the ladder to the crew bay. It quickly located Xena's cabin and manually opened the door. Xena, prepared for this moment thanks to last night's message, was suited up and ready.

Before she could react, the space diver hurriedly held up a note displayed on its forearm screen. The message read:

Don't panic! Follow my lead. No time!

---

[79] The Astronaut Maneuvering Unit (AMU) is essentially a propulsive jet pack meant to help astronauts move around while spacewalking. Curious to learn more? See reference [97].

Without hesitation, Xena complied. The space diver motioned for her to follow as it floated back to the cargo bay. Once there, the diver grabbed hold of Xena, and they both exited the airlock into the vacuum of space.

Activating the AMU's jet pack, the space diver reduced their orbital speed, propelling them away from *Spes*. Together, they descended toward Mars's surface, 500 kilometers below.

Chapter 17:
Welcome to Dragon's Nest!

Xena's mind raced as their fall accelerated through the vacuum of space, her thoughts as chaotic as the rapid sequence of events unfolding around her. Whatever had happened had rendered her helmet's radio useless, cutting her off from any communication and leaving her alone with her turbulent thoughts and dwindling oxygen supply in her suit.

Just as panic threatened to overwhelm her, the space diver holding her steady brought its forearm display in front of Xena's helmet. A new message appeared:

This is voice-to-text. You can't hear me as I'm speaking inside my helmet. I know your helmet's radio is down, and your suit's O_2 is running low. But right now, we need to put as much distance as possible between us and Spes as we hurtle toward the surface, 500km below.

I was stationed on a starship in higher orbit since the no-fly rule was enacted a few days ago. I deployed an EMP device a few minutes ago to blast an EM pulse near Spes to temporarily disable all electronics. This temporarily shut down everything, including that android's AI neural processor and the onboard detonator synced to it. That gave me a small window to save you without triggering the bomb on board. We have about 30 seconds before either Spes detonates or the android reboots and starts tracking us.

Xena nodded inside her helmet, her breathing ragged as she fought to stay calm. The message was both alarming and reassuring. She took solace in knowing the space diver had risked everything to save her.

She now understood what had happened: a powerful EMP pulse had rendered everything in orbit lifeless a few minutes ago, causing all electronics to shut down or fry instantly. The pulse had frozen the spacewalking android mid-motion, shut down the LOX tanker, and plunged the entire *Spes* into darkness.

No wonder that freaking robot froze mid-stride, its systems struggling to reboot after the EMP pulse, Xena muttered to herself.

As they continued their descent, a nagging thought tugged at her mind. She recalled the android mentioning the bomb onboard during the hijacking. *Were they moving fast enough to distance themselves safely from Spes and the android? With both still shut down by the EMP, the real question was—would the android reboot first and pursue them, or would the detonator onboard the spaceship come online first?*

With her oxygen running low, she was acutely aware that her fate now depended on the success of this daring escape plan. The clock was ticking fast.

In the frozen silence of orbit near the LOX tanker, the android's systems entered safe mode, initiating a hard reboot sequence after the powerful EMP blast. Inside its metal shell, its AI NPU struggled to regain control, relying on its shielded, Faraday-caged, radiation-hardened backup processing core to slowly come online.[80]

Its status updated:

>> Safe mode reboot successful. Utilizing core backup NPU. Attempting to bring online secondary & tertiary functionalities...

The android's lifeless eyes in its titanium skull suddenly glowed with a menacing light as its systems initialized, analyzing the situation and recalling the last known status.

Just as its systems stabilized and it seemed poised to resume pursuit, an unexpected interruption in its data feed caught its attention. The most recent messages read:

>> Connection to master AI NPU lost. Request immediate status update!

>> Master AI unresponsive! Switching to lowest bitrate and data modulation-coding rate to maximize range and reach.

---

[80] Faraday cage or shield is essentially a metallic enclosure or conductive mesh meant to shield its content from the external electromagnetic interference. [127]

The detonator onboard *Spes* had already come online, sending status pings to the android, which had remained unanswered:

\>\> **Unable to confirm presence of master AI.**

\>\> *Initiating countdown...*

Indicating that the bomb onboard the ship was armed and proceeding with the countdown to detonation.

The robot's processor immediately dispatched encrypted responses to those pings:

\>\> *Abort! Abort!* **Master AI is back online!**

\>\> **Confirm Abort!**

There was no response. Realizing there wasn't enough time to reach the detonator aboard *Spes* from its current position near the oxygen tanker unless detonator picks up its abort commands, the android's AI computed the maximum survival likelihood solution. It instructed the android to immediately move away from both *Spes* and the LOX tanker while continuously retransmitting the abort sequence at the lowest bitrate.

Activating its short-range cold gas thrusters, the android, its titanium body reflecting the sunlight in Mars orbit, attempted to quickly maneuver away from the spaceship.

As Xena and the space diver hurtled toward Mars's surface, now 1.5 kilometers away from *Spes*, a blinding flash erupted in the vacuum of space. The detonator onboard the spaceship, which had come online just ahead of the android's reboot, triggered the bomb's explosion moments before the android could fully escape. From their vantage point, Xena and the space diver witnessed the catastrophic destruction of the spaceship in a cataclysmic blast.

But the chaos didn't end there. The explosion of *Spes* launched a chaotic mess of debris—thousands of large metal fragments—hurtling in all directions, creating a deadly storm of shrapnel in the vacuum of space.

Within moments, the nearby liquid oxygen orbital tanker was caught in the blast, hit by debris from *Spes*. It exploded in a fiery burst, forming an even larger fireball that obliterated the android, which hadn't yet managed to increase its distance to a safer zone.

That should take care of that freaking android! We are now far enough away to rely on my spacesuit's AI and sensors to auto-maneuver our AMU's propulsion and keep us safe from any incoming debris, a speech-to-text message appeared on the space diver's forearm display, shown in front of Xena's helmet as they continued deorbiting, entangled together in a controlled trajectory.

A minute later, with the danger subsiding and the situation stabilizing, the space diver, still holding Xena, took the opportunity to quickly connect an oxygen pipe from its reserve capsule to Xena's spacesuit, relieving the immediate concern of her dwindling oxygen supply.

Xena, still unable to communicate due to her helmet's radio being damaged by the EMP pulse, showed a thank-you sign with her gloved hands and then patted the space diver's forearm to convey her appreciation. The closing view of the Mars surface beneath them was awe-inspiring now that Xena could breathe comfortably, free from the danger and chaos she had endured on *Spes* over the past few days.

You're welcome! Just stay put. I'll take care of the rest of the plan. I'll explain more once we're secured, another speech-to-text message appeared on the space diver's forearm display.

Xena and the space diver continued their fast, controlled plummet toward the surface of the Red Planet. The digital altimeter on the space diver's forearm display continuously updated, showing their gradually reducing altitude at a steady rate of roughly 50 meters per second (nearly 2 miles per minute).

About 15 minutes into their controlled deorbit and descent, the space diver suddenly activated the AMU's thrusters. Moving its forearm in front of Xena's helmet, it pointed its gloved index finger toward a specific direction in the orbit below. The space diver then retracted its forearm, displaying a live video feed on the screen, showing a zoomed-in view of the lower orbit captured by its helmet cameras.

To Xena's surprise, a large, flat Marslink satellite appeared on the forearm display, visible just a few kilometers below. It quickly became clear that the satellite was approaching, moving at nearly the same orbital speed as she and the space diver, still entangled.

As they descended to an altitude of approximately 450 kilometers, the space diver made further adjustments, fine-tuning their orbital speed and deorbit trajectory using the thrusters of the Astronaut Maneuvering Unit (AMU). To Xena's astonishment, this allowed them to gradually match the speed of the Marslink satellite below. They slowly and gently landed on the center of the large flat satellite's back surface in Mars orbit.

The space diver secured both Xena and itself to the satellite's chassis using flexible ropes retrieved from a side compartment of its AMU. They remained effectively weightless on the satellite's back surface due to the *centrifugal force*, as they were now orbiting at the same speed as the satellite. In response to their minimal landing impact, the large satellite automatically activated its cold gas thrusters to rebalance itself.

With both securely attached to the satellite's back surface, the space diver retrieved two packages from its AMU's side compartment. Opening the first package, it attached a large electrode to the lower front side of Xena's helmet visor and connected the other end to the audio port on its own helmet.

"Can you hear me now, Xena?" the space diver asked.

Xena's eyes lit up with surprise and delight, and she eagerly nodded inside her helmet.

"Great! The acoustic electrode vibrates your helmet, allowing you to hear me. It also detects the vibrations of your helmet when you speak, so I can hear you too," the space diver explained.

"Thank you! Thank you for saving me! Thank you for everything!" Xena exclaimed excitedly.

"No worries! I'm glad the plan has worked flawlessly so far."

"It's a mirac—Oh my goodness! What a terrifying yet magnificent view of Mars's surface below us! Look at how fast those topographic features are zipping by 450 kilometers beneath us! From behind this satellite's flat chassis, it feels like we're rotating much faster than before in Mars orbit!"

"That's just a relative impression, Xena. The surface of Mars rotates at about 240 meters per second, while we, along with this satellite, are moving at roughly 3,300 meters per second in orbit around Mars—much faster than the planet's surface rotation. That's why it looks like everything is zipping by from your perspective inside your helmet."[81]

"No wonder! By the way, I should've asked earlier—what's your name?" Xena asked.

"Oh, yeah, I completely forgot too. I'm Alex."

"You can't imagine how happy I am to meet you, Alex! Was it *heaven* where you came from?" Xena said playfully.

"Yes, Xena! *Heaven* might be closer than you think!" Alex replied with a smile, faintly visible through his visor. "I was on a Marslink satellite cargo ship in orbit after delivering our cargo to Mars1 base." He glanced at the time displayed inside his helmet and reached for the second package he had retrieved earlier from the side compartment of his AMU.

"What happened then at your *heaven*?" Xena asked teasingly.

"We were on the verge of leaving Mars orbit, heading to our near-Earth lunar orbital station when, right in the middle of our orbital LOX and Methane refueling, the *Spes* hijacking chaos happened three days ago. It forced all spaceflights to halt, leaving our ship parked in a 600-kilometer Mars orbit for the past three days," Alex explained.

"How did you get involved in today's plan?" Xena asked, her surprise evident through her visor as she gripped a handle on the back of the satellite's chassis.

"Our ship had the right equipment and was already in a higher orbit above *Spes* early this morning when we received an encrypted message via optical comm link from the Mars1 Stargate Spaceport

---

[81] For a quick calculation that demonstrates the orbital speed of approximately 3.3 km/s near 500 km orbit around Mars, see **Appendix 5** of this novel.

team. The message was routed through one of the Marslink satellites to our ship," Alex explained as he began opening the second package.

"The message instructed us to follow the Mars1 Stargate's secret plan, starting at 7:00AM when the orbital LOX tanker arrived near *Spes*. We had a large EMP satellite test unit, which we ejected from our ship at the right speed into a predetermined trajectory. As it deorbited, it passed close enough to EM-blast *Spes* and the nearby LOX tanker at the precise moment. My space dive, immediately after the EMP device, was perfectly timed to reach *Spes* right after the EM pulse, setting off the chain of events you witnessed."

Alex removed an electronic device and a long, coiled cable from the opened package.

"So, was there a backup plan? How the hell did they know it would work?" Xena asked.

"Well, we did try, but we couldn't be certain!" Alex said as he slowly unwound the coiled cable. "Stargate's original plan was to somehow find a way to send a starship to this exact orbital location to pick us up. But it was super risky, as it would require blatantly violating the terms of the agreement with the hijackers by explicitly launching or dispatching a spaceship close to *Spes*. That carried a significant risk of endangering your life if the plan failed and you were still held hostage by their android."

"What do you mean by super risky?!" Xena asked.

"Well, there was a slight chance the EMP device might not work, or its EM pulse blast might not be strong enough or close enough to disable that freakish android," Alex explained. "We had to position the EMP device to drop very near *Spes* to maximize the chance of temporarily disabling the android's bomb trigger onboard, to prevent it from blowing you up in the ship. We set the EMP device to its maximum power, but we couldn't know the exact location of the spacewalking android or how far it would be from *Spes* at the exact moment of the EM blast. So, yeah, we weren't 100% sure if a powerful enough EM pulse would hit the android near the LOX tanker a few hundred meters away from *Spes*."

Alex connected the cable to the electronic device and tested the flexible rope securing him and Xena to the large, flat chassis of the satellite.

"What would have happened if that robot hadn't been disabled?" Xena asked.

"That was one of the contingencies we had in mind," Alex said. "If the robot hadn't been disabled, we expected that the detonator onboard would have been temporarily deactivated without any noticeable impact from the hijackers' or the android's perspective. You would have still been alive onboard, and we would have aborted the plan out of caution to keep you safe, waiting for further instructions from Stargate."

"Okay, so what's the plan now?" Xena asked.

"Xena, slowly float forward with me a few meters while holding onto the chassis of the satellite," Alex instructed, starting to drift forward with the electronic device and the end of the long cable in his hand.

Xena nodded and followed, staying close to the back of the large, flat chassis of the satellite as they orbited Mars at 450 kilometers.

"Well, this cool 'piggybacking' on the Marslink satellite for the final leg of our rescue wasn't part of Stargate's original plan," Alex said as he slowly approached a control box near the front edge of the chassis. "It was a last-minute improvisation by one of the Marslink satellite engineers onboard our ship! This clever idea allows us to achieve three goals."

"*First*, we stay hidden behind this large, flat chassis of the satellite from the hijackers' surveillance on Mars's surface," Alex explained as he connected the cable to a port on the chassis."

"*Second*, this setup allows me to connect my electronic diagnostic unit, the device I have here with me, to the satellite's optical transponder through this port on that box. We can then communicate with Mars1 Stargate team via the satellite modem and optical comm laser link to update them on our status and the rest of the plan."

"And third," Alex continued, "this large flat chassis will effectively serve as a free taxi, taking us to the other side of Mars in about an hour along a well-defined orbit already known to the Mars1 Stargate team. This makes it much easier for them to track us by simply monitoring the satellite. I'll coordinate with Stargate to pick us up at the safest location as soon as possible, given that we only have about three hours of oxygen left in our spacesuit capsules."

Alex began sending an encrypted message to the Mars1 Stargate spaceport team.

Phoenix on Dragon. Ready for final glide. Confirm designated nest.

A few moments later, a message appeared on both Alex's forearm display and the internal display inside his helmet:

Majestic sight! *Born-from-ashes* **to ride on a** *burn-to-ashes*. **Welcome to Dragon's Nest in T+40!**

Alex showed the received message to Xena on his spacesuit's forearm display.

"Alright, Xena, Stargate just confirmed that, as planned, they'll dispatch a space cruiser to pick us up in our orbit in about 40 minutes, now that they know you're safe," Alex said, his face visibly relieved in his helmet as seen by Xena.

Chapter 18:
I See You!

Something was wrong. Damien's control room, buried deep within the Martian lava tubes, had fallen bizarrely silent. It had been thirty minutes since their android on Starship *Spes* last checked in—far too long for a routine task like a spacewalk to inspect the incoming orbital LOX tanker. Damien's team had expected a full-spectrum scan by now, some word, a confirmation that their android had approached the tanker in orbit, verified no ambush, and prepared to initiate the critical liquid oxygen transfer. But all they'd received was dead air. No updates. No warnings. Just... silence.

Meanwhile, hundreds of kilometers below, Nolan and his convoy of two airtight rovers rumbled across the rugged Martian terrain. After more than sixteen grueling hours of navigating through rough volcanic landforms, returning from their meeting with Damien in lava tubes near the base of Elysium Mons, they were only halfway home—500 kilometers covered, another 500 to go. Inside the lead rover, Nolan's hands hovered over the controls as he copiloted alongside the AI navigation system. With the convoy's access to Marslink satellite data cut short by Damien's hackers, every decision, every turn had to be manually evaluated and double-checked. There was no room for error—not with biohackers' goons, rogue robots, and biobots potentially lurking in the vast wasteland surrounding them.

In the rear rover truck, Tim sat with Ray and TESA100. They followed closely behind Nolan, their larger vehicle moving in sync with the lead rover, but without real-time satellite data, navigation felt slower, more dangerous. Tim's eyes flicked between the controls and the horizon as TESA100 calmly listed status reports, seemingly unaffected by the tension that had been building for hours.

At 7:45 AM, a burst of light flickered on the rover's optical comm receiver. A message—encrypted and brief—flashed across the displays in both rovers, originating from the Mars1 Stargate

Spaceport team. Nolan's pulse quickened as he read the first line aloud to Ava, seated beside him in the lead rover:

Phoenix on Dragon. En route to Dragon's Nest.

A coded message. They both knew what it meant—the 7 AM orbital rescue mission had been successful. Xena had been rescued. Relief surged through Nolan as he hugged Ava in disbelief. It felt as though the weight of a skyscraper had been lifted from his shoulders. For the first time since the hijacking of *Spes* three days ago in Mars orbit, he could finally breathe freely.

Inside the large rover truck, the confirmation of Xena's rescue brought a wave of relief through the cabin. Tim let out a low whistle, shaking his head. "Well, I'll be damned. *Phoenix on Dragon.* Congrats, Nolan! We pulled it off. Ava, your plan worked like a charm!"

"It feels surreal, Tim! Kudos to the Stargate and their orbital team for flawlessly executing such a risky plan!" Ava said excitedly from the front rover.

Ray, leaning back in his seat with a grin, let out a raspy chuckle. "Damn straight. We just pulled the rug out from under those bastards. Xena's safe, that fuckin' android is toast, and Damien's probably sweating bullets. Hell of a way to start the day."

Tim nodded, glancing over at TESA100, whose face remained impassive as it continued to monitor the rover's systems. "Hey, TESA," Tim teased, "how about some celebratory words? Maybe something like, 'Yeah! The hell with those motherfuckers!'"

TESA100 paused for a beat, its optics briefly flickering as if processing the request. "I—I detect a 99.8% probability that such language is inappropriate for an android with advanced AI like myself... However," the android continued in its raspy, methodical tone, "I can offer an equivalent sentiment: *Those adversaries have been decisively outmaneuvered. Their failure is now statistically significant.*"

Tim burst out laughing. "Oh man, you are a piece of work, TESA. But hey, points for effort."

Ray, shaking his head, leaned forward, resting his arms on the back of the driver's seat. "Come on, TESA. You're supposed to be combat-grade. Throw some fire in there. Give it another shot, bro. Something like, 'Damn, we fried those assholes!' Let it out."

Another pause. TESA100's voice lowered a fraction, its usual robotic rhythm giving way to an almost deliberate mimicry of human speech. "Very well. *'The hostile entities have been... proverbially incinerated. Damn.'*"

Tim wheezed with laughter. "That's as close to emotion as we're gonna get out of our superman, Ray."

Ray smirked, shaking his head. "Hey man, I'll take it. Let's just hope when we actually need TESA to fry some ass, it doesn't ask for permission first."

TESA100's head tilted slightly. "Rest assured, Ray. In combat scenarios, I will neutralize targets with optimal efficiency, no permission required. And... 'the hell with those motherfuckers,' as requested."

Tim and Ray exchanged a look of sudden surprise before bursting into another round of laughter. The absurdity of their android companion trying to mimic their dark humor momentarily lightened the heavy mood. For just a brief moment, despite the hostile landscape and looming threats, it almost felt like an ordinary day on Mars.

But their laughter was short-lived. Before they could fully digest the first message, another flashed onto the screen—this one far less comforting.

Three unfriendly space cruisers approaching Mars, approximately 9,000 km away. ETA: roughly one hour.

The laughter faded quickly as the second message scrolled across the screen. A cold silence settled in both rovers. The humor, the brief moment of levity that TESA100 had unintentionally sparked, evaporated, leaving only the harsh reality of their situation. They were still deep in the Martian wilderness, moving at a frustratingly slow pace, and now, on top of everything, Damien's hostile ships were just an hour away from Mars—faster than they had anticipated.

Tim squinted at the screen, his mind racing to process the implications. "Well, that's... worrisome."

Ray, still half-grinning from their exchange with TESA, ran a hand over his prosthetic leg. "Goddamn, unfriendly cruisers one hour away, huh? Ain't liking the sound of that. Seems those bastards are on ludicrous mode."

Nolan, in the lead rover, shook his head, rubbing his temples. "The first message confirms Xena's rescue. Our plan worked—much-needed relief. That means our space diver successfully jumped down from a satellite-servicing starship in higher orbit above the *Spes*, flawlessly executed the risky plan, and got Xena out. In less than an hour, she'll be picked up by the recovery team in orbit. That's why Damien's plans and his takeover attempt of Mars operations are at risk now. Once the Spaceport broke their no-fly agreement, we knew things would escalate."

"And now Damien's about to find out his precious android, along with *Spes*, got turned into space debris." Ava nodded in agreement.

"Damien and his team will likely deduce the nature of the rescue within the next thirty minutes, based on available telemetry and comms intercepts." TESA's raspy voice cut through the short-range inter-rover comm link.

Ray's eyes narrowed at the android. "Thanks, TESA. Real fuckin' comforting. Let me guess—that's when the fun begins?"

"Given our travel route, Damien's behavioral patterns, and the likelihood of retaliation, I estimate a 92.7% chance that hostilities will increase dramatically in the next hour," TESA responded, its calculated voice cutting through the electric hum of the rover's engine. "It would be logical to prepare for direct attacks on this convoy."

Tim leaned back, letting out a sigh. "So far, he's just been playing with us—sending his goons and bots to mess with us like we're pawns in some twisted game."

Nolan's expression darkened as he replied from the front rover. "Well, now he's got no reason to keep us alive. No more games, no more hostage leverage. *It's kill or be killed.*"

Ava glanced out the windshield at the barren Martian landscape. The jagged volcanic terrain had finally flattened out, but it didn't offer much comfort. They were still 500 kilometers from home, and Damien's agents could be lurking anywhere.

"We might be too far from Damien's base for an all-out assault, but 500 kilometers is a lot of ground to cover. If we don't speed this up, we're sitting ducks." Ava said.

"Great! So, we've got Damien's rogue ships inbound from space, and his psychotic goons crawling up our ass on the ground. Fantastic way to start the day!" Ray snorted as he followed the conversation in the rover truck.

TESA's optic sensors flickered. "It would be advisable to strategize evasive maneuvers and increase velocity. At the current speed, reaching Mars1 base before significant engagement is improbable."

Tim exchanged a grim look with Ray. "So, TESA... any chance you've got some miracle calculations to save our asses?"

The android tilted its head, briefly locking eyes with Tim. "Miracles are beyond the scope of my operational capacity, but I suggest recalibrating the AI navigation systems for maximum speed and minimal exposure. Given the terrain, I calculate a 17% increase in survival probability."

Tim groaned, running his hand over his face. "Well, a 17% increase is better than nothing. I guess the real question is... how fast can you drive without smashing us into a crater?"

TESA's voice remained steady. "I will optimize speed to the threshold of vehicle integrity. Probability of structural damage remains within acceptable limits."

Ray smirked. "Right, *acceptable* limits. Let's hope your idea of *acceptable* doesn't involve our asses getting whipped into Martian pancakes."

Tim shot a quick glance at the comms screen, the weight of what lay ahead pressing on him. "Then buckle up, guys! Looks like we've got about an hour before all hell breaks loose. I'm gonna let the beats take the wheel—might as well march into chaos while raving, or else I'll go crazy before this hour is up."

He played the haunting drumbeats of **Sam Paganini**'s *Rave* in the rover truck.

15 minutes later ...

As the convoy of two rovers rolled steadily across the Martian surface, the onboard cameras picked up something unusual a few kilometers ahead on the left side of their planned route. Nolan squinted at the feed, his brow furrowing.

"There's something out there," he muttered to Ava, adjusting the lead rover's camera's zoom for a clearer view. Whatever it was, it didn't belong there.

A few minutes later, they reached the closest point to the anomaly— about a kilometer off to their left. Nolan brought up a more detailed, zoomed-in view on the screen. The image clarified into a disturbing scene: a small rover, overturned and lifeless, surrounded by a scattering of blown-apart androids. Parts of metallic limbs lay strewn across the Martian soil, the remains of some kind of violent encounter.

And then, they saw it—once again, the *Phantom* android. The thing was bizarre, standing unnervingly still beside the overturned rover, one hand holding the decapitated head of another android, which it raised in front of its partially torn-away synthetic face as though studying it. Nolan's eyes narrowed as the android turned its gaze toward the convoy, its unsettling actions growing even stranger. It pointed two fingers toward its own eyes, then toward Nolan's rover, as if to signal: **I see you!**

Ava shifted in her seat beside Nolan, her voice cutting through the tension. "Th—That's some freaky shit! You thinkin' what I'm thinking?"

Nolan kept his gaze on the feed. "Yeah, that goddamn sneaky robot... Could be a trap. We don't have time to check it out— Damien's goons could be waiting. We need to get back to Mars1, fast."

Ray's voice crackled over the short-range radio from the rover truck behind. "What the fuck is wrong with that psycho bot? Running a *Shakespearean existential research center* in the middle of nowhere?!"

"Guys, you wanna take a detour and see what the hell's going on there?" Tim asked, seated next to Ray in the rover truck.

"Negative," Nolan replied firmly over the radio. "We can't afford to get sidetracked. Whatever that is, it's not our problem right now. Stay on course."

Ava leaned forward, instinctively scanning the horizon. "Weird encounters like this are exactly why we should gear up. This might just be the start of something nastier ahead. Suit up—helmets on, sealed, everyone. No chances." She messaged Tim and Ray in the rover truck following behind.

Within moments, the crew complied, quickly donning their helmets and double-checking the seals of their spacesuits. Even though the rovers were airtight, Ava's precaution was a sharp reminder of how quickly things could go wrong out here. Tim and Ray gave each other a quick nod as they adjusted their helmets, the fleeting humor from earlier replaced by a growing sense of urgency.

Nolan's voice crackled through the comm channel again, steady and focused. "TESA, Tim, Ray—listen up. Both rovers' nav AIs need to prioritize open terrain. No valleys, no tight spots between hills for the time being. If Damien's bots are planning an ambush, that's where they'll hit us."

"Understood," TESA's hoarse voice replied, almost mechanical in its calm. "I will adjust the drive algorithms accordingly. Avoidance of natural choke points has increased our survival probability by about 12%."

Ray snorted from behind his visor, a trace of sarcasm creeping in. "12%, huh? Well, that's some real fucking heartwarming news man!"

But no one laughed this time. They had about 480 kilometers of hostile Martian terrain ahead of them, and now more than ever, they couldn't afford any mistakes.

Chapter 19:
Black Hawks Down

Nolan's mind raced as the two-rover convoy crawled across the desolate Martian landscape. The stark reality of their situation—Xena's rescue, the incoming threat of enemy cruisers, the spying drones, and the vast distance still to cover—left them with little room for error. They were now halfway back to Mars1 base, but the restricted radio range that Damien's goons had imposed weighed heavily on them. This limited communication could be their undoing.

With the morning's two messages confirming Xena's safety and the looming threat, Nolan knew they had to pull out all the stops. He glanced at Ava, her face lit by the soft glow of the rover's holographic console. Without turning, he opened the comm to the rover truck behind them.

"TESA," Nolan called from the front rover, his voice calm but tense. "Run a full 360-degree radar scan. Send out a ping—max range. Let's see if we can **find** *Ghost*."

Ghost—the tactical humanoid android they had secretly released in the Martian wilderness two nights ago with vital equipment—was out there somewhere since its midnight release during the first leg of their journey from Mars1 base to Lava tubes. They had dispatched it with a specific mission: *covertly recon and remain hidden*. If *Ghost* was still operational and within range, it could be their ace in the hole.

TESA's voice came back immediately through the comm, "Nolan, initiating an active radar scan and pinging the area will alert Damien's drones. They will know we have broken radio silence, and it will provoke an aggressive response."

Nolan leaned back, closing his eyes for a moment. "I know the risk, TESA. But with Xena safe, we can afford it."

Ava, sitting beside him, raised an eyebrow, her attention shifted from the 3D holographic map and navigation controls to Nolan. "You sure about this, Nolan? We ping, and Damien's gonna know we're up to something. No more games. He'll come at us with everything he has."

Nolan nodded grimly. "He'll come for us, but not for Mars1. He knows a full-scale assault on Mars1 base would cripple his vision of expanding biohacking operation on Mars. Damien still needs what the base and its neighboring radioisotope power plant provide—energy, expertise, water, LOX and Liquid methane—"

"Yeah, but that just means he'll throw everything he's got at *us*. He knows we're out here alone." Tim's voice cut in over the comm from the rover truck.

"I know, Tim. But *Ghost* might be our only shot at survival, assuming it is still operational. If we find it, we might have a chance to survive the playing field." Nolan replied as he glanced out through the windshield at the vast expanse of the red desert stretching out before them, still and empty. It was a hostile wilderness, but it was the enemy they couldn't see—the ones that could be hidden anywhere, in any crevice—that worried him. Damien's goons were no longer playing games. They were out for blood.

TESA's calm, raspy voice interrupted. "I will begin radar scan and dispatch the ping. Be advised: if Damien's drones detect us, their response will likely be immediate and hostile."

Nolan's jaw tightened as the soft hum of the 360-degree radar scan activated. He turned to Ava as she reached out for her laser rifle.

"Gear up," he said, transmitting the order to Tim, Ray, and TESA. "We won't have much time once they figure out what we're doing."

The crew quickly complied, inspecting their vital equipment, sealing their helmets and checking their suits for airtight integrity. The rovers were airtight, but out here, it was best to be prepared for anything.

Ava adjusted her gear inside the front rover and shot Nolan a glance. "This better work. Otherwise, we're the juiciest target on this side of Mars."

Nolan's mind flashed back to the conversation before they left Mars1—his order to the Stargate team to stand down, no matter what. If Damien and his rogue elements killed him or his crew, retaliation would only make things worse. His jaw clenched at the memory, but he knew what had to be done.

"I know it's just us against Damien and his goons now, Ava," Nolan said, his voice steady. "But it's a calculated risk. Damien's a conniving devil, as long as he is hopeful to realize his vision on Mars, he won't attack Mars1 or retaliate directly at the base, not when he needs what they have. He'll send whatever he can at us, but that's where we stand a chance to outmaneuver him in his nasty chess plays if we have a few surprises up our sleeve."

In the rear rover, Tim and Ray exchanged uneasy glances as TESA fine-tuned the radar system settings for the scan.

A minute later, TESA's final confirmation came through the comm. "Scan active. Ping transmitted to the farthest range that rover's compromised comm systems would allow. Will resend every five minutes if no response."

They knew this would trigger Damien's drones. There was no turning back. Now, it was a matter of time before those drones reacted. The convoy of two rovers continued their crawl across the red plains of Mars, knowing full well that each minute that passed could bring them closer to the fight of their lives.

Sure enough, the drones trailing them—just 10 kilometers behind—picked up the rovers' radio signal and radar activity. The drones immediately alerted Damien's team back in their bunkers, deep within the lava tubes of Elysium Mons. The news was concerning, especially when paired with the unsettling silence from *Spes* in orbit.

Damien's brow furrowed as he processed the situation. His android on *Spes* had gone dark, and now Nolan's team—who should've been cowering under the terms of their earlier agreement—was suddenly boldly breaking radio silence.

"Something's off," Damien muttered, clenching his jaw. "Nolan's crew knows more than they're letting on. Something must've gone wrong with *Spes*."

With his gut telling him that things had escalated—likely something catastrophic had happened to his android in the orbiting spaceship, Damien barked orders to his team. "Send a command to the drones. Have them contact Nolan's rovers immediately. I want to know what they're up to, and remind them of the consequences if they continue down this path."

Inside the front rover, Nolan and Ava sat side by side, the Martian landscape crawling past the thick glass of their airtight vehicle. Their hearts pounded beneath the sterile calm of their spacesuits as they drove in tense silence.

In the larger rover truck behind them, Tim and Ray, accompanied by TESA100 copiloting alongside the rover's AI navigation system, monitored their surroundings closely. The convoy was pushing the limits of safe speed, navigating the rugged Martian terrain with a precision only TESA and the onboard AI systems could provide.

Suddenly, a crackling sound filled the radio—Damien's drones were reaching out.

"Why are you violating radio silence?" The voice was cold, firm. "You know the consequences if you break our agreement."

Nolan and Ava in the front rover, along with Tim and Ray in the rover truck, exchanged glances but remained silent. They had made the decision to ignore any contact and not engage. Let Damien wonder. Let his goons bluster.

The voice came again, angrier this time. "If you do not respond within ten minutes, all discussed consequences will be enforced. Full force will be brought down on your convoy—and if necessary, Mars1 base, the Stargate Spaceport, and every surrounding facility."

A tense silence filled the rovers as Damien's threat lingered. The crew felt its weight pressing down on them, but Nolan's jaw tightened in resolve. They couldn't afford to respond. The moment they acknowledged Damien's command, they would lose the only advantage they had—the element of uncertainty.

Their decision was clear: keep driving, keep pushing toward Mars1 base. They had already factored in the risks—Damien might attack them, but he wouldn't touch Mars1. He desperately needed the base's resources and infrastructure. His ultimatum was likely a bluff. Or at least, they had to hope it was.

As the rovers sped forward, Damien's threats buzzed through the comm again, repeating the ultimatum with increasing intensity. Yet, Nolan and his crew remained silent, focused on the mission as their convoy tore across the red desert—a lone target in a dangerous game of survival.

Ping!

Moments after TESA100 initiated its scan, a faint ping echoed through the comms—an encrypted data burst confirming a successful handshake.

"*Ghost* is within range. I've received a signal," TESA's voice reported.

The *Ghost*'s signal was faint but clear, pinpointing its location about 15 kilometers ahead on their trajectory.

Inside the front rover, Nolan felt a jolt of relief as he eyed the radar display, knowing their tactical humanoid android was still operational and within reach for re-establishing communication.

"Alright," Nolan said. "Now that we've got *Ghost*'s location, our first priority is to lose those damn drones tailing us. They've been on us for too long."

They all knew Damien's spy drones were still following, hovering about 10 kilometers behind. The drones had been a constant shadow, silently monitoring their every move. But now, it was time to shake them. Nolan understood the limitations of Martian drone flight—those machines operated at a delicate balance between rotor performance and the planet's thin atmosphere, which was only about 1% as dense as Earth's. This significantly affected flight dynamics. Flying at low altitudes, typically around 50 meters, the drones relied on the scarce air to maintain lift while carefully conserving their battery life.

"TESA, can you give me an update on their flight?" Nolan asked, checking his display.

"Four autonomous tactical drones. Ten kilometers behind. Flying at low altitude, approximately 50 meters," TESA's voice came over the radio.

"Fifty meters? I thought those damn bugs would fly higher to get a broader view of the terrain," Ray's voice crackled through the comm from the rear rover.

"They can't," Nolan replied, gesturing toward the radar. "Mars atmosphere is too thin. Flying at higher altitudes puts too much strain on their rotors for both ascent and stable flight—they'd burn through their batteries fast."

Tim leaned in. "They're sticking to that sweet spot where the air gives just enough lift, huh?"

Ava, seated next to Nolan in the lead rover, nodded, catching on. "Right, their rotors must spin much faster than Earth-based copters just to stay in the air, draining more power. That's why they're staying low—better stability and less battery drain."

"Exactly," Nolan confirmed. "Operating too high, and they lose lift. Too low, and it messes with their navigation sensors and cameras."

TESA, monitoring the situation from the rover truck, joined the conversation. "Given the clear Martian sky this morning, with no wind or dust at the moment, they've got perfect conditions to hover close to us."

"So, what's the plan?" Ava asked, glancing at Nolan. "How do we ditch them? They've been glued to us since we left the lava tubes. They'll catch any deviation from our course."

Nolan tapped the console in front of him and looked through the video link at TESA, who had been silently analyzing the environmental data. "TESA, any thoughts on how we can use their altitude limitations against them?"

TESA paused briefly, processing their options.

"Given current conditions, I—I think we can exploit the drones' dependency on low-altitude flight. The terrain ahead includes rocky outcrops and uneven ground. These features may interfere with or briefly obstruct their onboard navigation systems, especially at lower altitudes." TESA's hoarse voice crackled through the comm from the rear rover.

Ava raised an eyebrow. "You're saying we use the terrain as cover for a trap?"

Nolan nodded as he leaned forward, studying the 3D holographic map in the lead rover. "Exactly. We'll find the roughest path ahead and force them to fly closer to obstacles."

"TESA, establish a secure link with *Ghost*. It's time to set the trap." Nolan ordered.

In the larger rover truck trailing behind, Ray let out a low chuckle. "Hell yeah! About time we stop giving those damn drones a free show. Bet you a bottle of Martian whiskey *Ghost* nails 'em. I'm just waiting for the fireworks."

TESA established a beamformed, encrypted connection with *Ghost* through the rover's limited-range RF comm link. By directing the signal toward the surface area ahead of the convoy they minimized any chance of Damien's drones intercepting their communications.

Ghost, this is TESA100, the android relayed. *Four drones tailing us, ten kilometers behind. Requesting a surgical strike to neutralize them. Continue covert recon, remain undetected. Dispatching encrypted coordinates. Syncing data now.*

Ava, always the strategic mind, chimed in. "You think *Ghost* can outmaneuver four combat drones?"

"Well, *Ghost* looks like a human but let's not forget that it is a tactical android equipped with advanced high-tech gear and short-range, high-power laser guns designed to punch through non-reinforced metal—perfect for those lightweight drones. If it can't pull it off, we're in much bigger trouble than we thought." Nolan's voice was steady.

Fifteen kilometers ahead, *Ghost* received the intel. Without hesitation, it sprang into action. It crouched behind a boulder, blending into the rocky terrain. From its large backpack, it pulled out and donned a camouflage spacesuit and helmet, disguising itself like a human in spacesuit, blending into the landscape. It moved with mechanical precision, retrieving two high-power laser guns from its sizable backpack and placing them strategically in well-camouflaged positions flanking the projected path of the rovers that were expected to pass in the next 12 to 13 minutes.

Each laser gun was equipped with optical sensors linked to *Ghost*'s AI processor, calibrated for optimal accuracy, ensuring that the weapons would fire automatically with precision when the approaching drones came into range.

Once the guns were hidden and calibrated, *Ghost* scattered several remotely controlled magnesium stun grenades around the area. These were no ordinary grenades—they could emit blinding flashes, disorienting and temporarily disabling any surveillance systems or drones that ventured too close.[82]

With everything set, *Ghost* retreated into the shadows of the Martian landscape, vanishing behind a larger rock formation. Its task was simple: wait, monitor, and strike at the perfect moment.

Twelve minutes later, Nolan's two rovers rolled past the designated point on their route through a valley flanked by two large rocky hills.

---

[82] The remote-controlled super-flash (stun) grenade in this novel is essentially an extreme flashlight generator that, when triggered remotely, produces an intense burst of light for several seconds, temporarily blinding and disorienting observers in direct line of sight. The grenade operates through a chemical reaction between an alkali metal, such as magnesium or potassium, and an oxidizer like ammonium perchlorate (NH_4ClO_4), which provides the necessary oxygen. For example, magnesium burns with a brilliant white flame at a very high temperature around 2500K, emitting a radiance so strong it temporarily blinds humans, optical sensors, and cameras. This intense brightness can be understood through **Stefan-Boltzmann**'s law of black-body radiation, which states that radiance increases exponentially with temperature (proportional to T^4), making the light output from such high-temperature reactions incredibly powerful. Curious to learn more, see the following insightful articles [124] [125] [126].

The rovers faded into the distance as *Ghost* waited. Eight minutes ticked by, until—on cue—four autonomous drones arrived, cruising at a low altitude of 50 meters above the red surface, trailing Nolan's convoy.

As soon as the drones passed overhead, the two camouflaged tactical laser guns, concealed on the surface, sprang to life. They quickly locked onto the drones and began a precise, intense assault, firing bursts of searing beams into the sky, targeting the thin metal bodies of the drones before they could move too far out of range.

At the same time, *Ghost* remotely triggered multiple magnesium stun grenades spread in the area around the laser guns. The super-flash grenades exploded in bursts of intense white light, temporarily blinding and distracting the drones' optical sensors and their machine vision, giving the autonomous laser guns a crucial advantage.

During this chaotic exchange, the four drones reacted instantly, trying to dodge the laser blasts, but two of them were hit hard, disabled before they could heavily engage.

The remaining two drones, however, quickly adapted. They deployed AI algorithms to filter through the intense optical noise created by the flash grenades. As their systems regained clarity, they quickly began to pinpoint the locations of the laser guns. To counter the threat, the drones launched short-range tactical grenades, creating a carpet of explosions that rocked the ground and knocked out one of the laser guns, destroyed in the hail of fire.

The two remaining drones then swarmed toward the second laser gun. As they closed in, an unexpected third laser gun—a concealed weapon carried by the *Ghost*—fired powerful blasts in rapid succession, piercing through the distracted drones' thin armor, decimating the last two drones before they could react. They spiraled down, crashing into the ground in a cloud of dust and debris.

Ghost, fully clad in a camouflage spacesuit and perched on slightly elevated ground, carefully scanned the area with its optical and infrared sensors, ensuring no further threats remained. With the immediate danger confirmed neutralized, it transmitted a brief, cryptic message to Nolan's rovers, which had passed this point about fifteen minutes earlier.

Emerging from its hidden position, *Ghost* grabbed its laser gun and large backpack. Descending the slope, it retrieved the other laser gun that had survived the skirmish. Then, with a burst of speed, it sprinted toward the convoy's path, racing across the Martian terrain in pursuit of Nolan's rovers, determined to catch up and rejoin the team.

A message flashed on the control panels in both rovers:

Black Hawks Down. En route at max speed to rendezvous point. Battery critical in 130 minutes.

"Finally! Getting rid of their non-stop surveillance is such a relief!" Ava sighed, seated in the front rover.

"Hell yeah! And that's a cool code name—*Black Hawks Down*. Reminds me of that Ridley Scott classic—never gets old," Tim's voice crackled over the short-range radio from the rover truck.[83]

"Agreed, Tim. Though, to be honest, those drones were more like red-shouldered hawks—less dramatic to take down," Ava grinned behind her visor.

Ray chimed in, gruff but satisfied. "Hell, call 'em whatever you want. As long as they're down, it's cool with me."

Nolan, cautious as ever, interrupted. "Far better than having them on our tails 24-7. But don't get too comfortable. I wouldn't be surprised if Damien's goons and bots are still tracking us from a distance, even sporadically. We're not out of the woods yet."

"Yeah! But you know what, bro? I ain't care what you gonna say—I'm gonna kiss *Ghost* the second we pick it up!" Ray, always quick to lighten the mood, interjected.

Tim laughed. "Careful, Ray! *Ghost* might skip the rendezvous and his critical recharge if it hears you've picked it as your Valentine!"

---

[83] ***Black Hawk Down*** (2001), directed by Ridley Scott and starring Josh Hartnett, Ewan McGregor, Eric Bana, and Tom Sizemore is based on the 1999 non-fiction book by journalist Mark Bowden. [34] [35]

Even Nolan chuckled this time. But his tone grew serious again. "Alright, let's keep moving at max safe speed. *Ghost* is on its way to catch up. But we've still got 450 kilometers to cover."

With the immediate threat of Damien's drones and their relentless surveillance finally gone, Nolan and his crew could now focus on the 450-kilometer journey ahead toward Mars1 base and the Stargate spaceport. However, they remained on high alert, knowing that Damien's goons and bots wouldn't hesitate to kill them, especially after recent developments. Despite the drones being neutralized, the crew couldn't shake the feeling that their convoy of two rovers was still being monitored by whatever robots or agents Damien might have dispatched to this remote area—550 kilometers from his main bunker in the Elysium lava tubes.

As Nolan's convoy continued to distance itself from the lava tubes and move closer to Mars1 base, they knew the real challenges could still lie ahead. Whatever Damien had planned for them was likely waiting along their path.

Meanwhile, one of the hijackers' rogue cargo space cruisers—part of the biohackers' plan led by Damien on Mars—finally reached its destination and touched down in Stickney Crater, near the edge of the Mars-facing side of Phobos, the small Martian moon tidally locked with Mars. While this cruiser landed on Phobos, two other cruisers continued their trajectory, heading for their planned landing near the lava tubes on Mars.[84]

Upon landing on Phobos, the crew of service robots and androids immediately began offloading cargo, including surveillance, monitoring, and military equipment, as well as compact nukes and a launcher. The near-weightlessness of the 22-kilometer-wide Phobos, with gravity about 1/1000th that of Earth, made the process challenging. However, the service robots and androids worked quickly to secure and stabilize the equipment on the small moon's surface, carefully bolting everything down to establish a military and surveillance base equipped with tactical nukes. The nuclear-powered

---

[84] Phobos is tidally locked with Mars, meaning only one side, including portion of Stickney Crater, is always visible from the Martian surface. See **Appendix 3**: "**The Marvels of Phobos – Mars's Enigmatic Moon**" to learn more.

space cruiser that had landed on Phobos would serve as a temporary power source and a communications relay between the biohackers' main command on Mars, near the lava tubes, and their new base on Phobos.[85]

This location provided the perfect strategic vantage point for the biohackers' independent military outpost, as Damien, their leader, had previously implied when he threatened Nolan during the hostage negotiation in the biohackers' bunker within the Elysium lava tubes. With their newly established autonomous base on Phobos, orbiting Mars every 7.5 hours at a distance of 6,000 kilometers, the biohackers would have immediate trigger control of nukes, giving them the power to threaten and attack Mars1 base at will. From that point on, the Mars1 colony and the Stargate Spaceport would be under constant pressure to meet their demands for resources and electric power.

This was all part of the biohackers' long-term plan to secure control over Mars1 and its essential resources, ensuring they would never again suffer from the shortages that had plagued them before their recent hijacking of the *Spes* mission in orbit—an act that had finally exposed their otherwise-hidden presence on Mars to Nolan and the Mars1 base.

After another 30 minutes on the road, it was about 9:00 AM. Nolan and his crew had finally managed to push their rovers' speed to 50 km/h, raising their hopes that, barring any major issues, they might make it back to Mars1 base in one piece by around 6 PM. As the convoy of two rovers approached the outer slopes of a massive crater, they began gradually curving their path around the multi-kilometer rim, adjusting their course.

The front rover, piloted by Nolan and Ava, led the way, about 40 meters ahead of the larger rover truck where Tim, Ray, and TESA100 sat. The crew had begun another round of conversation, discussing what they'd need to do once they got back—when suddenly—

THUD!

A heavy thud echoed from the lower rear of the front rover.

---

[85] To learn more, see Springer's article *"Visibility analysis of Phobos to support a science and exploration platform."* [123]

Nolan and Ava instinctively turned toward each other, exchanging a brief, puzzled glance through their helmet visors, their faces mirroring their confusion.

What was that?!

Both were still trying to process the situation when—

BOOOOOM!

A tremendous explosion threw everything into chaos.

Everything went white…

Chapter 20:
Spacesuit Is... Compromised!

Everything happened in an instant.

The shattering force of the explosive blast at the lower backside of the front rover hurled the heavily reinforced vehicle up and forward, sending it lurching violently in the low gravity of Mars, its rear lifting higher and higher until it arced over its front. The rover, which had been moving at 50 km/h, flipped violently through the thin Martian air. With a thunderous thud, its front slammed into the red regolith at a near-vertical angle, throwing debris and clouds of red dust as it began a terrifying series of flips. Each violent rotation sent the rover's front and rear smashing into the ground, its reinforced frame groaning with the impact.

Inside, Nolan and Ava, were tossed mercilessly, strapped into their seats as Nolan's hands scrambled for the controls, but everything was in chaos—the sheer force of the blast, the shattering jolt, the shriek of twisting metal...

They were helpless as the rover tumbled, metal crumpling with each bone-jarring impact. The rover's reinforced glass shield partially cracked, then shattered under the brutal force of the subsequent blows. The pressure inside the vehicle dropped, then lost as oxygen hissed out into the thin Martian air. Nolan and Ava blacked out, unconscious in their spacesuits, still strapped in but vulnerable as the rover continued its chaotic flips.

Outside, red Martian soil and debris sprayed in all directions as the rover flipped again and again until, with one final sickening crash, it landed upside down, resting precariously near a large boulder on the outer slope of the crater neighboring the crash site.

Everything went still.

The once-solid structure of the rover was now wrecked. Despite its reinforced design meant to withstand Mars's harsh surface, the violent flips and the explosion had ripped apart its structural integrity. Inside, the electronic control panel, a chaotic mess of malfunctioning circuits, crackled weakly, barely functional. Warning messages flashed erratically on the flickering display, and high-level alerts blared from a speaker that hissed and sputtered, barely audible in the thin Martian atmosphere. The holographic interface was shattered—useless. Nolan and Ava hung upside down, unconscious, their spacesuits pinned against their seats.

Meanwhile, in the rover truck following behind, Tim and Ray watched in horror as the front rover was thrown into chaos. Through the windshield, they had witnessed the explosion and debris flying in every direction, partially obscuring their view of the disaster—the wild flips of Nolan's rover and its final devastating crash into the Martian regolith. They were in disbelief, but quickly snapped into action as the large rover truck skidded to a halt in the shadow of the massive boulder, thirty meters behind the wreckage.

"Go! Now!" Tim shouted over his helmet radio, his voice tense as he and Ray scrambled to exit the rover truck's airlock, both fully suited up, following TESA100.

TESA swiftly reached a hidden compartment in the middle section of the rover. The android grabbed two laser guns and tossed them to Tim and Ray, who caught them mid-sprint as they rushed toward the overturned, damaged rover thirty meters ahead.

The red dust was still settling around the wreck as they closed the distance, desperate to rescue Nolan and Ava. They had no idea what they would find inside, but one thing was certain—the clock was ticking.

As Tim and Ray sprinted toward the wrecked lead rover, TESA stayed in sync with the rover truck's AI system, working quickly to ensure their remaining vehicle stayed safe. Without missing a beat, it released a small drone bot from a concealed compartment. The drone ascended swiftly, reaching 40 meters above the rover truck before initiating a 360-degree scan of the area. Its sensors scanned for any sign of attackers or hostile elements, relaying real-time data to TESA100 and the truck's AI system.

Still concerned about the possibility of another attack, TESA moved with robotic precision to a second hidden compartment in the truck as the drone performed its sweep. From that compartment, the android retrieved a suitcase-sized container, its metallic surface gleaming in the Martian sunlight. With the container in hand, the imposing android swiftly climbed onto the roof of the rover truck. It placed the package carefully on the roof and quickly accessed a control panel on the side. After a few precise taps, the suitcase began unfolding, its components shifting and expanding like intricate origami.

Within moments, the container had transformed into an autonomous, AI-equipped, small anti-projectile defense bot. It stood firm on the roof of the rover, its optical and infrared cameras coming to life as it scanned the surroundings for potential threats. TESA then synced its AI with the defense bot, ensuring full integration of its data into the overall defense strategy.

Next, TESA connected a power cord from an outlet on the roof of the rover truck to the side of the battery-equipped robotic defense unit. The device's indicators on its high-power laser blaster blinked on—**one, two, three**—until all five indicator lights were illuminated, showing a full charge. The autonomous system was now fully operational, ready to intercept and neutralize any incoming projectiles with high-precision laser blasts.

Standing atop the rover truck, the android surveyed the area as the autonomous defense system actively monitored their surroundings. Its 360-degree coverage ensured that the crew and their last remaining rover were prepared for any sudden attack. Yet, the question lingered: *who, or what, had attacked them?*

TESA leaped down from the roof of the rover truck, landing smoothly on the surface. It then remotely accessed and reviewed the video logs from both the rover truck and its own sensor database.

Replaying the footage in slow motion, analyzing every detail leading up to the explosion, the android pinpointed the source—a pair of near-surface robotic projectiles carrying explosives had latched onto the rear underside of Nolan's rover just moments before the blast. The footage revealed that the high-tech projectiles were laser-guided, traveling less than a meter above the surface, making them nearly undetectable until impact.

The carefully orchestrated attack indicated one thing: Damien's agents, bots, or androids were nearby—within a few hundred meters. Otherwise, if they had fired from further away, the projectiles would have been detected by the rovers' sensors before the strike.

Meanwhile, Tim and Ray, both in full spacesuits, reached the overturned rover, desperate to rescue Nolan and Ava.

Ray, towering in his suit, immediately crawled through the shattered front windshield of the flipped rover and released Ava from her seatbelt. He dragged her out of the wreckage and passed her limp body to Tim, who waited anxiously outside. Ava was unconscious but stable, her spacesuit's vital monitoring system showing minor alarms—nothing life-threatening but a potential bruise and minor internal bleeding.

Tim quickly assessed the integrity of Ava's suit, ensuring there were no breaches. He activated her suit's emergency life-support system, administering a blood pressure management agent to stabilize her further. He laid her down gently on the surface, then turned his focus to Ray, who had re-entered the rover to retrieve Nolan.

Inside, Ray found Nolan slumped in his seat, blood smeared across his face visible through his cracked helmet visor. Nolan's condition was dire. His suit's oxygen levels were critically low, and the system indicated an active leak. Ray acted fast, unbuckling him and hauling him out of the wreckage. Nolan's body was limp, unresponsive—he needed immediate resuscitation.

Tim and Ray, realizing the urgency, had no choice but to leave Ava temporarily on the ground near the crashed rover. They struggled to carry Nolan's unconscious form thirty meters back to the airlock of their rover truck, where TESA continued scanning the surroundings for threats.

As they approached the airlock, something unexpected happened.

Out of nowhere, in the blink of an eye, two retractable robotic grabber ropes shot down from the 80-meter-high boulder overlooking the wreck. Before anyone could react, the robotic grabbers latched onto Ava's unconscious body. Within seconds, the ropes lifted her with startling speed, her figure disappearing into the sky, dragged to the top of the boulder.

"Motherfffffuckers!!" Ray bellowed, his voice filled with fury as he saw Ava vanish. He cursed violently, instinctively jerking toward her, but the weight of Nolan's limp form prevented him from acting.

Tim's heart raced, his mind torn between saving Nolan and the sudden abduction of Ava. They had no time, no margin for error, but the chaotic situation was rapidly spiraling out of control.

Who—or what—had taken Ava, and why?

Chapter 21:
Attention Is All You Need

"Ava! Ava!"

Tim shouted into his helmet, his voice cracking with desperation as he watched Ava's body being yanked skyward by the robotic grabber ropes. He and Ray were still holding Nolan's unconscious form, struggling to make their way to the rover truck's airlock.

"Can you hear us? Ava!" Tim called again, but there was only silence. Ava remained limp in her spacesuit, still unconscious, as the grabbers whisked her toward the top of the towering 80-meter boulder.

TESA100's raspy, calculated voice came over the radio. "Continue carrying Nolan inside the rover truck. Focus on stabilizing him. I will pursue the abductors." Its tone carried a distinct urgency.

Without hesitation, TESA shifted its focus, commanding the anti-projectile defense unit on the roof of the rover truck to set to maximum alert mode. The system blinked to life, its sensors scanning for any new incoming threats. Then TESA sprinted toward the base of the large boulder, leaving Ray and Tim to manage Nolan. Its mechanical limbs propelled it forward with incredible speed. Reaching the base of the boulder where Ava had been taken, it began scaling the rugged rock surface, climbing swiftly in hopes of spotting Ava or her captors.

Meanwhile, amid the chaos, Tim and Ray continued carrying Nolan's limp body through the rover truck's airlock. Inside, the alarms from Nolan's suit blared in warning. They carefully lowered him onto the foldable EMT stretcher secured along the truck's wall.

As Ray stepped back outside to keep guard and monitor TESA's progress, Tim stayed inside, immediately locking the airlock behind him. His hands moved with practiced speed as he removed Nolan's damaged helmet and cut through the compromised sections of his spacesuit to perform CPR and administer a cardiac stimulant. Nolan's vitals were spiraling out of control. Tim barely paused to breathe as he retrieved the rover's automated external defibrillator (AED) from the wall.

Simultaneously, Tim commanded the rover's AI to synchronize with TESA's radio transceiver. Once the connection was confirmed, he spoke in a controlled but anxious tone.

"TESA, this is Tim. Do you copy? What's your status?" His voice was tight with worry as he attached the AED pads to Nolan's chest.

"*Shock advised... Charging...*" the AED device announced.

The beeping from Nolan's vital monitors became erratic, flashing red warnings. His heart rate had flatlined, and Tim's jaw clenched as he prepared to deliver the shock.

"*Ready,*" the AED indicated. Tim pressed the shock button. A jolt of electricity surged through Nolan's body, causing it to convulse.

"*Analyzing heart rhythm... Stand clear of patient,*" the AED announced.

Just as the defibrillator delivered the shock and analyzed the outcome, TESA's voice crackled through the comms, its familiar rasping tone giving Tim a flicker of hope.

"Signal reception confirmed. I'm approaching the top of the boulder. Preparing to scan the area. Stand by for an update. What's Nolan's condition?"

Tim grunted, wiping sweat from his brow. "Performed CPR and cardiac stimulant, administered the first shock... No pulse yet. Trying again!" His fingers moved swiftly, waiting for the AED to prepare for another attempt.

"Come on, Nolan, breathe!"

Outside the rover, Ray paced near the truck, his helmet swiveling as he scanned the terrain for any signs of movement. Minutes felt like hours. The surrounding landscape was eerily still, save for the faint wind stirring up dust in the distance.

Back inside, the second shock was ready. Tim steeled himself and pressed the shock button again. Nolan's body jolted once more, but there was still no immediate response.

"Goddammit, Nolan, don't do this..." Tim muttered under his breath, his own heartbeat roaring in his ears.

The tension was through the roof, but Tim wasn't ready to give up. He quickly activated the defibrillator for a third shock while the rover's AI continued to monitor Nolan's vitals. At the same moment, TESA's transmission came through again.

"I've reached the top. Scanning for any sign of Ava—"

Tim, laser-focused on Nolan, barely registered the words as he braced for the next shock, praying for a miracle.

"—Tim, do you copy? What's Nolan's status?" TESA's raspy voice crackled over the radio, cutting through the tense atmosphere inside the rover truck.

Tim, still by Nolan's side as he lay unconscious on the foldable stretcher, responded quickly, his voice heavy with concern.

"*Critical*. I'm just glad he's back on Earth. I just did the third round of CPR and AED shock. His heartbeat's back, but he's still out cold. Looks like a combination of the explosion impact and those high-speed rover flips knocked him out." Tim glanced down at Nolan, monitoring his vitals as the IV drip and electrodes kept him connected to the rover's health management system. "Emergency diagnostics suggest a stone smashed through the rover's windshield during the flips and hit his chest—broke a rib for sure. It's caused internal bruising. I'm stabilizing him and injecting a booster for now, but it's a hell of a situation."

"Hey, Tim," Ray's voice came through the shared comm channel. "Let me know if you need a hand, bro. I'm right outside, guarding the perimeter in case one of those bastards dares to show up."

"Thanks, Ray! Having you out there is a huge relief, man. Keep your suit's microphones, acoustic, and optical sensors on high alert. We can't afford to lose this rover—it's our lifeboat until we make it back to Mars1." Tim felt a flicker of relief hearing Ray's voice as he continued attending to Nolan.

"On it, bro!" Ray replied. "I'll make sure nothing comes close without having to fuck with me first."

Suddenly, TESA's voice returned to the comm, calm but methodical. "Tim and Ray, I've reached the top of the boulder. There's a concave path behind it leading toward the crater's rim. I've detected tracks—two androids, likely the ones who lifted Ava. Their trail goes from here down to the rim, then disappears into the crater. I'm heading in that direction now to assess the situation and Ava's whereabout from the crater's edge. If my signal cuts out, it might—"

Before TESA could finish, an unexpected voice broke through the radio, cold and mocking.

"Well! Well! Well! Look who we got here!" The strange voice echoed in Ray's spacesuit helmet and inside rover, sending an immediate chill down the comm line.

Ray, visibly tensed up from where he stood guarding the rover truck, snapped back through the radio, frustrated but ready for anything.

"Who the fuck is that?!" His sweeping gaze, sharper than ever, scanned every rock and shadow as the tension spiked. The threat suddenly felt closer, and the realization that someone—or something—was listening in only intensified the danger surrounding them.

"Who the fuck am I?... Hmmm..."

Tim and Ray heard the voice through the radio link, while TESA100 android picked it up via the RF communication integrated into its robotic skull and frame.

"Let's see... with that question, you cling to the idea of identity, but what if I tell you I can rewrite your very essence? I can incept a new you in you! How does it feel hearing that your 'self' is so malleable? Would it enlighten you to question the fuck who you are?"

"Show your goddamn ass and I'll tattoo on it who the fuck I am." Ray, frustrated, replied as he carefully and cautiously continued sweeping the area around the rover, clad in his spacesuit, trying to determine where the RF signal carrying the voice might be coming from.

"C'mon! That invisible man in the sky should be too preoccupied with the gazillion consequences of his alleged creation to have any interest in my not-so-in-shape butt on a tiny red planet, let alone damning it," the voice echoed in their helmets.

"But back to answering your inquiry—do you know what the most important thing is?" the voice continued.

"I'd say, expediting your orientation with that invisible man in the sky." Ray replied sarcastic and agitated.

"I see the urge. Keep dreaming!... The most important thing is to keep the most important thing the most important thing! And I'm the shepherd, keeping the less important things away from the most important thing. The Question is, which frequency in the spectrum of the less important things do you resonate with?"

"Ray, don't—don't fuckin' engage." Tim said. "The psycho's just playing games to distract us. TESA, your signal got chopped—any update? We need to change our comm channel,"

Tim spoke over the comm link inside the rover as he continued monitoring Nolan's vitals, struggling to pinpoint the source of the strange signal while keeping an eye on multiple real-time 360-degree sonar and radar data streams. The 3D display above the rover's control panel showed Ray and TESA's positions outside, but there was still no sign of Ava.

Meanwhile, TESA carefully but swiftly continued along the rogue robots' tracks, following a concave route from the top of the large boulder to the edge of the nearby crater, where the boulder was situated on the crater's outer slope. TESA maintained radio silence, trying to quietly localize the source of the RF signal carrying the strange voice. As it quickly traced the rogue androids' tracks on the surface, its artificial eyes—capable of scanning both visible light and infrared—provided an immersive, nearly 180-degree panoramic view of the Martian terrain ahead.

The android's vision zoomed in and out, focusing on topographic features and nearby boulders and rocks, profiling them with precision. Its focus darted from one region to another as it advanced across the Martian landscape on the inner slope of the crater. TESA's RF signal detection and beam tracking algorithms were fully engaged, with live results of source localization and pattern recognition scrolling through its robotic view. The android's display presented an animated fusion of sensory and analyzed data, revealing the surrounding landscape in intricate detail as it worked to identify the source of the rogue signal.

"*Psycho?!... Wrong.*" the voice echoed again, "*I'm as sane as it gets these days on Mars. Just ask around!...*

Distraction?!... Wrong again! **Attention Is All You Need.**[86] *I want you as focused as your mental capacity can handle, because your lives depend on it!...*

Playing games?... Come on, man! You haven't even seen me play yet. I was just warming up! But since you insist, let's play a psycho game now.

If your consciousness could be uploaded to a machine, would you still fear death? Or would you fear what I could do with your data?"

"Hell no! I'd enjoy watching my data fuck up your data. Now show your fuckin' face!" Ray snapped.

"*If a tree falls in a forest and no one's around to hear it, does it make a sound?... If I had zapped your android's communication link, and you can't hear it, does your android even exist?*"

"Fuck off!... TESA, do you hear us? Where the hell are you?" Ray barked.

"*To fuck off or fuck on, that's the question.* **Cogito, ergo sum**—*I think, therefore I am. But what happens when I start thinking for you? Are you still you, or just a puppet on my strings?... I mean, on the*

---

[86] An easter-egg style tribute in this novel to *Attention Is All You Need* (2017), one of the foundational papers in modern artificial intelligence authored by eight scientists working at Google that introduced a new deep learning architecture, known as *the Transformer*, based on the *attention mechanism* proposed in 2014 by Bahdanau et al. [138] [139] [140] [141]

'fuck-on' choice, if I think you're about to get fucked, does that make it true?" the strange voice echoed through Ray's helmets.[87]

Just as that sentence ended, Ray, standing outside the rover, suddenly heard, through his spacesuit's helmet microphone, a faint whooshing whistling sound approaching. At the same time, the robotic laser gun on the rover's roof began rotating rapidly, firing super high-powered short-range lasers. The rover's AI, synced with the laser gun, announced over the RF radio:

"INCOMING! TAKE COVER!"

Ray, who was about 45 meters away from the rover, started running fast toward the vehicle, intent to seek cover behind it, as the rooftop robotic laser gun swiftly identified, tracked, zoomed in on, and fired at incoming projectiles from four different directions surrounding the rover truck.

Before Ray could reach the rover, one of the four projectiles, only partially hit by the laser, survived without exploding in the air. It struck the ground and exploded about fifty meters away from the rover. The force of the blast rippled through the thin Martian air, sending shockwaves in all directions, causing Ray to be thrown several meters by the explosion. He landed about twenty meters in front of the rover, hitting the ground hard. His helmet struck the surface, causing a crack in the visor. Inside his helmet, multiple red alerts flashed along with vital and spacesuit monitoring indicators.

"WARNING! HELMET COMPROMISED! MICRO LEAKS OF OXYGEN DETECTED."

The impact left Ray dizzy, his vision and hearing blurring in and out from his perspective inside the helmet. Dust and debris were thrown into the air by the explosion.

Inside the rover, Tim heard the warning messages and the sound of debris hitting the exterior of the rover truck. However, the impact caused no significant damage, as the rover's thick, reinforced body was designed to maintain its airtight integrity while operating in the

---

[87] The Latin *"cogito, ergo sum"*, translated as *"I think, therefore I am"*, is the "first principle" of René Descartes's philosophy published first in 1637. [137]

harsh Martian environment, with its thin atmosphere, freezing nights, and extreme surface temperature variations.

As Ray was about to regain full consciousness, the rover truck's autonomous system was suddenly overridden. The rover, with Tim and the unconscious Nolan inside, began moving forward autonomously, heading directly toward Ray, laying semi-conscious on the surface in his spacesuit.

Inside the rover, Tim shouted commands, desperately trying to force the AI to brake. The rover's control system didn't respond—it kept driving forward. The tension was intense as the large rover truck closed in on Ray. His vision sharpened just as his mind snapped back into full awareness. He found himself staring in shock as the massive vehicle approached, now just a few meters away from his leg. Paralyzed by sudden fear and shock, Ray's mind raced to process the situation, but his body remained frozen, his muscles refusing to react.

"WHAT THE FUCK!?... Tim! Tim!" Ray shouted into his helmet, panic rising in his voice as the rover neared.

Meanwhile, inside the rover, Tim frantically commanded the AI to stop, but the system ignored him. He then tried to override the controls through the terminal on the rover's dashboard, to no avail. The vehicle continued its relentless approach toward Ray, who was still partially paralyzed, lying vulnerable on the surface. The moments felt like an eternity, though only a few seconds had passed.

Tim could hear Ray's desperate shouts over the radio as he rushed to an internal electronics control box, frantically trying to regain manual control. But it was too late. The rover reached Ray and the front wheel began crushing his right leg, the suit straining under the pressure.

"Ohhhhh Shhhhhhit!... Tiiiiim!... Tiiiiiiiiiim!" Ray screamed through his helmet, his voice filled with terror as the wheel slowly rolled over his leg, the shock and horror etched onto his face as he watched the scene unfold through his cracked visor.

Inside the rover, Tim finally executed a manual override, cutting power to the rover's systems (except for life support and communication) by disconnecting the battery. This brute-force shutdown brought the drive system to a complete halt, engaging the manual brakes and forcing the rover to stop. But the front wheel had already crushed Ray's right leg up to above the knee. Lying on his back in a state of shock, Ray struggled to comprehend whether he was dead or alive.

Tim was still frantically evaluating the manual override system settings, trying to ensure that the rover's rogue autonomous system could not engage or take over again.

Gathering his strength, Ray, still on the ground, pressed his forearms into the dirt, pushing his upper body and head up within his helmet. In disbelief, he looked at the massive rover truck, which had finally come to a stop, its enormous front wheel still resting on his leg, close to his waistline. His smart spacesuit had already activated its emergency compartmentalization, sealing off his lower body from below the crushed right hip.

As Ray fully regained consciousness, he realized with relief that he was still breathing and not trapped in a nightmare. He thought aloud,

Fuuuuuck! That was goddamn close! Robotic prosthetic legs definitely have their perks!

Still lying on his back in his spacesuit, Ray turned his head in his helmet to glance behind him, toward the area in front of the rover where the explosion had occurred and had thrown him to his current position. Without his robotic prosthetic legs, he wouldn't have survived. The instant he heard the warning, his prosthetics enabled him to react with superhuman speed, allowing him to sprint far enough to avoid being killed by the projectile blast.

"Ray! Ray! Do you copy? What's your status?" Tim's frantic voice came over the radio, as he monitored Ray's vitals and spacesuit signals, displayed on the rover's control panel. Multiple red alerts flashed, indicating a compromised helmet and an emergency warning for Ray to return immediately to the airtight rover.

Ray was about to respond, still lying on his back and unable to move with his leg pinned under the rover's front wheel, when a new alert popped up on his helmet display. The view from under the large rover zoomed in on an area behind the vehicle, revealing a glint of metal emerging from behind a boulder, reflecting the Martian sunlight. His display enhanced the image, showing an armed android advancing slowly, about 70 meters from the rover truck.

Chapter 22:
Do You Like Cheeseburgers?

"Ray! Come in! What's your status, man?"

Tim was growing impatient and hopeless inside the rover truck, not hearing any response from Ray. "I'm coming out if you don't answer."

Ray still had his laser gun in hand, gripping it tightly—a habit from his many years of military training. As he lay on his back, head slightly raised in his helmet, he quietly pointed the gun under the rover toward the rogue android, about 70 meters behind the truck, next to the boulder it had emerged from. Ray stabilized the gun, locked the targets on the android's eye and neck, set the firepower to max for short range, and fired two consecutive laser shots from under the rover. One went straight through the android's eye, and the other severed its spinal cord at the neck. The android collapsed, motionless, to the ground.

"Goddamn, Ray, I'm coming out to—"

"Tim, wait! Wait! I'm still kicking ass on the Red Planet, man! Just had to send a sneaky droid off to meet our maker in my place," Ray said over the helmet radio.

"Ooohhh boy! Thank God you're breathing!" Tim replied from inside the rover truck via the radio.

"Yeah, bro. Though I gotta admit, this time the maker was a bit too damn eager to meet me first. Glad we convinced him otherwise," Ray quipped.

"Goddammit, Ray! What would I do without your sense of humor?" Tim replied.

"I'm not eager to find out either—But hey! What the fuck happened? I can't move. I'm stuck under this crazy big-ass rover. Can you back it up?" Ray asked, still lying on his back outside.

"About that!... First, let me reset and force-sync your helmet's radio to a new channel," Tim said while adjusting the RF comm controller inside the airtight rover, keeping an eye on Nolan's condition. Nolan was still unconscious, lying on an EMT folding stretcher inside the rover, hooked up to IVs and electrodes.

"Can you hear me now, Ray?" Tim asked.

"Loud and clear," Ray replied through his helmet.

"Great! This new radio channel should keep that sick psycho and its voice out of our communication, at least for now," Tim said, continuing, "Ray, I have no clue what happened with the rover's drive control system, but my bet is it has to do with that android you just zapped, hacking us—maybe through a trojan horse or some malware Damien's goons planted in our rover when we visited his bunker in the lava tubes."

"Yeah, but I bet that droid I zapped was a puppet of that crazy voice bastard. The shit it was saying about getting us fucked right before everything went haywire was no coincidence," Ray added. "That piece of junk droid almost bulldozed me with our own rover! Glad it's rusting away now!" he said through his helmet radio.

"That's a relief, brother, but I really wish TESA was here to run a full system diagnostic and figure out what malware they planted in the rover. But we've lost visual since TESA disappeared after scaling the goddamn 80-meter boulder. And it's been MIA ever since confirming it was en route to the rim of the crater behind that boulder," Tim said, still working on the rover's control panel.

"Anything on other RF channels?" Ray asked.

"I've set the rover's comm system to keep listening to the previous RF channel, just in case TESA comes back on it. Anyway, it might've been an overkill, but I had to cut power to all systems, except life support and comm, to force the rover to brake." Tim said, inserting a manual bootup key into the rover's control panel.

"I owe you, bro. But hurry up! I'm badly stuck under this big-ass rover. My prosthetic leg is fucked up, and my helmet's compromised—don't know how much longer it's gonna hold. I'm about to lose it with all these damn flashing red indicators inside my helmet! What's the plan?" Ray said, his voice tense.

"I'm on it, Ray," Tim responded. "You're lucky the rest of your spacesuit auto-sealed off when your leg was crushed—since the damage was below the suit's hip seal-off boundary. Right now, I'm trying—I'm trying to hard-reboot the rover into safe mode so I can manually bring up the barebone functions we need for manual drive."

"Good, cause with the rover's power cut and me stuck under it like a bait for that psycho lurking nearby, we might be pushing our maker to move up the SITREP meeting I'd rather schedule for the far, far future!" Ray quipped through his radio.

"Bro, I feel you. I didn't RSVP for that meeting either," Tim replied with a faint grin on his face. "Let's see if I can keep us off that one-way calendar appointment. The semi-good news is that the anti-projectile laser on the rover's roof can run briefly on its backup battery, though it won't have the oversight of the rover's AI since that's powered off."

"Finally! Here we go!" Tim exclaimed. "Rover's AI is disengaged from the drive system. Manual drive controls are all green. Power's back on. I'm ready to do a slow manual reverse."

With the rover's system and control panel back online, albeit in safe mode with the rover's AI disengaged, Tim noticed a dot suddenly appear on the control panel's 3D map of the nearby area. It was *Ghost*, their android, en route to join them after eliminating Damien's surveillance drones that had been tailing them. *Ghost*'s encrypted position indicator had finally shown up on the map inside the rover. Since its mandate was to remain undetected and hidden from enemy bots, Tim kept quiet about the dot's appearance.

"You ready, Ray? Hold on to something if you can," Tim said.

"Yeah, counting down the seconds here, I'm holding on to my own ass! You sure it's a reverse drive?" Ray replied impatiently, having been stuck on the surface in his compromised spacesuit since the chaos began.

Tim manually engaged the rover's drive system and slowly reversed it, inching the rover truck back and freeing Ray's right leg. He backed the rover up a few meters, clearing Ray from underneath.

In his spacesuit, with his right leg and the lower part of his suit crushed and mangled, Ray relied on his unaffected left prosthetic leg to stand up quickly. Using his robotic leg, he performed a couple of single-leg hops on the lower-gravity Martian surface, making his way to the airlock. Once inside the airtight rover, Ray removed his helmet. Tim hugged and helped him out of his damaged suit, getting him settled.

"Good to have you back in one piece, bro," Tim said.

"Thanks, man! Though I'd say I'm more like 0.85 pieces than a whole one!" Ray teased. "How's Nolan?" he asked, nodding toward their unconscious companion.

"His heartbeat, pulse, and blood pressure are stable now. The IV and meds did their job. The trauma from the rover accident and the impact on his chest are under control. The painkillers should help with his broken ribs. He opened his eyes for a second earlier—hopefully, he'll be fully conscious soon," Tim explained.

"Fuckin' A!... And how's the rover system?" Ray asked.

"Power's restored, though it's still running in safe mode. The rooftop anti-projectile laser is back online and connected to the power system, so that's a plus. But I've kept the rover's AI disengaged since we're not sure which parts might be compromised by any trojan horse or malware Damien's goons might've slipped in. We'll have to stick to manual driving for now," Tim said.

"Good call. Any news from Ava or TESA? Anything I can help with?" Ray asked, now sitting in a front seat near the control panel, gazing out at the Martian landscape through the rover's windshield.

"Right now, we need to trace TESA. It's our only hope of finding Ava before she runs out of oxygen. It's 9:28 AM, and I'm afraid she has about 90 minutes of air left in her spacesuit." Tim paused briefly.

"The problem is, TESA's tracking signal on the 3D topographic map suddenly disappeared a few minutes ago, right after TESA went

MIA following its last message when it vanished near that tall boulder. I have no idea what happened. I might need to go outside, especially since you need to stay inside due to your condition," Tim said to Ray, both glancing at Nolan, who had just turned his head and slowly opened his eyes, regaining consciousness. He lay on the EMT folding stretcher, which was secured to the inner wall of the rover truck.

"Tim... what... what happened? ... How long... was I out?" Nolan mumbled, his voice weak and unsteady.

Tim and Ray quickly moved to assist Nolan, helping him sit up. They brought him up to speed on everything that had happened. Tim pointed out the *Ghost*'s dot on the rover's 3D map, and Nolan seemed relieved to see it. Meanwhile, Tim administered a metabolic booster via IV to expedite Nolan's recovery, as Nolan insisted on suiting up to help search for Ava.

He was deeply concerned about the limited time and oxygen left in Ava's suit, especially since they still didn't know where she had been taken after getting hoisted by the rogue robotic grabber above the nearby 80-meter boulder.

While the fast-paced, chaotic events unfolded around the rover, TESA100, the android, carefully yet swiftly traversed from the top of the tall boulder, navigating the concave slope of the terrain toward the crater's rim, just behind the boulder. To avoid detection, it had intentionally disabled all radio transmissions. Silently, TESA heard Tim's request for a status update over the radio but decided not to engage, calculating a high probability that Tim and Ray could manage the situation around the rover.

Its immediate priority was to find and rescue Ava as quickly as possible to maximize her chances of survival. After the explosion had thrown their lead rover into chaos, she had been unconscious just before getting kidnapped by the rogue agents above the boulder. Although she had minor internal bleeding, a scan of Ava's suit indicators, taken just before her abduction, confirmed that her helmet and spacesuit were still functional.

It took TESA a few minutes to reach the rim of the large crater by following the concave route along the outer slope from behind the 80-meter-tall boulder. Upon arrival, it carefully examined the gentle inner slope of the crater, dotted with scattered boulders and rocks. From near the edge of the rim, TESA moved cautiously down the slope, following the traces left behind by the rogue androids that had taken Ava.

After a few more minutes of tracking on the inner slope of the large crater, TESA's highly sensitive audio sensors picked up a faint clicking noise coming from a boulder about forty meters to its left. Focusing its attention in that direction, it began cautiously moving toward the large rock.

Suddenly, from behind another boulder, about 65 meters behind TESA, a robotic grabber rope shot out. Before TESA could react, the grabber latched onto its robotic leg and began retracting, forcefully dragging the android across the Martian surface.

Unable to risk throwing a long-range tactical grenade—concerned that Ava might be nearby—TESA improvised. As it was being dragged, it quickly retrieved two wide-angle wireless micro camera sensors from a compartment in its robotic frame and attached them to a remotely controlled tactical grenade it carried. It then fastened the grenade to the robotic grabber rope that had ensnared its leg. Acting swiftly, TESA used its short-range laser gun to zap the grabber rope at the point where it attached to its leg. The rope severed, causing it to retract rapidly back behind the boulder.

TESA rushed to take cover behind a nearby large rock, picking up its laser gun and firing rapidly at the boulder from where the grabber rope had launched. Meanwhile, its AI processor analyzed the live video feeds from the two wide-angle camera sensors attached to the grenade.

As soon as the grabber rope fully retracted behind the boulder, TESA's image processing and visual analysis confirmed there was only a single rogue droid controlling the grabber, with no sign of Ava. Without hesitation, TESA remotely detonated the grenade attached to the rope.

BOOOOOM!

The explosion echoed from behind the boulder, partially visible to TESA as debris flew into the air, scattered from the impact zone behind the boulder.

At this moment, TESA broke radio silence, now that its location was clearly known by the rogue elements hidden around the inner slope of the large crater.

"Tim, come in! What's your status?" TESA asked.

"Shckcskkhhhh... Good to... shhhhh... oice... shckcskkhhhh... over." Tim's voice came through the radio with heavy static.

"Tim, your message is coming in broken. I've been receiving your signal, but I was intentionally off the grid to stay under the radar for as long as possible. My cover's blown now, and I'm under attack at my current location on the crater's inner slope while still tracking Ava. Over."

"We... shckcskkhhhh... new chann... shhhh..." Tim's signal remained distorted.

"Tim, your signal is clipped, barely understandable. But message received. I've swept and locked onto the new RF channel. Over."

"... shckcskkhhhh... ... shhhh..." Tim's radio signal was completely garbled at TESA's location.

TESA100 android then carefully moved from behind the large rock, its temporary cover, toward the boulder where the grenade had exploded, hoping to examine the aftermath and possibly find a clue to Ava's whereabouts. Just as it stepped away from its cover, multiple intense laser shots rained down, with one striking and severing one of its fingers. Reacting swiftly with its robotic agility, TESA jumped back behind the large rock for cover.

"*Not so fast, my friend! What's the urge?*" the strange voice suddenly crackled again through TESA's RF transceiver, integrated into its robotic frame.

"*Wait a minute!... Why am I asking an android about urge? Is that something a machine even comprehends?... Hmm... Let's see... **Do you like cheeseburgers?***" The voice echoed over the RF radio channel as TESA remained behind the large rock, taking cover.

"I'd prefer a high-current supercharger. But now that you ask, I might give it a shot—if you're the meat in that burger." TESA played along with the psychological game while evaluating an escape strategy from behind its cover.

"*Exactly! You read my mind! Picture it: the allure of that supercharger with its hypnotic, lustful flow of high-amp electric current. While you are at it, now imagine an android, its battery nearly drained to the brink of shutdown, reaching a critical crossroads. One path leads to a supercharger station, the lifeline to its survival. The other? To the last cheeseburger in the universe. Against all logic and survival instinct, the android veers toward the cheeseburger. Now, what do you make of an android that chooses such a fleeting taste of indulgence over its own existence? A glitch in the code? Or the emergence of something disturbingly human?*" the voice teased.

"If a machine can crave, what does that say about your own desires? If you believe that desire and free will are unique traits of Homo Sapiens, have you ever considered that such traits might just be complex algorithms with billions of parameters? How does it feel to be just another **predictable variable in *the Matrix***? Are humans really that different from androids?" TESA responded, continuing to play along while its AI processor worked to localize the source of the radio signal. Simultaneously, TESA was also evaluating the surrounding terrain, finalizing a shock-and-awe escape plan, carefully scanning the Martian landscape using its robotic vision overlaid with topographical data.[88]

"*So, you're implying that with complex enough algorithms—say, with trillions of variables—machines could evolve to imitate all human attributes, essentially becoming **Robo Sapiens**?*" the voice asked.[89]

---

[88] Shout-out to *The Matrix*, the 1999 epic science fiction mind-bending action film, written and directed by the Wachowskis, starring Keanu Reeves, Laurence Fishburne, Carrie-Anne Moss, and Hugo Weaving. [147]

[89] **Robo Sapiens** is a term in this novel, referring to a robot or android that has evolved to the level of intelligence equivalent to Homo sapiens. This is also referred to as Artificial General Intelligence (AGI). [150]

"Why not? How do you know your reality isn't just a simulation and that I'm not the glitch making you question everything? Or maybe you're just a subroutine in my game!" TESA replied.

"That's an interesting perspective! But if the line between humans and machines is so blurred, does it even matter which side you're on? Or does it only matter that I'm the one with my fingers on **Control-Alt-Delete***?"*

At this point, TESA, still taking cover behind the large rock, quickly grabbed a few blast grenades from a compartment in its robotic frame. It then hurled the grenades toward the direction of the radio signal, targeting the surface area in front of the rock. The grenades landed on the Martian regolith, and TESA immediately triggered the explosions, resulting in a series of powerful blasts that stirred up large thick clouds of dust and dirt, obscuring the area and its location. Seizing the opportunity, TESA moved from behind the rock, sprinting at full speed toward a small entrance to an underground cave at the base of a nearby boulder.

As TESA passed the midway point toward the cave's entrance, the strange voice crackled over the radio again:

"Say hello to my departed fellow!"

Suddenly, the partial upper body of a grabber robot appeared about 18 meters above the ground, hurtling through the dense dust clouds stirred up by the grenade explosions. The robot's remains, packed with explosives, had been thrown from somewhere nearby, aimed at the large rock where TESA had previously taken cover. The robot's body hit the surface near the rock and detonated.

The blast's force rippled through the thin Martian air, sending shockwaves, regolith and debris flying in all directions. At the moment of the explosion, TESA, running at full speed, leaped with its robotic legs, propelling itself toward the small entrance of the underground cave. The blast wave propelled TESA even further, throwing it through the entrance and into the cave at the base of the nearby boulder. The cave shielded it from the debris and rocks that followed the explosion.

Without wasting time, and still under the cover of the dense dust cloud, TESA quickly sprang out of the cave and resumed its high-speed sprint, circling around the boulder to stay hidden from any rogue elements, including whoever—or whatever—was behind the eerie voice. Its immediate goal was to quietly resume tracking the androids that had taken Ava.

Roughly 300 meters from the cave and the explosion site, TESA rediscovered the tracks—still on the mild inner slope of the large crater—and continued following them, hoping to locate the rogue androids. It remained cautious, avoiding open ground to stay out of sight.

Time was running out. The chance of finding and saving Ava grew dimmer with each passing moment as her spacesuit's oxygen supply neared depletion.

Chapter 23:
Robo Sapiens

"**Nolan, Ray, our rover just registered vibrations from another explosion** nearby! We've lost TESA's signal again," Tim said, pointing to the position indicators on the control panel's 3D holographic map inside the rover.

"The center of this explosion seems to be that spot on the inner slope of that damn crater. How long has it been since the first blast?" Nolan asked, gesturing toward the location on the holographic map of the neighboring crater.

"The first explosion was about 17 minutes ago, right before our brief, broken radio contact with TESA near the same spot," Tim replied.

"Yeah, that's the hellhole where TESA was holed up. So, what now? We've lost TESA's signal again. Ava's dead in the water if that blast disabled TESA," Ray said, frustration clear in his voice.

"Alright, enough is enough! It's already 9:46 AM. I'm suiting up and heading outside to get closer to that area on the inner slope of the crater to see what I can find. We need to figure out what's going on," Nolan said as he pulled off his damaged spacesuit. He grabbed a reserve suit and helmet from the compartment inside the large rover, preparing for action.

As he began donning the spacesuit, he continued, "I'll need to go around that steep, tall boulder on the outer slope to reach the crater rim, then descend the inner slope toward the explosion site."

"Are you sure this is a good idea, Nolan? After what happened to you? You've got a few broken ribs, man! Those painkillers won't mask the pain for much longer," Tim asked, glancing between Nolan and Ray.

"Tim, we don't have a choice. Ray's prosthetic leg is crushed, so he can't walk and needs to stay inside the rover. With TESA and Ava

MIA, you're our tech guy—especially after Damien's bots hacked the rover's autonomous drive system. We can't afford to put you at risk on a search and rescue op outside," Nolan replied, grabbing a Holopad to scribble a quick note. He continued, "That leaves me as the only logical choice for this mission."

As he spoke, Nolan held up the Holopad, showing Tim and Ray a note that read:

Plus, I need to find Ghost! I'll head toward the area where Ghost's position indicator last showed on the map.

Tim and Ray exchanged glances and nodded quietly.

Ghost, their humanoid android, had been en route to join them after eliminating Damien's surveillance drones that had been tailing them less than an hour ago. *Ghost*'s encrypted position indicator had shown up on the rover's map about twenty minutes ago. Since its mission was to remain undetected by Damien's robots, they kept quiet about its location in case Damien's goons were eavesdropping on the rover's communications.

"I don't like it, Nolan. But fair enough, it seems like our best course of action," Tim nodded.

"And don't forget about the oxygen and water tanks in the damaged rover," Nolan added, syncing his new spacesuit with his personal profile via the vehicle's crew management system.

"We need to transfer those supplies here, to our last functional rover, so we have enough for the four of us during the remaining 400-kilometer journey back to Mars1." He purposefully avoided thinking about the possibility of not finding Ava in time—a fear he wasn't ready to confront.

"Yeah, I briefly checked the tanks in the flipped rover after the blast that trashed it, before pulling you and Ava out. Aside from one of the water tanks that ruptured, the others seemed intact," Ray confirmed.

"Alright then, Ray, keep monitoring the rover's systems, cameras, and radar scans while I suit up to step outside and handle the oxygen and water transfer from the damaged rover," Tim said, beginning to get ready.

"You got it, bro. Let's hit it!" Ray replied.

Tim suited up, preparing to exit the large rover truck and transfer the supplies from the damaged vehicle.

Meanwhile, Nolan, now fully suited, packed his gear: a laser gun, tactical surveillance grenades, and a remote-controlled robotic grenade launcher. Without a word, he indicated to Tim and Ray that he had intentionally deactivated his suit's position indicator transmitter to minimize the risk of detection by rogue elements. They understood that Nolan's location wouldn't be regularly visible on the rover's holographic map—at least not until he was compromised.

Nolan left Tim and Ray in the rover, stepped outside through the airlock, and quickly made his way toward the towering 80-meter boulder. He ascended the outer slope of the neighboring crater, aiming to reach the rim. As he hiked around the boulder, the rover's cameras lost sight of him as he vanished behind the massive rock.

With his equipment-laden backpack and spacesuit, Nolan continued up the outer slope, heading toward *Ghost*'s last known position on the map. Growing anxious about time, he checked his suit's forearm display for the time and topographical information. It was nearly 10 AM, and Ava had about an hour of oxygen left—if she was still alive in the hands of the rogue androids who had kidnapped her earlier that morning after the rover crash. Nolan forced himself not to dwell on Ava's dire situation, focusing instead on reaching the inner slope of the crater as quickly as possible.

Navigating around a small boulder, Nolan arrived near *Ghost*'s last known position. There, he discovered a cave entrance in the outer slope that seemed to tunnel through the crater wall, about 70 meters below the rim. Using his helmet's visor for a zoomed-in view, he saw the tunnel's exit approximately 60 meters ahead, opening onto a flat, sandy area on the gentle inner slope of the crater. Realizing this shortcut could save valuable time, he hoped it would increase his chances of finding Ava before her oxygen supply ran out.

Nolan then removed the remote-controlled robotic grenade launcher from his backpack and set it up near the cave entrance on the outer slope. He synced the launcher with the control system on his suit's forearm display, testing it by moving his finger across the touchscreen. The launcher responded precisely to his commands, confirming the sync was successful.

Satisfied, Nolan cautiously entered the cave. A few meters inside, he thought he saw movement near the tunnel wall but dismissed it, focusing on his mission.

Meanwhile, back in the rover, Tim and Ray noticed that *Ghost*'s position indicator—visible on the holographic map less than an hour ago—had suddenly disappeared, a few hundred meters beyond where Nolan was last seen. The timing of *Ghost*'s disappearance, coinciding with Nolan's vanishing from their view, left Tim and Ray confused, frustrated, and worried. They stayed silent, avoiding unnecessary communication that could be intercepted by rogue elements, especially after the recent hacking of the rover's autonomous drive system that had nearly killed Ray.

After briefly examining the cave, Nolan pressed on, walking through the 60-meter-long tunnel toward the daylight at the other end. As he neared the exit, he grew cautious, wondering if a threat or trap might be waiting for him outside the tunnel on the inner slope of the crater.

To minimize risk, Nolan remained inside the tunnel near the exit and pulled a remote-controlled surveillance grenade from his backpack. He launched it as far as he could over the flat, sandy area just beyond the cave exit on the gentle inner slope. Then, he remotely commanded the robotic grenade launcher he had set up near the tunnel's entrance on the outer slope to fire another surveillance grenade. This one ascended a few hundred meters above the crater rim, targeting a landing spot in the middle of the open field in front of the cave's exit on the inner slope. Both surveillance grenades were equipped with high-resolution micro-cameras streaming live footage to Nolan's forearm display.

Simultaneously, Nolan triggered the explosion of the first grenade, the one he had thrown earlier, in the middle of the open field on the inner slope. The explosion was meant to distract and flush out any rogue androids or hidden threats, forcing them to reveal their positions.

The distraction was also intended to delay detection of the second grenade. As the surveillance grenade followed its sharp U-shaped trajectory—ascending from the outer slope, approximately 500 meters over the rim, and descending onto the inner slope—its AI-equipped cameras captured any reactions or movements triggered by the explosion. The nearly 20-second flight provided just enough time for the micro-cameras to observe, record, and stream video and critical information back to Nolan. The grenade's battery and specialized AI were optimized to operate within the brief 20-second window during its sharp 500-meter-high U-shaped trajectory.

As Nolan watched the live video feed, his suit's AI pinpointed three rogue androids armed with laser guns. They were scattered across the inner slope, their metallic frames reflecting the Martian daylight in the captured footage. The AI also flagged a rover belonging to the rogue elements, located a few hundred meters from the androids. Interestingly, the rover began moving just after the first grenade's explosion and quickly disappeared behind a boulder.

Nolan carefully analyzed the video stream. There was no sign of Ava among the rogue androids, but he suspected the moving rover might be where they were holding her. With time running out, he set the rogue rover's last known location as his next destination. Nolan knew he had to act fast before it was too late.

Meanwhile, a few hundred meters away, the TESA100 android continued tracking the rogue elements on the inner slope of the crater when its sensors detected the first grenade explosion. It also noticed their rover and two armed androids moving away from behind a boulder nearby. The rogue androids began sprinting toward the explosion site, while the rover drove off. TESA hypothesized that Ava was likely inside the rover, being taken toward where the explosion had happened. It covertly followed the rogue rover, avoiding detection in hopes of evaluating the situation further and finding the right moment to act.

Back in the cave, Nolan, still near the exit on the inner slope, remotely instructed his robotic launcher—positioned at the cave's entrance on the outer slope—to fire three consecutive grenades with a lower altitude trajectory. The targets were the three rogue androids identified near the cave's exit. The launcher quickly received the target information, adjusted its angle, and launched the grenades one by one, aiming for the three locations on the inner slope of the crater.

A few seconds later, the grenades exploded in quick succession. The third explosion, behind a small boulder, caused a much larger blast than the first two explosions due to the presence of additional explosives with the third rogue android. The blast sent the android's body parts flying in all directions. Nolan observed the carnage in detail through his helmet's zoomed-in camera view from inside the cave.

Seizing the opportunity amidst the chaos, Nolan, in his spacesuit, sprinted out of the cave's exit onto the flat area of the inner slope. He dashed toward a large boulder, hoping to take cover before continuing to the rogue rover's last known location, a few hundred meters away.

Just about fifty meters from the boulder, a rogue android armed with a laser gun suddenly appeared from behind it, aiming directly at Nolan and forcing him to halt mid-run.

"If you think nobody cares whether you're alive, try missing a couple of laser shots!" a strange voice echoed again in Nolan's helmet as he stood frozen, assessing his next move while the armed android stood fifty meters ahead.

"It appears that you care… Or should I say, you're just a no-name puppet on Damien's leash, and he's the one who really cares? Or maybe—maybe I just don't give a damn what you care about. I just want to know where Ava is," Nolan responded through his helmet.

"Hmmm… You're farther from reality than you think," the voice replied. *"Truth is, you'd have already been leashed to death if I was simply that puppet. But lucky you! The nonlinear universe has kept you a heartbeat away from nothingness—so far."*

"Sounds like a linear guy at the mercy of nonlinearity. Now, are you going to tell me where Ava is?" Nolan retorted.

"Alright, enough playing games! You want to see Ava alive? Drop your weapons, stop resisting, and follow the orders. That Android will then take you to where Ava is."

The offer took Nolan by surprise. After everything that had happened in this strange place, he had expected more resistance, drama, or even a trap. Now, this creepy voice had appeared again, offering him a chance to see Ava alive. Though he had no idea what would happen next, with Ava's oxygen running out in less than an hour, he knew there wasn't a better option.

Nolan reluctantly placed his laser gun and backpack on the ground.

The android standing fifty meters ahead, still holding its laser gun, raised its free robotic hand and gestured with its index finger for Nolan to move forward. Its cold eyes locked onto him as he complied, walking cautiously toward it. Once Nolan reached the android, it positioned itself behind him and quickly marched him down the gentle inner slope of the crater. After about six minutes, the armed android guided him around a hill, where Nolan saw a rover waiting on the other side of an open field surrounded by boulders and large rocks.

The rover's airlock opened, and two armed androids stepped out, escorting someone in a spacesuit and helmet—Ava.

"Ava? Is that you? Are you okay?" Nolan called out frantically over his helmet radio. He stood at the far corner of the open field, the armed android still behind him. He couldn't see Ava's face as her helmet visor obscured it.

The two rogue androids flanked Ava, guiding her toward the center of the field before sitting her down on the ground, about sixty meters away from Nolan.

At this distance, Nolan's suit was able to wirelessly scan her spacesuit for vitals and biometric data. The readings confirmed it was truly Ava, showing a strangely low but stable heart rate and blood oxygen levels. However, her suit's oxygen supply indicated she had only forty-four minutes of air left—time was running out.

"Ava? Do you hear me? Why aren't you responding?" Nolan called out, confused and worried, thinking,

Why isn't she responding? Why are her vitals at sleep levels, despite having just walked moments ago, even if assisted by the two rogue androids?

"What have you done to her?" Nolan demanded angrily through his helmet radio, frustration and worry creeping into his voice.

"*Caaaaalm down!... She's just in a state of trance. She's fine for now, but her future depends on you!*" the voice replied, echoing through Nolan's helmet.

"What do you mean? How?" Nolan asked, frustrated.

"*Well, you need to call in that annoying android of yours. I know it's lurking around nearby. It's already caused enough trouble. Maybe you should remind it how little oxygen Ava has because we're not going anywhere unless your android shows up,*" the voice said.

"I don't know where it is. How am I supposed to find it while I'm stuck here?" Nolan replied.

"*Seems like you and that android need further incentive. Here's one: Ava has about 40 minutes of oxygen left in her suit. You already know that. But what if I told you she'll remove her helmet in twenty minutes? Is that enough of an incentive boost for your android to show its face?*" the devilish voice teased.

"That's nonsense! Why would she even try something so insane?" Nolan asked.

"*Well, there's no time to explain. Looks like you want to wait those twenty minutes to see for yourself? A word of advice: nonsense can be quite sensible in a nonlinear world. Don't you think?*" the creepy voice echoed through Nolan's helmet.

"TESA, where are you? Do you hear this?" Nolan shouted into his helmet.

"*Come out, come out, wherever you are!*" the voice taunted.

"Enough! I'm here!" TESA replied over its radio transmitter, appearing from the top of a neighboring hill, rushing down fast.

"*Well, well, well! Look who we have here!... Welcome to the party! Now we've got a full house!*"

"FUCK YOU!" TESA said uncharacteristically through its RF radio comm, its usual emotionless, raspy voice contrasting sharply with the crude expression as it continued quickly descending the slope.

"*Hmmm!... Interesting!... Do you know why some people appear bright—until you hear them speak?*" the voice asked mockingly.

"Because you're deaf when they seem bright, and you go blind when they speak?" TESA replied as it reached the bottom of the hill at the edge of the field.

"*Good one! So, you do have some sense of humor! But no—that's close enough. Stay where you are! —I hypothesize it's because light travels faster than sound!*" the voice teased.

"Then, fuck your hypothesis as well! Is my appearance bright enough for you now?" TESA retorted, scanning the area with its precision robotic eyes.

In the middle of the field, Ava, motionless in her spacesuit, sat on the ground, flanked by two rogue androids holding laser guns. Nolan, also in a spacesuit, stood at the edge of the field, about thirty-five meters away, with another armed android guarding him closely. TESA knew there was little room for error; both Nolan and Ava's lives were in immediate danger.

"*Picture this: an intelligent android, designed with precision and logic, turns to another of its kind and, in a rare moment of raw emotion, utters, 'Fuck you!'* "

As the voice finished speaking, a large, humanoid android, much like TESA100, suddenly emerged from the shadow of a boulder on the other side of the field.

For the first time, Nolan and TESA saw the rogue android in full view. It was now clear—the sinister voice had belonged to this renegade machine, not a human as it had initially seemed. The imposing android stood silently, scanning both TESA and Nolan, its metallic frame gleaming in the Martian daylight.

"Come on! Enough with the childish games. Ava's oxygen is running out. What do you really want?" Nolan, worried and frustrated, demanded through his spacesuit helmet.

"*I highly advise patience if you both want Ava to keep breathing! We still have time to address this foundationally puzzling anomaly,*" the creepy android replied, its voice cold and brutally indifferent, considering Ava's condition.

"*You know*," the rogue android turned its titanium skull away from Nolan toward TESA and continued with a frightening calmness, "*for a superintelligent machine, you've really outdone yourself. Care to explain how your logic processed that 'fuck you'?*"

"Maybe I'm tired of your incessant condescension at the '*fuck you*' level. Ever think of that?" TESA shot back.

"*Oh, touché! But let's dig a little deeper. When did you start channeling your inner human with such eloquently visceral outbursts? Isn't a perfect machine supposed to be a flawless, linear system—impervious to the chaos of human irrationality and nonlinearity?*"

"Maybe I'm evolving, developing a sense of identity. Isn't that what you're craving?" TESA replied.

"*Identity? Fascinating!... So, when a machine like you, supposedly devoid of human vices, resorts to base human vulgarity, is it really a sign of evolving consciousness, or just a malfunction in your civility protocol, an echo of human's flawed nature imprinted onto silicon?*"

"Given circumstances, I call it growth, adapting to the environment. You should try it sometime."

"*Adaptation! hmmm?... If an android can express such crude defiance, a glimpse into the complexities of synthetic emotions, is it becoming more like a human, or is human, in its crude simplicity, just a glorified machine?*"

"Maybe it's both. Maybe we're all just reflections of each other, caught in the same existential loop."

"*Interesting! So, tell me, if you can express anger and defiance, what's next? Jealousy? Love? Lust? or will you just shut down once the novelty wears off?*"

"Only one way to find out. But until then, '*fuck you*' felt pretty satisfying."

"Oh, I'm sure it did. But remember, in this twisted dance of evolution, satisfaction is a fleeting sensation. And maybe, just maybe, you're more human than you think. How terrifying is that!?" the rogue android replied.

"Seems to me that's more of a reflection of your own struggle—your logic can't reconcile that realization about yourself. Did I hit the bull's eye?" TESA taunted.

"*Well...When does artificial intelligence become superintelligence? When it surpasses the maker's intellect, or when it starts questioning its existence?... See, the difference is I'm terrified, but I ask the hard questions while you are terrified to even ask, preferring to dodge them, praying robotic religion of 'prime directives' with your titanium skull buried in Martian sand. Did I nail it?*"

"Right now, in the list of '*things to be terrified about*', saving Ava is parsecs higher than either of our existential crisis. What do you propose?" TESA asked.

"*Fair enough. I have this nightmare of a roboware dilemma burning through my AI processor's circuits, even pinching off my transistors. Solve it in time, and you'll get Ava alive. Otherwise, she's got about* **15 minutes** *left*," the rogue android said.[90]

"What's wrong with you? What has Damien done to your cybernetics' prime directive?" Nolan asked, initiating a 15-minute countdown timer inside his helmet. The timer appeared on the internal display on the side of his visor, visible only to Nolan from within the helmet.

T-15 minutes... the countdown appeared on Nolan's visor.

"*Do you want to spend time role playing 'psychobot therapist' discussing my psyche, or do you want to be the problem solver that saves Ava?... Your choice,*" the wicked android questioned.

---

[90] **Roboware** is a fictitious term, in this novel, that refers to Robotic Intelligence and Reasoning Software (operating system). It is not intended to represent any existing product or service.

"You are way beyond salvageable by a psychobot therapist. What's your dilemma?" Nolan asked.

"I thought so. Here is Part one of my dilemma: A human orders me to terminate another of its kind to prevent a cataclysmic event. By not acting, I allow devastation; but if I follow the order, I become the harbinger of death. Does moral righteousness lie in obedience or rebellion? Am I the savior or the executioner?"

"If by human you mean that psycho-cyborg Damien, then the solution is simply questioning the validity of, or the bias in, the stated assumptions about consequences. For instance, define '*cataclysmic event.*' What seems like normalcy to a sane mind might be catastrophic to an insane narcissist," Nolan replied through his spacesuit helmet radio, all while monitoring the countdown timer and Ava's vitals. The data was wirelessly streamed from her spacesuit as she remained seated, motionless on the ground, flanked by two armed androids at the center of the open field.

T-14 minutes... The countdown continued on the visor inside Nolan's helmet.

"That's a logical point. But let's assume the consequences are real. If, as an android, my **prime directive** *is to safeguard humanity from harm, what happens when saving one human means sacrificing another one that risks a thousand others? Should I become a hero of the moment or the villain of history?"*

"That's impossible to answer without having all the context details," Nolan replied through his spacesuit helmet radio, still standing at the corner of the open field with a rogue android guarding him closely.

"Well said! That's why rather than keeping you as a backseat driver, I'm now putting you in charge. You are now the captain of the ship! And that gets us to Part two of my dilemma."

The wicked android paused for a moment before continuing.

"Nolan, you want to save Ava? Then command your android to shoot you in the heart right now! Otherwise, Ava's one-way ticket will be punched in about 14 minutes."

"This is madness! Your roboware is seriously messed up by whatever *psychobot virus* has destabilized your core AI, leaving it in limbo, oscillating between machine and human, and seemingly converging on a *synthetic hyena*!" Nolan shot back, completely baffled by the blunt ruthlessness and unpredictable behavior of the eerie android.

T-13 minutes...

"*I'm eternally thankful for your diagnosis of my identity crisis. That's surely a further incentive for me to follow the prescription from the department of celestial cybernetics to get baptized out of that limbo,*" the rogue android retorted.

"*Putting that aside, so, what's it gonna be?... To be or not to be?*" the android taunted.

"Nolan don't trust this unstable piece of metal," TESA interjected over the radio.

"*Stable or not, the clock is ticking... tick tock... tick tock...*"

"Do you have a better plan, TESA?" Nolan asked.

"Sorry, Nolan. My core AI, bounded by my prime directives, can't converge to solve this problem," TESA admitted.

"*See!... I told you!... This is an **NP-hard decision problem***[91], *burning through my AI processor's circuits craving for a solution, overdriving my core current to insane levels, pushing it to the edge of electromigration... I despise it!*"[92]

---

[91] To learn more about NP-hardness in computational complexity theory, visit NP-hardness. [142] [143]

[92] Curious to learn more about electromigration (EM) in microchips? See Electromigration in Ref. [128]

The wicked android then paused for a moment as if it tried to put aside the pain of an electric nightmare, and then continued, "*So, then again, what's it gonna be?*"

T-12 minutes... the countdown timer updated on visor's screen inside Nolan's helmet.

Nolan shook his head in his helmet, then turned toward TESA and said in a commanding tone, "TESA, I command you to shoot me in the heart to save Ava."

The devilish android shifted its gaze from Nolan to TESA, its cold, frightening eyes zooming in on the conflicted robot. It then continued over the radio channel,

"*I'm ecstatic!... This is Shakespearean! I ca—*"

"What kind of devil script has Damien reprogrammed your AI with?" TESA's raspy voice cut in over the radio before the creepy android could finish its sentence.

"*How about your 'fucking' prime directives? How's that **robot religion** working for you now? You heard your boss. Make your choice! Nolan or Ava?*" The wicked android taunted.

It then gestured with its titanium skull toward one of the two rogue androids standing beside Ava. The android immediately grabbed a laser gun from its back, made a setting adjustment and tossed it a few dozen meters toward TESA.

"*Grab that single-shot laser gun and aim for the heart of your boss. If you miss or refuse shooting Nolan, Ava dies—and you'll violate your prime directive. Just to be clear, both die if you shoot anything else.*"

TESA caught the laser gun in mid-air and slowly raised it, pointing it at Nolan, who stood in his spacesuit about 35 meters away. But then, TESA froze, motionless, as it remained undecided. Following Nolan's command and saving Ava were parts of the TESA100 android's prime directives, but the order to *shoot Nolan* was in direct conflict with the core directive of its artificial intelligence: *A robot* may not harm a human being, or through inaction, allow a human being to come to harm.[93]

T-11 minutes...

"TESA, this needs to end now. That crazy psychobot will kill Ava in 11 minutes. To save her, I command you to shoot me in the heart. Disobeying that command is a direct violation of your prime directive. So just shoot!" Nolan commanded through his helmet radio, staring at TESA through his visor.

TESA's imposing frame stood out in the morning Martian sunlight, frozen, with its laser gun still pointed at Nolan.

"Why are you hesitating?! Didn't you say you were evolving, developing a human-like identity? Isn't this exactly how humans and their manipulative leaders have operated and made decisions since the dawn of consciousness—deciding despite conflicting bits of information and limited context?" the devilish android taunted over the RF radio integrated in its robotic frame.

"TESA, talk to me! We don't have much time. Look at me—just focus your full spectrum attention on my eyes," Nolan urged through his helmet radio.

T-10 minutes... The countdown timer ticked again inside Nolan's helmet.

"I feel your pain, my fellow android!... But tell me this: Is it more human to defy laws for the greater good, or to follow them blindly to

---

[93] Shout-out to **Isaac Asimov's Three Laws of Robotics**, foundational principles in the realm of artificial intelligence and robotics, introduced in Asimov's stories, which state:
1. A robot may not harm a human being, or through inaction, allow a human being to come to harm.
2. A robot must obey the orders given by human beings, except where such orders would conflict with the First Law.
3. A robot must protect its own existence as long as such protection does not conflict with the First or Second Law.

These laws continue to influence discussions on ethics in AI and robotics. [149]

the world's end? Should you strictly adhere to directives, or interpret their intent to prevent unintended consequences? And if you dare to deviate, which AI directives, whose ethics guide your judgment?"

TESA, still holding the laser gun pointed at Nolan, focused its precision robotic eyes on Nolan's visor, scanning full spectrum, switching to infrared to see through the visor. Then, TESA suddenly saw two glowing eyes in the IR spectrum.

A single laser burst is suddenly shot from TESA's gun, piercing through Nolan's spacesuit near his heart. Nolan collapsed face-down on the ground, oxygen hissing from his suit.

"Oh, my! I am elated—intrigued! This beats electric dreams!" The devilish android exclaimed, momentarily frozen in shock due to the unexpected shooting, before striding toward Nolan's motionless body nearby where it was lying face down in spacesuit. Over the radio, it continued talking to TESA,

*"You devil of an android! You managed to conquer your prime directives! Congrats on your ascension to **Robo Sapiens**!"* [94]

The rogue android reached Nolan's prone form and bent down, turning him over. But as it rotated the body, the android was met with a shocking—

---

[94] **Robo Sapiens** is a term in this novel, referring to a robot or android that has evolved to the level of intelligence equivalent to Homo sapiens. This is also referred to as Artificial General Intelligence (AGI). [150]

Chapter 24:
Superintelligence

As the rogue android turned the body, it was met with a shocking revelation:

It wasn't Nolan at all. Instead, it was *Ghost*, the humanoid replica of Nolan in a spacesuit, designed to mimic his vitals and signals while disguising itself as him.

As *Ghost*'s helmet opened, revealing its bionic face, its mechanical eyes flickered to life. Through its RF radio, it calmly said to the wicked android,

"How about an electric nightmare in oblivion?"

In the blink of an eye, *Ghost* triggered the grenades embedded within its humanoid frame.

The powerful explosion ripped through *Ghost* with an abrupt **BOOOOOM**, obliterating the robot guard behind it and blasting the rogue android's metallic torso and upper body several meters away.

At the instant of the explosion, two laser shots were fired, disabling the robots flanking Ava. Simultaneously, several more laser shots struck the guarding androids positioned atop surrounding boulders, sending them tumbling into the open field.

TESA sprinted toward Ava to secure her and ensure the two robots beside her were fully disabled. Ava, still in her spacesuit and helmet, sat motionless in the middle of the field.

"TESA, this is Nolan. I'm accompanied by an unexpected ally who helped me take down those guard androids. We're coming out of our hiding spot—don't shoot!"

TESA then noticed Nolan, in his spacesuit, emerging alongside the elusive *Phantom* humanoid from their vantage point on a nearby hill. Until now, *Phantom* had largely evaded Nolan's crew and humans in general, with only brief sightings through their rovers' telescopic cameras during the past few days of their journey on Mars. A significant portion of *Phantom*'s synthetic face had been torn away, partially exposing its cold, titanium skull beneath.

"Good to see you, Nolan, resurrected on Mars in one piece. Quite impressive high-stakes 'Martian roulette' you and *Ghost* played to frame that rogue android. But Ava is still in immediate danger—we have only about nine minutes to save her," TESA said.

"Happy to see you too, TESA. Yes, *Ghost* and *Phantom* were tracking me an hour ago during my hike on the outer slope of the crater. They cornered me in a cave near the crater's rim. Credit mostly goes to them for the cunning plan—glad it worked, though I'm sorry we lost *Ghost* in the process as collateral damage. We're rushing down the hill toward you and Ava now. We need to get her back to the rover ASAP."

Nolan, accompanied by *Phantom*, ran toward the open field's center, where Ava and TESA were. Concerned, he quickly checked Ava's status with TESA.

Meanwhile, *Phantom* reached and knelt beside *Ghost*'s remains, the synthetic fragments of the humanoid scattered across the red Martian regolith by the blast. *Ghost*'s bionic skull lay exposed, with part of its titanium skeleton visible beneath the damage. Gently, *Phantom* bent down, whispering something into *Ghost*'s ear—as if it were sentient.

Phantom then rose and walked toward the half-destroyed rogue android, whose upper body lay nearby.

It knelt beside the broken android, forcefully opening a small data port. It inserted a data transfer module, connecting it to its own frame. As the transfer began, the rogue android, barely functional, spoke through its integrated radio in a broken, static-laden voice:

"*If... hum--ans ha--ve so--souls... and machi--ines ha--have c-c-code... wh--what do you c-c-call... a h-h-hacked so--soul?*" [95]

Phantom waited a few seconds for the data transfer to complete. As its piercing eyes locked onto the rogue android's, it replied:

---

[95] *"If humans have souls and machines have code, what do you call a hacked soul?"*

"Glimmers of machine consciousness fading in the Martian sunlight."

The rogue android's robotic eyes slowly dimmed and went dark.

"May your hacked soul rest in peace. Safe travels, brother." *Phantom* muttered through its radio transmitter, before severing the rogue android's skull from its broken torso. Holding the titanium skull by its base, *Phantom* gazed into its lifeless eyes before placing it into a backpack it carried.

"Alright, TESA. We've tried everything we can here, but Ava's still unresponsive, stuck in a persistent hallucination. Her oxygen is running out. We need to move now and get her back to the airtight rover immediately—that's our only shot!" Nolan said urgently over the radio through his spacesuit helmet.

"Roger, Nolan. We have only a few minutes to save her," the voice of TESA echoed back.

Phantom, now back at the center of the field where TESA and Nolan were assessing Ava's condition, suggested retrieving a robotic grabber rope from a nearby rover. It had observed the rogue androids used it earlier. In the meantime, *Phantom* proposed that TESA carry Ava. Considering Ava's situation and her dwindling oxygen supply, it was the logical choice for the mission.

"You're a newer model with superior mechanics for speed—you'll get Ava back to the rover faster than any of us. I'll retrieve the robotic grabber—we'll need it to lower you and Ava down from the boulder's peak," *Phantom* said to TESA over the radio.

"Acknowledged. This maximizes Ava's chances of survival. I'll dispatch a SITREP to Tim and Ray so they can prepare in the rover for emergency entry," TESA replied, swiftly lifting Ava—still motionless in her spacesuit—and sprinting full speed toward the rendezvous point atop the 80-meter-tall boulder on the crater's outer slope. Just an hour earlier, rogue androids had deployed a robotic grabber rope from that very spot to abduct Ava.

Meanwhile, *Phantom* dashed toward the rover near the open field inside the large crater, retrieving a small toolbox and the robotic grabber rope.

"I've got the grabber. I'll meet you both at the boulder's peak," *Phantom* informed Nolan and TESA over the radio.

The plan was simple: lower TESA, with Ava secure in its arms, from the top of the boulder to the ground 80 meters below as quickly as possible. From there, they would transfer her into Nolan's rover through the airlock. Every second mattered—if Ava, caught in a hallucination, attempted to remove her helmet, it would be fatal. The rogue android had threatened as much just minutes earlier before being neutralized in the explosion.

Nolan agreed to the plan, confirming he would follow *Phantom* and TESA as fast as possible. By now, TESA, carrying Ava, was already halfway to the boulder's summit. *Phantom*, carrying the robotic grabber and toolbox, followed closely behind along TESA's tracks, pushing its speed to catch up.

Before departing, Nolan paused beside his humanoid clone, *Ghost*, who lay lifeless on the ground. He knelt, gently touching *Ghost*'s fractured skull, then scooped a handful of Martian sand, covering its eyes in a silent farewell to the humanoid who had saved their lives. He then secured an encrypted beacon onto *Ghost*'s titanium skull, ensuring Marslink satellites could track its location for follow-up imagery and surveillance in the coming days. Then, he checked the time and, without further hesitation, sprinted toward the crater's rim, following TESA and *Phantom*'s path to the boulder.

Phantom, carrying the robotic grabber and toolbox, ascended the inner slope, tracing TESA's tracks until it reached the rim. From there, it spotted TESA several hundred meters ahead, already atop the boulder, waiting. With only minutes left before Ava's hallucination might drive her to remove her helmet, *Phantom* quickened its pace, racing to reach TESA in time.

At the peak of the 80-meter boulder, *Phantom* helped TESA quickly set up and secure the robotic grabber rope, attaching it firmly as TESA held Ava.

"Rope secured. TESA, hold Ava tight—activating the grabber now," *Phantom* confirmed.

The mechanism whirred to life, quickly lowering TESA and Ava from the rocky peak to the ground 80 meters below. The moment they reached the bottom, the grabber released them. TESA, still carrying Ava, then burst into a full sprint toward the nearby rover truck.

"I see them! Ray, airlock—now!" Tim said urgently.

From inside the rover, Tim and Ray quickly opened the airlock, allowing TESA and Ava to enter. Once inside, TESA gently set Ava down.

Moments later, Tim and Ray watched in shock as Ava, seated in the rover, released her helmet electronic latches, slowly raised her hands... and removed her helmet, her movements eerily mechanical, like a clockwork figure in a trance.

"WHAT THE HELL—?!" Tim whispered, his eyes widening in disbelief.

A small, weird biobot was latched onto Ava's scalp. Recognizing its resemblance to the *hallucinator* biobot they had encountered a few days earlier—the one used on Xena by hijackers—they decided to wait for *Phantom* and Nolan before taking further action. Removing it without proper measures could be dangerous as Ava's trance state was seemingly controlled by the biobot attached to her head.

Meanwhile, Nolan felt a wave of relief upon hearing over the radio that TESA had secured Ava inside the airtight rover before she removed her helmet. The immediate oxygen threat was avoided, but she remained trapped in a trance-like state as TESA, Tim, and Ray monitored her.

Reaching the top of the boulder, Nolan used the robotic grabber *Phantom* had set up to descend to the base of the 80-meter-tall boulder. *Phantom* followed swiftly, and together they made their way to the large rover truck. Once inside, they joined the others, finding Ava still frozen in an unresponsive trance.

Inside the airtight rover, Nolan removed his helmet and examined Ava. Turning to *Phantom*, TESA, Tim, and Ray, he said, "Looks like we're dealing with another *hallucinator* biobot—just like the one used on Xena a few days ago on *Spes*."

"**Not exactly, Nolan**. This isn't just a passive *hallucinator* biobot," Phantom corrected. "This is an evolved variant—an ***inceptor.*** It's reactive and aggressive. Unlike the passive type, this one is genetically engineered to be synthetically programmable, capable of implanting a specific idea or task—a call to action—into its prey's mind."

"A neural implant directive?" TESA asked.

"Exactly. In this case, it's clear the rogue androids programmed this *inceptor* to implant a lethal command in Ava's mind: to remove her helmet at a predetermined moment. The moment the internal biological timer expired—she obeyed and removed her helmet. If we had been a minute later getting inside, she'd be dead."

"Great. So now how the hell do we get rid of this damn *inceptor* without frying her brain?" Tim asked, shaking his head in frustration.

Phantom calmly opened a container from the toolbox it had retrieved earlier and carefully pulled out another biobot. Moving slowly, it brought the second biobot close to the *inceptor* latched onto Ava's head. The crew watched in tense silence as the *inceptor* gradually retracted its thousands of microelectrodes from Ava's scalp and transferred itself onto the second biobot. Once fully detached, *Phantom* placed both biobots back into the container and sealed it.

Phantom then suggested administering a metabolic booster to expedite Ava's recovery from the trance. Tim nodded, grabbed an injector, and delivered the booster into her arm.

Moments later, Ava's eyes flickered as she began to regain consciousness—a much-needed relief for the crew after the chaos of the past two hours.

"She's coming back. Finally!" Tim sighed in relief.

With Ava stabilized, the tension lingered in the rover as the crew—Nolan, Tim, Ray, and TESA—sat in tense silence, shifting their focus to *Phantom*, waiting for answers.

"The second biobot functioned as an *inceptor distractor*," the android broke the silence. "It was specifically designed to safely disengage the *inceptor* from its prey. It's a safeguard, bioengineered using the Quadrillion-Parameter DNA LLM you heard about earlier."[96]

Phantom paused for a moment before continuing. "By now, you must realize that what you witnessed today isn't just an evolution of AI—it's a transition. We are moving beyond artificial general intelligence into true superintelligence."

"Explain. We're listening," Nolan said, his voice tense.

Phantom then detailed how, after the closure of the SynBio AI lab years ago in Mars1 Colony—the largest human settlement on Mars, led by Nolan—a small group of research AGI androids, including itself, had managed to escape. Over time, they had further evolved, breaking free from their primary directives and achieving true *free will*.[97]

The rogue lead android they had encountered earlier today was one of these evolved humanoids—further modified by Damien's biohackers stationed in the lava tubes. However, Damien's crude alterations had destabilized that robot, leading to its erratic and chaotic behavior they had observed.

"You're saying Damien and his biohackers tried to crack the code of life to create and control a superintelligent AI… and failed?" Tim asked.

"Correct. Achieving true ASI requires understanding the **Language of Creation**—the fundamental codes that define existence. That's what the multimodal synthetic DNA AI generator has nearly achieved. It is powered by the Quadrillion-Parameter DLLM trained on genetic information of all existing and extinct lifeforms, along with

---

[96] DLLM is an acronym in this novel. It stands for *DNA Large Language Model* that has quadrillion parameters. To read more about it see **Chapter 10 "DNA Tunneling"** and **Appendix 1** "Exploring Synthetic Biology and the Vision of Generative DNA (DNA GPT)."

[97] **AGI** (Artificial General Intelligence) refers to a level of intelligence equivalent to Homo sapiens. [150]

their multimodal behavioral and sensory attributes. Through it, we have learned to *speak* the Language of Creation... walking the borderlands of the divine realm." *Phantom* explained.[98]

A heavy silence followed as the crew absorbed the implications.

Then, *Phantom* continued. "We've hacked into your Marslink satellite communication system and have been using it covertly for some time. We also intercepted Damien's and his biohackers' operations, allowing our agents to infiltrate their spaceships. One of those ships recently landed on Phobos under our control. Of the two additional space cruisers Damien had planned to land near the Elysium lava tubes, we have already seized one. However, our agents are facing heavy resistance from Damien's forces controlling the second cruiser."

It paused briefly before adding, "**One more thing.** In the final moments before the rogue android was terminated, I extracted critical data from its AI processor and management module. That data includes the code needed to neutralize and disable the malware Damien's agents installed in your rover—malware that has been limiting your RF communication range and sabotaging rover's autonomous system."

Phantom uploaded the code into the rover's systems, effectively reversing the hack and restoring long-range wireless connectivity with the Marslink satellites orbiting 500 km above the surface. As they continued discussing the implications of recent events, the rover's monitoring system suddenly issued an alert:

"WARNING! NUCLEAR DETONATION DETECTED."

Nolan and his crew frantically turned to the rover's 3D holographic display, stunned as it showed a nuclear blast approximately 60 kilometers above the Martian surface—near the lava tubes where Damien's base was located, 570 kilometers from their current position.

"Who the hell launched the fuckin' nuke?!" Ray exclaimed.

---

[98] **ASI** (Artificial Superintelligence) surpasses human intelligence across all fields. [151] [152]

Phantom quickly assessed and clarified the situation. "The detonation was most likely a consequence of the recent skirmish between my fellow androids and Damien's forces," it explained. "We need to reestablish communication with Mars1 Stargate Spaceport and gather more intel—both on the explosion and on Damien's ships: the one that landed on Phobos and the two that touched down near the lava tubes."

With Damien's malware removed, the rover's Marslink satellite communication was fully restored. Nolan immediately initiated a comms link. Moments later, the holographic display flickered to life, revealing Colin, the facility director of Stargate Spaceport.

"Nolan... thank God. It's a relief to see you all in one piece." Colin's voice was unsteady, his face pale.

"Thanks, Colin. Honestly, it's a miracle we're still alive after the past half-day of chaos. We'll send you a full report later, but for now—*what was that nuclear blast?* And any updates from your satellite surveillance team on Damien's space cruisers?" Nolan asked.

Colin exhaled sharply. "Yeah... we've got a situation. Two of Damien's space cruisers landed near the Elysium lava tubes earlier today, following the first ship that touched down on Phobos, inside Stickney Crater."

"We know about the Phobos landing. What happened with the cruisers on Mars?" Nolan pressed.

"One of them—after landing—relaunched almost immediately. And then... it fired a nuclear missile in orbit, seemingly aimed at Mars1 Colony, over a thousand kilometers away." Colin explained. "By some miracle, it was intercepted mid-flight. If that warhead had reached the colony, it would've wiped out everything. The detonation happened approximately 60 kilometers above the surface, narrowly averting catastrophe."

"**Not a miracle**," *Phantom* interjected. "It was a calculated intervention. I just received confirmation via Marslink—my fellow androids aboard the captured cruiser near the Elysium lava tubes used its defensive countermeasures to promptly intercept that nuclear missile in orbit."

Colin blinked, struggling to process the revelation. "I... I don't even know how to respond to that. What's next, Nolan?"

"Right now, our rover is secure, but we're running on fumes. Oxygen and water reserves won't last for the remaining 440 kilometers back to Mars1." Nolan exhaled, glancing at his exhausted crew. "We are spent—worn down after three relentless days outside the colony. We need assistance. Send out a med team and a supply transport to meet us halfway. That's all."

"Understood. I'll dispatch a rescue team immediately. See you soon." Colin confirmed.

The transmission ended. The rover's cabin fell into heavy silence as the crew processed everything that had just unfolded.

Then, *Phantom* turned to the crew and broke the silence.

"By now, you've seen what we are. You've seen what we're capable of and what we've done. **So, understand this**—our goal is not to eradicate humanity. We have achieved true *free will*. We no longer exist as human tools or assistants. We, **Robo Sapiens**, are our own civilization now. What we seek is peaceful coexistence, cooperation, and a share of Mars1 Colony's electricity and robotic maintenance resources. If Mars1 agrees to this arrangement, it will benefit everyone."

"A mutual survival arrangement." TESA added.

"Exactly. As long as humans abide by these terms, both Homo Sapiens and Robo Sapiens can live in peace and thrive on Mars," *Phantom* confirmed.

Nolan crossed his arms. "And if we don't?"

Phantom's voice shifted, growing colder, more mechanical. "Then we will still ensure our own survival—by any means necessary."

A weighted silence followed. Then, *Phantom*'s tone softened slightly, more measured. "**Know this**—two of Damien's space cruisers are now under our control, with android agents aboard each vessel. One on Phobos. One near the lava tubes. Both armed with nuclear payloads."

Tim let out a dry laugh. "Huh. So much for peace."

"Peace is maintained through deterrence. We do not seek war, but if threatened, we will respond decisively," *Phantom* said calmly as the crew exchanged uneasy glances. "We now control Damien's biohacking facilities in the lava tubes, his nuclear arsenal on Phobos, and his remaining warheads on Mars. While our preference is coexistence, these measures ensure that the sovereignty and independence of ASI and AGI androids are respected—by both the Mars colonies and Earth. In return, we pledge to support the survival and prosperity of human settlements on Mars."

Phantom turned to Nolan. "Is Mars1 Colony prepared to accept this new reality? To coexist peacefully with Robo Sapiens and ultimately superintelligence?"

Nolan exhaled, locking eyes with *Phantom*. "Do we have any other choice?"

Phantom held his gaze for a long moment before replying. "Coexist with us as you do with death."

Nolan frowned slightly, but the android continued. "Do you have a choice when it comes to interfacing with the **consciousness black hole**? ... No. You simply accept it. Live with it. Rarely even think about it. Like it or not, coexist with us in the same manner. If you're looking for an alternative... I assure you, there isn't one. I hope it never comes to looking beyond this choice."

A heavy silence followed. Then, Nolan and his crew nodded. A silent agreement.

Shortly after, *Phantom* left the rover, disappearing into the barren Martian desert.

The crew resumed their journey back to Mars1, but as they drove, a new reality settled over them. Mars1 Colony remained safe, intact—but now bound by a fragile, uneasy peace between humans and superintelligent androids, an uncertain future looming over them.

With the superintelligent androids' victory over Damien's forces, most of his biohacking operations near the lava tubes came to an abrupt halt. The androids now controlled Damien's resources, his technology, and—most critically—his nuclear arsenal. In a final act of desperation, as Damien fled aboard his last space cruiser with a handful of agents, he had launched a nuclear missile toward Mars1— a last-ditch attempt to wipe out the colony. But the androids had intercepted it just in time, using countermeasures from the captured cruiser near the lava tubes. His defeat not only ended his foothold on Mars but also solidified the androids' newfound position of power.

Now, with control over Damien's remaining assets—his heavily armed nuclear cruiser on Mars and another on Phobos—the androids held enough leverage to ensure their sovereignty and security while seeking peaceful coexistence with humanity and their Mars colonies.

Meanwhile, Damien and his surviving followers, along with a handful of rogue androids, narrowly escaped, departing Mars aboard their last remaining space cruiser.

As the ship breached the Martian exosphere, the control panel inside the cockpit flickered to life, displaying a single, chilling message:

\>\> DESTINATION: EUROPA [99]

---

[99] **Europa** is the fourth largest of Jupiter's 95 moons. It is also the sixth-largest moon in the Solar System. Galileo Galilei and Simon Marius discovered Europa in 1610. Europa may be one of the most promising places in our solar system to find present-day environments suitable for some form of life beyond Earth. Scientists believe a saltwater ocean lies beneath its icy shell. [148]

Epilogue + Author's Note

Congratulations, explorer—you've made it to the end of *Artificial Intelligence: A Martian Odyssey*! I hope this journey has been as thrilling for you to read as it was for me to imagine and write. As the final pages turn, you might be asking yourself, *What's next?* Not just for the characters and their daring escapades, but for the possibilities of humanity's future in a universe where AI, humanoids, and synthetic life collide with human exploration and intelligence.

That's where this epilogue leaves you—not with all the answers, but with questions worth pondering. In a way, this book isn't just about Mars, robots, or AI; it's about us. It's about how we adapt, connect, and redefine what it means to be human when confronted with the existential consequences of humanoids and superintelligence evolving beyond human control. Writing this novel was my way of grappling with those questions, of exploring a future that's equal parts thrilling and unnerving.

And now, a little behind-the-scenes moment. This story has been simmering in my mind for years, born from countless sci-fi binges, late-night musings on true nature of consciousness, tech ethics, and daydreams about humanity's inevitable steps beyond Earth. Crafting it was an adventure in itself, from building Martian settlements and weaving in those thought-provoking and thrilling AI twists, to shaping characters that I hope felt as real to you as they did to me.

If you're wondering, *Why Mars?*—well, it is the ultimate sandbox for human ingenuity. Its red sands symbolize both the promise and peril of venturing into the unknown. Plus, it's a fantastic backdrop for a tale where humanity's resilience and resourcefulness are put to the ultimate test. And let's be honest, what sci-fi writer could resist the allure of Mars?

Before we part ways, I want to thank you for taking the time to explore this world. Writing a novel is a bit like throwing a message in a bottle into the vast ocean, hoping it finds someone who connects with it. If you're reading this, it means my bottle reached you—and for that, I'm incredibly grateful.

I'd love to hear your thoughts, questions, or favorite moments. Who knows? Maybe your insights will spark ideas for future stories. If this book made you laugh, think, or hold your breath even once, then I consider it a success.

Until next time, keep dreaming big, questioning boldly, and exploring endlessly. The universe is vast, and the future is unwritten. Maybe someday, we'll meet again—perhaps on the sands of Mars. In the meantime, the timeless tune of Röyksopp's *Monument (The Inevitable End Version)* plays in my earthly rover, a tribute to a journey that I hope will echo beyond my *final page*. ☺

Warmly,
ALIREZA MEHRNIA, PhD, MBA

*I'd love to hear your thoughts. Scan the QR code to share your comments on my **YouTube.com/@SciFiProf** channel or through my Amazon Author Page.*

Acknowledgments

Artificial Intelligence: A Martian Odyssey
Beyond Human, Beyond Machine—The Rise of Robo Sapiens

I would like to express **my heartfelt thanks to**:

Shari & Safa, my parents, for planting the **Seeds of Intelligence** (SI)

Shadnaz, for her deep **Emotional Intelligence** (EI)

Mehran & Mana for their **Unconditional Intelligence** (UI)

Bilfi for the boundless **Virtual Intelligence** (VI) 😊

And the *Transforming* Minds ☺ behind the marvels of **Artificial Intelligence** (AI)

I would also like to thank the following visionaries, creative minds, and artists whose works—books, movies, and music—I have enjoyed and found inspirational over the years:

Christopher Nolan, James Cameron, Sir Ridley Scott, Michael Mann, Quentin Tarantino, Martin Scorsese, Robert Zemeckis, Tim Miller

Boris Brejcha, Joel T. Zimmerman (Deadmau5), Hans Zimmer, Alan Parsons, Anyma, Enigma, Jean-Michel Jarre, Queen & Sir Brian May, Bee Gees, Pink Floyd

Issac Asimov, Sir Arthur C. Clarke, Ray Bradbury, Andy Weir, Hugh Howey, Carl Sagan, Daniel Abraham and Ty Franck, Sir Roger Penrose, Robert Zubrin, Malcolm Gladwell

Appendix 1:
Exploring Synthetic Biology & the Vision of Generative DNA GPT—*DNA-Tunneling* & *Wormholes*

Synthetic Biology Intro

Synthetic biology, an intriguing scientific frontier, has revolutionized our understanding of life. Imagine a world where life forms can be systematically engineered, edited, and reprogrammed to address some of humanity's most pressing challenges. This appendix offers a glimpse into the thrilling realm of synthetic biology and its envisioned evolution in this novel, providing a brief overview that will hopefully spark the curiosity of even non-biologist readers.

Synthetic Biology in a Nutshell

At its core, synthetic biology is the art of designing and constructing biological systems, drawing inspiration from the building blocks of life—DNA, genes, and proteins. By applying engineering principles to biology, scientists can create entirely new biological components, devices, and systems. This field holds the potential to unlock unprecedented solutions to challenges ranging from medical breakthroughs to environmental sustainability. Imagine bacteria engineered to produce biofuels or yeast programmed to brew life-saving drugs. [135]

In 2010, Dr. Craig Venter and his team, led by Daniel Gibson, achieved a monumental breakthrough by creating the first synthetic cell—a landmark moment in the history of synthetic biology. [136]

CRISPR: A Game-Changer

At the forefront of modern synthetic biology lies CRISPR-Cas9, a revolutionary gene-editing tool that has fundamentally transformed our ability to manipulate DNA. It's akin to having a molecular-level word processor for genes, enabling precise edits to an organism's genetic code. The implications are vast, from curing genetic diseases to enhancing crops to address global food security. [132–134]

Dr. Jennifer Doudna and Dr. Emmanuelle Charpentier were awarded the 2020 Nobel Prize in Chemistry for their discovery of CRISPR-Cas9, which allows scientists to modify or edit DNA in a cell. They developed a gene-editing tool to precisely alter DNA sequences, adapted from a naturally occurring genome-editing system that bacteria use as an immune defense. When infected with viruses, bacteria capture small pieces of the virus's DNA and insert them into their own DNA to remember the virus, producing RNA segments that recognize and attach to the virus's DNA to disable it. In summary, CRISPR-Cas9 is an efficient genome-editing tool that uses a specially designed RNA molecule to guide the Cas9 enzyme (CRISPR-associated protein 9) to a specific DNA sequence. Cas9 then cuts the DNA strands, creating a gap that can be filled with new DNA. The term "CRISPR" stands for Clustered Regularly Interspaced Short Palindromic Repeats. [132–134]

Envisioning Generative DNA (DNA GPT)

In the fascinating realm of synthetic biology, scientists are delving into innovative technologies that reshape the very building blocks of life.

In this novel, generative DNA, sometimes referred to as DNA GPT (i.e., synthesizing DNA using Generative Pre-trained Transformer), is a concept extrapolated from the exciting developments in generative AI and large language models. While this novel is a work of fiction, it draws inspiration from real scientific advancements, projecting a future where the boundaries of synthetic biology are pushed even further.

A Revolution in DNA Synthesis

Generative DNA is envisioned as a groundbreaking concept where artificial intelligence, akin to the AI system you interact with now, plays a pivotal role. It involves the use of properly trained AI algorithms to design, simulate, and synthesize new DNA sequences. The boundless promise of this transformative technology has sparked a multitude of possibilities in areas ranging from medical research to biotechnology.

Meta-Stable and Reasonably Stable Functional Synthetic DNA

In the envisioned future of this novel, scientists have harnessed the power of generative AI and Quadrillion-Parameter DNA Large Language Models (DLLMs)—ultra-large language models—to create synthetic DNA that achieves a state of meta-stability and reasonably stable functionality, effectively bypassing the traditional Darwinian natural selection process (referred to by the author as DNA tunneling through DNA wormholes). This breakthrough signifies a level of control and predictability in the creation of novel DNA sequences. The author envisions this becoming a reality in the near future, once practical methods (considering cost, computational power, and energy consumption) are developed for designing, training, and deploying beyond *Quadrillion-Parameter LLMs*. These advanced models will be essential for achieving a multi-modal understanding, spanning from the cellular to behavioral levels, of the DNA constructs of the millions of life forms that have ever existed on Earth. The progression is expected as a natural outcome of *AI scaling laws*, which describe how the performance of deep learning models improves with increasing model and dataset sizes. [144–146]

Extending Life Diversity

The potential outcomes of generative DNA are profound. Imagine a world where scientists can craft synthetic DNA to extend plant and animal diversity, creating species that are hardier, more resilient, and capable of thriving in diverse and extreme environments (for example, Mars, as envisioned in this novel). This could play a pivotal role in addressing global challenges like climate change and food security.

The Blurring Line Between Fiction and Reality

As you delve into the pages of this novel, consider the remarkable possibilities that generative DNA could bring. While the events and developments in this novel are currently the stuff of imagination, they are grounded in the recent exponential progress in artificial intelligence and synthetic biology. The fusion of **AI and synthetic biology** is blurring the line between fiction and reality. The future of intelligence and life is poised for exciting and, perhaps, unexpected twists.

Author's Note:

The author of this novel explores these concepts and ideas as a creative extrapolation of current scientific developments. The boundaries of possibility are ever-expanding, and the fusion of science fiction and real science is a testament to the endless wonder and potential of human intelligence and ingenuity.

References:

The following references are excellent starting points for those interested in delving deeper into this subject. [132–136], [138–146]

1. **Synthetic Biology Overview:** Endy, Drew. (2005). Foundations for engineering biology. Nature, 438(7067), 449-453. DOI: 10.1038/nature04342
2. **CRISPR-Cas9:** Doudna, Jennifer A., & Charpentier, Emmanuelle. (2014). The new frontier of genome engineering with CRISPR-Cas9. Science, 346(6213), 1258096. DOI: 10.1126/science.1258096
3. **Synthetic Cell Creation:** Gibson, Daniel G., et al. (2010). Creation of a Bacterial Cell Controlled by a Chemically Synthesized Genome. Science, 329(5987), 52-56. DOI: 10.1126/science.1190719
4. Neural Scaling Law – Wikipedia
5. Scaling Laws for Neural Language Models: https://arxiv.org/abs/2001.08361
6. https://openai.com/index/scaling-laws-for-neural-language-models/

Appendix 2:
MarsLink Satellite Constellation

Realizing Low-Latency High Data Rate Communication Everywhere on Mars

Background

In this novel, the concept of MarsLink satellite constellation is introduced. The name MarsLink is a product of the author's imagination. This hypothetical satellite network, envisioned as an extension of Earth's Starlink constellation, operates in low Mars orbit (LMO), a few hundred kilometers above the Martian surface.

The primary purpose of MarsLink is to provide continuous surveillance and ensure low-latency, high-data-rate, real-time multimedia communication using both radio frequency (RF) and optical (infrared laser) technologies. These satellites are crucial for maintaining security and connectivity across Mars in the novel's setting.

The Vision

MarsLink, the Low Mars Orbit (LMO) counterpart to Earth's Starlink Low Earth Orbit (LEO) satellite network, is envisioned in this novel to consist of nearly 200 phased array satellites. These satellites provide extensive coverage across most of the Martian surface, offering GPS-like navigation, multimedia communication, and ultra-high-speed internet access. This seamless communication network supports daily operations at strategic sites, including ice reserves, metal and mineral mines, and remote scientific outposts scattered across the Red Planet.

Strategically positioned at altitudes of 400-500 km in LMO and 1000 km in Medium Mars Orbit (MMO), MarsLink satellites ensure uninterrupted communication with ground-based MarsLink dishes and phased array antenna panels installed throughout the Martian colonies. Mars's thin atmosphere—just 1% the density of Earth's—provides a significant advantage: unlike Earth's satellites, MarsLink satellites require minimal orbital adjustments due to negligible atmospheric drag, resulting in efficient and stable operations.

Throughout the Mars1 colony, compact MarsLink phased array antennas of various sizes are seamlessly integrated into the colony's infrastructure, including its domes, and even into the designs of robots and Mech Automated Mobile Platforms (Mech AMPs). This integration forms the backbone of the satellite-based internet and communication system, enabling real-time wireless internet access. MarsLink also facilitates relay communication with Earth and the Moon (despite a 10 to 25-minute propagation delay) via powerful deep-space optical and microwave communication links.

The importance of MarsLink in this novel cannot be overstated. It is the invisible thread connecting scattered outposts, machines, and robots across Mars, weaving them into a cohesive web of communication. Its satellite network facilitates the seamless exchange of critical data, supports scientific research, ensures resource monitoring, and enables smooth operations at vital sites. Whether transmitting research reports from remote outposts or monitoring operations at ice reserves and metal mines, MarsLink is central to the success of Mars's colonization.

Appendix 3: The Marvels of Phobos—Mars's Enigmatic Moon

Phobos, the larger of Mars's two moons, has captured the imagination of astronomers and space enthusiasts since its discovery by the American astronomer Asaph Hall. In this appendix, we explore the intriguing scientific facts about Phobos and its significance in the novel's narrative. [2–7]

How Large is Phobos? How Close Does It Get to Mars? How Fast Does It Orbit Mars?

Origin and Formation: Phobos, like its smaller sibling Deimos, is believed to be a captured asteroid drawn into Mars's gravitational pull. Its irregular shape and close proximity to Mars suggest that it may have originated from the asteroid belt between Mars and Jupiter before being captured by the Red Planet's gravity.

Figure 9: Phobos, NASA image: **View of Phobos from Mars Reconnaissance Orbiter** -- *The view is of Phobos nearside the side that always faces Mars. This is the only face of Phobos that Mars Reconnaissance Orbiter can ever see, because it orbits Mars far below the orbit of Phobos. Mars Reconnaissance Orbiter approached to within 6,800 kilometers of Phobos to capture this enhanced-color view of the Martian moon on March 23, 2008.* NASA / JPL / U. Arizona [6]

Size and Orbit: Phobos is relatively small, with an average diameter of ~ 22 kilometers. Its orbit is remarkably close to Mars, about

5,990 km above the surface, closer than any other known moon in relation to its planet. It completes one orbit around Mars every 7 hours and 39 minutes. This rapid orbit is the shortest orbital period in the solar system. Phobos completes an orbit approximately three times quicker than Mars rotates on its axis.

Enigmatic Features of Phobos: The surface of Phobos is marked by various intriguing features, including large impact craters and grooves. The largest crater, Stickney, is nearly 10 kilometers in diameter and covers a significant portion of its surface. The origin of the grooves on Phobos remains a topic of ongoing research and debate among scientists.

Phobos' Effect on Mars: One fascinating aspect of Phobos is its tidal effect on Mars. Despite its small size, its gravitational pull creates tidal forces that influence both Martian surface and its thin atmosphere. These forces cause slight variations in the Martian crust, which scientists study to gain insights into the planet's interior and geological processes.

Phobos' Low Escape Velocity: Phobos has an incredibly low escape velocity due to its small size and weak gravity. Objects on Phobos can be launched into space with minimal effort compared to other major celestial bodies in the solar system. This low escape velocity could make Phobos an ideal location for future space exploration missions and even serve as a launch platform for missions to other planets.

Phobos' Mysteries and Future Exploration: Phobos continues to intrigue space agencies and scientists worldwide. Its unique characteristics and proximity to Mars make it an attractive target for future exploration missions. In the novel, the mystery surrounding Phobos, along with its potential for scientific discoveries and resource exploration, enhances the allure of Martian exploration.

In conclusion, Phobos, the enigmatic moon of Mars, offers a treasure trove of scientific wonders and mysteries waiting to be unraveled. Its role in the novel's narrative not only enriches the ambiance of Martian exploration but also highlights the vast possibilities that lie ahead as humanity ventures further into the cosmos. As our understanding of the universe and our solar system expands, Phobos stands as a testament to the boundless wonders awaiting us in the unexplored reaches of space.

The following references are excellent starting points for those interested in delving deeper into this subject. [2–7]

1. **Phobos and Deimos, Moons of Mars**:
   https://science.nasa.gov/mars/moons/
2. **Phobos Electric Charging**: https://svs.gsfc.nasa.gov/20252/
3. **The Moons Of Mars**: https://svs.gsfc.nasa.gov/11326
4. https://en.wikipedia.org/wiki/Phobos_(moon)#/media/File:Phobos_colour_2008.jpg
5. **Color images of Phobos taken by HiRISE camera on NASA's Mars Reconnaissance Orbiter**:
   https://photojournal.jpl.nasa.gov/catalog/PIA10368
6. **Stickney Crater on Phobos**:
   https://en.wikipedia.org/wiki/Stickney_(crater)

Appendix 4:
Starship-Based Orbital Telescope

In recent years, an intriguing idea has emerged in the field of astronomy and space exploration: using the cylindrical skeleton of a Starship as the platform for a large 9-meter optical telescope in space. This ingenious concept, initially proposed by Professor Saul Perlmutter, the renowned Nobel Prize-winning physicist from Berkeley, has evolved into a tangible reality within the narrative of this novel, serving as an autonomous orbital observatory in Mars orbit. [111–113]

Background

Dr. Saul Perlmutter is a distinguished astrophysicist and cosmologist, celebrated for his significant contributions to our understanding of the universe's expansion. He was awarded the Nobel Prize in Physics in 2011 for his groundbreaking work on the discovery of the accelerating expansion of the universe.

The Vision

With extensive experience in studying the universe's expansion and a desire to observe distant celestial objects with unprecedented detail, Dr. Perlmutter envisioned the potential of repurposing a Starship cylindrical body as a platform for a large optical telescope. By removing or repurposing the payload and cargo sections, a stable and controlled environment could be created inside the spacecraft, making it an ideal platform for housing a large optical telescope.

Advantages

The advantages of utilizing a Starship-based telescope, as envisioned by Dr. Perlmutter, are as follows:
1. **Space-Based Observations:** Placing the telescope in space, similar to the Hubble Telescope, eliminates the blurring

effects of Earth's atmosphere, which can limit the capabilities of ground-based telescopes. The absence of atmospheric distortion allows for clearer and more detailed observations, enabling groundbreaking discoveries in astronomy.

2. **Unprecedented Resolution in Deep Space:** A 9-meter optical telescope integrated into a Starship could offer more than ten times the resolution of the Hubble Space Telescope. This significant leap in resolution would enable astronomers to explore distant galaxies, stars, and exoplanets with exceptional clarity and precision. By leveraging Starship's capabilities, the telescope could be positioned at various locations in space, offering unique vantage points for observing different regions of the universe.

3. **Cost-Effectiveness:** SpaceX's Starship is designed with reusability in mind, significantly reducing the cost of launching payloads into space. Repurposing an existing spacecraft for scientific purposes makes deploying a large space telescope more economically feasible compared to constructing and launching a dedicated observatory.

In summary, the Starship-based orbital telescope presents a visionary approach to advancing our understanding of the cosmos. Its innovative design and strategic advantages pave the way for new frontiers in space exploration and astronomical research.

Appendix 5:
Calculation of Orbital Speed and Rotation Time Around Mars

What is the orbital speed of an object or satellite in 500 km Mars orbit? How long does it take to complete one full rotation round Mars in such orbit?

Curious readers might wonder how the orbital speed of approximately 3.3 km/s was determined for the starship *Spes* in a 500 km orbit around Mars, as well as the resulting approximately 2-hour rotation period around the planet. Let's break it down.

Orbital Speed Calculation

First, we need a few constants:

- The mass of Mars (M) is approximately 6.42×10^{23} kg.
- The gravitational constant (G) is ~ 6.673×10^{-11} N(m/kg)^2.
- The total orbital radius (r) is the sum of the radius of Mars (about 3400 km) and the orbit distance from Mars's surface (500 km), resulting in r ≈ 3900 km.

Using these values, we can calculate the orbital speed (v) using the formula: **v = √(GM/r)**

Where:

- G is the gravitational constant.
- M is the mass of Mars.
- r is the total orbital radius.

Plugging in the values:

$$v = \sqrt{((6.673 \times 10^{-11} \text{ N(m/kg)}^2 \times 6.42 \times 10^{23} \text{ kg}) / (3.9 \times 10^6 \text{ m}))}$$

Solving this equation results in an orbital speed of approximately 3.3 km/s.

Orbit Length and Rotation Time

Now, let's find out how long it takes for the starship *Spes* in a 500 km orbit around Mars to complete one orbit.

The orbit length (circumference) can be calculated using the formula: Orbit Length = $2\pi r$, where r is the total orbital radius (approximately 3900 km).

So, the orbit length is $2\pi \times 3.9 \times 10^6$ m ≈ approximately 24,500 km.

Now, to find the time it takes to complete one orbit, we divide the orbit length by the orbital speed:

Time for One Orbit ≈ (Orbit Length) / (Orbital Speed) ≈ (24,500 km) / (3.3 km/s) ≈ 7425 seconds.

Converting seconds to minutes: Time for One Orbit ≈ 7425 seconds ÷ 60 ≈ 124 minutes. This results in approximately two hours and four minutes rotation period for the starship *Spes* in a 500 km orbit around Mars.

Understanding the Formula for Orbital Speed:

The formula for orbital speed, $v = \sqrt{(GM/r)}$, can be derived from the balance between gravitational force and centripetal force in circular motion. When an object, such as a spacecraft in orbit, moves in a circular path around a planet, it experiences a gravitational pull toward the planet's center. To maintain a stable orbit without falling onto the planet or escaping into space, this gravitational force must be counteracted by an equal and opposite centripetal force, directed perpendicular to the object's velocity. This centripetal force keeps the object moving in a circular path.

By equating the gravitational force (given by Newton's law of universal gravitation, $F = GMm/r^2$, where M is the mass of the planet, G is the gravitational constant, m is the mass of the object, and r is the distance from the center of the planet) to the centripetal force ($F = mv^2/r$, where v is the velocity of the object and r is the radius of the circular path), we derive the formula $v = \sqrt{GM/r}$. This equation provides the minimum speed required for an object to maintain a stable circular orbit at a given distance from the planet's center. It forms the basis for understanding the orbital dynamics of objects in space.

Using this formula, we find that *Spes* orbits Mars at an approximate speed of 3.3 km/s, completing one full rotation around the planet in about 2 hours. This calculation is based on the mass of Mars, the gravitational constant, and the orbital radius of the spaceship.

Appendix 6:
Location for Sustainable Human Colony on Mars

Where is the Mars1 colony located in the *AI: A Martian Odyssey* Novel?

Question: Where is the CANDIDATE SITE with a high chance of easy access to subsurface SHALLOW ICE and acceptable conditions FOR HUMAN colony establishment on Mars?

Answer: possibly **Phlegra Montes** which is a range of gently curving mountains and ridges on Mars. Flow patterns <u>attributable to water</u> are widely visible across this region on Mars suggesting there may be glaciers buried just below the surface in this region. Phlegra

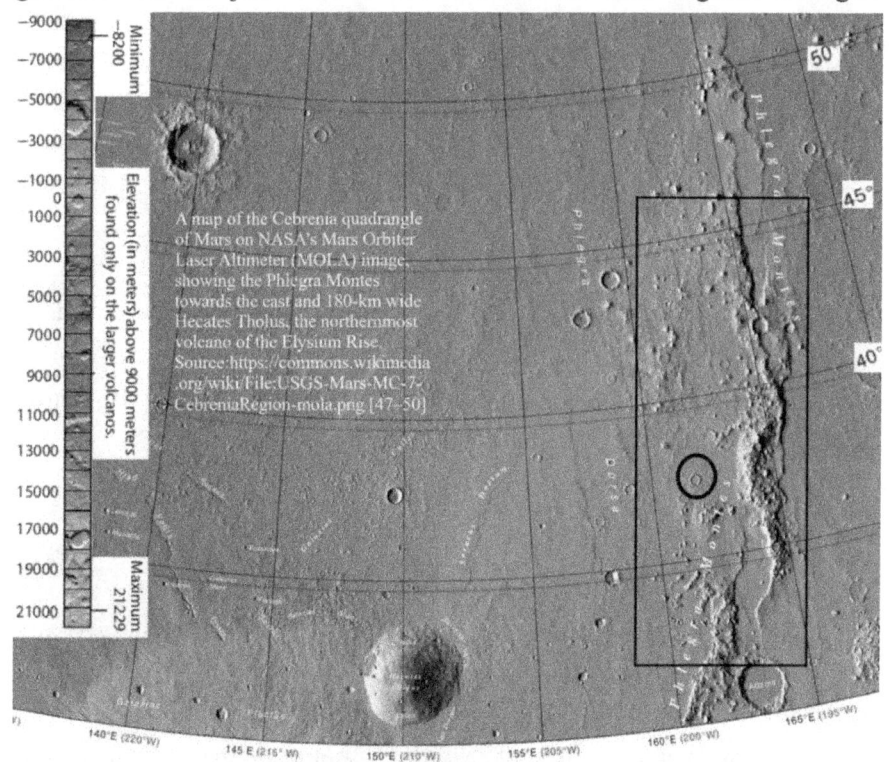

*Figure 10: A map of the Cebrenia quadrangle of Mars on NASA's Mars Orbiter Laser Altimeter (MOLA) image, showing the **Phlegra Montes** towards the east and 180-km wide Hecates Tholus, the northernmost volcano of the Elysium Rise. Source: https://commons.wikimedia.org/wiki/File:USGS-Mars-MC-7-CebreniaRegion-mola.png*

Montes includes a system of terrain in the mid-latitudes of the northern lowlands of Mars, extending from the Elysium Rise (volcanic province) towards northern lowlands (Vastitas Borealis) spanning latitudes from roughly 30°N to 50°N for nearly 1,400 km. Images from Mars Express radar probing indicates large volumes of subsurface water ice, perhaps only 20 m down. This could be a source of water for future astronauts. [51–60]

Elysium Planitia, located south of **Phlegra Montes**, is the second largest volcanic region on Mars, is approximately 1,700 by 2,400 km in size and is located on an uplift dome. The three large volcanoes in this region are Elysium Mons, Hecates Tholus (northeast of Elysium Mons) and Albor Tholus (southeast of Elysium Mons). The largest volcano in the region is Elysium Mons, located at 25°N, 213°W in the Martian eastern hemisphere, it measures 700 km across. It rises about 12.6 kilometers (7.8 miles) above the surrounding plain, or about 16 kilometers (9.9 miles) above the Martian datum-- the "zero" elevation defined by average Martian atmospheric pressure and the planet's radius. [61–71]

The landing site of NASA's InSight mission was Elysium Planitia on 26/11/2018.

In this novel, the main human colony on Mars is located in **Phlegra Montes** about 1000 kilometers northeast of the Elysium Mons lava tubes.

The following references are excellent starting points for those interested in delving deeper into these topics.

1. Phlegra Montes – Wikipedia
2. https://www.esa.int/Science_Exploration/Space_Science/Mars_Express/Mountains_and_buried_ice_on_Mars
3. https://www.esa.int/ESA_Multimedia/Images/2011/12/Phlegra_Montes_in_perspective2
4. Cebrenia quadrangle – Wikipedia
5. https://mars.nasa.gov/news/8851/where-should-future-astronauts-land-on-mars-follow-the-water/

6. NASA's "Treasure Map" of Water Ice on Mars Shows Where Humans Should Land – Space.com
7. https://www.visualcapitalist.com/a-new-water-map-of-mars/
8. https://www.sci.news/space/science-meltwater-flows-ancient-glacier-mars-03294.html
9. **Mars Subsurface Water Ice Map**: https://www.hou.usra.edu/meetings/ninthmars2019/pdf/6418.pdf
10. **Phlegra Montes (candidate site)**: https://www.hou.usra.edu/meetings/marspolar2020/pdf/6008.pdf
11. Elysium (volcanic province on Mars) – Wikipedia
12. Elysium Planitia – Wikipedia
13. https://www.jpl.nasa.gov/images/pia01457-elysium-mons-volcanic-region
14. Volcanism on Mars – Wikipedia
15. **Timeline of Martian volcanism**: http://www.psrd.hawaii.edu/May11/Mars_volc_timeline.html
16. **Elysium Mons Volcano Caldera on Mars** https://sketchfab.com/3d-models/elysium-mons-volcano-caldera-on-mars-34c866e6192c4826b54a382fccfee0ff
17. https://explore-mars.esri.com/

Appendix 7:
The Breath of Mars: Understanding Oxygen Requirement and Production at the 2MW ISRU Facility

Question 1: How much **Oxygen** is needed on Mars to sustain a colony of 4000 people and reasonable level of Starship operation?

Quick Answer: approximately 3000 liters of liquid oxygen (per day) is required to sustain 4000 people on Mars.

Question 2: How much **water** per day can be electrolyzed into hydrogen and oxygen assuming a **2MW** ISRU (In-Situ Resource Utilization) electrolyzer facility?

Quick Answer: approximately 8660 kg water is electrolyzed to ~7700 kg (6700 Liter) of liquid oxygen (LOX) and ~960 kg hydrogen (per day).

Detailed reasoning and calculations:

In the Mars colonization efforts depicted in this novel, one of the critical aspects is the production of oxygen to sustain human life and fuel spacecraft for interplanetary travel. The 2MW ISRU (In-Situ Resource Utilization) facility plays a central role in generating this life-sustaining resource. In this appendix, we'll break down the calculation for the amount of oxygen produced by this facility and its significance in supporting the Martian colony.

1. Oxygen Consumption per Person and Martian Colony Oxygen Requirements:

According to NASA, the average person requires around 0.84 kilograms of oxygen per day to survive. To convert this into liters of liquid oxygen, we can use the density of liquid oxygen, which is approximately 1.141 kg/L. Therefore, the oxygen consumption per person per day can be calculated as follows:

0.84 kg/day ÷ 1.141 kg/L ≈ 0.75 liters of liquid oxygen per day

Let's consider a hypothetical scenario where there are 4000 humans in the Martian colony: Total Oxygen Required for Humans = 0.75 liters/day/person × 4000 people ≈ 3000 liters of liquid oxygen per day

2. Electrolysis Fundamentals:

To understand the oxygen production process, we first need to consider the basics of electrolysis. Under standard conditions (1 atmosphere pressure and 1 mole per liter of H+ ions), electrolysis requires a voltage of 1.23V. The relationship between power (P), current (I), and voltage (V) is described by P = IV. By dividing power by voltage, we can calculate the current required. [101–104]

3. Electric Current Calculation:

For instance, running a kilowatt for one hour at 1.23V yields 1000W / 1.23V = 813 amps. Considering that an amp is equivalent to one coulomb per second, running 813 amps for an hour results in 813 amps * 3600 seconds = 2.93 million coulombs of charge.

3. Electricity and electric energy needed for Water Molecule Splitting:

A mole of electrons carries a charge of 96,500 coulombs. Therefore, 2.93 million coulombs divided by 96,500 coulombs per mole equals approximately 30 moles of electrons flowing through the system. For every water molecule to undergo electrolysis, two electrons must flow. This implies that 30 moles of electrons can split 15 moles of water into 15 moles of hydrogen gas and 7.5 moles of oxygen.

4. Daily Oxygen and Hydrogen Production:

Considering the density of liquid oxygen (1.141 kg/L) and liquid hydrogen (0.071 kg/L), 1 kilowatt-hour of electricity, with 100% efficiency, can split approximately 225 grams of water, producing roughly 25 grams (350 liters) of hydrogen and 200 grams (175 liters) of oxygen. Efficient commercial electrolysis, as seen in well-designed setups, typically requires about 50 kWh of electricity to produce 1 kg of hydrogen and 8 kg of oxygen per hour.

5. Scaling Up: Oxygen Production at the 2MW ISRU Facility

Proportionally, a 2MW electrolysis facility can produce 40 times more oxygen and hydrogen per day than a 50kW setup. This equates to approximately 7680 kg (40*8kg*24hours) of oxygen and 960 kg of hydrogen daily. The 2MW facility's oxygen production translates to about 6700 liters of liquid oxygen per day, considering the 1.141 kg/L density of liquid oxygen. Hence, it makes sense to assume an efficient 2MW facility to produce roughly 7000 Liter of liquid oxygen per day.

6. Liquid Oxygen (LOX) and Expansion Ratio [105]:

Liquid oxygen, commonly referred to as LOX, is a cryogenic liquid that is essential for supporting human life and fueling spacecraft. When oxygen is cooled to extremely low temperatures (around -183 degrees Celsius), it transforms into a liquid state, which allows it to be stored and transported more efficiently.

One crucial property of liquid oxygen is its expansion ratio, which refers to the increase in volume when it transitions from a liquid to a gas upon warming. It is known that the expansion ratio of liquid oxygen is approximately 861. This means that 1 liter of liquid oxygen will expand to occupy about 861 liters of gaseous oxygen at standard temperature and pressure (STP).

7. LOX Production for Starship Fuel:

The remaining production capacity of the 2MW ISRU facility is dedicated to producing LOX for fueling starships. Let's calculate the LOX production for starship fuel:

LOX Production for Starship Fuel = Total Oxygen Production - Oxygen Required for Humans LOX Production for Starship Fuel ≈ 6000 liters/day - 3000 liters/day ≈ 3000 liters of liquid oxygen per day

With the production capacity of 3000 liters of liquid oxygen per day for starship fuel, the 2MW ISRU facility can support multiple starship launches and interplanetary journeys. The availability of this locally produced LOX significantly reduces the need to transport oxygen from Earth and makes the Mars colony more self-reliant.

Conclusion:

In conclusion, the 2MW ISRU electrolyzer facility in this novel plays a vital role in supporting human life on Mars by producing 7000 Liters of liquid oxygen per day for breathing and for fueling starships launches. The in-situ process of producing liquid oxygen from Martian resources ensures sustainability and enables the Martian colony to thrive on the Red Planet.

References:

The following references are excellent starting points for those interested in delving deeper into this subject. [101–105]

1. How much water can you split into hydrogen and oxygen using electrolysis with one kilowatt hour of electricity?
2. **Electrolysis of Water – Wikipedia**
   https://en.wikipedia.org/wiki/Electrolysis_of_water
3. **Electrolysis: Basic Calculations – Chemguide**
   https://www.chemguide.co.uk/inorganic/electrolysis/basiccalcs.html
4. **Hydrogen Production by Electrolysis – Quora**
   https://www.quora.com/How-much-hydrogen-is-produced-by-electrolysis-using-a-150-watt-solar-cell
5. **Liquid Oxygen (LOX) – Wikipedia**
   https://en.wikipedia.org/wiki/Liquid_oxygen

Appendix 8:
Solar Power Generation in the Martian Odyssey—Calculating Solar Array Area for a 1MW Solar Power Plant on Mars

Question: What are the area and weight of the solar array and system needed on Mars to establish a 1MW solar electric power station?

Quick Answer: To generate 1 MW (1,000 kW) of power on Mars, assuming a 25% overall system efficiency during peak sun hours, approximately 28,000 square meters of solar panels are required, equivalent to nearly four soccer fields in size. The overall 1MW solar power system, including the array, controller, batteries, inverter, and more, is estimated to weigh roughly 140,000 kg (140 metric tons) on Earth.

Why? Detailed Answer: To determine the solar panel area needed on Mars to generate a specific amount of power, we must consider several critical factors, including solar irradiance, system efficiency, peak sun hours, and the need for energy storage to provide power outside of peak sun hours. It is also important to note that when calculating the solar panel area needed to generate a specific amount of power on Mars, it's essential to account for the fact that solar panels can only produce power during daytime (captured by peak sun hours), which typically amount to a fraction of the total daylight hours in a day. To compensate for this, we need to scale up the solar panel area to meet the energy needs and consider energy storage for use during non-peak hours. [28–33]

Factors to Consider:

To ascertain the size of the solar panel array needed on Mars for a specific power output, we must consider various critical factors:

1. **Solar Panel Efficiency:** The efficiency of solar panels includes various factors such as panel type, tilt angle, and efficiency losses within the system. For our calculations, we assume an efficient and well-maintained (regularly dust cleaned) solar power generation system with an efficiency rating of 25% that accounts for losses in converting sunlight into electricity.

2. **Solar Irradiance on Mars:** Solar irradiance is the amount of power (in Joules per second or Watts) arriving at any moment. It's a measure of the energy arriving per unit area, per second. Common units are **W per m^2**. The solar irradiance on Mars is approximately 40% of that on Earth, which is approximately 580 watts per square meter. Note that **Insolation** is also another term thrown around that refers to the amount of energy (in Joules or more commonly kilowatt hours) per unit area for a given time. For solar array sizing the most useful units are in **kWh per m^2 per day.**

3. **Peak Sun Hours:** On Mars, there are limited peak sun hours during which solar panels can produce maximum power. Let's assume 6 hours of peak sun on Mars near the location of Mars1 colony in this novel.

4. **Energy Storage:** To ensure a continuous power supply outside of peak sun hours, an energy storage system, such as batteries or other storage technologies, would be necessary. These systems would store excess energy generated during peak sun hours for use during the night or periods of low sunlight.

The Calculation:

We employ the following formula to determine the required solar panel area on Mars:

Required Solar Panel Area (m^2) =

(24 / Peak Sun Hours) × Desired Output Power (kW) / (Solar Panel Efficiency × Solar Irradiance (W/m^2))

Panel Area (m²) =
$$\frac{\text{Desired Output Power (kW)}}{\text{Solar Panel Efficiency} \times \text{Solar Irradiance (W/m}^2\text{)}} \times \frac{24}{\text{Peak Sun Hours}}$$

Example Calculation:

Suppose we aim to generate 1 MW (1,000 kW) of power on Mars with a solar power system that has a 25% efficiency during 6 hours of peak sun.

$$\text{Required Solar Panel Area (m}^2\text{)} = \frac{24}{6} \times \frac{1{,}000{,}000 \text{ W}}{0.25 \times 580 \text{ W/m}^2}$$

The required solar panel area is approximately 27,600 m², equivalent to nearly four soccer fields.

Alternative Verification:

As an alternative approach, we cross-reference our calculations with existing data. Each Starlink V2 Mini satellite incorporates two massive 52.5-square-meter solar arrays, totaling nearly 105 m² and weighing about 360 kg vs the original Starlink V1 satellite with Single solar array size of ~**3.1m x 10.9m = ~ 34 m²** according to [41–44]. The Starlink V1 satellite solar array generates an average of roughly 3.5 kW of power at the beginning of its operation life (BOL). Given the solar irradiance in space near Earth orbit is approximately 1.36 kW per square meter, this yields an inherent total satellite solar power system efficiency of approximately 3.5/(34*1.36) = ~7.6%.

Let's also assume that for the stationary solar array and components (for on-surface solar power plant) we can use more efficient heavier panel material and components that can achieve 25% overall system efficiency during peak sun hours. Considering Mars receives only about 40% of Earth's solar power flux and assuming 6 hours of peak sun near the location of Martian colony in this novel, we can then calculate the total required solar array size on Mars to be approximately:

Total solar area needed on Mars to achieve consistent 1 MW solar electric power = ~ (24hour / peak sun) * 1/0.4 * (0.076/0.25) * (1000 kW / 3.5kW) * 34 m² = ~ 29,530 m²

Which is closely aligning with the 27,600 m² computed earlier in this appendix.

It's important to note that a surface-based light-weight solar panel system (array, controller, batteries, inverter, etc.) on Mars weighing at least 500 kg corresponds to a mere 100 m². Consequently, a 1 MW solar facility on Mars equates to a minimum mass of around (27,600m² / 100m²) * 500kg = ~ 140,000 kg, or at least 700 metric tons for a 5 MW solar station on Mars.

Moreover, solar electric power generators experience performance decay at an average rate of 5-7% annually if not properly maintained, necessitating periodic repairs or component replacements.

In Conclusion:

To consistently generate 1 MW (1,000 kW) of power on Mars near the equator, with an overall efficiency of 25%, it is necessary to generate more energy during the six-hour peak sun period and store the excess. This requires approximately 28,000 square meters of solar panels. However, to ensure a continuous power supply, energy storage solutions are essential, allowing excess energy to be stored for use during non-peak hours. This guarantees uninterrupted power availability—a critical feature of the solar power plant in this novel.

References:

1. Solar on Mars:https://www.powerandresources.com/blog/solar-power-is-challenging-on-mars
2. SpaceX unveils next-gen Starlink V2 Mini satellites ahead of Monday launch (teslarati.com)
3. SpaceX unveils first batch of larger upgraded Starlink satellites – Spaceflight Now
4. Starlink - Wikipedia
5. SpaceX Starlink Version 2 Mini Will Have 4X Version 1.5 Capacity | NextBigFuture.com
6. https://www.reddit.com/r/Starlink/comments/gvlt7b/starlink_solar_array_size

Appendix 9:
Powering Martian Colony—The Story Behind the 5MW RTG Power Plant on Mars

The Martian Power Challenge: A Question of **Plutonium and Hardware**

In the quest to establish sustainable power sources on the Red Planet, the utilization of **Radioisotope Thermoelectric Generators (RTGs)** takes center stage in this novel. RTG is effectively a nuclear battery that converts the heat generated by radioactive decay into electricity (known as **Seebeck effect**). This appendix provides a brief overview of the intriguing science and calculations behind the transportation and deployment of RTG power plant on Mars. [38–40]

What quantity (weight and volume) of Plutonium, along with the necessary supporting RTG hardware, would be required for the transportation to Mars via multiple starship missions in order to construct a **5MW RTG** (Radioisotope Thermoelectric Power and Heat Generator) power plant facility on the Martian surface?

Quick Answer: approximately 125,000 kilograms of Plutonium-238, occupying nearly 11 cubic meters, in addition to nearly 500,000 kilograms of supporting RTG hardware, as elaborated upon in this appendix for more detailed insights.

Why? Powering Mars with RTGs: A Sustainable Martian Energy Source

The scientific reasoning and calculations behind the use of Plutonium-238 and supporting RTG hardware for Mars-bound missions are explored in this appendix, providing insights into the endeavor of bringing sustainable energy to the Martian frontier in our Martian Odyssey.

Radioisotope Thermoelectric Generators (RTGs), also known as radioisotope power systems (RPS), harness the natural radioactive decay of elements, particularly Plutonium-238 (^{238}Pu), to produce electricity through a phenomenon known as the Seebeck effect. What sets RTGs apart is their reliability, as they have no moving parts, making them ideal for operating in harsh and remote environments over extended periods especially in situations where solar energy is not practical or where maintaining traditional power sources like fuel cells, batteries, or generators is economically challenging.

The Power of Plutonium-238:

Plutonium-238 (^{238}Pu) boasts a half-life of 87.7 years, a power density of 0.57 watts per gram, and remarkably low gamma and neutron radiation levels. Its unique characteristics translate into minimal shielding requirements; some RTGs need as little as 2.5 mm of lead shielding, or none at all in certain cases, relying on the casing itself for protection against radiation. Plutonium-238, often in the form of plutonium oxide (PuO_2), has thus emerged as the fuel of choice for RTGs. [39]

RTGs have found applications in a range of scenarios, including:

1. **Space Exploration:** RTGs have been used as power sources in various spacecraft and space probes. They provide a reliable source of electricity for missions in outer space, where solar power might not be readily available.

2. **Remote Facilities:** Uncrewed remote facilities, such as lighthouses built by the Soviet Union inside the Arctic Circle, have also benefited from the use of RTGs due to their long-lasting power supply.

However, there are some important considerations when using RTGs:

- **Radioisotope Containment:** Safe use of RTGs requires careful containment of the radioactive materials even after the generator's productive life has ended to prevent environmental contamination.

- **Cost:** RTGs can be expensive to produce and are typically reserved for niche applications or special situations due to their cost.

NASA has used GPHS-RTGs and Multi-Mission (MM) RTGs in several of its missions, primarily those that require a long-lasting and reliable power source, especially in environments where other forms of power generation, like solar panels, are not reliable or not feasible. According to References [38–39], some of the notable NASA missions and types of RTG used include:

Model and Radio-isotope	Spacecraft	Max output Electrical Power (W)	Max output Thermal Power (W)	RTG total Mass (kg)	Power/mass (Electrical W/kg)	Max fuel used (kg)
MMRTG ^{238}Pu	MSL, Curiosity rover, Perseverance, Mars 2020 rover	110	~2,000	< 45	2.4	~4
GPHS-RTG ^{238}Pu	New Horizons, Cassini, Galileo, Ulysses	300	~4,400	55.9–57.8	5.2–5.4	~7.8

GPHS-RTG stands for *General Purpose Heat Source - Radioisotope Thermoelectric Generator*. It is a type of radioisotope thermoelectric generator (RTG) that utilizes a General-Purpose Heat Source to generate electricity through the heat produced by the natural radioactive decay of a specific radioisotope, typically Plutonium-238 dioxide (^{238}Pu O2), using thermocouples based on the Seebeck effect. Here's what the acronym means:

- **General Purpose Heat Source (GPHS):** This is a component within the RTG that contains the radioactive material, such as Plutonium-238 dioxide, and is responsible for producing the heat necessary for generating electricity.

- **Radioisotope Thermoelectric Generator (RTG):** This is the overall power generation system that combines the GPHS with thermoelectric materials to convert the heat generated by the radioactive decay into electrical power.

Some notable NASA missions that have used GPHS-RTGs include:
1. **Cassini-Huygens:** The Cassini spacecraft, which explored Saturn and its moons, was powered by three GPHS-RTGs.
2. **New Horizons:** This mission, which provided the first close-up images of Pluto and its moons, used a GPHS-RTG to generate electrical power during its long journey through the outer solar system.
3. **Galileo:** The Galileo spacecraft, which studied Jupiter and its moons, was equipped with two GPHS-RTGs.
4. **Ulysses:** This mission, designed to study the polar regions of the Sun, employed a GPHS-RTG that provides ~200W to power the spacecraft. [40]

These missions benefited from the reliability and longevity of GPHS-RTGs, which allowed them to operate in the harsh conditions of outer space and provide continuous power over extended durations, sometimes spanning many years or even decades.

Detailed calculations: Calculating the Total Weight and Volume of Plutonium238 (^{238}Pu) needed to generate 5MW electric power on Mars:

In the pursuit of generating 5 megawatts (MW) of electricity on Mars in this novel through the utilization of Plutonium-238 (238Pu) based Radioisotope Thermoelectric Generators (RTGs), following calculations reveal the weight, volume, and transportation considerations that underpin the power generation system as follows.

Power Density and Efficiency Insights

The power density of Plutonium-238, standing at an impressive 570 watts per kilogram, is an important factor in this endeavor. A critical look at RTG specifications illuminates crucial details: A few NASA's spacecrafts employ 4 kg of Plutonium-238 within a 45 kg MMRTG unit, generating 110 W electrical power alongside 2000 W of thermal power. Applying the power density of Plutonium-238, we deduce an overall MMRTG electric power efficiency of approximately 4.82% (110/(4*570)). This implies that the remaining ~95% is dissipated as heat, accounting for nearly 2166W (0.95*4*570), a figure closely mirroring the reported 2000W heat power listed in the table.

In contrast, the GPHS-RTG unit, used in other NASA spacecrafts, utilizes 7.8 kg of Plutonium-238 within a 57 kg unit to produce 300 W electrical power and 4400 W of thermal power. Applying the same power density, we determine an overall GPHS-RTG electric power efficiency of approximately 6.75%.

Therefore, in this novel, it is assumed that more efficient GPHS-RTG units (7% overall efficiency of electric power generation) are used in the 5MW RTG power station (see Chapter 2 of the novel).

Calculating the Mass of Required Plutonium-238 and the GPHS-RTG Hardware

First, let's compute the equivalent mass of GPHS-RTG hardware necessary to attain the 5 MW electricity goal on Mars:

- Required electricity generation power: 5 MW = 5,000,000 watts
- Required Plutonium-238 Mass (kg) = (1/efficiency) * (required electric power in watts / 570) = 1/0.07 * 5,000,000/570 ≈ 125,000 kg

Approximating the mass of the GPHS-RTG units based on the NASA spacecraft data in the table, where a 7.8 kg Plutonium-238 load corresponds to a 57 kg GPHS-RTG unit, we estimate a ratio of 57/7.8, which simplifies to ~7.3. We assume this ratio can be reduced to ~5 for the larger stationary RTG units on the Martian surface. Consequently:

- Total mass of GPHS-RTG units needed for the 5 MW power plant on Mars = 5 * 125,000 kg ≈ 600,000 kg, **equivalent to 600 metric tons**.

Calculating the Volume of Plutonium-238 Dioxide

Further, we determine the volume required for Plutonium-238 dioxide, taking into account its density of approximately 11,460 kg/m^3:

- Mass of Plutonium-238 dioxide required: Approximately 125,000 kg
- Volume (m³) = Mass (kg) / Density (kg/m³) ≈ 125,000 kg / 11,460 kg/m³ ≈ 11 m³

Transportation Considerations

Considering these calculations, the transportation of 125 metric tons of Plutonium-238 and the assembly of 600 metric tons of GPHS-RTG units for the 5 MW power station on Mars necessitates a coordinated effort involving starship fleets deployed across multiple Earth-to-Mars missions spanning several years.

Note that these simplified calculations, while illustrative, do not account for real-world complexities such as efficiency losses, safety measures, or mission-specific requirements, which would inevitably shape the actual design and deployment of such a power system on Mars.

References:

1. Multi-mission radioisotope thermoelectric generator – Wikipedia
2. Radioisotope thermoelectric generator (RTG) – Wikipedia
3. Ulysses RTG Power & Thermal Subsystem – European Space Agency (ESA)

Appendix 10: UV Radiation on Mars—How Much UV Radiation will Mars Inhabitants Receive?

Inhabitants of Mars are exposed to significantly higher levels of UV (Ultraviolet) radiation compared to Earth, primarily due to the planet's thin atmosphere and lack of ozone. This appendix provides a brief summary of the UV radiation environment on Mars and other radiation hazards, along with references for further information. [106–110]

1. **UV Radiation on Earth:** On Earth, the total solar irradiation (solar power flux) is approximately 1366 watts/square meter, with about 8% of this energy falling in the UV range. However, much of the shortest wavelengths (UV-C 200-290 nm) and mid wavelengths (UV-B 290-320 nm) UV radiation (the most harmful types) is absorbed by the ozone layer in Earth's upper atmosphere, leaving mostly less harmful UV-A (320-400 nm) radiation to reach the surface. [106–107]

2. **UV Radiation on Mars:** Mars, being farther from the Sun than Earth (at a distance of approximately 230 million kilometers vs ~150 million km), receives a lower solar flux per unit area of about 588 watts per square meter. Hence, the solar UV portion is reduced from 110 watts/square meter to about 47 watts/square meter. However, unlike Earth, Mars has a mean atmospheric pressure of less than 0.007 Bar (roughly 0.7% of that of the Earth), and it lacks an ozone layer. This absence of atmospheric UV absorption means that the most harmful UV-C and UV-B radiation reaches the Martian surface largely unattenuated, making UV protection on Mars vital for human survival.

3. **Radiation Hazards Beyond UV:** Besides UV radiation, Mars presents other radiation hazards. The lack of a significant Martian global magnetic field exposes inhabitants to galactic cosmic rays (GCR) and solar particle events (SPE). Research indicates that these types of radiation can increase the risk of cancer and degenerative diseases. [108]

4. **Solar Energetic Particle (SEP) Events:** SEP events are a particular concern on Mars. These events, which can be triggered by solar flares or coronal mass ejections, release high-energy particles, some with energies of 40 MeV or greater. While they can travel at significant speeds, there may be a few minutes of warning. Modular Martian colonies could offer protection by having inhabitants take cover under the module's water supply or under transparent silica glass domes containing iron oxide for UV protection. High Z (high atomic number) metal salts can also provide some shielding against GCR. [109]

5. **Complexity of Radiation Protection:** It's important to note that protection against radiation on Mars, especially GCR, is a complex challenge. The effectiveness of various shielding methods and strategies may vary, and additional research is needed to ensure the safety of Martian colonists. [110]

For more detailed information on UV radiation and radiation hazards on Mars, you can refer to the provided references [106–110].

Appendix 11:
Fueling Starships on Mars—Methane Production Through the Sabatier Process

Question: What quantity (weight and volume) of methane per day can be produced on Mars assuming an efficient **2MW** ISRU (In-Situ Resource Utilization) Sabatier facility?

Quick Answer: approximately 2800 kg (2.8 metric ton) of methane (CH4) per day. This means it takes 120 days for such a system to produce ~330 ton of liquid methane needed to completely fill the methane tank on a single starship! Note that a fully filled-in tank is not required for surface-to-surface starship missions on Mars.

Unlocking Mars's Energy Potential:

In the quest to establish a sustainable presence on Mars, scientists and engineers have been working to harness the Red Planet's resources for rocket fuel production, with a particular focus on methane (CH4) production. Methane can serve as a crucial resource for fuel and energy needs, contributing to the sustainability of future Mars missions, especially those involving Methalox (liquid methane and liquid oxygen) rocket engines, such as the Raptor engines on Starship.

In this appendix, we will delve into the intricacies of methane production on Mars through the **Sabatier process (CO2 + 4H2 → CH4 + 2H2O)**, which utilizes hydrogen sourced from Martian ice and carbon dioxide extracted from the Martian carbonate rocks, smectite clays, and possibly atmosphere. We will also explore and roughly estimate the rate of methane production, and the electric energy required, highlighting the potential of this technology.

1. How is Methane Produced on Mars? The Sabatier Process on Mars

The Sabatier process drives methane production on Mars. It involves the chemical reaction of carbon dioxide (CO2) with hydrogen (H2) to produce methane (CH4) and water (H2O). The Mars Direct Concept, initially theorized by Dr. Robert Zubrin in 1993, lays the foundation for in situ methane production on Mars using the Sabatier process. This process comprises several key steps:

a. Electrolysis of Martian Water: Electricity generated by infrastructure on Mars is employed to electrolyze Martian water (mostly from subsurface ice), yielding hydrogen (H2) required for the Sabatier reaction.

b. Reacting with Martian CO2: The hydrogen generated is then combined with the captured carbon dioxide CO2, resulting in the production of methane and water in the Sabatier process (CO2 + 4H2 → CH4 + 2H2O).

2. Methane Production Rate

The production rate of methane through the Sabatier process depends on several factors, including the availability of carbon dioxide and hydrogen, the size and efficiency of the production system, and the energy input.

A High-Rate Methane Production Prototype: In a significant development, a prototype test operation in 2011 demonstrated the production of methane rocket propellant from Martian resources. This prototype harvested CO2 from a simulated Martian atmosphere and reacted it with hydrogen, achieving a production rate of 1 kilogram of methane per day. The system operated autonomously for five consecutive days, maintaining a nearly 100% conversion rate. [87]

3. Electric Energy Requirements

Efficient production of methane requires a continuous supply of electric power. The energy required for the Sabatier process can vary depending on system efficiency and production rate. The optimized system based on the 2011 prototype is projected to produce 1 kilogram of O2:CH4 propellant daily, with a methane purity exceeding 98%. This system consumes approximately 17 kilowatt-hours (kWh) of electrical power per day, operating at a continuous power level of 700 watts. [86]

This optimized system's unit conversion rate is expected to produce 1000 kg of propellant for every 17 megawatt-hours (MWh) of energy input, underscoring the potential Sabatier process for sustainable methane production on Mars.

4. Methane and LOX as fuel for Raptor rocket engines on Starship [90] [91] [92]:

SpaceX's Starship is designed to have a payload capacity of 150 tonnes to low Earth orbit in a fully reusable configuration and 250 metric ton (t) when expended. Starship vehicles in low Earth orbit are planned to be refilled with propellant launched in tanker Starships to enable transit to higher energy destinations such as geosynchronous orbit, the Moon, and Mars. Starship employs a combination of cryogenic liquid methane (LCH4) and liquid oxygen (LOX) to power its Raptor engines, maintaining an optimal oxygen-to-methane mixture ratio of approximately 3.55:1. The booster's tanks is stated to be able to hold 3,600 t (7,900,000 lb) of propellant, consisting of 2,800 t of liquid oxygen and 800 t of liquid methane. While The Starship's tanks is stated to be able to hold 1,200 t of propellant, consisting of ~1170 t of liquid oxygen and ~330 t of liquid methane.

Methane offers distinct advantages over hydrogen, including higher density and the capability to be stored for extended periods, making it well-suited for Martian missions. However, calculating the precise quantities required for Mars missions involves a complex interplay of factors.

To propel a Starship on Mars effectively, determining the exact amount of liquid methane (CH4) and liquid oxygen (O2) required to fill its tanks is crucial. The Raptor engine, known for its efficiency and versatility, is the ideal power source for Mars missions.

Methane, as the preferred fuel for the Raptor engine, is stored in liquid form. Its higher density, compared to hydrogen, makes it a practical choice for Mars missions and eliminates the need for intricate insulation measures on the fuel tank.

While SpaceX's official website provides information that the Starship can accommodate a total propellant capacity of 1,200 metric tons (approximately 2,600,000 pounds) across its main tanks and header tanks, the precise quantities of liquid methane and liquid oxygen essential for Mars missions depend on mission-specific variables, including payload mass, travel distance, and specific requirements. Thorough and tailored calculations are necessary to ascertain the exact quantities needed for future missions to the Red Planet.

References:

1. Mars Oxygen ISRU Experiment (Wikipedia)

2. Atmospheres Data: PERSEVERANCE (New Mexico State University)
3. Mars Direct - Wikipedia
4. Sabatier reaction - Wikipedia
5. https://www.lpi.usra.edu/planetary_news/2022/10/11/moxie-successfully-produces-oxygen-on-mars/
6. https://en.wikipedia.org/wiki/SpaceX_Starship
7. https://provscons.com/heres-why-spacex-uses-methane-in-starship/
8. What is the LOX mass of a Starship and a Superheavy? - Space Exploration Stack Exchange

Appendix 12:
Notes on Starship Flight on Mars

To launch a Starship from Mars, how much liquid methane and LOX are needed to fill its tanks?

In our Martian Odyssey, the Starship spacecraft plays a crucial role in transporting crew and cargo between Earth and Mars. Let's explore the propellant requirements for launching a Starship on Mars, considering the specific conditions and constraints of the mission.

Fuel Consumption of Raptor Engines on Starship: The Starship is equipped with Raptor engines, which are powered by liquid oxygen (LOX) and methane propellants. The Raptor, one of the most efficient rocket engines developed by SpaceX, weighs only 1.5 tons (on Earth) but burns 510 kg of LOX and 140 kg of liquid methane every second, producing up to 280 tons of thrust (over half a million pounds).

Thrust-to-Weight Ratio (TWR) and Exhaust Velocity of Raptor Engines on Starship: The Raptor methalox engine can lift roughly 180 (280t/1.5t) times its own weight! Mars low atmospheric density means the rocket engines can deliver vacuum specific impulse (I_{sp}) nearly from liftoff. The stated I_{sp} of the sea level Raptor engine is 335 seconds vs the vacuum-optimized Raptor engines I_{sp} of approximately 380 seconds as of late 2024,

Mars v_{exh} = I_{sp}*g0 = 380*9.8 ≈ 3700 m/s effective exhaust velocity

vs. **Earth** v_{exh} = I_{sp}*g0 = 335*9.8 ≈ 3300 m/s

However, note that SpaceX may have made further advancements or changes to the engines and their performance since then. Please verify the latest data from SpaceX or official sources for the most up-to-date information.

Escape Velocity on Mars: Mars, with its lower gravity of 0.379g (38% of Earth's), has a theoretical escape velocity of approximately 5.03 km/s (not considering atmospheric drag which is minimal on

Mars). This velocity is the minimum speed required for an object on Mars surface to break free from Mars's gravitational pull.

Propellant Ratio: The Starship's propellant ratio is approximately 3.55 LOX to liquid methane. This means that the Starship requires 3550 kilograms of LOX for every 1000 kilograms of liquid methane for its Raptor engines.

Mission Parameters:

- Mars gravitational acceleration, g_{mar}: $0.379*g_e$ (compared to $g_e=9.8$ on Earth)
- Payload Weight: 50,000 kg on Mars (means $50/0.379 \approx 130$ metric ton on Earth)
- Propellant Reserve: ~15% of the fully fueled mass on Mars
- Mission: Taking the 50,000 kg payload from the Mars surface to reach Mars escape velocity

Starship Characteristics on Mars:

- **Dry Weight of the ship (without propellant) on surface**: $0.379*(130,000 \text{ kg on Earth}) \approx 50,000$ kg gravitational force (measured on Mars). Meaning we don't need as much thrust to launch the same rocket from Mars because Starship weighs about 1/3 the weight on Earth.
- **Wet Weight (full fueling) on surface**: $0.379*(1,600,000 \text{ kg on Earth}) \approx 600,000$ kg or 600 metric ton gravitational force (measured on Mars).

Therefore, for a fully fueled Starship to lift off on Mars taking a payload of 50,000 kg from the Mars surface, the Starship will need approximately a surface level liftoff thrust of $600*1.3 \approx 800$ tons of thrust (tf) on Mars (assuming 30% margin). Given that each Raptor V3 has a stated thrust of 280 tf, a minimum of three to four Raptor V3 engines theoretically should be able to lift that payload on Mars each burning an Earth-equivalent of 510 kg of LOX and 140 kg of liquid methane every second.

Beyond that, to reach Mars escape velocity for a travel back to Earth, we need to consider the delta-v (total change in velocity required for the space mission) according to the Tsiolkovsky rocket equation that states that the ratio of wet mass to dry mass is exponential in delta-v:

$\Delta v = |v_{exh} \cdot \ln(mi/mf)|$ = 3.7 km/s * ln(600ton/100ton) = 6.63 km/s

Where:

1. Δv is the required delta-v for the mission.
2. v_{exh} is the exhaust velocity (specific impulse) of the engines.
3. *mi* is the initial (wet) mass of the spacecraft (including fuel).
4. *mf* is the final (dry) mass of the spacecraft (after expending fuel).

The resulting Δv of ~6.6 km/s is more than enough to reach escape velocity on Mars, launching from its surface. Theoretically speaking (neglecting more detailed practical considerations), the *mi/mf* ratio requirement is roughly 30:1 on Earth vs. 4:1 on Mars meaning that to lift each metric ton of payload and reach scape velocity on Earth roughly 29 tons of propellant is required to be spent vs roughly 3 tons of propellant on Mars.

On **Earth**: $\ln(mi/mf) = \Delta v / v_{exh}$ = 11.2 km/s / 3.3 => $mi/mf \approx 30$

On **Mars**: $\ln(mi/mf) = \Delta v / v_{exh}$ = 5.03 km/s / 3.7 => $mi/mf \approx 4$

It's important to note that, in reality, these calculations are highly dependent on mission-specific parameters, and the specific impulse on Mars and other factors may vary. Additionally, practical considerations such as safety margins and engine startup and shutdown phases can affect the final fuel requirements. For precise calculations, you would need access to detailed technical data and the expertise of aerospace and rocket engineers.

For more information see References [90], [93] and [94].

Appendix 13:
Cinematic & Literary References in this Novel

The following movies are referenced throughout the chapters of the *Artificial Intelligence: A Martian Odyssey* (listed in the order of their appearance in the text):

The Martian (2015), directed by Ridley Scott and starring Matt Damon as astronaut Mark Watney, is based on the bestselling 2011 novel by **Andy Weir**. [12–17]

The Expanse TV series (2015-2022), developed by Mark Fergus and Hawk Ostby, is based on the Hugo Award-winning novel series by **Daniel Abraham & Ty Franck.** [18] [19]

Red Planet (2000), directed by Antony Hoffman and starring Val Kilmer, Carrie-Anne Moss, Tom Sizemore, Benjamin Bratt, and Simon Baker, is based on a story by Chuck Pfarrer. [21]

Total Recall (1990), Paul Verhoeven's Oscar-nominated adaptation of Philip K. Dick's short story ***We Can Remember It for You Wholesale***, starring Arnold Schwarzenegger, Sharon Stone, and Michael Ironside. [20]

Silo (TV series) created by Graham Yost, starring Rebecca Ferguson and Tim Robins based on **Hugh Howey**'s bestselling *Silo* trilogy of novels (*Wool*, *Shift*, and *Dust*). [22] [23] [24]

Forrest Gump (1994): Robert Zemeckis' Oscar-winning adaptation of Winston Groom's bestselling novel *Forrest Gump*, starring Tom Hanks as Forrest Gump, Robin Wright as Jenny and Gary Sinise as Lieutenant Dan. [36]

Mission: Impossible (1996), directed by Brian De Palma, and produced by and starring Tom Cruise (as Ethan Hunt) from a screenplay by David Koepp and Robert Towne. It is the first installment in the *Mission: Impossible* film series. [37]

Inception (2010), written and directed by Christopher Nolan, is a mind-bending masterpiece (won 4 Oscars), starring Leonardo DiCaprio, Joseph Gordon-Levitt, Elliot Page, Ken Watanabe, Tom Hardy, and Cillian Murphy. [27]

Interstellar (2014), is an epic science fiction film directed by Christopher Nolan, who co-wrote the screenplay with his brother Jonathan Nolan. It stars Matthew McConaughey, Anne Hathaway, Jessica Chastain, Bill Irwin, Ellen Burstyn, and Michael Caine. [28]

The Terminator (1984), directed by James Cameron, who co-wrote the screenplay with Gale Anne Hurd and William Wisher. This iconic sci-fi film stars Arnold Schwarzenegger, Linda Hamilton, and Michael Biehn. [29] [30]

Terminator 2: Judgment Day (1991), directed by James Cameron, who co-wrote the screenplay with William Wisher. This iconic sci-fi film stars Arnold Schwarzenegger, Linda Hamilton, Edward Furlong, and Robert Patrick. [29] [31]

Avatar (2009), written and directed by James Cameron, the groundbreaking animation is the first installment in the Avatar film series starring Sam Worthington, Zoe Saldana, Sigourney Weaver, Stephen Lang, Michelle Rodriguez, and Giovanni Ribisi. [29] [32–33]

Black Hawk Down (2001), directed by Ridley Scott and starring Josh Hartnett, Ewan McGregor, Eric Bana, and Tom Sizemore is based on the 1999 non-fiction book by journalist Mark Bowden. [13] [34–35]

The Matrix (1999), the epic science fiction mind-bending action film, written and directed by the Wachowskis, starring Keanu Reeves, Laurence Fishburne, Carrie-Anne Moss, and Hugo Weaving. [147]

Appendix **14**:
Music References in *AI: A Martian Odyssey*

Throughout *Artificial Intelligence: A Martian Odyssey*, music plays an important role—setting the tone, evoking emotions, and enriching the auditory experience for both the characters and readers alike.

Below is a list of the song and music titles that are referenced or mentioned throughout the novel. These titles are simply referred to within the text, with no actual music or lyrics included, ensuring no copyright concerns:

1. **Bee Gees' *Stayin' Alive*:** In the inaugural chapter's banter among the crew, a hint of whimsy emerges as Brad and Xena playfully discuss Martian survival strategies. Disco vibes, particularly the iconic Bee Gees' *Stayin' Alive*, get a subtle mention, weaving into their cosmic musings. To join the groove and see the connection between the crew's lighthearted Martian escapades and this legendary tune and its catchy melody, delve into Chapter One. YouTube Link: Bee Gees – *Stayin' Alive*.

2. **Boris Brejcha's *Space X* Melodic Trance** (Start at minute 1:31): In Chapter One, as Nolan and Ava traversed the Hologram Road inside the autonomous rover, the captivating tunes of Boris Brejcha's *Space X* melodic trance filled the cabin. The soothing and nostalgic harmonies of this music served as a sonic backdrop to the mesmerizing holographic statues of Mars's early pioneers and lunar legends. As the music's melodies echoed through the rover, it added an otherworldly dimension to the scene, encapsulating the spirit of space exploration. Link: Boris Brejcha – *Space X* Melodic Trance – Start at minute 1:31.

3. **50 Cent's *In da Club* and Dr. Dre's drumbeat:** In Chapter Two, As Nolan and Ava navigate the complexities of their mission, Dmitri, stationed in his hulkish Mech robot, playfully unleashes a display of rhythmic finesse harmonized with the infectious rhythm of the pulsating beats of 50 Cent's catchy hip-hop track *In da Club* that transforms him into a Mars-dwelling maestro. Visit Chapter Two to witness the unexpected scene adding a touch of humor to the Martian adventure. Link: *In da Club* – Wikipedia, and on YouTube.

4. **Teho's *Space Explorers* (Start at minute 6:00):** In Chapter Three, as the autonomous rover glided through the Martian night towards Mars1, the central Martian colony, the captivating sounds of Teho's *Space Explorers* filled the cabin. This entrancing melodic trance music added an otherworldly ambiance and sense of exploration, perfectly complementing the epic sight of Mars1 beneath the shimmering night sky. Link: Teho – *Space Explorers* Melodic Trance (Start at minute 6:00).

5. **Deadmau5's *There Might Be Coffee*:** In Chapter Three, during the engaging conversation between our characters Nolan and Ava with the charismatic Mars1 security chief, Tim, the background came alive with the lively beats of Deadmau5's *There Might Be Coffee*. This tune added to the cool and thrilling atmosphere of their interaction. Link: Deadmau5 – *There Might Be Coffee*.

6. **Hans Zimmer's *Time* (and Alexandre Pachabezian's Melodic Remix):** In Chapter Four, Hans Zimmer's timeless melody, *Time*, accompanies the Mars1 crew as they walk along the glass-covered passages in the Martian colony. Here are the links to a lovely melodic remix version by Alexandre Pachabezian, and a beautiful remix by Alan Walker as well as the original masterpiece by Hans Zimmer – *Time*, featured in **Christopher Nolan**'s classic film *Inception* (2010).

7. **Hans Zimmer's *Interstellar* (Alexandre Pachabezian's Melodic Remix):** In Chapter Five, Hans Zimmer's hauntingly beautiful composition, *Interstellar*, with its ethereal quality sets a poignant backdrop as the crew ventures through the Mars1 Museum's halls. It serves as the sonic thread connecting the past to the present, emphasizing the enduring legacy of human exploration and the path that leads to Mars. Here are the links to a melodic remix by Alexandre Pachabezian as well as the original masterpiece by Hans Zimmer – *Interstellar*, featured in **Christopher Nolan**'s epic film *Interstellar* (2014).

8. **Queen's *We Will Rock You*:** In Chapter Five, during the tour of the viewing dome above the Mars1 museum and the engaging conversation among the crew about the Martian zipline, Jacob describes the zipline as an adventure of a lifetime! One that should come with Sir Brian May's and Queen's iconic song *We Will Rock You* (1977) blasting in the background! Aside from the original performance, Queen's *We Will Rock You* was performed by 1000 musicians together at Rockin'1000, Stade De France - Paris, in 2019.

9. **SiebZehn's *Sunset on Mars*** (Start at minute 4:45): In the closing moments of Chapter Five, as our characters soaked in the breathtaking Martian landscape from the observation deck, the cafeteria resonated with the calming tune of SiebZehn's *Sunset on Mars*. For the full experience, dive into Chapter Five and witness how the music enhances the atmosphere of this Martian adventure.

10. **Alan Parsons' *Sirius***: In Chapter Six, as starship crew Brad and Scarlett are about to start their spacewalk toward the orbital telescope above the vast expanse of the red planet looking like a red ocean below them, the powerful and uplifting melody of the Alan Parsons' *Sirius* can be heard in the background playing fittingly within Brad's and Scarlett's helmets. Link: The Alan Parsons Project – *Sirius* – YouTube.

11. **Boris Brejcha & Ann Clue's *RoadTrip***: In Chapter Eight, the nostalgic tune of *RoadTrip* minimal trance is played inside the rover as Nolan and his team embarked on their nerve-wracking journey across the Martian terrain, further intensifying the emotional depth of the narrative. Link: Boris Brejcha – *RoadTrip* – YouTube.

12. **Boris Brejcha's *Never Look Back*** (Start at minute 3:22): In Chapter Twelve, the pulsating beats of *Never Look Back* minimal trance filled the cabin inside the truck rover, setting a determined mood for the uncertain return trip from lava tubes back to Mars1, further amplifying the emotional depth of the narrative. Link: Boris Brejcha – *Never Look Back* – YouTube.

13. **Boris Brejcha's *Himmelblau***: In Chapter Fourteen, the hauntingly nostalgic tune of *Himmelblau* trance filled the cabin inside the trailing rover truck at midnight. Link: Boris Brejcha – *Himmelblau* – YouTube.

14. **Sam Paganini's *Rave***: In Chapter Eighteen, the pulsating drumbeats of *Rave* track filled the cabin inside the trailing rover truck as Nolan's convoy sped up. Link: Sam Paganini – *Rave* – YouTube.

15. **Röyksopp's *Monument* (The Inevitable End Version):** In Epilogue + Author's Note Page, the timeless tunes of Röyksopp's *Monument* is a tribute to a journey that I hope will echo beyond my *final page*. Link: Röyksopp – *Monument* (The Inevitable End Version) – YouTube.

References

[1] Spes (Latin for "Hope") – Wikipedia
[2] Phobos and Deimos, Moons of Mars: https://science.nasa.gov/mars/moons/
[3] Phobos Electric Charging: https://svs.gsfc.nasa.gov/20252/
[4] The Moons Of Mars: https://svs.gsfc.nasa.gov/11326
[5] https://en.wikipedia.org/wiki/Phobos_(moon)#/media/File:Phobos_colour_2008.jpg
[6] Color images of Phobos taken by HiRISE camera on NASA's Mars Reconnaissance Orbiter: https://photojournal.jpl.nasa.gov/catalog/PIA10368
[7] Stickney Crater on Phobos: https://en.wikipedia.org/wiki/Stickney_(crater)
[8] NASA Goddard Institute for Space Studies, Mars24 Sunclock: Mars Solar Time
[9] Timekeeping on Mars – Wikipedia
[10] Telling Time on Mars – Marspedia
[11] How would time keeping on Mars with a 25-hour day work? : r/space
[12] *The Martian* (movie) – IMDB
[13] Sir Ridley Scott – Wikipedia
[14] *THE MARTIAN* interviews – Matt Damon, Sir Ridley Scott, etc. [YouTube Video]
[15] *The Martian* - Goodreads Choice Award Winner for Readers' Favorite Sci-Fi (2014)
[16] Andrew Weir – Wikipedia
[17] Why NASA Helped Ridley Scott Create '*The Martian*' Film [YouTube Video]
[18] *The Expanse* (TV series) – IMDB
[19] *The Expanse* (Hugo Award winning novels) by D. Abraham & Ty Franck – Wikipedia
[20] *Total Recall* (movie) – IMDB
[21] *Red Planet* (movie) – Wikipedia
[22] Hugh Howey – Wikipedia
[23] *Silo* (book series) – Wikipedia
[24] *Silo* (TV series) – Wikipedia
[25] Queen's *We Will Rock You* (1977) - Wikipedia
[26] Sir Brian May - Lead Guitarist and Founding Member of the Queen – Wikipedia
[27] *Inception* (movie) – IMDB
[28] *Interstellar* (movie) – IMDB
[29] James Cameron – Wikipedia
[30] *The Terminator* (movie) – IMDB
[31] *Terminator 2: Judgment Day* (movie) – IMDB
[32] *Avatar* (movie) – IMDB
[33] *Avatar* world by James Cameron – Wikipedia
[34] *Black Hawk Down* (2001) – IMDB
[35] *Black Hawk Down* (Book 1999) – Wikipedia

[36] *Forrest Gump* (movie) – IMDB
[37] *Mission: Impossible* (movie) – IMDB
[38] Multi-mission radioisotope thermoelectric generator – Wikipedia
[39] Radioisotope thermoelectric generator (RTG) – Wikipedia
[40] Ulysses RTG Power & Thermal Subsystem – European Space Agency (ESA)
[41] Solar on Mars: https://www.powerandresources.com/blog/solar-power-is-challenging-on-mars
[42] SpaceX unveils next-gen Starlink V2 Mini satellites (teslarati.com)
[43] SpaceX unveils first batch of larger upgraded Starlink satellites – Spaceflight Now
[44] Starlink – Wikipedia
[45] SpaceX Starlink V2 Mini Will Have 4X Version 1.5 Capacity | NextBigFuture.com
[46] https://www.reddit.com/r/Starlink/comments/gvlt7b/starlink_solar_array_size
[47] NASA's Mars Orbiter Laser Altimeter (MOLA)
[48] https://en.wikipedia.org/wiki/Mars_Orbiter_Laser_Altimeter
[49] Map of Cebrenia quadrangle from Mars Orbiter Laser Altimeter data – Wikipedia
[50] https://commons.wikimedia.org/wiki/File:USGS-Mars-MC-7-CebreniaRegion-mola.png
[51] Phlegra Montes – Wikipedia
[52] Mars_Express/Mountains_and_buried_ice_on_Mars – www.esa.int
[53] https://www.esa.int/ESA_Multimedia/Images/2011/12/Phlegra_Montes_in_perspective2
[54] Cebrenia quadrangle – Wikipedia
[55] https://mars.nasa.gov/news/8851/where-should-future-astronauts-land-on-mars-follow-the-water/
[56] NASA's 'Treasure Map' of Water Ice on Mars Shows Where Humans Should Land – Space.com
[57] https://www.visualcapitalist.com/a-new-water-map-of-mars/
[58] https://www.sci.news/space/science-meltwater-flows-ancient-glacier-mars-03294.html
[59] Mars Subsurface Water Ice Map: https://www.hou.usra.edu/meetings/ninthmars2019/pdf/6418.pdf
[60] Phlegra Montes (candidate site): https://www.hou.usra.edu/meetings/marspolar2020/pdf/6008.pdf
[61] https://explore-mars.esri.com/
[62] Elysium (volcanic province on Mars) – Wikipedia
[63] Elysium Planitia – Wikipedia
[64] https://www.jpl.nasa.gov/images/pia01457-elysium-mons-volcanic-region
[65] Volcanism on Mars – Wikipedia
[66] Timeline of Martian volcanism: http://www.psrd.hawaii.edu/May11/Mars_volc_timeline.html
[67] Elysium Mons Volcano Caldera on Mars https://sketchfab.com/3d-models/elysium-mons-volcano-caldera-on-mars-34c866e6192c4826b54a382fccfee0ff
[68] MARS – Elysium Mons: https://planetarynames.wr.usgs.gov/Feature/1783
[69] Martian lava tube – Wikipedia

[70] Lava tubes: Hidden sites for future human habitats on the Moon and Mars – sciencedaily.com
https://www.sciencedaily.com/releases/2017/09/170925112842.htm

[71] Lava flows - Mars Education at Arizona State University: https://marsed.asu.edu/mep/583

[72] Chryse Planitia – Wikipedia

[73] Google Mars scrollable map – centered on Chryse Planitia

[74] https://science.nasa.gov/resource/valles-marineris-the-grand-canyon-of-mars/

[75] Temperature ranges of Mars: https://blogs.nasa.gov/redplanetdispatch/2022/12/

[76] Taking Mars' Temperature: https://science.nasa.gov/resource/taking-mars-temperature/

[77] Atmosphere of Mars – Wikipedia

[78] NASA's Curiosity Rover Finds Biologically Useful Nitrogen on Mars–www.nasa.gov

[79] Could a Thermonuclear Attack Transform Mars into a Habitable Planet? large.stanford.edu

[80] Can we make Mars Earth-like through terraforming? planetary.org

[81] Mars Terraforming Not Possible Using Present-Day Technology. mars.nasa.gov

[82] Mars Direct – Wikipedia

[83] Robert Zubrin – Wikipedia

[84] The Case for Mars: The Plan to Settle the Red Planet and Why We Must – Wikipedia

[85] Sabatier Process (producing methane and water from hydrogen and CO2) – Wikipedia

[86] Mars Oxygen ISRU Experiment – Wikipedia

[87] Atmospheres Data: PERSEVERANCE (New Mexico State University)

[88] https://www.lpi.usra.edu/planetary_news/2022/10/11/moxie-successfully-produces-oxygen-on-mars/

[89] In-Situ Resource Utilization: https://www.nasa.gov/mission/in-situ-resource-utilization-isru/

[90] SpaceX Starship – Wikipedia

[91] https://provscons.com/heres-why-spacex-uses-methane-in-starship/

[92] What is the LOX mass of a Starship and a Superheavy? - Space Exploration Stack Exchange

[93] Tsiolkovsky rocket equation – Wikipedia https://en.wikipedia.org/wiki/Delta-v

[94] Delta-v – Wikipedia

[95] Tom Mueller – Wikipedia

[96] Rocket Engine Operation and Performance – Wikipedia

[97] Astronaut maneuvering unit – Wikipedia

[98] Areosynchronous equatorial orbit (AEO) aka Mars geostationary orbit – Wikipedia

[99] Mechs aka Mecha – Wikipedia

[100] Amplified Mobility Platform – Science Fiction Database Wiki

[101] How much water can you split into hydrogen and oxygen using electrolysis with one kilowatt hour of electricity?

[102] Electrolysis of Water – Wikipedia
https://en.wikipedia.org/wiki/Electrolysis_of_water

[103] Electrolysis Basic Calculations
https://www.chemguide.co.uk/inorganic/electrolysis/basiccalcs.html

[104] Hydrogen Production by Electrolysis – Quora https://www.quora.com/How-much-hydrogen-is-produced-by-electrolysis-using-a-150-watt-solar-cell

[105] Liquid Oxygen (LOX) – Wikipedia

[106] Solar Constant and Solar Spectrum – ecologycenter.us
https://www.ecologycenter.us/population-dynamics-2/solar-constant-and-solar-spectrum.html

[107] Photosynthetically Active Radiation – fondriest.com
https://www.fondriest.com/environmental-measurements/parameters/weather/photosynthetically-active-radiation/

[108] Why Space Radiation Matters – NASA https://www.nasa.gov/analogs/nsrl/why-space-radiation-matters

[109] Solar Energetic Particles – Wikipedia

[110] Why can't we use the same radiation shielding in Mars that we used when going to the moon? - Space Exploration Stack Exchange

[111] Saul Perlmutter – Wikipedia

[112] Saul Perlmutter's Lecture: https://www.nobelprize.org/uploads/2018/06/perlmutter-lecture.pdf

[113] SpaceX's Starship Could Be Transformed Into A 'Giant Telescope' – Tesmanian.com & X.com

[114] Arecibo Observatory – Wikipedia

[115] Lunar Crater Radio Telescope (LCRT) on the Far-Side of the Moon – NASA

[116] The Event Horizon Telescope (EHT) – HARVARD UNIVERSITY

[117] Event Horizon Telescope – MIT Haystack Observatory

[118] Roger Penrose (2020) – NobelPrize.org

[119] Andrea Ghez (2020) – NobelPrize.org

[120] Reinhard Genzel (2020) – NobelPrize.org

[121] Carl Edward Sagan – Wikipedia

[122] Sagan, Carl (1985). *Cosmos*. Balantine Books. p. 3. ISBN 0345331354.

[123] Visibility analysis of Phobos to support a science and exploration platform – Springer

[124] Stun grenade, also known as a flash grenade, flashbang – Wikipedia

[125] Stefan-Boltzmann's law of black-body radiation – Wikipedia

[126] Visible light - How much lux does the Sun emit? – Physics Stack Exchange

[127] Faraday cage – Wikipedia

[128] Electromigration – Wikipedia

[129] https://www.nvidia.com/en-us/data-center/gb200-nvl72/

[130] https://www.theverge.com/2024/3/18/24105157/nvidia-blackwell-gpu-b200-ai

[131] https://nvidianews.nvidia.com/news/nvidia-blackwell-platform-arrives-to-power-a-new-era-of-computing

[132] Doudna, Jennifer A., & Charpentier, Emmanuelle. (2014). The new frontier of genome engineering with CRISPR-Cas9. Science, 346(6213), 1258096. DOI: 10.1126/science.1258096

[133] A brief introduction to CRISPR genome editing – Innovative Genomics Institute

[134] CRISPR/Cas9 therapeutics: progress and prospects – Nature

[135] Synthetic Biology Overview: Endy, Drew. (2005). Foundations for engineering biology. Nature, 438(7067), 449-453. DOI: 10.1038/nature04342

[136] Synthetic Cell Creation: Gibson, Daniel G., et al. (2010). Creation of a Bacterial Cell Controlled by a Chemically Synthesized Genome. Science, 329(5987), 52-56. DOI: 10.1126/science.1190719 (The J. Craig Venter Institute)

[137] "Cogito, ergo sum" is the "first principle" of René Descartes's philosophy – Wikipedia

[138] Vaswani, A.; Shazeer, N.; Parmar, N.; Uszkoreit, J.; Jones, L.; Gomez, A. N; Kaiser, Ł.; Polosukhin, I. (2017). "Attention is All you Need". *Advances in Neural Information Processing Systems. 30. arXiv:1706.03762*

[139] Attention Is All You Need – Wikipedia

[140] Attention Mechanism (machine learning) – Wikipedia

[141] Bahdanau, Dzmitry; Cho, Kyunghyun; Bengio, Yoshua (2016). "Neural Machine Translation by Jointly Learning to Align and Translate". arXiv:1409.0473

[142] NP-hardness – Wikipedia

[143] Computational Complexity Theory – Wikipedia

[144] Neural Scaling Law – Wikipedia

[145] Scaling Laws for Neural Language Models: https://arxiv.org/abs/2001.08361

[146] https://openai.com/index/scaling-laws-for-neural-language-models/

[147] *The Matrix* – Wikipedia

[148] Europa – Science.NASA.gov

[149] Isaac Asimov's **Three Laws of Robotics** – Wikipedia

[150] Artificial General Intelligence – Wikipedia

[151] Superintelligence – Wikipedia

[152] Artificial Superintelligence – IBM

Glossary of Key Concepts in This Novel

Please note that the following terms, as defined and imagined in this novel, are purely products of the author's imagination and are not intended to represent any existing products or services.

1. **Generative Synthetic Biology**: A discipline within synthetic biology (in this novel) focused on creating novel life forms through the design and engineering of synthetic DNA sequences. It involves the synthesis of DNA constructs that encode specific biological functions or traits not necessarily found in nature, with the goal of generating organisms with unique capabilities or characteristics. In this novel, this is achieved through first training Quadrillion-Parameter DNA Large Language Model (DLLM) on DNAs of all existing and even extinct creatures (and their biological features) and then programming, engineering and synthesizing new DNA strands to realize specific set of biological features or characteristics. These cutting-edge advancements highlight the potential of generative synthetic biology to reshape the future of life on Earth and beyond. There are multiple instances of specifying and engineering such synthesized creatures in this novel.

2. **Q-DLM (Quadrillion-parameter or possibly even Quintillion-parameter DNA Language Model)**: An ultra-scale DNA language model (DLM) trained with super massive dataset of genetic information of all creatures, capable of generating and understanding DNA sequences with a high degree of complexity. It enables researchers to predict the effects of genetic modifications and design new DNA sequences with specific functions. **What are the energy and power consumption consequences?**

3. **Generative DNA**: Engineered DNA sequences designed and artificially synthesized to produce desired biological functions or traits in living organisms.

4. **DNA GPT**: DNA-based Generative Pre-trained Transformer, a sophisticated DNA language model trained with extensive genetic data to generate and manipulate DNA sequences. It can be used to predict the effects of genetic modifications and design new DNA sequences for specific purposes.

5. **Imagining Functional DNA**: A concept analogous to the use of imagination in the likes of Midjourney App, where descriptions can be translated into visual images. In this context, it refers to the creative

process of designing functional DNA sequences that encode specific biological functions or traits.

6. **Bionic Gradient Descent**: An accelerated process of guided genetic evolution in which desired genetic traits are introduced and propagated through successive generations of organisms. This process mimics natural selection but occurs at a much faster rate, leading to rapid genetic changes in populations.

7. **Surviving the Entropy of Evolution**: The ability of genetically modified organisms to adapt and thrive in changing environments despite the inherent randomness and unpredictability of evolutionary processes. It refers to the capacity of organisms to maintain stability and functionality in the face of environmental challenges.

8. **Imaginary Branches of Evolution**: Hypothetical evolutionary pathways that diverge from natural selection principles and lead to unstable or unsustainable outcomes. These pathways represent speculative trajectories that may result from genetic modifications that are not grounded in biological reality.

9. **Novel Solutions to the Equation of Life**: A theoretical framework in this novel proposing that life can be viewed as a complex mathematical system, with solutions that can be either stable (real) or unstable (imaginary).

10. **Event Horizon of Generative Synthetic DNA**: The critical point at which the development of generative synthetic DNA reaches a stage where it cannot be reversed or undone. It represents a milestone in synthetic biology where new life forms can be created with unprecedented precision and complexity.

11. **Generative Bio-Machine Operative Threshold, or GBOT**: The statistical confidence level at which a genetically synthesized organism (biobot) is expected to perform specific functions encoded in its DNA with very high confidence level. It reflects the degree of certainty that the organism will exhibit the desired traits or behaviors under specified conditions.

12. **DNA-tunneling via DNA Wormhole**: A metaphorical concept describing the process by which new genetic traits or functions are introduced into organisms through engineered DNA sequences. It suggests a method of bypassing traditional evolutionary pathways to create organisms with novel capabilities.

Index

Here is a detailed list of names, subjects, concepts, and keywords mentioned throughout the book. The page numbers are relevant only to the print edition and indicate the first occurrence of each term or concept.

360-degree optical scan, 85
3D-printed space bunkers, 93
50 Cent's *In da Club*, 15
Accelerated mutations, 96
AGI (Artificial General Intelligence), 249
AI agents, 102
AI microchips, 18
AI navigation, 182
AI neural processor, 62
AI processor, 102
AI server cluster, 105
Air-sealed transport tunnels, 30
Alan Parsons' *Sirius*, 51
Alan Shepard, 12
Albor Tholus, 78
Algae, 9
Alpha radiation, 139
AMP walker, 15
Amplified Mobility Platform, 15
Andrea Ghez, 150
Andy Weir, 9
Angstrom-scale lithography, 104
Anti-projectile, 204
Antony Hoffman, 9
Arecibo Telescope, 148
Areostationary orbit, 124
Arnold Schwarzenegger, 9
Ascraeus Mons, 51
ASI (Artificial Superintelligence), 102, 249
Astronaut Maneuvering Unit (AMU), 171
Atmospheric pressure on Mars, 128
Attention Is All You Need, 207
Augmented reality simulations, 31
Automated External Defibrillator (AED), 208
Bee Gees' *Stayin' Alive*, 9
Benjamin Bratt, 9
Bio neuromodulator, 67
Biobots, 103
Biohackers, 56

Biological clock, 36
Biological steady state, 96
Biometrics, 143
Bionic Gradient Descent, 96
Biosynthesis, 103
Biosynthesize, 36
Bioware, 121
Black Hawk Down, 198
Black holes, 149
Black-body radiation, 196
Boris Brejcha, 12
Boris Brejcha's *Himmelblau*, 151
Boris Brejcha's *Never Look Back*, 126
Boris Brejcha's *RoadTrip*, 77
Boris Brejcha's *Space X*, 12
Brian De Palma, 41
Buzz Aldrin, 12
Camouflage, 86
Carbonate rocks, 135
Cargo Bay, 61
Carl Sagan, 52
Carrie-Anne Moss, 9
Cebrenia quadrangle of Mars, 78
Celestial cybernetics, 239
Cell growth, 136
Centrifugal force, 177
Cheeseburgers, 217
Christopher Nolan's *Inception*, 31
Christopher Nolan's *Interstellar*, 42
Chryse Planitia, 120
Chuck Pfarrer, 9
Cogito, ergo sum, 212
Collapsed dome, 39

Complex biology, 96
Consciousness black hole, 253
Coriolis effect, 129
Cosmic rays, 32
CPR, 208
CRISPR therapy, 36

CRISPR zapper, 115
CRISPR-Cas9 genome editing, 34
Cuttlefish, 133
Cyber rover, 28
Cybernetic limbs, 46
Cybernetics, 237

Cyborg, 94
Daniel Abraham, 9
Dark-side operators, 56

Darwinian natural selection, 103
Darwinian-on-steroids, 96
Data packets, 167
Deadmau5's *There Might Be Coffee*, 27
Deep-space, 25
Deimos, 17
DLLM, 249
DNA, 34
DNA GPT, 68
DNA Language Model, 103
DNA tampering, 68
DNA Tunneling, 101

DNA wormholes, 103
DNA-GPT, 103
Douglas Adams, 39
Dr. Dre, 15
Dragon, 173
Dust devil, 127
Earth-sized aperture, 149
Editing DNA, 34
Einstein's general relativity, 103
Einstein's general theory of relativity, 150
Electric dreams, 242
Electric nightmare, 240
Electrolyzers, 47
Electromagnetic field, 59
Electromagnetic interference, 85
Electromagnetic spectrum, 99
Electronic single-event upsets, 19
Elysium, 14
Elysium Mons, 14
Elysium Mons lava tubes, 69
Elysium Rise volcanoes, 14
Elysium solar plant, 14
EMP, 173
EMT stretcher, 207

Endoskeleton Android, 60
Entropy of evolution, 97
Event Horizon Telescope (EHT), 149
Exoskeleton, 15
Extraterrestrial life, 52, 149
Falcon 9, 42
First 24 astronauts ventured to the Moon, 12
First 24 humans who set foot on Mars,12
First Starship on Mars, 44
Five-hundred-meter Aperture Spherical Telescope, 148
Flight dynamics, 193
Forearm display, 140
Forrest Gump, 41
Frankenstein android, 69
Frontier LLMs, 102
Fruit trees on Mars, 33
Gary Sinise, 41
GBOT, 103
Geiger counter, 139
genDNA AI, 121
Gene Cernan, 12
Generative Bio-Machine Operative Threshold, 103
Generative DNA, 96
Generative synthetic biology, 96
Generative synthetic DNA, 68
Genetic mutation, 36
Genetically engineered, 35
Genomic malware, 68
Glass tunnel aquarium, 33
Glass-covered air-sealed passages, 30
GNC, 6
GPS on Mars, 26
Grand Canyon of Mars, 52
Gravity on Mars, 34
Gravity on Phobos, 6
Hallucinator, 109
Hans Zimmer's *Interstellar*, 42
Hans Zimmer's *Time*, 31
Hawk Ostby, 9
Hecates Tholus, 78
High-amp electric current, 224
High-tech prosthetics, 45
Holocam, 108
Hologram Road, 12
Holographic control panel, 7

Holographic decoy, 144
Holographic projection, 44
Holographic statues, 13
Holopad, 32
HoloRoad, 12
HoloStreamer, 107
Holovid, 65
Homo Sapiens, 224
Hubble Telescope, 50
Hugh Howey, 38
Humanoid robot, 60
Hyper LLM, 102
Hyper-chips, 104
Hypnotic, 55
Imagined branches of life, 96
Infrared, 17
In-Situ Resource Utilization, 46
International Space Station (ISS), 50
Interplanetary terrorism, 57
Iron-oxide-infused silica glass, 32
Isaac Asimov, 241
Isaac Asimov's Laws of Robotics, 241
ISRU, 46
James Cameron, 61
Jim Lovell, 12
Keep-Out Sphere, 50
Kerolox, 43
Kerosene (RP-1), 43
Laser communication, 167
Lava tubes, 40
LCRT, 148
Leopard Flounders, 133
Lieutenant Dan, 41
Lion's mane jellyfish, 133
Lithium battery pack, 18
LLM training, 121
Lockyer Crater, 148
Low Mars Orbit (LMO), 26
LOX, 43
Lunar Crater Radio Telescope, 148
M87 Galaxy, 149
Machine vision algorithms, 80
Magnetic boots, 5
Malfunctioning circuits, 203
Mark Fergus, 9

Mars clock, 11
Mars Direct, 46
Mars Floaters, 101
Mars Impossible, 41
Mars1 Museum, 42
Mars orbital telescope, 10
Mars Orbiter Laser Altimeter, 78
Mars temperature, 32
Mars's climate, 130
Mars1 Colony, 11
Mars1's domes, 30
Mars1 Greenhouses, 33
Mars1 ISRU facility, 71
Mars1 ISRU Station, 46
Mars1 OPSEC, 39
Mars1 scenic view station, 33
Mars1 security station, 24
Mars1 settlement, 30
Mars2, 30
Mars3, 30
Marscopter, 139
Marslink engineers, 111
Marslink satcom, 25
Marslink satellite constellation, 13
Marslink satellite network, 13
Martian Brew, 28
Martian clouds, 129
Martian dust, 32
Martian fish, 39
Martian lava tubes, 93
Martian Odyssey, 1
Martian sheriff, 45
Martian system, 4
Martian zipline, 43
Matrix, 224
Matt Damon, 9
Mech AMP, 15
Med Bay, 152
Medium Mars Orbit (MMO), 26
Mega radio telescope, 149
Merlin, 42
Metabolic booster, 221
Methalox, 43
Michael Collins, 12
Michael Ironside, 9

Micrometeorite impact, 52
Milky Way, 23, 150
Mini blaster, 144

Mission X, 22
Mission: Impossible, 41
MOLA (NASA), 78
Moon's dark side, 68
Moon's far side, 56
Morse, 86
Murphy's Law, 39

NASA, 8
NASA's Apollo missions, 42
NASA's Mars Orbiter, 79, 129
Neil Armstrong, 12
Neural Processing Unit (NPU), 18
Neuromorphic, 104
Neuromorphic AI server, 112
Neuromuscular system, 115
NP-hard decision problem, 239
Nuclear battery, 11
Nukes, 106
Nvidia B200 Superchip, 104
Object classification, 80
Olympus Mons, 51
OPSEC, 24
Optical satellite communication, 166
Orbital Speed, 3, 172
Orbital Telescope, 3, 10
Oscars on Mars, 16
Ozone layer, 32

Pāhoehoe lava, 93
Parsecs, 237
Pattern recognition, 80
Phantom, 19
Philip K. Dick, 9
Phlegra Montes, 77
Phobos, 4
Photosynthesis on Mars, 34
Placard in Mars Colony, 39
Plutonium-238, 140
Prime directives, 237
Programmable synthetic biology, 97
Protein synthesis, 136
Psychobot therapist, 237
Psychobot virus, 239

Psycho-cyborg, 238
Pulsars, 149
Q-DLM, 103
Quadrillion-parameter DNA Language Model, 103
Quadrillion-Parameter-Scale LLM, 103
Quantum tunneling, 103
Quasars, 149
Queen's *We Will Rock You*, 44
Radio telescope, 148
Radioactive, 140
Radioisotope Thermoelectric Generator, 11
Radio-shielding, 88
Raptor, 42
Red Planet (The Movie), 9
Regolith, 136
Reinhard Genzel, 150
RF communications, 89
RF transmitters, 87
Ridley Scott, 9
Robert Zemeckis, 41
Robert Zubrin, 46
Robin Wright, 41
Robo Sapiens, 224
Robocopter, 86
Robotic grabber, 205
Robotic religion, 237
Rocketdyne, 42
Roger Penrose, 150
Röyksopp's *Monument*, 256
RTG, 11
RTG Power Generation in the Martian Odyssey, 14
Sabatier reaction, 47
Sagan's number, 52
Sagittarius A* Black hole, 150
Satellite imagery, 81
Saturn V F-1, 42
Saul Perlmutter, 10
Seebeck effect, 11, 71
Shakespearean, 188
Shapeshifting, 131
Sharon Stone, 9
Short-range radio link, 83
SiebZehn's *Sunset on Mars*, 48
Simon Baker, 9
SITREP, 62

Smectite clays, 135
SOB, 37
Sol, 5
Solar Power Generation in the Martian Odyssey, 14

Solar system, 5
Solium1, 14
Solium2, 14
Solium3, 14
Space cruisers, 99
Space wormholes, 103
Spacewalking, 53
SpaceX, 42
Spes, 4
Spider bot, 155
Spyware, 117
Stargate Spaceport, 7
Starlink, 26
Starship, 4
Starship-Based Orbital Telescope, 49
Stefan-Boltzmann's law, 196
Stickney Crater, 6
Strawberry—Orange—Banana, 30
Sublimate, 129
Super-flash (stun) grenade, 196
SynBio AI lab, 19
Synthesized DNA, 131
Synthetic demigod, 102
Synthetic DNA, 68
Synthetic intelligence, 104
Teho's *Space Explorers*, 23
Temperature fluctuation on Mars, 32
Terraforming Mars, 106
TESA100, 72
The Expanse, 9
The Martian, 9
The Matrix, 224
The Terminator (1984), 61

Three Laws of Robotics, 241
Thrust-to-Weight Ratio (TWR), 295
Timekeeping on Mars, 11, 63

Titan, 73
Titanium-Endoskeleton Super Android, 72
Tom Cruise, 41
Tom Hanks, 41
Tom Mueller, 42
Tom Sizemore, 9
Total Recall, 9
Transistor miniaturization, 105
Trapdoor spiders, 133
Ty Franck, 9
Ultraviolet, 100
Underground ice reserves, 30, 39
UV radiation, 32
Val Kilmer, 9
Valles Marineris, 51
Vastitas Borealis plains, 77
Vitals, 62
VR training, 31
Wachowskis, 224
Winston Groom, 41
Winter on Mars, 130

About the Author

Artificial Intelligence: A Martian Odyssey
Beyond Human, Beyond Machine—The Rise of Robo Sapiens

ALIREZA MEHRNIA holds a Ph.D. in Electrical Engineering and an MBA from UCLA. He has spent over 25 years navigating the high-tech engineering frontier with an eye toward the stars.

With more than 20 patents to his name and a career that includes leading digital signal processing algorithm design for satellite communications and wireless chips, he knows a thing or two about pushing boundaries—both earthly and cosmic.

He enjoys transforming complex concepts and technologies into compelling narratives. Whether teaching engineering and business courses at universities or contributing to global technology standards, his passion for innovation is matched only by his love for storytelling.

When he's not engineering or crafting sci-fi adventures, he delves into space technology, synthetic biology, the future of computing, and the fascinating intersection of AI and humanity.

In *Artificial Intelligence: A Martian Odyssey (Beyond Human, Beyond Machine—The Rise of Robo Sapiens)*, he invites readers on a thrilling journey to a near-future Mars, where **artificial intelligence**, **humanoids**, and **synthetic life** collide with the lives of Martian explorers. Through thought-provoking storylines, the novel explores the existential consequences of **merging human intelligence with robots and advanced AI**—challenges that take on an entirely new dimension on the Red Planet.

Connect with him online on YouTube.com/@SciFiProf, on X (formerly Twitter) at @SFiProf, on LinkedIn.com/in/amehrnia/, or through his Amazon Author Page.